CHAOTIC CUPIDS

WHEN LOVE GOES AWRY

Executive Editors

KEVIN J. ANDERSON AND
ALLYSON LONGUEIRA

Editorial Team

CL FORS, MEAGAN FRIEDMAN, ADELAIDE
HALLIDAY, AMY LIZ HARRISON, BETH ILER,
STACE JOHNSON, JARED NELSON, LORI
PARKER, HAILEY SWANBOM,
AND CATHRYN UBER

WFP

WORDFIRE PRESS

CHAOTIC CUPIDS
When Love Goes Awry

Executive Editors
Kevin J. Anderson and Allyson Longueira

Editorial Team
CL Fors, Meagan Friedman, Adelaide Halliday, Amy Liz Harrison, Beth Iler, Stace Johnson, Jared Nelson, Lori Parker, Hailey Swanbom, and Cathryn Uber

EBook ISBN: 978-1-68057-751-8
Trade Paperback ISBN: 978-1-68057-752-5
Hardcover ISBN: 978-1-68057-753-2
Cover painting by C.L. Fors
Designed by Allyson Longueira

Published by WordFire Press, LLC
PO Box 1840 Monument CO 80132
Kevin J. Anderson & Rebecca Moesta, Publishers
WordFire Press Edition 2025
Library of Congress Control Number:
Printed in the USA

Join our WordFire Press Readers Group for sneak previews, updates, new projects, and giveaways. Sign up at wordfirepress.com

CONTENTS

Foreword   v

CLOSED EYES AND OPEN HEARTS   1
Brie Tartaglia

CELESTIAL BODIES   16
J. L. Smyser

HIT POINTS   30
J.E. Birk

FORGET-ME-NOT   45
Robert Luke Wilkins

NYLAH ZIMMERBACH AND THE GHOST OF THE
PENDRAGON   49
Erica S. Peck

FOR ALL LOVE IS PRAYER   59
Lynne Sargent

RABBITS AND RASPBLUERRY WINE   62
Jennifer M. Roberts

DAPHNE   78
Allister Nelson

THE NECESSARY ARRANGEMENTS   80
Lynn Strong

DEATH TAKES A WIFE   96
J.M. Reinke

THE GLOBE CRYSTALS ARE NEVER WRONG   106
Angel Martinez

DAMNED IF I DO   122
Morgan West-Burnham

TELL ME ONCE AGAIN   138
Gary Smith

FOR THE LOVE OF FARKAKTEH PHONES   140
Sara Itka

THE TIES THAT BIND   157
Lia Wu

ALLIE'S AWAKENING 170
R.A. Johnson

POSSESSIVE LOVE 184
Leslie Kung

CUPID'S AROS 199
Kay Hanifen

(RE)WILD AT HEART 214
Caitlin Barbera

STAR-CROSSED 230
Diana Olney

WITCHFUL THINKING 237
Kristi Charish and Sebastien de Castell

THE BOTANIST AND THE MEDICINE WOMAN 262
CMarie Fuhrman

CURSED 276
Hadley H. Hudson

Acknowledgments 289
Copyright Information 291
About the Editors 293
About the Illustrator 295

FOREWORD

Is that love in the air?
Or chaos?
Or both?

When you're an editor with an open call for submissions, you never know what the slushpile will produce. Sometimes, it's a delightful surprise; other times, it's a head-scratcher. Occasionally, you ask yourself, "What were they thinking?"

Chaotic Cupids: When Love Goes Awry had plenty of surprises for our editorial board. And the stories themselves shaped the very nature of the anthology.

It started out simple and straightforward enough. This is the sixth annual anthology put together by the Publishing MA graduate students at Western Colorado University. Each year, as a cornerstone of their classwork, the cohort of students creates and produces an original anthology from start to finish. They brainstorm and develop the concept during their summer in-person residency in the mountains of Colorado. Past anthologies have been about movie monsters, masks, fairy-tale mirrors, evil mermaids, and magical cats.

This year, the students took a more romantic turn with their idea for an anthology of fantastical romance stories, imagining all the mayhem that a literal or metaphorical Cupid could cause in the characters' lives. Working together, they wrote up a call for submissions and distributed it widely. Our program receives generous funding from Draft2Digital, which allows us to pay professional rates for the stories—and that means we get a lot of submissions!

This year, the students had to weed through nearly four hundred manuscripts submitted by writers from all around the world. The stories that came in were quite a surprise, though—not what we were expecting. Some writers applied the guidelines very literally and produced stories about actual meddling Cupids, while others took more literary license and used their imaginations to create far-ranging stories. We saw a lot more hard science fiction stories than we had counted on, as well as some gritty horror, modern urban fantasy, high fantasy, and ghost stories.

The editorial team rejected the first batch of stories that didn't make the cut, then did a second round of culling, then a third. It was like a literary version of *Squid Game*. Finally, they narrowed the slush pile down to only the very best tales—all of them publishable stories, all of them loved by at least some of the editorial team. But more than fifty stories still remained, and we could only buy 23.

That final "Thunderdome" call—two stories enter, one story leaves—is one of the hardest but most instructive experiences in their entire graduate degree program. But they did it. It was a hard-fought process, but we had our final selections, and the students could write their last round of rejections ... and issue the contracts.

When we looked at the final choices, however, our original title of *Confounding Cupids* didn't quite fit. This book has more wild, madcap mayhem than simple romantic confusion. So we changed the title to *Chaotic Cupids*, but the love still goes awry.

Once again, our Publishing students have done a remarkable job producing an anthology of entertaining and thought-provoking stories. If you'd like to check out some of the previous anthologies, you can find them all at wordfirepress.com/gpcw.

For more information about Western Colorado University's Graduate Program in Creative Writing, see western.edu/department/graduate-program-in-creative-writing/.

Now, turn the page and enjoy stories about love as chaotic as the feeling itself.

—Kevin J. Anderson and Allyson Longueira, Executive Editors

CLOSED EYES AND OPEN HEARTS

BRIE TARTAGLIA

Stories about hunting Cupid to remove a love spell always skipped the part about climbing a cliff to get to him. They never mentioned him living in a stone shepherd's hut that was bigger on the inside than the outside. And as I snuck into the hut wielding a solid rose-gold arrow like a throwing dart, expecting to find piles of lovers recovering from the throes of passion, I found the god of love's sanctuary full of piles of something else entirely: scrolls.

Racks of parchment covered the wall. Open rolls full of neat scrawl lay next to white feather quills. I aimed the arrow at the god who stood at the center of it all. Cupid was tall and young with roguishly unkempt black hair, but not boyish, built like a reclusive scholar whose only exercise came from climbing ladders to get to higher shelves. I faced his bare, tanned back and white dove wings —of course they wouldn't be from a gutsy bird.

Why am I doing this? said the traitorous voice in the back of my head who'd fought me every step of this journey. I had nicknamed her "Arrow," since she came from one of Cupid's arrows, the same one I was lining up to throw. All she cared about was that I hadn't seen the object of my—her affections in weeks.

I should be out finding my beloved Blandus instead, Arrow whined.

Really? That "beloved" ruined the reputation I'd built up over the last decade as a folk hero by urging me to leave all my honorable mercenary jobs to pay attention to him. The morning after I tried to find a compromise with Blandus, I found his bedroll empty and this mythical arrow hiding in his quiver. An oracle explained that it was one of Cupid's arrows, that it forced me to fall in love with him. The revelation unveiled the truth, that the part of me yearning for him was like a leech. He was another person who wanted to chain me down, no better than the family I left.

"You must pierce the owner of the Cupid's arrow that pierced you, using the very same arrow, to undo its spell," had been the oracle's solution. And who owned Cupid's arrows besides Cupid?

The god still had his head down studying something. He wouldn't stay this careless, and I only had one piece of ammunition.

I stared at the arrow, holding it by its shaft. Arrows should be shot or thrown, but my aim was horrible, and the oracle used the word "pierce." I could do that better at close range.

I picked my way between parchment rolls and approached the god. Attacking someone from behind wasn't my style, but I would do anything to get my freedom back. Holding my breath, I stabbed between his wings.

The arrow's head turned clear and glassy like a ghost as it entered his back.

Cupid keeled over with a pained grunt. His wings burst out in a panicked frenzy.

I jumped back, letting go of the arrow. Nothing felt different. I went over the list of the best nights I ever had. All of them were with Blandus. Sleeping under the stars together, laughing at pompous aristocrats' silly hair styles, stumbling on an undiscovered hot spring. My life had better friends and lovers before Blandus came into it, but all of them paled in comparison to that carefree blond and his stupid, dimpled smile.

"Why didn't it work?" A lump balled in my throat. I followed the oracle's directions exactly, didn't I?

"That depends. What were you trying to accomplish by

stabbing me with an *arrow*?" Cupid folded his wings in and reached over each shoulder for the arrow shaft. The tips of his long fingers barely brushed the rosy metal.

"Getting my life back." I swiped away hot tears from my eyes. So my first plan failed, but I figured out my best jobs on the fly. I could salvage this. "So tell me what in Hades *will* work."

"I'm too preoccupied at the moment." He reached under his wings, but a heap of feathers blocked him. His eyes were squeezed shut, leaving him to feel around. "Blasted wings. Do pull this out. It's not doing either of us any good stuck in me."

"Then stop flailing like a headless chicken." I braced one hand against his bare back, my pinky brushing a couple feathers.

"I wouldn't be if you hadn't put an arrow in my back." He rubbed his still-closed eyelids like someone would rub their temples during a headache, surprisingly calm, mildly annoyed at worst. "People have stolen my arrows before, but no one ever returned one quite like this."

"What?" I yanked back, hard. The arrow slid out of Cupid like his skin was water. I stumbled back a couple steps with the shaft clutched in my white-knuckled fist. "If anyone stole this thing, it's Blandus, and he stuck me with it. You own it, so sticking you should've fixed me."

"Ah, the satyr with the weakness for warrior women. That explains why my mother captured him." Cupid rolled his shoulders and stretched his wings some. A few stacks of loose parchment fluttered to the floor as the plumage bumped them. "You were on the right path. Piercing the one who owns the arrow that pierced you will undo the arrow's effects. Unfortunately for you, Blandus technically owned the arrow when he pierced you, despite having stolen it. You need to find him, but he is in my mother's custody and out of your reach."

I blocked out Arrow's protests that I needed to rescue Blandus from Cupid's mother, Venus. As validating as it was to hear my suspicions were right all along, it didn't help the hot humiliation. Tensing my forearms and curling my fists didn't help either. I couldn't punch a feeling into submission. "Then how do I fix this? I just want my life back."

"I suggest you vow celibacy and see if a temple to Vesta would be willing to take you in."

"How is that fair?"

"It isn't, but Blandus is beyond your reach, and rejecting compulsive feelings for him will only quicken your descent into love madness." He held out his hand, palm up and waiting. "Now give me the arrow. I'll prick you and let you be on your way. I'm behind on my work."

I raised an eyebrow at him, even though with his eyes shut he wouldn't appreciate it. He couldn't expect me to give him the arrow, not when taking back my freedom while keeping my sanity required it. The existence of the Arrow persona in my head hinted I didn't have much time left until love madness set in. Victims of that malady saw their passion turn to obsessive pining until they couldn't bear to keep living without their lover. And why wasn't Cupid looking at me, and why ask to stick me?

"You can't resist your arrows," I announced as the pieces of the game fell into place. "You can't open your eyes, or you'll fall in love with the first living thing you see."

His nonchalant expression crinkled with a frown. I took that as a yes.

"Fine, I'll give you the arrow," I said, knowing he could hear the smile in my voice, "but only after you take me to Venus and help me stick Blandus."

Cupid crossed his arms over his chest and shook his head. "That's a horrible idea. Every mortal who crosses her ends up with a petty trial that either takes their will to live or kills them outright."

"It's better than trying to be a Vestal Virgin in my thirties."

"You don't understand—"

"No, you don't understand." I slipped the arrow into the quiver at my hip and grabbed his shoulders. "I don't hate falling in love. It started off pretty nice. But being stuck in it when I don't want to be, it's fracturing me. There's another person living inside me trying to convince me to give up my freedom and like it, the way my family wanted. Nothing is dragging me back to that life. Not some magic arrow or satyr, not you or your mother, not even the Fates."

Cupid comically gaped at me with a slack jaw and his eyes staying sealed shut, like a mortal never had the audacity to interrupt him. Then he pursed his mouth in consideration, wings rustling at his back, and his frown returned.

"I can't fly in this condition," he said, his plumage settling. "I'll need you to be my eyes."

I swept my arms around him in my tightest bear hug.

"Th-This can't end well for you," he stammered, just like all my friends when I'd grown into my chest early. I pulled away to find his tawny cheeks as rosy as his arrow.

"I'll succeed and get my life back or fail and die. Either way, this love spell *will* come off."

WE SET off from the shepherd's hut, deeper into the mountains. Cupid held onto my shoulder and gave directions as we climbed through the rugged terrain. Healthy gusts whipped against my bare arms and legs the whole way, and goats bleated at me in mocking laughter before hopping away. Once darkness fell, we made camp in the shelter of a small cave surrounded by enough foliage to keep a fire.

"What's your name?" Cupid asked as I stretched.

Had I given him a name? I guess not. "Little Amazon."

"An Amazon without a bow?"

"I'm not actually an Amazon, just trained by one, and she agreed my aim is awful."

He shook his head, as if refocusing his thoughts. "I mean your real name."

Was it smart to give him my real name? I hadn't told anyone, even Blandus, just in case they'd heard of me and tried taking me back to my family. Then again, what bounty could my parents offer that would tempt a god? Besides, he could probably find out on his own later. Might as well save both of us the trouble.

"Psyche." I winced as guilt twisted my insides.

What right does a puny god have to know my name over the love of my life? Arrow's biting commentary came with the cramps. She'd been quiet 'til then, content I was on my way to find Blandus.

Cupid raised his eyebrows so high, he accidentally opened his eyes. He covered them with his hand before I caught a glimpse of their color. "The raven-haired princess whose beauty rivaled Venus? I heard you were kidnapped by a giant, fire-breathing serpent."

"That's what they told everyone?" I guffawed, holding my stomach as my eyes watered. My laughter died as something dawned on me. "Wait, why do you know about that? My parents only spread that 'Venus's rival' tripe so they could attract more suitors. It couldn't have reached..."

"Of course it did." He moved his hand away from his newly closed eyes and pressed his mouth into a cynical line. "She even sent me to deal with you."

Words failed me, and scalding embarrassment boiled in my face. It was one thing hearing about me, but he'd seen me. Over a decade ago when my face was caked with paint and powders and the rest of me was weighed down by too much fabric and gold. Had he spotted me sobbing and punching at locked doors after being caught with a guard's stolen sword, screaming for my family to let me out?

"I was supposed to make sure you married an older aristocrat, Aquila I think." Cupid scowled at the notion. "I came to the engagement dinner. Neither of you were compatible. He was sweet enough, but he rarely left his home in the city. He needed someone who could host his political parties and care for him in his advanced age. You picked at your calluses under the table and wore an excruciating smile."

"And he was the best of the suitors my parents picked." My family had set a guard to watch me every moment of every day until my wedding, when they wouldn't have to pay back my dowry.

The smile and the picking were my nerves as I waited for the right moment to sneak to my room and climb out the window. But the guard was always there, lurking and loyal to my parents, and I wasn't strong enough to overpower him yet.

"As soon as you left the table, though, I saw the plan brewing behind your eyes. Your determination and ferocity were obvious, even hidden under all your heavy finery. I couldn't snuff that out." A fond grin flickered like a candle flame across his lips. "Your guard on the other hand kept trading glances with another guard. Those two had all the signs of a deeper connection. They were going to be a match on my list, so I pushed them together instead of you and the aristocrat, and went on my way."

"So *you* made him run off." My keeper had excused himself once I reached my room and never returned. That decision let me escape, find my mentor, and make a whole new future for myself. I never knew it was from anonymous generosity by a minor god. "How do you feel now that you've gotten to see how it turned out?"

"That depends. Are you happy?"

Not without Blandus, Arrow cut in, as an ache of longing spiked through my chest. I massaged my sternum and ground my teeth against the icy despair building under it. Usually those waves passed if given enough time. How much longer until they consumed me? Any honest reply to his question caught against a growing lump in my throat. "Whatever happened to those guards?"

"They are happily retired and running their own goat farm." Cupid puffed his chest and his feathers, proud and suitably distracted. "Further evidence my system works, no matter what my mother says."

I sat, ready to dig into my rations. "Stories were wrong about you two being close, eh?"

"We get along," he said with a stiff shrug I didn't believe for a moment. "We just don't agree on parts of my role."

"Like?"

"She wants me to do it like she would." He wrinkled his nose.

"The constant lovers and liaisons, the jealous competitions. It's all so excessive."

"So you tried it, got tired of it, and buried yourself with your scrolls?"

Red crept up his neck.

"Don't tell me you've never tried it."

The red inched to his ears.

"Have you ever even been in love?"

"Making the matches has always been the good part. Finding where people are compatible, beyond the physical and emotional passion, is like solving an ever-changing riddle." Cupid lit up with a dazzling smile that spread a pearlescent glow from his feathers to his feet. What color were his eyes when he got like this, and were they half as stunning?

I caught myself gaping and snapped my jaw shut.

The moment shattered as he cleared his throat and the light withdrew back into his gangly self. "Like I said, I have a system, and it works very well. Why do I need personal experience when my work speaks for itself?"

"If your system works so well, wouldn't you want to try it?"

He either didn't have an answer or kept it to himself.

I KNEW we had reached Venus when the constellations in the night sky flipped around and the weather changed from gusty to balmy. Gray stone and green firs turned to flowering trees and crystalline pools. I squinted and sneezed at the overwhelming colors and aromas at first. Nude statues in provocative positions filled Arrow with idea after idea, each punctuated by pangs of growing desperation. Doubt dribbled into the cracks of my determination and froze to widen them. If this kept up much longer, I might not have enough resistance left to put the arrow in Blandus when I saw him.

I described and Cupid guided us toward a great marble-pillared courtyard. Platters of honey-drizzled, suggestively shaped vegetables sat with floods of open oysters and pomegranates. I would've laughed at the feast of aphrodisiacs if it hadn't spurred Arrow's frenzy as much as the statues.

The goddess of love, clothed only in her waves of curly hair, lounged in a seashell-backed throne at the head of the courtyard. Unlike her son, she had an abundance of pale, scintillating curves. I blinked, only to find her shape had changed to a brown-skinned, blonde beauty with willowy grace. I blinked again, checking my eyes, only to find her as bronzed, muscular, and fire-headed as my Amazon mentor. Her appearance constantly shifted between dizzying combinations of feminine ideals as I forced my eyes to stay open.

I swallowed to wet my dry mouth. My parents had been colossal fools to ever compare my looks to hers.

"It smells like you're hosting guests, but I don't hear any obnoxious moaning," Cupid said in a disinterested monotone. "I haven't interrupted anything, have I?"

"Your visits are never an interruption, sweet son. My company won't be here for a few hours yet," Venus replied, her voice a harmony of high sweetness and throaty allure. She glanced to me and gave me the narrow-eyed assessment of a potential rival. "Have you changed your mind about coming to my parties? Your companion is pretty as mortals go, and sturdy enough to keep up for the first few hours."

Cupid's entire head from collar to crown turned beet red. Sounded like a fun time to me—

I am not some hussy who passes herself around a party, not without Blandus to enjoy, Arrow screeched. The same pain as when someone knifed me in the gut tore through my viscera. I doubled over, ripping myself away from Cupid, Venus, the decadent surroundings. I squeezed my eyes shut and blocked it all out. Sweet, calming darkness engulfed me and dulled the edges of my feelings.

Arrow recalled images of Blandus's dimpled smile, his woodsy smell, his sarcastic commentary about the nobles who gave us jobs. No, this couldn't be what soothed me. I had to remember the secrets he hid from me, the way he disregarded my wants, how he used a stolen mythical arrow to coerce me into trusting him. This was a curse, and never what I wanted. I forced my eyes open and held my head between my hands. My fractured halves had to stay separate. I wasn't Arrow, Arrow wasn't me.

Cupid brought his arm around my shoulders. His eyes searched behind his closed lids with bald concern. If I sounded awful enough to alarm a god, I must be bad. I'd been hiding and bearing with it so well, but the presence of a goddess of passion personified was too much. I'd underestimated Arrow and the true progression of my love sickness. Could I really overcome her?

"This mortal helped me find the arrow the satyr, Blandus, stole," Cupid lied as he addressed his mother, and I didn't speak up to correct him. "She fell victim to the arrow before you captured him. I need to see him and undo its effects."

"Who is she?" Venus pursed her tantalizing mouth. "She looks familiar."

"Does that matter? I owe her a boon, and she's verging on madness."

"If who she is doesn't matter, then give me her name."

For the love of the gods, I didn't have more time than a goddess to play this game. "Psyche," I answered with phlegm thickening in my throat. "It's Psyche."

"My my, no wonder I didn't recognize you at first. You used to be a waif. The muscles have made you much lovelier. A thief Blandus may be, but I can't fault him for his taste." Venus cast an appreciative leer over my shuddering self. "As far as I'm concerned, my son leading you here fulfills his debt to you, so now you deal directly with me. I don't grant something for nothing, especially not to mortals who dare compare themselves to me."

Cupid spoke up. "That was her parents—"

"What have I told you about interrupting my fun?" Venus threw him a pitiful pout. "This is why I worry about you. You have no sense of theatricality, no drama, no presence. Our work drains us if we don't enjoy it, and you aren't even trying to fake enthusiasm."

"We can discuss this later, Mother." Cupid hunched his shoulders nearly to his ears, and his wings followed suit. "Kindly tell Psyche what you want in exchange for letting her meet with the satyr."

"Watch and learn." She tossed some errant red-to-black-to-violet hair over her shoulder with feline smugness. "Psyche, here is the trial you must pass. My son needs a lesson in desire. He seems fond enough of you. Give him a memorable first kiss, and don't try to cheat him either. I want real feeling behind it."

I'd rather die! Arrow declared. New agony streaked through my guts, cutting into my knees. I stumbled forward, but managed to catch myself. Arrow would let me get away with a generic peck, maybe something deeper if it meant reaching Blandus, but not if I had to enjoy it. But if I refused? I was already on Venus's grudge list because of an outrageous rumor. How much worse would she punish me if I implied some satyr—the *love of my life* according to Arrow—was better than her son?

I peered over at Cupid, measuring his reaction. He shrank away at first. This would be easier if he opened his eyes and let himself be carried away, but first kisses were precious. Mine had been my first step to claiming my independence. His should be special too, not a means to an end for his mother's scheme. But I had to pass this trial to free both of us.

"You really haven't ever had a kiss from anybody?" My heart pounded through my ears. Arrow's raving mounted. *He's not worthy of even my scraps. I don't care if he's a god or an ant, the only one my heart wants is Blandus. I can't betray him like this, I won't!*

"Never," Cupid answered, red flaring in his complexion again. He stayed rooted to his place, not compromising the moment by opening his eyes, but not backing away from me either. "Go on. Do what you have to."

"Forget about your mother." I cupped both his cheeks and leaned my forehead against his, blocking Venus from my periphery. I spent the last of my willpower on an idea that could make everyone happy, if I could just hold out a little longer against my compulsion.

"Remember back to the night you first saw me." My voice dropped to my softest whisper, keeping any words between us. "You said I looked determined and fierce, but truth is I was terrified. I planned on running away that night. The guard was the only thing in my way, and I had no idea how to get past him. But he left his post that night because of you. I was able to get away, become the Little Amazon and travel wherever, doing whatever I wanted. You did match me that night, with my true self, with my freedom."

He nearly blinked, his thick lashes fluttering before he caught himself. He faced me with a parted, full mouth. Pearly light overcame the blush in his cheeks. He glowed as much as when he described his passion for giving people lasting happiness with his matches.

Part of me wanted to deviate from my plan and close the distance between our mouths. A flutter of something new and comforting sparked in my belly. I'd never felt this kind of open intimacy with anyone before. What would it be like to explore—

A glacial chunk of utter despair slammed into my chest, caving in the fragile, genuine affection. I couldn't break, not yet. Just a little longer.

"Thank you." I tapped my lips against the tip of his nose, and hoped Venus couldn't tell the difference with my hands in the way.

Cupid tentatively reached out, fingers brushing my waist. Did he want to keep going, to pull me tighter to him? I wanted him to.

Arrow's cry pierced through my mind. It overcame me, overwhelmed me. Arrow was me. I was Arrow. My own cry pierced through my mind.

I crashed to my knees and tears cascaded down my cheeks. Snot choked my nose and phlegm clogged my throat as I rocked, clawing at myself. How could I feel something so pure for someone else, even for an instant? How had my heart betrayed me, betrayed him? "I'm scum, I'm lower than scum."

"Hold on." Someone knelt beside me, Cupid, the source of my shame. He was so brilliant with the rainbow slivers in his aura—

no, my traitorous, vile heart shouldn't admire him. "She passed your trial. Now bring the satyr."

"I've never seen you so bright before," Venus said. "What makes her so different from anyone else?"

"It's not about her!" Cupid rose with his wings spread, a genuine god showing his full power. "I'm like this because she listened. You've never seen me like this because you never paid attention. My work is helping people find real, lasting happiness. Physical desire can be part of that, but that's not as important to me as it is for you, it never has been." He hooked his arms under mine and held me up until I could stand on my own. "Pay attention now and get the satyr."

Venus smiled broad and proud, showing all of her cycling, vibrant teeth. I'd seen that smile on my own mother at both my sisters' weddings when she realized her babies were all grown up.

I breathed heavier with anticipation as Venus scooped her open palm up through the air. As soon as she brought Blandus out, I would beg for his freedom, or insist that she let me stay with him in his prison.

A short man rose out of the floor of the courtyard. His blond ringlets bounced, revealing tiny goat ears before settling into place again. Gold chains and cuffs as fine as jewelry bound the rest of his human physique to the stone.

"Sweetheart!" Blandus beamed as he spotted me, hope bringing out his dimple. "Quick, trade yourself for my freedom. You'd do anything to get me out—"

"Who said you could speak, thief?" Venus snapped her fingers, and Blandus's jaw snapped shut.

I started forward, ready to run for him. Would Venus really accept my life in trade for his?

"Psyche, remember what you came here for." Cupid caught my arms and lined himself up behind me, chest inhaling and exhaling against my back. He spoke next to my ear. "If you get too close to him, you might not be able to do this. Stay here, with me. Take the arrow and throw it into him."

"But I love him, I don't want to hurt him." I looked between

Blandus and Venus, unsure how to stop her from stealing my true love away again.

"Are you sure it's not the arrow making you feel that?" Cupid patted around my hip until he came to his arrow in its leather quiver. He guided my hand to it. "If you two are a true match, piercing him will only prove it."

Yes, if I could prove to Venus my love was real, she might take pity on me and let Blandus go. I scrambled to pull out the rose-gold arrow, the weapon radiating in Cupid's light. "But my aim is awful."

"Mine won't be. Even with my eyes closed." The god set his hand over my arm, ready to guide my shot. "Let me help."

I raised the arrow and drew back my arm. A fog I hadn't known was there lifted. Guided by Cupid's subtle pressing, the arrow point lined up to Blandus with perfect clarity. I took a steadying breath and launched it.

The arrow lodged in Blandus's chest, its shaft turning translucent.

My mind went quiet. My chest seemed empty, hopeful. My muscles stayed calm as I lowered my arm and stepped away from Cupid. I thought over the best nights I ever had. Climbing out the window of my childhood bedroom to find freedom, beating my mentor for the first time in a spar, a whole tavern cheering for me after we took down a local invader. No more Blandus.

Arrow was finally dead.

Venus tugged Cupid's arrow free from Blandus's chest and walked it back to her son. She whispered something to him before slipping it into his hand and sauntering back to her prisoner. The goddess threw me a sly wink as she wrapped her arms around Blandus and evaporated with him.

I stood facing Cupid in the courtyard, just the two of us, surrounded by a risqué feast and bursts of floral intensity. The perfect setting for an adventure's end, or a romantic beginning.

"Here." Cupid held the arrow out, its tip facing me. "I'd like to be able to see how lovely you've become for myself."

He gripped the shaft and nudged it forward. His arrow's head passed through my tunic and disappeared into my stomach. The excited flutter from our near-kiss flared to new life in my chest, hardy and resilient without Arrow to dampen it. Whether it didn't last beyond this courtyard or continued for years to come, it was all mine.

Cupid opened his eyes, and they were the same rose-gold as his arrow.

About the Author

Brie Tartaglia is an Italian-American fantasy author who talks with her hands (in American Sign Language). After years writing and editing fiction, nonfiction, and comics from her native swamplands, she escaped to the mountains and obtained a Masters in Creative Writing and Publishing. When not consuming or telling stories, she's prepping for her next renaissance festival, artistic excursion, or scalding mug of over-steeped tea. Join her adventures at *brietartaglia.com*

CELESTIAL BODIES

J. L. SMYSER

Year 1

I don't think you ever knew this, but I saw you before the mission began. It was during the candidate gala before the selection process. We were all assessing one another and trying to figure out who had the best chances of going on the terraforming mission. Mostly academics with occasional military personnel. None of us had any real idea of what it would take.

Through the crowd of candidates, I saw you in all your confident splendor, smiling and talking to others with genuine curiosity. You easily pivoted from one conversation to another, bringing out a different side of you for each. The clever astrophysicist. The experienced astronaut. The radical scientist. It all came to you with ease, like you knew you had one of the positions already and were simply looking for your partners.

I, on the other hand, orbited the party, stuffing my face with appetizers. Also confident, but in a different way. Confident they'd never pick the disgraced aerospace engineer to be a "hero of humanity." I had to pull some frayed strings just to be at the gala.

Things might have turned out differently had I met you then, but I was too nervous. It was the first time since high school that I had butterflies in my stomach. Sorry, I should say moths. You were right. They are cooler.

We finally met a few months later—I as the official terraformer of Venus, and you for Mars. The selection process was grueling, but proving I had learned from my professional mistakes ended up being a point in my favor. I double checked every bit of calculation. Refused to cut corners, and somehow impressed them. All because I knew first-hand that one misplaced integer could get someone killed.

It was easier for you, but I still think you were trying to put up a brave face.

We weren't expecting to be the only ones. With the war going on, and the restriction of resources, the government couldn't justify sending whole crews up to space. If anything happened to us, they'd send up a replacement. It was ridiculous meddling and a complete lack of foresight. You called us glorified button pushers. We both laughed it off at the time, but mine was fake. I was terrified.

Months of strenuous preparation together can bond two people. So many boring training videos, thick manuals to memorize, and brutal cryogenic acclimatization. I don't remember any names or faces of anyone we worked with, but I remember us. The late-night study sessions. The beach trip where you told me about your fascination with moths. But my favorite night was the bar, where you destroyed me in every game of astro-billiards.

You tried to throw the final game of the night by sending your last ball careening around the suspended sun, but I still managed to lose when my ball failed to slingshot around the Earth and knocked yours into the pocket. You poked your fun at me—the space genius who struggled with a game of gravity and planetary physics. Instead of making excuses, I latched on to being called a genius. The number of times someone acknowledged me like that could be counted on one hand.

Poorly misjudging a moment, I leaned in for a kiss, failed, and played it off as something else to avoid embarrassment. I know you saw through that. There was no point in trying again. We'd soon be farther apart from each other than any other two people in history. A 100 million kilometer long-distance relationship was infinitely discouraging. I wish I was wise enough to know you wanted me to try again at least once before we were separated. But I'm not the only one to blame here. You didn't make a move either.

Your birthday came around soon after. I got you that luna moth pupa, thinking it'd be a nice pet until takeoff. Paid a collector a fairly decent amount for it, since moths were pretty much extinct in the wild in those days. Unfortunately, I didn't realize the lifespan of an adult luna was about a week. A little embarrassing, but you assured me beauty is fleeting.

Finally, it was time to say goodbye to the planet on which we had lived our entire lives. According to allied space agencies around the world, we were the last bastion of hope for humanity's survival. And not one of them would be around to see that hope come to fruition. With our technology, they estimated a few thousand years of terraforming before shuttles could begin ferrying people over to Venus and Mars. But we were all hopeful more tech would be developed and sent to us as needed to speed the process along.

You were sent up first. Off to the terraforming station already in orbit around Mars. I liked to imagine you could look out the window of the shuttle and see me waving you off. My launch was set for the day after. I couldn't sleep that night.

Luckily, they'd give us a direct line of communication in our stations. Otherwise I'd be alone again. It was funny, actually. I had chosen this because there was nothing else in my life. No family. No prospects. Just a dead-end job teaching math at a community college. This one-way trip leaving everything behind was supposed to be a sacrificial choice in a way. Instead, it became a new starting point to my life.

❧

Year 2

People at mission control weren't really ones to hold a fun conversation. Only being able to talk to them during the trip made the months feel like an eternity. So even though we were only going to be together through a digital screen, I couldn't wait to get onboard the station.

After boarding, I looked out the bay windows to Venus. The station would run mostly on its own, but I still felt a tremendous weight on my shoulder while floating around this sulfuric cocoon about to be forced into a transformation. All I could think about was sharing this overwhelming feeling with you.

I was hardly settled in before I set up the quantum communicator and called. You were clearly waiting for it because you picked up in a few seconds. Seeing you light up my screen sent me into a panicked joy. And we talked for hours.

Every day, I'd find an excuse to call. I'd pretend my atmospheric dampener controls were broken, or the artificial gravity was wonky, or my living quarters needed some decorating —all so I could need your help. You, on the other hand, never pretended anything. Without a greeting, you'd call with a question to trip me up. *What if we're in a space equivalent of a fishbowl? Do you think it would hurt to go through a black hole? Is it ethical for us to change entire planets?* I got used to having an existential crisis during breakfast.

We worked out, played chess in silent contemplation, and occasionally talked until we fell asleep. Even if I wasn't your closest friend, you were mine, so I was desperate to draw out these calls—forcing myself to make small talk like my life depended on it. It got to the point where mission control complained they couldn't always get through to us. They made empty threats to replace one of us, so we agreed to cut down on our calls to each other.

That was around the time the news broke back on Earth about my involvement in the space station disaster that killed three astronauts on board. Mission control put out a statement on my behalf to the media, but what people said back on Earth didn't matter to me anymore. I only cared what you had to say, and made myself sick to my stomach by obsessing over it. I waited for you to make that call rather than me desperately reaching out and potentially pushing you away. When you finally did, you were more concerned about why I didn't tell you than anything else.

So after many years, I finally talked about my tragic measurement and the people I got killed. They traced the mistake back to me, and I lost everything. I wanted to go to each funeral, but during the first one, the mother of the astronaut made a scene and kicked me out. I couldn't bring myself to go to the next two. From then on, I shut myself off from the world as much as I could.

Just when I could feel the overbearing weight of loneliness creeping over me again, you forgave me. Although you'd never call me a math genius again, at least you had the compassion to do what no one else could—not even myself.

Year 3

CRYOSTASIS DAY CAME. When everything was in place, the only thing left to do was wait. Set it and forget it for 100 years. For me, the drastic change was a relief. I had no family to miss, people would forget my name, and the disaster would be a footnote in history. But you had parents, grandparents, siblings, friends. They'd be gone. Long dead. They sent you final messages, and you sent each of them one in return. I still can't imagine how hard that was. During our final talk before stasis, you tried not to cry in front of me. Even when I said it's better to let it out, you held firm with that brave face.

Year 103

CRYOSTASIS WAS LIKE GESTATION, except instead of us changing, everything else did.

There was no more mission control. It had become space command—a new branch of the military—and we had been retrofitted with ranks. Not a good sign. Diplomacy had failed at some point. Probably many times over. But we were away from all that. They didn't tell us the details, and we didn't ask. It wasn't our priority.

This became our new normal. Wake up. Meet the new faces in charge. Work for a month or so. Go back into stasis...

Year 180

...AND WAKE UP ONCE MORE, never to see those faces again. On Earth, new conflicts were fought, borders changed, tech transformed, and people lived and died. But to us, it was like falling asleep one night and waking up the next morning. The only change for us was Venus slowly losing its golden luster and Mars getting moldy with algae.

At the very least, you were my constant, and I yours.

Year 233

DURING ONE OF our vacation days, we had a meal together. Well, I suppose "meal" is not the best word for it. It was our standard fare. Space command had sent us new rations designed to last for a thousand years in the preservation chamber. No more luxuries like a steak dinner with wine, but the company was what mattered.

It was then I shared the mythology of Venus and Mars—the goddess of beauty and the god of war. Their union created Cupid. Love conquered war. How fitting it was for us to be hovering over those two planets, I suggested. It went over your head. You thought I meant the endless wars on Earth would be stopped by our terraforming mission.

Perhaps I was too subtle. Or perhaps you were deflecting.

I hoped it was the former.

Year 291

You woke up later than I did. It was only a week, but that kind of cryochamber malfunction was strange, and could be detrimental to our tight schedule. Space command was of no help. For whatever reason, this new generation seemed to be less enthused by our mission. So you tinkered with it yourself, assuring it would be fine the next time. You refused to let me double check. It was your confidence that made me trust you, but my thoughts festered with the anxiety that you didn't trust me.

Year 352

Space command had become Intergalactic Central Base. They sent us new tech to install for the stations. It arrived on the first day we came out of stasis. They were playing it fast and loose with these timelines. Had either of us not been up to the task due to post-stasis sickness, or had your cryochamber malfunctioned again, we could have messed up the retrieval—ruining trillions of dollars of equipment.

Despite that, we were amazed by how advanced Earth had gotten. The additions were way beyond anything we studied. Nanobot surface scattering. Biosphere pumping. Tectonic stabilizers. Once we got it all up and running, we'd make habitable planets in a quarter of the original time. But, unfortunately for us, it required months of studying to comprehend. It became invasive.

There were times I didn't see you for days. For one excuse or another, you were too busy. After several weeks without a call, I worried about your health. As even more days passed without even a simple message, there was no greater thought in my mind than the familiar assumption of being ignored. A feeling I thought I had left behind became exacerbated by the emptiness of space.

Finally, when you did call me back, I was cold and distant.

You didn't deserve that.

Year 604

Silence. Awaking from our longest span in stasis, we were met with silence. Our comms to each other were perfectly fine, but the ICB, or whoever was in control at that point, was gone. No messages. No calls. Nothing.

With that fake optimism I'd come to know well, you suggested their comms were momentarily down and they'd be in contact again shortly. I wanted to believe that, and maybe I did for a while. But eventually, the eerie feeling of dead silence could no longer be shaken from my bones.

We *were* alone.

Our only hope was to believe the ship colonies had embarked and were standing by until the terraforming was complete. Otherwise, we had no reason to keep going.

There was a part of me that wanted to ditch the mission and use my fuel reserves to get to you, but I wasn't sure I was up to that task. Life and death calculations had to be made. You said it wasn't a good idea. I respected that decision, and resented it.

Year 712

BECAUSE WE ONLY HAD EACH other, we returned to our previous routine of talking every day. In fact, there was hardly a time when the comms were off. And in those moments of rekindled connection, I fell into a deeper love than I ever knew. I kept falling in love over and over again like you were the Venus I orbited around. Endless falling toward a celestial body without ever touching it. That was something that needed to be said before it was too late.

So I finally told you.

And you knew. You had always known and felt similar, but something held you back.

Year 800

I DON'T KNOW what we were to each other. There was hardly a second we were alone. We laughed like a couple. Had date nights like one. There was some semblance of a normal relationship despite the fathoms of space between us. But you never said you loved me. Maybe it was too soon. Maybe it was the distance. Whatever it was, I pretended to be fine with it.

It was as if we were both afraid of losing each other and it manifested in completely opposite ways. Like you were trying to keep the moth in its cocoon, and I was trying to force it out. Neither of us wanted it to die, but both our methods were killing it.

Year 852

HUNDREDS OF YEARS passed without anything from Earth. Things fell apart on our stations. Every time we woke from stasis there'd be something new to repair. Without guidance from Earth, some of our tech was left broken. If something couldn't be fixed, we did our best to make sure it wouldn't cause further disruptions to the station. Losing luxuries was fine, but we worried something vital would deteriorate. If one of us lost power, life support systems, or even the ration preservation chamber, that would be the end of our mission—or worse.

Year 910

OUR LAST SPRINT to the finish line was near. Terraforming calculations told us we needed only one more cryostasis sleep of fifty years. Venus and Mars were soon to be completely sustainable for life. Then we could use the last of our fuel reserves to surface our planets and be the first to settle on a new home.

Right before our stasis, I was once again going to bring up the idea of using my fuel reserves to come to you. I wrote down compelling arguments and rebuttals to any rejections I could think of, but all of that crumbled when you picked up the call—shaking.

Trying to laugh it off, you revealed you almost died on a spacewalk outside of the station. While repairing a solar panel, the cable snapped, nearly flinging you off into space. My mouth fell agape, horrified.

You said everything was fine. You weren't.

You said the shaking was too many caffeine pills. No, that was the adrenaline. And fear. And exhaustion, all mashed behind your fake grin.

I was furious. I couldn't stop myself from snapping at you for being reckless. For nearly getting yourself killed. For trying to fix everything by yourself without letting me know beforehand. For lying about being okay when you weren't.

Why couldn't you stop trying to be brave?

But you saw that as selfishness. Claimed I only wanted you to be safe so I wouldn't be alone again. Maybe it was true, but I didn't want it to be, so I called you a coward for not loving me. You ended the call.

As I prepared for stasis, every word echoed through my head and pricked me with regret. Sometimes thoughts immediately before entering stasis don't have time to enter long-term memory. I wrote something on my hand to remember.

Year 960

APOLOGIZE. That's what I wrote. It took a moment for my post-stasis brain to recall the fight.

My Venus was no longer the milky yellow it once was. It was no longer plagued with storms and volcanic eruptions. It was beautiful, like a second Earth. Although, it was beautiful before, too, in its own way.

I pondered this while my call to you kept ringing and ringing. When you didn't answer, I sent a video recording of my apology, but it bounced back with an error. The Mars station's communicator was down.

My stomach fell to Venus like a crashing satellite.

I checked the station's log history. Every month, each station sent out and received a ping to record functionality. There hadn't been a ping from Earth for 500 years, but the Mars station updated every month on schedule. Which meant the station wasn't destroyed.

Over the next week, I made all the necessary calculations to get to you. The station was made of modular sections. Some were unnecessary and needed to be undocked to lighten the load. I double- and triple-checked my calculations. No more mistakes. Even a little one meant crashing or being cast off into space forever. When the preparations were complete, I instructed the computer to blast out of Venus's orbit.

After a few months, I approached Earth for a flyby gravity

assist. It was always going to be a dangerous proximity, but I didn't expect such a dead-looking planet. Above the ashen clouds in the atmosphere was a wall of debris and wreckage swirling around the planet. Even if there was anyone left underneath, no shuttles could get out of that safely. Had my slingshot been any closer, a hypervelocity impact from a fragment of that detritus could've scattered my remains across Earth's orbit.

But my luck came through, and our old home flung me off to Mars. To you.

I let my station send out a ping to find yours. The computer used the last of my fuel reserves to slow down and course correct into docking.

The docking modules latched.

Sealed and pressurized.

Doors opened.

Down the module corridor, I saw nothing. I had hoped you'd come to see me, even if it meant getting into another fight. As long as I knew everything was all right. But you weren't waiting for me, so I entered to find you.

The first thing I noticed in your station was the false gravity was turned off. Even in your living quarters, which was strange. There was soft lighting—accentuating the glow of Mars through the bay window. After a short search of this quiet station, I found you. Gently floating. Alive. Breathing through the medkit oxygen tank.

Aged fifty years.

Without uttering a single word, I pieced it together. Your cryochamber malfunctioned again and woke you up early. You couldn't fix it. It was still you, but a version of you who lived an entire life without me—without anyone. Your eyes were filled with loneliness. Fifty years with no one to talk to but yourself and the station computer. You faced my greatest fear for all that time.

Although the lack of gravity was easy on your bones, you turned it on again for us to sit and have a chat. You finally acknowledged that you loved me once, but only realized it a long time after the argument. Despite that, you had to stop loving me after ten or fifteen years of waiting. It was a past you had to get over. Which you did. Breaking the comms was supposed to keep me away.

Then you landed the final blow. Your family's history of cancer. The station's health diagnostic report said you had less than a year. Maybe even as low as four months.

I told you to get in my cryochamber, but you refused. Even if they had a cure, Earth wasn't coming to save us. But that's not what I wanted. So I explained myself. If you lived a full life without me, I was going to live a full life without you. And after fifty years, we'd live our final days together. It would be brief, I noted, but reminded you beauty is fleeting.

Year 1009

NOW I KNOW why you fell out of love. You had so much strength for continuing on day after day. I can't blame you for leaving something behind. At least I was lucky enough to have a goal to keep pushing me forward.

For the first twenty years of your sleep, I finished the final touches to Mars's terraforming. I focused on one particular area before planning our descent. I used the station's power source and terraforming tech to make this final spot of land into the perfect home. A luscious green spot on a once-dead planet. For the final decades, I built and furnished our lovely log cabin using the nearby forest. The station had schematics for other things, like making clothes and growing crops to feed myself real food instead of rations.

Freshly out of stasis, you took all this in, teary-eyed and groggy. I guided you to a bench in front of the cabin. There, I showed you the reason why I let you out a year early. In the terraforming tech was the inclusion of thousands of different types of insects, worms, birds, and rodents to ensure optimal biodiversity. You had long ago requested one specific creature to be included in that package.

And so, we finally sat together after so many years apart. You laid your head on my shoulder, and we enjoyed the sight of the luna moths taking flight on Mars.

Author Bio

J. L. Smyser is a teacher by day, vigilante by night, and co-owner of Blue Feathered Quill Publishing. He squeezes in his writing time by scribbling on any scraps of paper or sticky notes, and the cats that use him as furniture are his muses. His notes app is filled with ideas he'll probably never get around to using, none of which will be deleted "just in case". The curious reader will be able to find other stories he's written once he realizes they will never be perfect. His ultimate goals in life are writing something for *Star Wars*, making up a word that gets put in the dictionary, and becoming immortal. On any given day, you can find him somewhere in Colorado trying his best.

HIT POINTS

J.E. BIRK

We were in the Milan airport when I climbed onto a moving luggage carousel.

"Lucas?" Matt's voice was high and frantic. "What are you doing?"

Ever since the accident, Matt had shadowed me like a puppy keeping watch over its owner, and I wasn't so numbed by grief that I couldn't understand his reasoning: he constantly worried I'd decide to pack it all in and join Chloe by doing something like sticking my head in the oven or taking up a diet of nothing but Cheetos and vodka. And now he seemed concerned I was throwing myself onto the mercy of a conveyor belt moving less than a mile per hour.

"Don't worry!" I called back as I attempted to crawl past a large neon-pink duffle bag and nearly fell over a backpack the size of my torso. "The die fell out of my pocket while I was grabbing my suitcase. I just need to find it!" Then I saw it: the object I carried with me everywhere. Bright purple, with twenty gold numbers inscribed across each of its faces in Comic Sans, my favorite font. Chloe and Matt both teased me about my obsession with that font, but as I always told them, someone had to love poor Comic Sans.

Chloe had the die made as a gift for our tenth anniversary. Matt knew what it meant to me, and he relaxed and nodded in easy understanding while the crowd around us let out gasps and mutterings in shocked Italian. Thanks to my two-hundred-day Duolingo streak, I could pick up just a few words: *man* and *crazy* and *hospital.*

"I can reach it!" I lunged for the die, which was keeping pace with a Louis Vuitton suitcase. "Gotcha!" I grabbed hold of it, but then quickly lost my grip. The die flew up into the air, I leapt for it, and the next thing I knew I was falling past a swirl of Ls and Vs and bright pink cloth while Italian words soared past my ears and the floor rushed toward me.

Well, drat. Maybe I really was going to kick it on a luggage carousel after all. So much for letting Cheetos and vodka do the job. I was making a last grab of hope for the Louis Vuitton when strong arms latched onto me, breaking my fall in an athletic twirl that brought me down to the ground much more gently than I was anticipating...except I never actually hit the ground. Instead, I landed with an *oof* on top of my best friend. Matt clasped his arms around me as he somehow managed to fit in another roll across the tiled floor that quickly cushioned both our falls.

Applause shattered the air around us. "Whew!" Matt's dark curls fell across his forehead as he helped me sit up. "You're okay, right? Lucas?"

Okay was a relative term. Physically, I was fine. But was I reeling from landing on top of the best friend I'd been having uncomfortable feelings about for the last three months, after I'd finally started to come out of the grief fog I fell into after my wife passed away? Was I deeply regretting agreeing to travel halfway across the world with said best friend on a trip my wife and I had always planned to take with him? Was I, in fact, questioning many of my life choices to date?

Yes, yes, and yes. Still, the baggage claim of the Milan airport didn't seem like the best time to mention any of that. So I just took a breath, nodded, and let Matt help me stand.

Applause sprang up again, all of it directed at Matt. He blushed, ever humble, and said something in Italian, because his Duolingo streak was two hundred and fifty days and because Matt managed to be naturally gifted at anything he tried. Even rescuing his best friend from a death-by-suitcase scenario.

I straightened my hoodie and studied the small object now sitting in my palm. It had been zipped into the side pocket of my travel pants when we walked into baggage claim. I was absolutely sure of it. I'd carried that die with me everywhere for years, both before and after Chloe's death. It was the best gift she'd ever given me and one of the most important physical objects in my life, even more important than the wedding ring she'd slipped on my finger the day we said our vows. When it traveled somewhere with me, I treated that die with more reverence than I gave my wallet or my car keys. I'd been keeping tabs on it the whole way from Denver; I had better awareness of that die than I did of my passport. How had it gotten onto that conveyor belt?

And that's when I began to wonder: could a ghost inhabit a twenty-sided die?

❧

CHLOE WAS THE FIRST, and only, person I'd ever said *I'm bisexual* out loud to.

It's not that I was ever hiding it, exactly. It's just that fully realizing you're not straight when you're a guy in your thirties who's in a committed, monogamous relationship with a woman is...well, awkward? Even telling Chloe was a challenge, and she and I had been together since we were nineteen.

"Can I be bisexual if I'm only in love with you? Or pansexual? At my age?" I blurted the words out over morning coffee at our kitchen counter one day. Chloe, a middle school teacher, had endless patience for my word vomit. She shrugged, unfazed.

"I don't think there's an age limit on bisexuality or pansexuality, hon. Does this mean we can start ogling Rob Lowe together? Because it's really hard for me to play it cool when *911: Lone Star* is on." She took another sip of coffee while I sat there, stunned. And from then on, we played *eff, marry, date* together whenever we found ourselves staring at the same guy.

There was a freedom in saying those words to her. Freedom in realizing that falling in love young with the woman of my dreams didn't preclude or change feelings and wonderings I'd had for long portions of my life. There was freedom in accepting that realization for myself. But my bisexuality was all so theoretical, and every time I opened up my mouth to tell someone besides Chloe, I froze. Would it change things? Would it change how they looked at me? Or at my relationship with Chloe?

And Matt...what would he think? That question haunted me, and I never told him. The closest I ever came was one night when we were all watching the hockey playoffs together. Matt spent an average of three nights a week at our house. Eating dinner, playing board games, watching whatever happened to be on television. The three of us had been attached at the hip since we'd met in college, and we'd moved into the same condo complex in Denver after Chloe and I got married.

When the game ended that night, Matt's head was in Chloe's lap and his feet were in mine, because he was too tall to properly fit on our couch. He was half-drunk on the tequila seltzers he pretended not to like, since macho marathon runners who work in hedge funds aren't supposed to drink anything but IPAs and Michelob Ultra. "I'm so glad I didn't go on that date tonight," he mumbled against Chloe's jeans.

She and I exchanged a look. Matt dated plenty of women, but none of them ever seemed to stick. None of them ended up coming to our apartment more than once before Matt broke up with them.

"What date?" Chloe asked him.

Matt sighed. "Another setup by my team at the office. They think it's depressing that I'm still single." He sighed and flipped like a fish across our laps. "They don't believe me when I tell them

I like my life how it is. I like being with you two. You're all I need. My family." He was slurring the words slightly by then, and soon after that he started snoring.

Chloe and I managed to get ourselves out from under him and tuck blankets around him. Then we tried to find the kitchen counter under a load of takeout containers, and I thought about what truths we owe to the people we call family. "Someday I'll tell Matt," I finally whispered to Chloe.

Chloe frowned and pursed her lips. "You should tell him if you want to. Just remember," she added. "You don't owe anything to anyone, babe. You only owe your world to yourself." Then she kissed me on the cheek and went back to tying up trash bags, and I wondered for the twenty bazillionth time how I'd gotten so lucky. *Me.* I was just a high-school history teacher with a penchant for snark, a paunch around the middle, and a not-so-slight addiction to *Dungeons and Dragons.* And here I'd landed the most perfect woman in the world. Except when we argued over whose turn it was to unload the dishwasher.

I never did come out to Matt. And when Chloe went off the road in that rainstorm, I swore to the universe that I'd unload the dishwasher for the rest of our days together if she just made it out of the hospital. After she passed away on the operating table, I found I couldn't look at our old dishwasher anymore.

Every single night after her death, Matt came over to eat dinner with me. We did all the dishes by hand together, and he never once asked me why.

I WAS STUDYING the die as Matt navigated our miniature rental car through the winding, tight roads of Tuscany. I would have been white-knuckling it every time a truck came around the corner, but Matt just waved cheerfully and inched the car past other vehicles without breaking a sweat.

"Do you think Chloe knows?" I asked him. "That we finally made it here?" The three of us had been slow-planning this trip for years, never quite getting around to taking it. When the one-year anniversary of the accident started to creep up, Matt appeared in front of me with plane tickets and an itinerary.

"I think we need to go," he said. "For her."

Matt swallowed, and I watched his Adam's apple as it moved. He focused on keeping the car steady around a hilly curve, and for a moment I thought he wasn't going to answer me.

"Yes," he finally whispered. "I think she knows, Lukey." I blinked back tears when he used the nickname Chloe had always called me.

He took his hand off the stick shift and moved it slightly toward mine. My vision went fuzzy around the edges. Matt and I touched all the time; physical contact was a natural and very real part of our relationship. But holding hands crossed an unmarked and unspoken boundary we'd never ventured over before.

Matt hesitated, just for a moment. And then he dropped his right hand and let it rest on mine.

It was warm and familiar. Soft and hard at the same time. Reminiscent of recent dreams that left me sweaty and wondering how any person who considered themselves a decent human could start having *those kinds* of dreams about his best friend only nine months after his wife's death.

When he lifted his hand away from mine to shift gears again, I felt the loss the same way I still felt the emptiness on the right side of my bed at night.

Matt swallowed again. I couldn't look away from his Adam's apple. "Chloe would be proud of us for finally coming here. And we're going to have a great time. I'm sure of it."

AND FOR THE first few days, we did have a great time. Or at least, Matt did. And I did too, in theory. It's hard not to enjoy yourself in a place where every meal makes your taste buds sing and the wine is cheaper than water. But each morning when I slipped the twenty-sided die into whatever secure pocket I had ready for it that day, I knew I was waiting for its next move.

That move came in a family-owned restaurant in the local village where Matt and I were staying. It was a restaurant Chloe had chosen for us. Ever the planner, Chloe had left behind a whole notebook filled with brainstorming for this trip we'd never managed to take together. Next to this restaurant's name, in the notebook's margins, she'd written *MUST GO HERE.*

So we'd decided to go for the full Tuscan dinner experience: apps, pasta, steak the size of our arms. The works. I was elbow-deep in burrata cheese when I jiggled the side of my zipped jacket pocket to check for the die and felt a distinct absence of weight.

"Oh no." Only my missing die could drag me away from the best cheese I'd ever tasted in my life. Matt was slurping away at some kind of pepper sauce, blissfully unaware of my panic as I leapt under the table like a dog after a table scrap.

"Signore?" someone said.

"Lucas?"

Great. Now I'd alarmed the server *and* Matt. "Don't worry about me!" I called through the tablecloth. "Just...need to find something!" I scrambled as I squinted at the hardwood floor. Where could it have gone? I was simultaneously shocked and not surprised at all when I found the die sitting perfectly on the toe of Matt's white sneaker.

"Didn't you feel it?" I asked as I popped up from under the table like some kind of possessed jack-in-the-box, shocking the poor waiter, who was probably all of sixteen. He'd already had to endure me accidentally ordering a car as a main course; the poor guy didn't need me trying to explain *this* situation in my piss-poor Italian. What even was the Italian word for sneaker, I wondered, as Matt shook his head and smiled.

"No, I didn't." He laughed as he helped me stand back up. "How does that thing keep getting away from you? Thank goodness you found it."

I left the die next to my water glass for the rest of the meal, eyeing it like a misbehaving child. And then, Matt said something during dessert.

"I wish we could thank Chloe for finding this restaurant."

His words were wistful. Sad. He'd loved her as much as I had, in a different kind of way. A love that had its own power. I reached over, like I might take his hand the way he'd taken mine in the car. But we both hesitated, and all the oxygen seemed to leave the space around us as we stared at each other. Eventually, I dropped my hand first.

I used it to grab hold of the die instead. I held it so firmly on the walk back to the car that it left indentation marks in my palm.

❧

THAT NIGHT, I sat outside the villa apartment we'd rented. Matt was inside showering, and I was spinning the die over and over. Rolling it. Contemplating it.

"Chloe," I whispered to the die. "Are you here?"

I'm not sure what I expected. For Casper to pop out of the ancient stonework of the building, cheerfully musing in Chloe's voice about ghosts and other sides and crossovers? Or maybe I expected the die to jump into my hand, spin itself through the air, and land on twenty on the patio table in front of me.

Nothing happened. Nothing. I sighed and stood up, maybe a little too quickly, and I pushed into the patio table by accident. The die moved, twisted, and twirled on an edge. I blinked as I watched to see what number it landed on.

Sixteen.

My heart pounded just a little faster in my chest as memories scattered through me.

College. Matt and Chloe and me, out at a bar, silly drunk on Irish car bombs right after the end of finals. That was our senior year, and we were talking about what came next.

"I wish I knew the future," Chloe said, tilting slightly on the bar seat. "I want to know if we'll all still be *us* in twenty years." She'd giggled then, high and light with that lilting laugh she had.

"You know. The Three Musketeers!" The predictable nickname had been given to us by one of our philosophy professors, and it had stuck. A large percentage of the faculty and staff around our small college campus called us that whenever they saw the three of us together.

"Nobody knows the future," I told her. Matt was listing against the hand he'd propped his face up on, studying us intently, the way he so often did. I always wondered what he was thinking when he looked at us that way, but I never asked.

"Let's see what the odds are," Chloe announced. "Give me your die!"

A twenty-sided die had been my good luck charm for years, and I kept one on me at all times. I'd had one in my pocket the day I met Chloe and Matt in a freshman composition class. The one I had back then was a boring old die I'd gotten in a set, nothing like the one Chloe would give me more than a decade later. I pulled out the die and handed it to her.

"I'm going to roll the die," she said gleefully. "The higher the number, the better the odds are that we'll stay this close, all three of us. The more hit points, the bigger the chance we have!"

I groaned and rolled my eyes. Of the three of us, I was the only one who regularly played *Dungeons and Dragons*, and I was forever correcting both Chloe and Matt about their use of proper terminology. "You're using hit points wrong," I told Chloe. "Hit points are when—"

"Boring!" Chloe announced cheerfully. "Can't I just roll the die and yell out a number of hit points? Hit points sounds *fun*."

"We should definitely yell out hit points," Matt said, almost dreamily. "And you should definitely roll the die and make it tell us what our chances are. Kind of like that Rush song." He hummed something for a minute before he started to sing some off-key lines. Something about *fate* and *bones*. Chloe and I both looked at him blankly. Just as my love of D&D eluded the two of them, Matt's love of prog rock went right over both of our heads. And to be fair, neither Matt nor I could comprehend Chloe's obsession with binging Food

Network shows for hours on end. She didn't even like to cook.

"Okay, that settles it." Chloe held up a hand. "We're rolling the die, got it? Higher the number, the better our chances." She narrowed her eyes at me. "And whatever number we roll...I'm calling them hit points, Lucas."

I decided I was too drunk to argue.

"Oh, sacred die that Lukey is obsessed with," she whispered. "Predict the future." She spun the die on the bar, and we all sat up straighter as it clicked and moved against the wood. When it landed on 16, I let out a laugh of relief.

"Sixteen hit points!" Chloe said gleefully. "The die says our odds are good!" Matt started singing again, and soon after that Chloe puked all over the bar's ancient jukebox.

Now, in the middle of Tuscany, living out Chloe's lost travel dreams, I stared at the die which had so easily hit that same number once again. I leaned down and studied it. Pursed my lips and thought. And then I took the shot.

"Chloe," I said to the die. "I'm going to roll again. What are the chances of things going well if I finally tell Matt?"

I flipped the die up into the air and held my breath as it launched itself back down in space to land on the table.

Seventeen.

I sat there for a long time, staring at that number.

Not quite maximum hit points, as Chloe would have said. But awfully close.

THE NEXT DAY, Matt drove us to Sienna. It was raining, and Sienna was hilly, and Matt and I hoisted umbrellas as I tried desperately to keep up with him while he charged up nearly vertical roads toward whatever caught his interest. We were laughing and joking and living the kind of day we used to live all the time back in college, back before adulting and paychecks and the inevitability of loss aged us as it had. I let myself fall into the moment, and it wasn't until the rain finally let up that I realized the die, once again, had magically escaped the zippered pocket of my jacket.

"Matt!" I said his name in a panic as I turned out the lining of the pocket, but he just nodded, ever cool-headed. We started retracing our steps. I was both shocked and not at all surprised when we spotted the die right next to the steps of a small bistro.

"Pranzo!" Matt called as he lifted the die in the air. Even I knew pranzo meant *lunch,* and I followed Matt inside.

Right away it was clear that this restaurant wasn't like the others we'd been eating in. It was covered in American rock memorabilia, and the owners seemed to have a particular penchant for the band Rush. Matt's eyes were wide as we ate the signature soup of Tuscany, a concoction of bread and tomatoes originally created by peasants, while he hummed along with every song that came on in the background.

Matt was frowning at the restaurant wall when he snapped his fingers. "Hey, I know this restaurant's name! It was in Chloe's notebook." He blinked hurriedly, and I looked away from the wetness in his eyes. "She had it on her list because she thought I'd like it."

Something lodged in my throat, and my vision crowded with one number: *seventeen.*

"Matt," I blurted out in a rush. "I'm bi. Or pan, maybe. I never was very good with labels." I shook my head. "And I'm sorry I never told you," I added.

And then I waited, heart pounding like the bass line of the song that played behind us. I waited to see if I had enough of Chloe's hit points in me. Waited to see if her odds played out in my favor.

"You don't have anything to be sorry for. Thank you," Matt finally whispered. "For telling me. You can't know what that means to me, Lucas. And I—I want you to know that—"

The words seemed to lodge in his throat then, and he stopped. He shook his head, and I didn't push him to go on. I knew better than anyone how words could get trapped inside of you and refuse to come out.

We finished the soup and started a silent walk back to the car. I was breathing out the feeling of being wholly, one hundred percent *me* in front of a person who meant so much to me. We were nearly back at our parking spot when I felt one of Matt's hands brush against mine.

We both turned to look at each other at exactly the same moment. I sucked in all the questions I wasn't ready to ask, and Matt frowned as he looked down at our arms.

And then he lifted his palm and slid it under mine.

I held in a gasp I didn't want him to hear as we both focused on walking straight ahead. I clung to him with one hand and the die with the other. I thought about the night in the pub when Chloe had first rolled that die and hit sixteen.

I saw that night so differently now. Just like the nights after Chloe's death, when I would lay in bed, so stricken with loneliness that sleep looked to be a million miles away. Matt often appeared out of nowhere on those nights, as if I'd somehow conjured him. He'd sat in the chair across from my bed, across from Chloe's cold, abandoned space in the sheets. He'd promised me that I wasn't ever going to be alone. Because he wouldn't allow it.

I could see so many things differently now. I held up the die, and it glinted in the bright sun, its silly font sparkling.

"Someone has to love Comic Sans," I whispered.

"I think we should go to that town with all the castles today," Matt said conversationally the next morning. I was slurping down espresso while he ate fruit.

"We're in Italy, for crying out loud," I told him. "There's freshly baked pastry on the counter, and you're eating strawberries and yogurt for breakfast. This is blasphemy."

He laughed. "I'm going for a run. Be ready when I get back?"

So I asked her again while he was gone. I had to.

"Chloe," I whispered to the die, just after Matt had addled my brain by putting on spandex under his running shorts. "I'm not sure if I should take another risk. I need you to tell me the odds, Chloe. Please."

I dropped the die onto the grass next to our apartment's patio, and it hit the ground with a soft thud. I sucked in a breath when I saw the roll.

Nineteen.

I could almost hear Chloe's voice in the air: *nearly maximum hit points, Lukey!*

I got ready to leave, but I couldn't seem to look away from the die the entire time; my eyes were all but attached to that one number. Nineteen. We were both quiet on the drive, and I finally put on a podcast so Rick Steves could tell us all about our forthcoming trip: about San Gimignano, a town of medieval towers. We parked in a lot below the town, already half-filled with other early summer tourists, and we started walking up the winding road toward the entrance of the village.

Matt frowned as I held the die between my thumb and forefinger. "Think it's going to take off on us again today?" he asked, but there wasn't much whimsy in his voice. We were both watching the die carefully, almost reverently, when a gust of wind shot through the air and the die flipped out of my right hand. Matt gasped at the same time I did, and we both moved to catch it at the same moment.

Our hands closed on it at the same time that our bodies came together, pushed against each other in time and space by a twenty-sided die. The air around us was still, and I wondered for a moment if I'd imagined that gust of wind. But I knew I hadn't. I was sure of it.

"Matt," I whispered. "Do you want me to..."

He pressed his forehead against mine. He was breathless and sweating slightly, and Matt was never breathless. Three miles into a run, Matt wasn't breathless. The corners of his mouth were tilted up in something like a smile.

"What did the die say?" he asked me.

He knew. Because of course he knew. Just like he knew not to load the dishwasher, or knew when I was being haunted by an empty bed, he knew when I'd been rolling the die without him, asking questions to an empty sky that maybe wasn't so empty after all.

He always knew.

"Nineteen," I answered softly.

He smiled then. Full-on smiled. "Good odds," he said evenly.

He leaned in all the way toward me as I leaned into him. The first touch of his lips to mine was different than anything I'd ever felt before, and also completely familiar in every way. It was home and away all at once. It was fireworks and being wrapped in the comfort of my favorite everyday blanket all at the same time. It was old and it was new. And I took it all in like a drowning person breaking the water's surface for a first gasp of air.

I'm not sure when we finally broke apart. It was either minutes or hours later. Matt kissed my forehead, and I'm sure I heard him murmur three words.

"Thank you, Chloe."

❧

AFTER THAT, there were topics others would have probably said we should have discussed. Labels. Fears. Secrets. Pasts. Presents. Futures. But we didn't talk about any of those things. Instead, we walked between towers, hand in hand, eyes locked together on the sky. We ate a massive portion of pasta for dinner and went back to the villa. We drank wine and listened to prog rock. We kissed some more. Matt got ready for bed, and I held up the die.

"Chloe," I said. "I'm going to roll one more time, okay? Tell me the future." I opened my hand and let purple and gold fall from it.

The die rolled twenty.

Maximum hit points.

About the Author

J.E. Birk, also known as Johanna Parkhurst, writes beloved and bestselling LGBTQ+ fiction and romance. She firmly believes in giving her perfectly imperfect characters the happily ever afters they all deserve. J.E./Johanna is a long-time lover of all types of genre fiction, and she's proud to be the director of the MA/MFA Genre Fiction program at Western Colorado University.

J.E./Johanna was raised in Vermont and is now adulting in Colorado with intermittent success. She enjoys paddleboarding, skiing, and traveling. She does not enjoy vacuuming. You can learn more about J.E.'s books by visiting her website, www.jebirk.com, and signing up for her newsletter.

FORGET-ME-NOT

ROBERT LUKE WILKINS

My lover lies near me, beautiful and still, as the first of five promised flowers sprouts from her dead left eye. I don't know its name. It has a short, strong stem, with seven pointed yellow-orange petals and a sweet, unfamiliar smell.

I love the brightness of the flower, the warmth of it. Not cool, like the pale blue forget-me-nots she adored, that bloom in clusters now around the trees and shrubs that span the wilds between our small stone cottage and the river, the place she called her garden.

Five blue-stone plant pots wait ready, each a half hand-span tall, and loosely filled with soil I collected from the river's edge. I take the flower's stem between my thumb and forefinger, and pull—it resists for a moment, and then her eye lifts out along with the roots.

Perhaps that's good. Perhaps it'll help it to grow.

I press my thumb into the soil of the first pot and make a hole, deep and wide enough to take the flower's roots, eye and all. I set the seedling home, brush the soil back around to cover, and press it down gently.

The seeds she gave me are in a pouch at my hip, and three more remain. I place one into her empty left eye socket. The seedling sprouts of the second flower are already piercing the lens of her right eye, but it's not ready. Not yet.

I take the first potted flower inside, and set it on the window-ledge behind the kitchen sink, to be sure it catches the sun.

HER BODY IS in full bloom, now, her eyes long gone. Day by day, she joins the garden.

From the front step of our cottage, I can see the whole of it, to the end of my vision—but close by, on the south side, a twisting tree struggles. It's a fruit tree, one I don't know. Like the others, even out of season, it should blossom and fruit, but instead I can see its leaves yellowing, their tips curling. I've already given it water, carried all the way from the river, but that didn't help. It needs more than I know how to provide.

But I can care for her flowers, her dusk stars. I know how to feed them, and how much water to give. The five blue-stone pots stand on the ledge behind the sink, the leftmost one already empty, but the other four host the seedlings. The newest is small, and each in turn is larger than the last. The fourth is now twice the height of the pot it sits in, and with three yellow-orange star flowers in bright bloom.

It's ready.

I take the pot and pull the flower out, roots and all, then shake it so the soil falls away, revealing copper roots that gleam darkly in the fading sun. I turn it, watching the light shift and dance, and then I slip it into my mouth, down into my throat, careful not to bite or chew. It must be whole, must *remain* whole.

For a moment, it seems I can taste the sweetness of the flower's fragrance—then nausea floods me as its roots scrape my throat. I ache to vomit it back up, repel the intruder, but I kneel and close my eyes to focus, to suppress the impulse. The second time is not so bad as the first, but the first flowers in my stomach make it trickier. I have to wiggle the new plant to help it past, then push until it's out of reach of my fingers, and fight to swallow it.

That part is hard. It takes many tries.

But then it's done, and I can feel the new flower heads brushing the inside of my stomach alongside the old. I stand again. The sun has almost completely set, and I miss its warmth—but I feel glad, satisfied, as I look at the three remaining pots.

The next will be ready in less than a week.

It's dark as I stand outside, but the glow of dawn is building at the horizon. Her body is gone, now, and the garden complete, waiting with me. The sun rises at last, and the morning mist begins to burn away, but for a moment I catch a chill on the air, as though the winter in the skies far above thinks it might find a way through to the garden. It never will.

I walk over to the struggling Silverpear tree, and force my hands down into its tangled roots, the earth soft and warm as I dig. Soon I find what I'm seeking, grasp it, and draw it out. A watch beetle, two inches long, gleaming blue-purple in the washed-out morning light. Silverpear roots can confuse them, and left alone, both beetles and tree will die.

But not today. I press the beetle to my lips, a floral kiss by which its brethren may know to follow, then carry it to a blackberry bush at the edge of a nearby willow copse. It burrows into the ground, out of sight. The beetles will thrive there, and the blackberry bush will be glad to shelter them.

I return to the cottage, and sit at the front step. I can feel my lover, now, stirring within me. Not awake yet, but soon—and when she wakes, my time will draw to a close. But for a little while at least we will linger together, she and I, entwined.

Later, when the spring breaks, she will find another. But I hope, at least, that I will not be forgotten. I have left a small mark of myself to be seen and remembered by, just to one side of my cottage's front step. Five clusters of Forget-me-nots, in five bluestone pots. They've always been my favorites.

About the Author

Born in England to a mad painter-poet and a voracious book-hound, Robert began writing in his toddler years, with beat-poetry about smashing a neighbour's cucumber frames. When he got older, he fell in love with fantasy and science fiction, and never really looked back. These days, he calls the USA home, and he lives there with his wife and their two ragdoll cats, Mochi and Teddy. His stories have appeared in *Kaleidotrope, PodCastle*, and Canada's *On Spec* Magazine, amongst others. You can find him online at robertlukewilkins.com or as @robertlukewilkins on BlueSky.

NYLAH ZIMMERBACH AND THE GHOST OF THE PENDRAGON

ERICA S. PECK

The Pendragon was a squarish building of dingy pinkish-gray stone, the shortest high rise on a block of very tall ones, and Nylah Zimmerbach found it disappointing due to its lack of actual dragons.

Her parents had called their new apartment a *coup*, whatever that meant, because of its proximity to her father's new job, and because of the Very Reasonable Rent for a doorman building, which turned out to be on account of the ghost.

"The what?" sputtered Nylah's father the day they moved in.

"The ghost," said the doorman, whose name was Virgil, and who had just explained why Elevator Two was out of order. "She's been moody lately. But don't worry," he continued, "she never does any harm. We call her Ella, 'cause she's in the *ele*-vator." His eyes crinkled as he chuckled at his own well-worn joke.

Nylah decided that a real live ghost was almost as good as dragons, and resolved to learn more about it.

Most of the residents she talked to seemed content to avoid the ghost. Nobody could tell her how it came to be in Elevator Two, and nobody seemed overly concerned about the frequent shutdowns and occasional bleeding walls.

"Could be worse," said Mr. Lipman from 14D, their across-the-hall neighbor who always smelled of mothballs. "Could be rats, or bad water pressure."

Nylah made a point of taking Elevator Two whenever she could in hopes of befriending the ghost. She left it offerings of sandwiches and candy and a bracelet she made out of plastic beads and a pipe cleaner.

Several weeks later, she arrived in the Pendragon's lobby after a particularly harrowing day at her new school to find Elevator Two standing open. She entered without thinking, and as soon as the doors closed she slumped against the dented metal wall and let loose the angry tears she had been holding back since lunchtime. It took her a moment to notice that the elevator had stopped on twelve and the doors remained closed.

Nylah wiped her face and stood. "Is that you, Ella?"

"Not Ella," said a low, raspy voice like stones grinding together in the darkness.

The lights dimmed and reddened. Deep, maniacal laughter echoed around the elevator car, and a stream of blood oozed from the corner of the control panel.

Nylah shut her eyes and took a deep breath. "Look, Ghost, I've had a bad day and I'm not really in the mood. Can we do this another time?"

The laughter died. The lights flickered uncertainly.

"Are you not...terrified?" asked the voice.

"Not really," said Nylah. "Sorry, but a disembodied voice in an elevator just isn't that scary compared to what happens at school."

The metal walls shivered in a huffy sort of way. "I find that doubtful."

"Oh yeah? At lunch today I got my period and bled all over my seat, and when I stood up Lydia Simmons pointed and made barfing noises."

"Oh dear."

"That's not even the worst of it," said Nylah. "Claudia Mitchell found a sketch I drew of Robert Weber and told everyone I had a crush on him, but I don't, he just has interesting bone structure." Nylah's cheeks warmed a little because she did have a crush on

Robert Weber, but she wasn't about to admit that to anyone, not even an elevator ghost.

"Hmmm. That is...unkind."

"Right? And Lauren Andrews said I'm too bony and ugly for anyone to ever like me. And that my back looked like it had boobs. And then everyone called me Nylah Nippleback." She hunched her shoulders, curling deeper into a self-conscious ball. "It's not my fault I'm skinny and my shoulder blades poke out."

"These are indeed foul torments," rasped the voice. "How did you punish your enemies? Did you make them eat their own entrails?"

Nylah sighed longingly. "I wish, Ghost."

"Not *Ghost*," it rumbled. The closed doors gave an exasperated little rattle.

"All right, what should I call you then?"

"I am Sangclamorax the Bloodletter, Hastener of Inevitable Pain, Lord of the River of Screams."

"Oh," said Nylah. After a moment's consideration, she asked, "Why are you in the elevator?"

There was a brief pause, and then: "I just am."

"Are you stuck here?"

The atmosphere in the elevator car shifted from menacing to melancholy. The streams of blood on the walls trickled to a stop.

"Aw, you're stuck in here, aren't you?" Nylah found an unbloody spot on the control panel and patted it. "I'm sorry. That must suck."

THUS BEGAN Nylah Zimmerbach's friendship with Sangclamorax the Bloodletter (Rax for short), the Pendragon's resident demon, which was way better than a ghost, and almost as good as a dragon.

Nylah brought Rax cough drops and lemon tea for his raspy voice, along with baked goods pilfered from her mother's kitchen. Rax comforted Nylah on bad days with creative suggestions of the best ways to torture and maim the children at school who bullied her. He was her best and only friend.

During their mutual tenure, they enjoyed many fascinating conversations, but when Nylah asked how Rax became trapped in the elevator, he offered only cryptic explanations like "an inexcusable moment of inattention," or "thinking with the wrong head."

Nylah didn't know what Rax looked like when he was visible, but she was intrigued by the notion that he had more than one head. That might explain the echoey quality of his voice. But when she asked him about the number of heads or what they looked like—wolfish, or lizardy, or, dare she hope, dragonesque?—he only laughed his sandpaper laugh and changed the subject.

NYLAH WAS A SMALL, pointy child when she first met Rax, in some ways old for her age and in others very young, and in the early grips of an exceedingly unkind puberty that seemed determined to gift her with all the unpleasant symptoms, such as mood swings and spots and cramps, and none of the ones she considered advantageous, such as *womanly curves*. To make matters worse, all the other girls at her school seemed to be developing womanly curves all over the place, while she remained as plain and angular and lonely as ever.

"They're right, Rax," she said through sobs one especially bad day when her back ached and an enormous zit throbbed in the center of her forehead and she wanted to punch everyone. "I'll never have a boyfriend because I'm too ugly. No one will ever like me. I don't even like me."

"I like you," said the demon, "and I like very few beings. These foolish child-women are not worthy of your envy. They are as insects beneath your claws. Someday you will find a nice mortal boy who appreciates your beautiful, tender soul. One who will not betray you and leave you disincorporated and trapped in a metal box."

Nylah, always on the lookout for clues to explain Rax's imprisonment, tucked that tidbit away to ponder later. "How will I know he's the right one?" she asked aloud.

"When you are with him, you will know peace."

Nylah nudged the wall next to her with a bony elbow. "I always feel peaceful around you, Rax."

"So it is with me, dear child, but I am not a *mortal boy*. I can never be that for you. When you find the right one, his touch will send magic flowing through your veins. He will be respectful and supportive. He will aid you in seeking out your enemies, rending their flesh from their bones, and bathing the streets in their blood."

"Aww, Rax, You're such a good friend. You always know just what to say to cheer me up."

ABOUT TWO YEARS into their association, Nylah noticed a change in her friend. He seemed distracted and moody. The walls bled with less gusto than usual.

"What's up with you, Rax?" Nylah asked. She had brought her sketch pad and was drawing a picture of a red unicorn with claws and fangs in an effort to cheer him up.

The metal walls shivered with a great demonic sigh. "Next October will mark my one hundredth year in this wretched box. It feels as though I have been bound here, invisible and impotent, for an eternity. And yet..."

"And yet, what?"

"Nothing."

"I'm sorry, Rax," she said. "I wish there was something I could do to help."

The metal walls groaned inward slightly—Rax's closest approximation of a hug. "You do help, dear child, by spending time with me. Your company has been the only bright spot in my existence in the last ninety-nine years. That is a glorious beast, by the way. I particularly like the gore dripping off its horn."

Nylah wasn't fooled; there was something he wasn't telling her. That evening she brought him a double batch of salted caramel blondies—his favorite—and he seemed to perk up a little. No amount of prodding would get any information out of him, though, so she let it go.

❧

THE NEXT WEEK brought a flurry of excitement as a new family moved in down the hall from Nylah. Most exciting of all, they had a son about her age.

Her parents invited his family to dinner the day after they moved in, because being *neighborly* was very important to Mrs. Zimmerbach. The son was slightly chubby, and he wore sweaters that were too big, and his parents had made the unfortunate decision to name him Cornelius Augustus Pratt.

He was exceedingly shy and polite and said very little during dinner aside from "I prefer to be called Gus" and "Please pass the yams."

Nylah liked him instantly and decided she would try to befriend him. He seemed terrified of her, but not in a bad way.

A few days later, Nylah ran into Gus outside the elevators on her way downstairs. Elevator Two opened at her approach and she stepped inside, but the boy hung back.

"Aren't you coming?" asked Nylah.

"Isn't that the elevator that's..." He looked both ways down the hall, as if checking that the coast was clear. "...The one that's *haunted*? My dad said not to use it."

"It's fine," said Nylah. "I use it all the time. C'mon." She snagged him by the trailing sleeve of his sweater and dragged him into the elevator with her. The doors closed. His hand wriggled in its sleeve like a trapped animal, so she let it out, then grabbed it and squeezed it reassuringly.

Just as she'd hoped, the lights flickered into red and the elevator jerked to a halt. Blood oozed down the walls. Deep, booming laughter echoed around the tiny space. Gus yelped and trembled, and his hand, still clenched in Nylah's, started to sweat.

"Knock it off, Rax," said Nylah. "I want to introduce you to somebody."

GUS RECOVERED QUICKLY from his initial shock, and agreed with Nylah that a demon was way cooler than a ghost. He took to joining her for many of her visits in the elevator. An afficionado of Egyptian things (on account of having lived in Cairo when he was small and his father had a job there), he often entertained his new friends with stories from Egyptian mythology. He was working on an Isis and Osiris fanfic that Nylah thought had real promise.

Nylah listened to his stories and drew pictures to go along with them. She also drew Gus. He had interesting bone structure, and the dimples that sprouted in his round cheeks when he smiled presented an interesting shading challenge. She did her best to get him to smile often. For the pictures, of course.

The bullies at school picked on Gus just as much as they did Nylah, but it was easier to take with someone to stick up for you. Gus got a three-day suspension for punching Robert Weber after he said Nylah looked like a bad Halloween decoration.

"Totally worth it," said Gus a few weeks later, when his mom finally let him out of his room. The control panel's buttons glowed in approval. Gus blushed and ducked his head and wouldn't meet Nylah's eyes.

HALLOWEEN SEASON ROLLED AROUND. Virgil decked out the lobby with elegant but spooky floral arrangements and many residents decorated their doors with skeletons and pumpkins.

Nylah and Gus had decided they were too old to go trick-or-treating, but they still paid their friend a visit with some of the iced ghost cookies Mrs. Zimmerbach had baked for the entire floor.

Rax seemed especially melancholic, shuddering the walls and flickering the lights dramatically, but accepted one of the ghost cookies. Nylah shot Gus a worried glance as she deposited it into the emergency phone box.

"Everything all right, Rax?" Gus asked.

The demon heaved a great creaky sigh. "All will be well. It is just the season."

It took Nylah a long time to get to sleep that night. She had not liked Rax's vibe in the elevator one bit. It reminded her of that part in *The Lion, the Witch and the Wardrobe* where Aslan got really sad right before he sacrificed himself to the White Witch. Then she snort-laughed, because Rax was about the furthest thing from Lion Jesus she could think of.

Nylah was just starting to drift off when the clock struck midnight. A rumbling sound like giant stones tumbling down a mountain jolted her awake, and the building began to vibrate. She knew instantly that it had something to do with her demon.

She expected her parents to wake up as well, expected to see all her neighbors stumbling out of their doors in their nightclothes, but only Gus met her in the hall. They raced to the elevator together. It was waiting for them, doors trembling as if it were a great effort to hold themselves open. They crashed shut the moment she and Gus came through, and the elevator began to descend.

It shuddered and creaked the whole way down, picking up speed. Nylah and Gus hugged the walls, holding on to the railings for dear life. The elevator rattled to a stop on the first floor and the doors opened. Thunderous laughter boomed all around them, dark but somehow joyful, welling up from the bottom of the elevator shaft and echoing through the lobby. Something scaly and invisible brushed against Nylah's calves, and she could just make out a dark serpentine shadow as it slithered past them, out of the elevator, and across the lobby's black-and-white checkerboard floor.

And then Elevator Two was just an elevator.

Rax was gone, without a word.

The next day, she and Gus met in the stairwell at the end of the hall. It just didn't feel right to meet in the elevator without Rax.

"A hundred years," said Nylah. "He said this month would be a hundred years since he got trapped in the elevator."

"Maybe that was, like, the end of his prison sentence," said Gus.

"I guess so," said Nylah. "I'm happy he's free, but I miss him so much." Their voices bounced all around disconcertingly, not at all like in the familiar confines of the elevator. She huddled closer to Gus so she could whisper. "He was my only friend. Except you, I mean."

"I know," said Gus, "Me too." And he slipped an arm around her and pulled her into a hug.

He had never done that before.

His body was cushiony but solid, like an expensive orthopedic mattress, and the circle of his arms felt overwhelmingly peaceful.

Nylah decided she would do just about anything for more hugs like this one.

"I had the weirdest dream last night," she said, and told it to him.

In the dream, Nylah was a powerful sorceress, and Gus was her partner in dark magic. They wore matching purple robes. At her command, their shoulder blades extruded from their backs and spread into great leathery bat wings. They launched into the air above the schoolyard and rained terrible vengeance upon her former tormentors with fangs and claws and fire, assisted by a two-headed dragon wearing a pipe-cleaner-and-bead bracelet. Together, the three of them slashed and stabbed and scorched and laughed and high-fived, until the blacktop was littered with charred entrails and severed limbs, and then they had sandwiches and lemon tea.

When all the sandwiches were gone, the dragon wiped its mouths with a dainty napkin and rose. "I must go, children," he said. One of his heads leveled a glowing red gaze on Gus. "Promise you will never betray her. Always respect and care for her."

Gus swallowed hard, but drew himself up straighter. "Yes, sir. Always."

"See that you do," said the other head, blowing a prim huff of smoke from its nostrils. "Or I shall find you in the afterlife and drown you in the River of Screams."

It was the best dream Nylah ever had.

At some point while she spoke, Gus had taken her hand and woven their fingers together; his grasp was strong and certain, and not at all sweaty.

"I had the same exact dream," he said. "It was the best one I ever had."

He bent his head and kissed her, and Nylah could swear that the brush of his lips against hers felt a little bit like magic.

About the Author

Erica Peck is a mild-mannered stay-at-home-mom, freelance editor, former data analyst, and lapsed drama major. She is a member of To Live and Write in Alameda, Bay Area Romance Writers, the Editorial Freelancers Association, and ACES: the Society for Editing. In her spare time, she reads, writes stories, and sings soprano in a 40-voice symphonic chorus. She lives in the San Francisco Bay Area with her family and is currently working on her debut novel, a steamy paranormal romance, under a pen name. You can find more of Erica's short fiction (and the occasional poem) on her blog at soundcheckingthevoid.com, follow her on Bluesky at @shydogs.bsky.social, and learn about her editing services at ericapeckedits.com.

FOR ALL LOVE IS PRAYER

LYNNE SARGENT

The monks murmur, *"Ringrender,"* bowing as I walk towards the altar. I can see their eyes wander to the cut of my muscles and the sharp edge of my heavy blade. My heartbeat quickens and I want to run but I keep my pace steady as I approach. As I kneel to pray, I cannot help but let my tears cut runnels through the gold face paint they have anointed me with, and there I whisper, so quiet that only our god can hear.

I do not know how a god's memory works, if you remember falling in love with Zel the way the stories tell, but I remember the day that I fell in love with Senaton. I was fourteen, and it was the last time I was simply Arhis, not yet Ringrender, not your Shining Blade. Then, Senaton was the bronze and noble one shining up in the stands. I swear I won that first match in the arena because the fluttering in my heart when I saw him up there, watching me, lifted my very body, making me light and swift as never before.

I shouldn't have been fighting to impress him. I should have been fighting for my life, for even then I knew the arena so often meant death. Now, fighting for life seems the only just reason to fight. But I was young and had just seen my first, my only love. I'm sure you think I was a silly boy, believing in love at first sight, believing that I, an orphan gutter rat could dare to love a noble.

Except I won that fight, and who better to train with the king's son than the youngest-ever winner of the *Ilnultha*. You know, they instituted an age limit because of me. I still don't know if it is because they couldn't bear a slave chit of a thing beating the arena's lifers, the ringmasters themselves, or because they finally figured out how barbaric it was to have a child in there for the full three days of slaughter.

Perhaps with the perspective of your immortality I still seem a silly boy at thirty-five, but Senaton always loved me too, you know. I'm sure you had better things to be looking at at the time, but I still remember his devilish smile the first day we sparred, the whispered, "You were glorious," as we wrestled under Cateleyna's tutelage. Three weeks later he dared me to race him in a swim across the Synola stretch, and we laid together naked, drying ourselves in the sun in the seclusion of the far shore.

'I will ensure you inherit a glorious country,' I promised him, the first time we made love together under the stars in his garden. How we planned, how we schemed to create opportunities for my glory that I might one day become his partner, his consort, the best father to whomever he chose to adopt as his own son someday.

You know the rest, of course. How the Inosians assassinated the king, started the war, and raised the devils. That is where you came to know me when you gave me this sword.

Now, I hold forth the sword which was gifted to me. The shining, iridescent blade attached to a silver hilt, crackling with electricity that harms all but me. Now I offer it back.

Without this, I could not have saved Senaton's life, I might have lost my love and my country. I thank you for that, and for all that you have done to patronize this country, but I supplicate myself now because I do not want it anymore.

Senaton writes me letters telling how his advisors broker a political marriage. I have not seen my love in eight months; we were not apart so long even in the war. They say until I leave here a demigod, blessed with immortality it is too risky for so much of Kilaka's power to be together in the same place lest Inos's remaining sorcerers attack. And afterward they say I cannot be with him, not even as his concubine, lest my glory insult his husband.

Please, I beg you.

I do not want to be a demigod. I do not want to be Ringrender, nor the Shining Blade. I don't mean to snub you, or reject your honored gifts, but I have never fought for you. All this glory was only ever for Senaton, and the ability to be with him is all I wish as a reward, and reward I deserve. I spent a decade in a gutter. I should have died fighting in the ring at fourteen. It is that boy who promises you now that if you grant me this wish I will praise you all my days. I know it will not matter for I will be nothing and no one once again. No one except for his.

I cannot help but devolve into weeping, let the monks whisper if they will. But it is not a monk's voice that echoes through the hallowed hall. It is something deeper, more primal. Even when I received the blade you never spoke to me, but now I hear you speak, *"And who do you think would dare deny a demigod's desires?"*

A wind blows through the hall. It smells like sun on clear water, like Senaton's perfume, like roses blooming in spring. I can barely open my eyes there are so many tears.

"You have the power now, and you deserve him. You claimed my sword once, now take it and claim your happiness also."

I am back in our garden. I use the sword to stand. When I look up, Senaton is there, and I am shining in his eyes.

About the Author

Lynne Sargent is a queer writer, aerialist, and holds a Ph.D in Applied Philosophy. They are the poetry editor at Utopia Science Fiction magazine. Their work has been nominated for Rhysling, Elgin, and Aurora Awards, and has appeared in venues such as Augur Magazine, Strange Horizons, and Daily Science Fiction. Their work has also been supported through the Ontario Arts Council. To find out more, visit them at scribbledshadows.-wordpress.com.

RABBITS AND RASPBLUERRY WINE

JENNIFER M. ROBERTS

Clarissa closed her eyes as the sharp tang of raspbluerry wine sent a shiver through the back of her throat. A fitting drink for one dining alone. Already the happy conversation buzzing around the restaurant undermined her resolution not to wallow. Well, she was entitled. Clarissa sipped at her wine again, ignoring the bustling dining room to focus on the four faces that smiled up at her from a photo propped against her water glass. A birthday gift, the glossy printout boasted several creases, evidence of how often Clarissa folded it to make it fit into various pockets.

"You left me," Clarissa muttered, despite the fact her lonely state was no fault of theirs. Vince and Doug had offered her a place on their family excursion to Mars. They'd kept their word to make her an honorary aunt to the children born from her donated eggs. Birthdays, babysitting, weekly game nights.

She'd canceled more often than not these past few months. Too busy. It was a poor excuse, but one she could put into words without inviting a pity party. Truthfully? The bigger the children got, the closer Vince and Doug grew, the happier their little family became over the years, the harder it was to be near them. The light of their domestic bliss was more blinding than a solar flare.

Clarissa shifted her attention to the view. The entire wall was glass, tilted and mirrored to avoid sight of the lunar surface in favor of the stars. Earth hung like a Christmas ornament between glittering strings of lights. Today, the Pacific was prominent, a vast expanse of blue of a sort that Clarissa, born here on Lunar Colony III, had never seen anywhere else. Earthers spent more money than she would earn in a year to fly up here for a meal with that view. Even at lunchtime on a Tuesday, the place was full.

Clarissa rolled her tongue through a mouthful of wine, wondering when the buzz would start to take the edge off her nerves. The aroma of rare truffles, exotic spices, and perfectly braised meats tickled her nose. At three hundred currents a plate, the Dome represented the pinnacle of culinary achievement. But Clarissa hadn't managed to order any food yet. She simply sipped her wine, searching for the dark points between the stars and wondering if the lonely expanse felt as empty and cold as the lump inside her chest.

Maybe, this had been a mistake. Usually, Clarissa saved her free meal, a perk offered to all restaurant staff annually, for something special. Something fun. Maybe, moping at home would be better for her mental health than moping in public. Unfortunately, the public space offered a key advantage: witnesses. She swirled her wine, looking at the happy photo through the amber liquid. It gave the image a sunny tint that made it feel even less real. Could four people ever actually be that happy?

"It's you!"

The excited exclamation made Clarissa flinch, her hand clenching around the stem of her wine glass as she waited for the rush of panic and the declaration from the person who had spotted her that they should call the police.

"Hello!"

The voice held no panic, only eager cheerfulness as if greeting an old friend. A man stood in front of her table, positioned squarely in front of the Earth so that the black of space framed him. Like a Greek god stepping out of the heavens. The metaphor was not far off; square jaw, blond hair that glowed in the soft lamplight, but a barrel chest and wide belly even his well-cut suit could not hide. Clarissa's experienced eye recognized silk and the S on the cuffs; Sylvester, one of the premium brands manufactured here on Lunar Colony III.

Rich, handsome, and proud of his local heritage. Also bad at facial recognition.

"Sorry, I think you've got the wrong person."

"What? But you—black dress, long black hair, corner table, the bottle of raspbluerry wine—" His eyes flicked over her, the tabletop, and then down to his pocket. "Oh!" With a bright smile, he pulled out a yellow carnation and settled it on the edge of his breast pocket with a self-explanatory pat. "I'm Gary. Your date."

Clarissa almost wished she had a mouthful of wine. There would be something satisfying about spewing it across the table in shock. As it was, all she could do was stare. "Date?" The carnation felt like something out of a book. "A blind date?"

"Yes. I—" Gary's brows drew together as his expression fell. "Oh. I see. You don't like what you see. That's all right."

"No!" Clarissa nearly jumped off of her seat, face flushing. "I like—I mean—I'm not here for a blind date. Sorry."

"You're not?"

Clarissa shook her head. "This is a solo affair."

"Well then—" Gary turned a slow circle to survey the room of diners, most dressed as well as he was. Clarissa barely fit in, in the neutral black she wore when working as hostess up front. Gary shook his head. "I don't see anyone else who matches the description."

"Sorry." Clarissa turned back to her wine, but the man did not move, hovering like a lost bunny in need of a mother.

"Would you like to go on the date?"

Would she like to eat expensive food while enjoying the view of his strong jaw and sunny smile? This could either be the beginning of a charming romantic comedy, or a horror story.

Clarissa scowled. "Why? I'm not the person you came here to meet. Don't you want to find out where she is?"

Gary shrugged. "It's not like we've been exchanging letters and have fallen in love or anything. I'm here for an Experience."

Clarissa's eyes grew as wide as the empty bread plate in front of her. "Oh."

She'd seen Experience dates get started off here before. All of the hostesses knew about the company. An elite matchmaking service, they offered not only an opportunity to meet a potential mate but also to have a curated evening of experiences—the most extreme, the most romantic, the most expensive. If this man had set up a date through The Experience, then a dinner at the Dome was just the beginning.

"I'm not looking for a date."

"Great." Gary's smile grew. "You can have an entertaining evening with me, and I'll be able to tell my brother that I tried it and it didn't work out."

"Your brother?" Just the way Gary said the word, Clarissa knew. This was a family drama, and she was merely an accessory to the main plot.

Gary gave a resigned sigh that Clarissa felt reflected in the depths of her soul. His mouth twisted, looking as if he was searching for the right way to explain. Clarissa held up a hand.

"Good enough for me. Please. Sit."

Gary's mouth hung open for a moment. "Really? You don't mind?"

"I'm drinking a bottle of raspbluerry wine alone. Company can only make this day better."

His head tilted, suddenly wary. "Why the wine?"

"My sister."

Gary's eyebrows rose. He had a very expressive face, Clarissa noted. She braced herself for the demand for further explanation, but he just nodded. "I understand."

"So." Clarissa set her glass aside, the better to focus on her dinner date. "What is included in our Experience package today?"

"Well, dinner—"

Clarissa waved to the menu. "Get whatever you want. I'm not hungry."

"No?" Gary flipped the menu over to the back, a cheeky grin on his face. "Not even for dessert?"

Clarissa's resolve to wallow in raspbluerry wine until everything faded to a numb haze vanished as soon as the dessert flights arrived. Cheesecake cups, chocolate truffles, and frozen crèmes. Clarissa dove into the sugar. Gary sat back, watching with a look of awe as the desserts vanished. Until she went for the rum-truffle with hazelnut crust.

"Um." The word was tentative, but his finger swift as he knocked Clarissa's hand aside. "Could I have that one?"

"Oh! Yes. I—" Clarissa took stock of the decimation on the plate, only a few crumbs and smears remaining. "Sorry. We can order another."

"No. I don't need anything else. Just. This." Gary lifted the truffle to his lips, closing his eyes as if any distractions would ruin the moment. His mouth worked and he let out a sigh that made Clarissa flush with embarrassment. As if she were witnessing something private. Something more intimate than chocolate.

"Good?"

"Mm." Gary swallowed slowly and opened his eyes to the empty plate. "That's odd, they made it with fig jam instead of rum."

"Fig?" Clarissa's voice creaked. "That's—they don't usually make it that way. I'm glad you ate it."

"Why?"

"I'm allergic. That could have killed me."

Glary looked down at the chocolate smear on his fingers, then back up at Clarissa. "Wow." He licked his finger. "They really are the best thing. Do you want to try the order again and I'll make sure it's the rum version before you try it?"

"It's okay. I've had them before. They're okay."

Gary's lips parted and he gave a small gasp, as if he'd been stabbed in the back. "Okay?"

"The orange crème is better."

"No. Never. Not possible."

"Have you tried it?"

"Why would I, when there's true perfection to be had?"

"Now, if you haven't tried it—" Clarissa turned to flag down a waiter, and froze as if someone had dropped a frozen crème down her back. Two police officers stood in the doorway, heads bent over the hostess station. "So sorry, but maybe you should go now." Her chair nearly toppled sideways, she stood up so fast.

Gary stood with her, sensitive blue eyes crinkled with concern. "Are you okay?"

"Absolutely not. I started this day drinking raspbluerry wine alone and ended it with a man who hates oranges." Clarissa gripped the chair back to steady herself as the police officers approached.

Gary, following her gaze, narrowed his eyes curiously. "Are they here for you?"

"Yes. I'm sure they have more questions." She'd hoped, after the first round of interrogation, that they would figure out she didn't know anything. After the second round, she'd hoped they would not think to look for her here. Apparently, there had been a development.

"Oh."

"It's not you, Gary. I'd love to keep arguing about desserts, but things are about to get complicated. You don't need that."

"We could get out of here."

"What?" She felt stupid asking him to repeat the statement, but with her focus on the approaching law enforcement, the words she'd heard could not be the words he'd said.

"We could get out of here. The Experience has a whole slate of activities ready for me and my date. If you want to put that," Gary gestured to the cops, who had paused to let a waiter carrying a tray of appetizers pass, "off for a bit."

"There is nothing I would love more."

Gary gripped her hand and nodded toward the back. "Come on then."

SHE EXPECTED her breath to fog the glass, the stiff suit to constrict her movements, the oxygen to taste stale and recycled. Nope. The Experience catered to a clientele base that considered comfort as essential as water or vitamin D. The faceplate in her helmet refused to fog, the oxygen tasted as crisp and clear as if she were standing in the arboretum, and the suit fit her like a second skin.

"Hmph." Gary's voice came through the radio in high definition. He shifted his feet, dragging a toe through the lunar dust. "The boots are a bit loose."

Clarissa laughed, surprised she could summon such a joyful noise on a day like today, but grateful for the diversion. She spread her arms wide. "We've got the entire Herman crater to ourselves and that's your complaint?"

"I have narrow feet, and in twenty-five years they've never adjusted for it."

"You've been doing lunar walks for twenty-five years?" Clarissa gaped, more stunned by her partner in crime than by the vista that surrounded her. "How old are you?"

"Twenty-six." Was that a hint of a blush beneath his helmet? "My dad thought we should learn surface safety as soon as we could walk."

"Huh."

Gary tipped his head. "Have you never—is this your first—?"

"Most lunar residents never walk the lunar surface, you know. It's mostly tourists on vacation out here, and—"

"You were having dinner in the Dome."

"I work at the Dome." Clarissa closed her eyes, as much to avoid seeing his reaction as to take in a breath for a mental reset. He'd been so kind, and downright relatable about dessert. She'd forgotten for a moment just how different his life was from hers. They lived in the same lunar module, which was less than ten miles across at its widest point. Yet they were worlds apart.

Why did she care what he thought? She was on the lunar surface. Moonwalking. Every child's dream.

Clarissa opened her eyes to take it all in properly. High crater walls rose around them, cradling a sculpture garden. Panels that gathered sunlight to convert to energy were far more than flat black squares. Instead, sculpted shapes rose out of the lunar surface, geometric patterns that evoked a feeling of something recognizable while refusing a clear definition.

In this garden, Clarissa vaguely remembered from a school lecture, the viewer could see what they chose. Was that why the cluster of figures to her left looked like a family pulled into a group embrace?

"You should come look up here. When you're ready." Gary's tone was excited without any hint of impatience. Was he always happy? With his charmed life, probably.

Except that he was here, on a blind date he didn't want. Family was complicated no matter the income bracket.

Clarissa held out her hand and let Gary lead her up the edge of the crater, out of the garden to an unobstructed view of the wide lunar plain.

"You wanted to get away."

Clarissa's gasp, even amplified by the suit's comm system, felt like a whisper in the face of the vast, empty expanse. She was a tiny speck on the surface. Invisible. Unimportant.

Untouchable.

"This. Is..." Clarissa had no words, and Gary did not try to supply any. For a long moment they simply enjoyed the peace.

"Your family came up here a lot?"

"Well." Gary crossed his arms with a rueful tone. "My brother tried to destroy as many sculptures as possible, and when Dad told him to stop, he tried to forcibly test my rocket boot system." Clarissa didn't need the meaningful pause to catch his meaning. Gary's brother had tried to throw him off the lunar surface. Only his suit's safety systems had kept him from floating away.

"I hid up here," Gary finished. "Came to like this spot."

"I can see why. If I could escape here, I'd build my own module."

"They'd still find us."

"Yeah." Clarissa let out a sigh. Chatter crackled in the background of her comm system. Police trying to get authorization to call her back in? "I couldn't even get away from my sister on Pluto."

"You've been to Pluto? But there's no surface walking there. No stars." Gary lifted his hand to the sky. "You can feel alone here but know there's more out there. Pluto is just tunnels."

"It wasn't as bad as you think. But I'm glad to be home."

"Glad to be drinking alone in the Dome?" His tone was soft; not trying to make some sort of point, just genuinely curious.

"Well, that's a special circumstance." Clarissa paused, but those blue eyes fixed on her, anxious to hear more. "I've got a sister. If she were out here with me, she would definitely be testing my rocket boot systems."

His face fell. "I'm sorry."

"I'm not." The new voice was a hiss, soft and sharp. It sent a chill through Clarissa. She froze, all senses on high alert, waiting to see which way she needed to run. Something solid hit her abdomen hard, then expanded with a wet squelch. Air hissed through her helmet, the new gas bringing a sharp tang. Something soft but strong wrapped around her neck, twisting. Clarissa gasped, fighting the gas, the noose, and the weight on her chest.

"What's wrong? What do you need?" Gary asked anxiously.

Clarissa floundered to form a clear thought. Everything had gone hazy. "My suit—is—attacking me."

"Your med lights are all going off. Every emergency system at once." Gary gripped her arm tight as a sharp blast from her boots threatened to send Clarissa careening into space. Gary slapped her ankles, cutting the power to the rockets. Clarissa reached for him, but her fingers failed to respond.

The gas must be some kind of numbing agent, but judging by her growing headache, it was being pumped into her helmet without any oxygen in the mix. She gasped, mouth flapping like a fish. Gary's grip tightened and for far too long all Clarissa could do was hang on as he ran, scattering a cloud of moondust around them. Then the starscape changed to bright lights. She was on the floor. Her helmet came off and clarity returned, partnered with a headache that made her wish she'd stuck with the raspbluerry wine.

"We need emergency services!" Gary bellowed above her.

He'd saved her. Protected her. She stared, still stunned by the gas and lack of oxygen, as Gary marshaled a surprisingly large number of people to pull her out of her suit, check her vitals, and settle her on a couch in the waiting area. His hand gripped hers tight and refused to let go.

Blue eyes met Clarissa's again, and his brows furrowed. "You're staring. Am I—?"

"No. It's just..." Clarissa winced at her sore ribs. "You're...nice."

Gary gaped.

Clarisa wriggled her fingers in Gary's hand. "This is feeling like a date, though. I thought you didn't want that."

Gary considered their linked hands for a moment, then tightened his grip. "I didn't want one of the spoiled, entitled women my brother usually sets me up with." His face darkened. "I'm so sorry. This is all my fault."

"What?" Clarissa scrubbed at her face, willing the numbing agent to dissipate faster. "This was my sister. I heard her voice in my helmet."

"Yes, but my brother's company set up this whole thing," Gary countered.

"I bet my sister made the call. She wants me dead."

"Dead?" Gary repeated, going pale. "That fig-filled truffle—" He paused, his finger ticking the air like he was connecting dots. "My brother used to say he thought it would be fun to run an assassination company. Said it was a perfect partner for the dating company. Set them up, then when the honeymoon is over help them get rid of each other. I thought it was a joke."

"And you're his alibi for the test run."

"What?" Gary looked startled.

"What better way to see if he can get away with murder than to use an escaped criminal and his own brother. "

"Criminal?"

Clarissa grabbed the remote and flicked the button that turned on the large screen on the other side of the room. Her face hovered in the corner no matter what else the screen displayed. Red letters under the image read: DANGEROUS CRIMINAL. CALL EMERGENCY SERVICES IF SIGHTED.

Gary's eyebrows drew down and he leaned forward, studying the picture. Finally, he said slowly, "That's not you."

Warmth bloomed in Clarissa's stomach, flooding her body with relief. "You can tell? We're identical twins. Only our parents and a few friends see the differences."

"It's in the nose, and—" Gary shrugged. "I don't know. She's not you." He frowned, turning back to Clarissa. "This—Alexis—wants you dead?"

"I heard her voice when my suit went haywire. She probably thinks she can pass my body off as her own, and steal my life." Gary continued to stare. "I know it sounds unbelievable, but she's done it before. I—" Clarissa pulled her hand out of Gary's grip. "I should go to the police. They can keep me safe until she's caught."

"At least they'll believe you." Gary hunched his shoulders. "You're right, it's going to look like I planned this."

It felt like the time Clarissa's sister had dumped ice water over her head. She reached for Gary's hand again. "You can wait with me. Perfect alibi."

"Until the next time he tries something like this." Gary shook his head. "Maybe I should go to that job on Titan my brother keeps going on about. At least there I'd be out of his way." He looked as if he'd fallen into a Plutonian mushroom pit, with no way out and no hope of seeing the stars again.

Clarissa knew that feeling. She reached for his other hand, and his blue eyes landed squarely on her. "They're working together, and they're using the date Experiences to try to kill us. That gives us the advantage, because we know where they'll strike next. If we play our cards right, we can catch Alexis, and she'll turn your brother in."

Gary frowned. "Next we're supposed to go swimming with the bioluminescent snails—"

"Probably poisoned the slime."

"Then dancing in the Weightless Wonderland."

"Ohhh! I always wanted to see that place. Definitely don't want to die when they suddenly switch on the gravity, and we both go splat."

"And after that a rabbit farm. They have real grass and—"

Clarissa nearly choked. "A rabbit farm?"

"Yeah, with real—" Gary's eyes narrowed. "Why?"

Clarissa was already on her feet, pulling Gary with her. "I'll explain on the way."

⁂

"Grass." The word was a hushed whisper, and Gary dropped reverently to his knees to place a hand on the soft green turf. "With real dirt."

"Yeah." A smile tugged at Clarissa's mouth despite the fact she knew they needed to focus on the whole attempted murder thing. "First time?"

Gary nodded, then turned to Clarissa with a jealous expression. Not the possessive jealousy Clarissa had seen so often on her sister, but an aren't-you-truly-lucky look. "You've been here before."

Clarissa shrugged. "I work here."

"I thought you work at the Dome."

"I have more than one job." Part-time gigs could not pay the bills solo. What would he think of her other two jobs? "There will be time to enjoy the grass later. Right now, we have to pretend this is a real date."

Gary shook his head, stroking the grass. "We can't do that. Your friend needs this for the rabbits."

Clarissa laughed at Gary's serious tone. "We won't ruin it by lying down on it."

"But—"

"We can't insult this space by doing anything less." Clarissa flopped onto the grass, arms spread wide. The green sprigs tickled her ears, and the soft earth smelled like home. This space was the last place she had been truly happy. Before Alexis tried to kill her the first time. Before Doug and Vince got busy with their family.

Gary cleared his throat. "There are five patches of grass on this colony. We can't—"

"My friend lets his kids play soccer on this grass. It's not that fragile." She ran her hands through the soft blades. "See? Flexible. It'll bounce right back after we get up."

"Okay." Gary still sounded uncertain, but he settled next to Clarissa, hands on his stomach. His eyes cast upwards, to the wide glass window that formed the ceiling. The starry sky gave the grassy nook a mystic feel, especially with the musky scent of rabbits and the sound of the small creatures rustling around in the hutches that lined the walls. "So the plan is to lie under the glass ceiling that your sister will try to drop on us. This feels like we're helping them kill us."

"The glass has five fail safes she doesn't know about. Vince installed them after the kids came along. We've also got police surrounding the place and on the roof."

"They didn't believe you, and they think this plan is crazy," Gary said.

"Doesn't matter what they believe, they're here."

"You think she'll be stupid enough to come here in person?"

"Absolutely." Clarissa frowned. "Don't worry, we'll figure out how to prove your brother was in on it."

A warm arm encircled Clarissa's shoulders and she curled into Gary's wide chest, which thrummed as he spoke. "Make it look like a date, hmmm?"

Clarissa nodded, surprised at how well her cheek fit in the crook of his neck. "Romance stuff. You know."

"Ha!" The laugh was soft. "Not really. I'm not very good at this, hence why my brother thinks I need blind date setups."

"Not good at this?" Clarissa tipped her head back to get a better look at his face, startled again by how much he resembled the sun. Warm. Bright. Not just his features, but everything about him. His kindness, his cheer in the face of what had been a very difficult life. "Your brother is an idiot. Let's not talk about him. Or my sister. Right now it's just you and me."

Gary shifted, turning sideways to face Clarissa even as his eyes flicked toward the ceiling. She could feel him tensing, surprised at the muscles hidden beneath his soft belly. "There are five police officers waiting on the roof."

Clarissa let out a steadying breath. Could Gary feel her trembling? "We can't look. She might already be watching."

"So why rabbits?"

"What?" Clarissa tried to connect the question to anything about their recent conversation, and failed.

"Why work here?"

"I wanted to do something different. Something Alexis wouldn't want any part of. Cleaning up rabbit poop was the best I could come up with."

"We're back to your sister. Sorry."

"It's okay. But why haven't you seen grass before? If you had the money to go for regular lunar walks, you could definitely afford a ticket to the Greenhouse." Clarissa had only seen the recreational park from a distance, one had to pay to get within fifty feet of the place.

"My dad wanted my brother and me to be tough, and grass is soft."

"Sorry." Clarissa huffed. "Someday, will we be able to talk about our lives without running into stories about our psychotic families?"

"I have snails."

Clarissa blinked, once again startled by his change in subject. "Snails?"

"Yeah. I found one when we went swimming in the old caverns the first settlers dug, and I brought it home. Hid it from my family and went back for a new one every year. They live in a tank by my bed, and neither my brother nor my father care about them."

A giggle bubbled up out of Clarissa, unexpected. It was the second time he'd made her smile tonight. "Snails? Ewww."

"You work with rabbits. That's worse."

"Rabbits are soft and fluffy and adorable."

"Rabbits are stinky, have little wiggly noses, and—" Gary froze, eyes flicking to the ceiling. "Did you hear that?"

A creak came from above, then the sound of a boot thudding against glass. Gary flinched.

"Ignore it." Clarissa put her hands around Gary's face, blocking his view of the ceiling. "We can't help, we just have to wait for the police to do their job. It'll be all right. I promise we're safe here." She pounded the ground three times. A steel sheet shot out from the wall, a shield between them and the ceiling. "See? Fail safes."

Gary let out a long breath. "Safe. I've never really felt—" He wrapped his hands around her head, burying his fingers in Clarissa's hair. His grip tightened as thumping came from above again. "I need a distraction."

"Of course." Clarissa moved forward and captured Gary's lips in hers. Soft, warm, and delicious. For a moment nothing existed but the two of them. Finally, the sounds above went silent and then a knock came at the door.

"You two okay in there?"

Clarissa pulled away with a gasp. Gary held up a thumbs-up to the police as Clarissa called, "We're fine. Did you get her?"

An enraged scream in the background gave Clarissa her answer. "You can't do this!" Alexis's protests faded as the police marched her away.

"So, that happened." For a moment Gary stared at Clarissa while she waited, breath stuck in her throat. The threat was gone. This weird, maniacal, magical night was almost over.

Time for goodbye. Clarissa knew she needed to say the words, but they refused to make their way to her lips. Instead she simply stared at Gary in awkward silence while the grass tickled her ear.

"Do you want to do this again?" Gary asked. "Dinner, I mean, without the murder. Someplace simple. Cheap. Not cheap cheap, I mean—"

"I know what you mean." Could this be real? It was too early to tell, but Clarissa knew one thing. Gary was the best thing to come into her life for a very long time and she wasn't about to let him go.

She inhaled deeply the smell of earth and grass, and allowed a slow smile to spread across her face. "It's a date."

About the Author

Jennifer M. Roberts earned her BA in History, but prefers to dream of how things might have been rather than focusing on how things really were. She hails from the Midwest and enjoys cooking, contra dancing, and historical re-enactment. Her fiction ranges from sci-fi adventures to epic fantasy to historical romance. An ordained minister, Jennifer has performed over 50 wedding ceremonies. She enjoys helping real-life couples find the right words to express their vows, and helping fictional couples find their way to a happily ever after. You can learn more at jmroberts.com.

DAPHNE

ALLISTER NELSON

You loved me as a youthful flower,
but the floods came, divots of rivers
in my delta, stretch marks as I carried
our water babies, and we lost ourselves—

To the farm and fallow seasons, to tenderness
of years easing the spark, routine treachery,
but also? Softness, faith that my thorns and

Browning leaves would not deter you, and I
found, the Apollo of my laurel tree had turned
into a gardener, Asclepius—Father to Sun:
God to Healer, and I understand age,
and reason

as our marriage, and I: have found God
in your arms, time and again, so when

my petals grow seeds, and I carry the fruit

of your fire into the sleeping soils, know this:
we live on in the roses and rain.

And my Apollo?

This
was all

Worth
it.

The bark? The branches?

Your kiss.

About the Author

Allister Nelson is a multiple Pushcart Prize-nominated author whose work has appeared in *The British Fantasy Society, Apex Magazine, ILLUMEN, Eternal Haunted Summer, Renewable Energy World, Frontiers in Health Communication, The National Science Foundation, Luna Station Quarterly, Prismatica Press, Coffin Bell, FunDead Publications*, and many other venues. Her work has been translated into Polish and Spanish, nominated for Poland's top fantasy prize, and appeared in anthologies alongside Graham Masterston, Bill Willingham, Jane Yolen, and Alan Dean Foster. In her spare time, Allie is a wanderer of graveyards, weaver of fables, caster of literary aspersions, and gazer at alien starships. Her backlist and available works can be found at her site allisternelson.com

THE NECESSARY ARRANGEMENTS

LYNN STRONG

H ave you heard? Roshana's probably got to get married to that fat old prince who lusts after his stableboy! That's if she can't win the younger prince at the ball, and hundreds of women are coming ..."

"What a fate worse than death!" The Kyndric handmaids giggled behind their hands.

Roshana rattled the door handle more loudly than she would have otherwise, and managed half a curtsey when they all scrambled to their feet and curtsied to her.

She wasn't feeling merciful today. She waited for them to settle like flower petals in the garden before she said, "His Highness Theodric is a most accomplished lutenist, I've heard. We would have music to enjoy with each other."

The stammered apologies and whisperings rustled like moth wings in the moonlight.

Roshana didn't let herself think too much about Prince Theodric, though. Her own mother and Theodric's sister Amalia had recently determined to see Roshana wedded to Theodric's nephew Amalric. Who was by all reports young and handsome and charming, with exquisite manners and alluring dance skills and, one had to assume, a young man's lusts.

It was pointless to think that Theodric might have been happy to pay court to his stableboy and speak of music and poetry with his wife, and that Roshana might have preferred it that way. Amalric was second in line for the throne of Kyndra, but his mother could push for him to become the first in line once he had an heir of his own. It had been known for decades that Theodric was not so inclined, and Kyndra's throne came with expectations that the bloodline *would* continue.

Roshana's mother had reason to push her into Amalric's arms, too. Their family's holdings in Mirshan were rich in trade but not in warriors, and a year ago her brother had sailed off to find the truth behind the legends of those fabled silk-spinning moths. He had never been heard from since. A prince from a foreign land of towering blond axe-wielders would make many powers think twice about how much they could encroach on the trade routes through the Mirshani lands.

It wasn't that Roshana disliked children, in the abstract. Many of the local children she'd met through her Kyndric language tutor were bright and curious and liked singing along with her lute. But the business of getting herself a child involved so much backstabbing gossip even before the actual siring, and the less Roshana had to think about the siring, the better.

Especially if she wasn't one of the women who could conceive at the drop of a veil. If her husband had to try and try, and keep trying, for months or years or...

If she had to be married for her family's protection and her mother's ambitions, she would have preferred at least a chance to talk with the older prince who was happy with his stableboy. She could have worked with that. A man who was happy with his lover would trouble her less.

Nobody had any idea what the young Prince Amalric actually wanted; he was much too discreet to feed the gossips.

She supposed he'd needed to learn that discretion the same way Roshana had, if his royal Kyndric mother was as much like her royal Mirshani mother as it seemed.

THE BALL WAS PREDICTABLE. She was thrown into a dance with Prince Amalric as soon as their families' handlers could arrange it. He was, as promised, young and slim and terribly handsome and a magnificent dancer, and so very, very polished.

Prince Amalric was excruciatingly polite. The perfect smile, the perfect degree of a bow over her hand, the perfect bit of poetry —*too* perfect, because he'd done his homework. He knew verses she'd written herself. He quoted her own poetry back to her, in her own native language. He'd clearly practiced. It sounded like words, not like sounds he'd memorized by a singer's rote.

If she'd actually been interested, Roshana was sure it would have been quite flattering that he'd put in the work, that he took such attentive interest. Or even that he did such a flawless job of imitating that interest when he needed to.

She wasn't as good at the dance of courtship as he was. It galled her to admit it. She had been so busy dreading the ball that she hadn't studied how to divert his attention with anything other than his well-known interest in dancing. And Kyndric dancing involved much holding hands and holding waists and spinning until a little dizzy and gazing into each other's eyes.

Intellectually, Roshana understood the dances were designed to set off the same sorts of desires as a peacock's mating displays, getting hot and flushed and giddy and staring at someone's mouth from close enough to count the freckles on his cheeks, to see the blood rising under pale Kyndric skin.

Intellectually, she understood. The rest of her wanted to throw up.

With a faint crook between those perfect golden eyebrows, Prince Amalric said, "Would you like a breath of fresh air, my lady Roshana?"

"Please."

THE BALCONY WAS SO MUCH BETTER. The wind was cold and crisp and biting, and it was only the second story. Roshana thought she might not break both her legs if she jumped down and ran.

Softly, behind her, Prince Amalric said in a breaking voice, "I'm trying. I truly am. I've studied, I've rehearsed—I'm so sorry if it's not good enough."

That cut through her frantic thoughts like a sharp blade through the grass. "What?"

"You are a beautiful and intelligent young woman, we both know our parents are determined, I'm ... I'm trying very hard not to be terrible. And if you can tell this—this isn't my first choice ... then that's *not your fault*—"

"Goddess's grace, you too?" Roshana blurted out.

"I'm sorry, what ...?"

"Not your first choice," Roshana said. "Or not your choice at all. Is there someone else you *would* choose?"

"Of course not," he said, in immediate reflex, a gallantry that had been trained into him as deeply as a show horse's gaits. Then, a moment later, he admitted softly, "I have always known I would not be the one to choose. But I've sometimes wondered what it might be like to *have* a choice I could make."

"You're here at a ball for your own birthday with a hundred women competing for ..." Then Roshana heard herself, and said, "Oh."

"I'm not the judge," Prince Amalric said. "I'm the trophy that one of you is going to win. Most likely at a private auction where my mother and grandfather hold the gavel. Though your mother has clearly made an outstanding bid so far."

"*Oh,*" Roshana said. "Oh, Goddess." She took another look over the edge of the balcony.

"My lady, please—"

"No, not that," Roshana said. "I'm just thinking, do we both want to run away? With each other? Because if they think we're living in sin with *each other*, they might even leave us alone."

For a moment, he looked terribly tempted. But then he said, wearily, "I couldn't do that to Uncle Theo. Something would happen to poor Hal. Someone would get Hal out of the way. And some woman would have to obviously carry an heir. Very obviously, very publicly, because Uncle Theo's preference is so well known."

"And we couldn't *all* run away together," Roshana said. "… could we?"

"They might let two of us go," Amalric said. "They wouldn't let all of us go. I can't take more than another few minutes out here, even. If it were anyone but you, Mother would have had us interrupted already."

Roshana sighed. "Might we find a few private minutes with your uncle and his stableboy?"

"His master of the horse," Amalric said. "Hal is no more a stableboy than you or I."

"I'm sorry," Roshana said. "I had only ever heard him called that. It's just that if you had asked me last night, I would have assured you I would rather choose your uncle."

Prince Amalric blinked. He had clearly never heard *that* from a young woman before in his life. But he rallied valiantly. "Because he is the Kyndric heir, and more useful to your family?"

"Goddess's mercy, no. Because he already has Hal. So he'd be less interested in me."

"Oh," Prince Amalric said, and for the first time Roshana saw something very human in his eyes, and something very understanding. "Because you were also not allowed to have a first choice? And absolutely not allowed to choose no one at all?"

"Of the lot of us, I'm the only one with a womb," Roshana pointed out. "Something useful has to come from it."

"In a gentler world, I might hope that rather than something useful, someone you could love could come from it."

"Talk to our mothers about that," Roshana said. "They have made plans for the arrangement of our loins, along with the grandchildren engendered thereof. Most likely in perpetuity."

Amalric laughed; she wasn't surprised that he had learned to laugh like a song, but the little snort at the end was surprisingly unregal.

"I must dance at least until midnight with the daughters of at minimum eight other realms lest I set off a diplomatic spectacle," he said. "But my uncle is likely in the third floor conservatory, and you could claim interest in the lute collection."

"Thank you, I will," Roshana said. "And it will even be true."

&.

HIS HIGHNESS THEODRIC was almost as described; he was a soft, fat man, though not quite old. His hair and beard had once been a wren-like brown, but were now streaked through with a striking silver. The lines at the corners of his eyes spoke of both laughter and weariness, along with years of squinting at books and lute strings with not-fully-adequate candlelight. He clearly had not expected to attend the ball, because he wore a soft loose tunic and breeches more at home in his lover's stables than in the palace ballroom.

He had also not expected his nephew's almost-but-not-quite princess-to-be to seek him out in his own conservatory, wearing a gown that *was* intended for the palace ballroom. The trailing hem of her gown rustled on the carpet. Theodric looked up from his fingering on the neck of a lute, blinked, and nearly toppled over the candlesticks as he scrambled to his feet in order to bow to her.

"Welcome, my lady Roshana—I'm sorry, I wasn't expecting company. *Mirhaban y'a sabhrin.*" He bowed again, this time with a hand over his heart in the Mirshani manner, and Roshana thought Amalric must have learned his Mirshani from his uncle; their accents were nearly identical. "You are most welcome to make yourself at home as family do, for we hope that you will find yourself a part of our family. Amalric is in the ballroom; I can show you the way if you wish?"

"Actually," Roshana said, "I'd hoped I might speak with you, your Highness."

Theodric showed his surprise more clearly than his nephew; perhaps the lessons slipped from his grasp when he was startled in his own music room, in his night-clothes, on an evening when everyone's undivided attention was to be focused upon Amalric.

Then the bewilderment cleared like fog melting beneath the sudden summer sunbeam of his smile.

Theodric was a handsome man when he smiled, Roshana thought, no matter what her gossiping maids whispered of a fat old man who chased stableboys. She could see the family's echo of Amalric's beauty in the dimples in his cheeks and the warmth of that smile.

"Oh—the poetry, yes, of course! The poetry, the music, yes? Even here we have heard of your skill with both word and song, my lady."

Roshana couldn't help smiling back. Somehow it was easier to hear from a man whom she knew had no physical interest in her, who appreciated music as she did.

"It would be an honor to share music with a poet and musician of your renown, your Highness," she said. "And your nephew assures me that his evening's dance card is overfull."

"Oh dear," Theodric said, with the same crook between his brows as Amalric. "My sister will be most wroth with me if I distract you with music's wanton allure, and you cannot claim a dance with my far more charming young nephew. If we asked Hywel to find a time—"

"Your Highness," Roshana said, "if we may have a moment's privacy?"

Theodric cleared his throat, and a young page by the door bowed and slipped out.

"Yes, my lady?"

"Your Highness, it seems to me that among the frenzied arranging of royal pedigrees, no one has bothered to ask any of us what we want. But if anyone had asked me last night which of the Kyndric princes I would prefer, I would have named you."

Theodric all but collapsed back into his chair, like a puppet with cut strings.

"I—but—you—why on *earth* would you—?" he stuttered. "You're young, you're beautiful, so is he—it unites two realms, he'll have the inheritance once you have an heir. Why on earth would you *not* prefer him?"

"Because you have music, and you have Hal," Roshana said. "Because you *wouldn't* want me that way. We could share our music with each other, and be content in that. And—I suppose someone is going to have an heir from me, one way or another. But nobody has asked Amalric what he wants either. Not about a wife, not whether he wants to be heir, not any of it. The court has obviously told him what they expect from him. Did anybody ask him what he wanted?"

"I tried," Theodric said wearily. "I tried, many times. He told me he was sure he could be the prince his mother and I needed him to be. I tried to tell him I would love him even if he couldn't. I don't know if he believed me."

"He believed you, I'm sure," Roshana said. "Because he loves you too. He couldn't run away and abandon you to what the court would do to you and Hal if he left and there wasn't another heir."

"Ah, hellfire." Theodric ran both hands down his face. "If he gets the chance? If both of you get the chance—take it. Go. Get yourselves free of this lineage mess. I'm old enough to be canny. I'll work something out."

"That's what I'm saying," Roshana said. "Let's work something out. You and me and Hal and Amalric. Let's make our own arrangements."

"Whatever do you mean by that?"

"Well, for one thing, which of you actually *prefers* to be the Kyndric heir? Which of you *wants* the diplomacy and the bureaucracy and the court infighting and all the rest?" Considering that, she said, "I've got to admit, all of us running off to sing our madsongs to the hills in some tiny island full of sheep and crags? That is looking better and better."

"I'm accustomed to it by now, I suppose," Theodric said. "I've been heir for half a century, it leaves some familiar wheel ruts in a man's soul. I wouldn't know what to do with myself if I weren't the heir, if I couldn't hand out the baking prizes at the festivals and sponsor the bardic circles and crown a poet with a circlet of bays every so often. Not to say that Amalric wouldn't be a magnificent king if he needed to be—the boy was raised to shoulder his duty like a soldier and smile through it like a bard. But I'm not certain it would be *good* for him."

Roshana nodded. "And if they marry me to him before he even has a chance to find his Hal, whoever that is for him—or whether that's anybody at all? You know him better than I do. Tell me if I'm wrong that he'd smile and nod and keep anything else he might want behind his teeth for the rest of his life, because it's his ground-into-the-soul wheel-rut duty to be flawless."

"You're not wrong," Theodric said. "And if I were a better man, I would be able to take that burden from his shoulders as well. But I'm not a better man. It's become quite clear over fifty years of effort that I simply cannot ..." He hesitated, and sighed, and admitted in a very quiet voice, "I cannot persuade my body to cooperate with one particular, essential part of an heir's duties."

"The man that you are is a good man," Roshana said. "And the man that you love must be a good man too, or I think that you would not love him as dearly as you do. You seem to be an excellent judge of character, if I may judge by the insights in your poetry."

"You've read my work?" He seemed surprised, and a bit embarrassed. "I often think that if I were not the heir, much less lavish attention would be paid."

"Of course I've read your work," Roshana said. "You are one of the two men I've been told I must attempt to marry. Of course I've read your work. And of course, if I were given a choice, I would choose a man who lets me see his soul. His own soul, not the mirror he has been commanded to polish to the point where not even he can see his heart in it."

"Even if what you see reflected in that soul is that I am a notorious fat old lecher who cannot properly please a woman as other men do?"

"Especially then, your Highness," Roshana said. "Because I have also been informed that I am a frigid outland witch who could not hold a man's interest with a whole fleet's worth of fishing nets. And I would be *entirely* pleased to craft songs with you during our days, and teach our children music in a dozen languages, and kiss your cheek in the evenings as you take to your own bed with your own beloved. If only there were some less mutually unpleasant way of getting another heir into the line."

"If you were a man, it would be easier to misdirect," Theodric said. "But it is more difficult to mistake who is giving birth to a child."

"Goddess's own truth, that." Roshana struggled with herself for a moment, then admitted, "So long as I am being terribly scandalous, I have never before tasted a cup of your Kyndric alcohols, and this conversation seems to call for it."

"Would mead suit well enough?" Theodric said, gesturing to a dew-gleaming ewer half full of some golden-amber, sweet-smelling liquid. "Brewed from honey, and the conversation could use a touch of sweetness as well."

"I bow to the voice of your greater experience, your Highness."

Theodric poured the mead into a pair of blown glass cups, only a couple fingers-depth at a time.

Roshana sipped at hers as cautiously as he did at first, but the taste of it widened her eyes. It tasted like sunshine in a glass, sweet and floral and warming all the way through to her toes; she drained her glass in a swallow, and asked, "May I have another?"

"Careful," he warned, and filled her glass with elderflower water next. "Your head will regret it in the morning if the mead sneaks up on you, and I would not have either of us make an arrangement of such sensitivity when drink-addled. Let us save another glass for the toasting, if we come to an arrangement that suits us all."

"Well, Amalric's dancing at least until midnight, he said," Roshana said. "Could we speak with your beloved in the meantime? I will make a terrible mess of this gown if I wear it into the stables. So I'd love to, of course."

Theodric passed both hands over his face again, in a gesture that looked almost like a prayer for mercy. "Let me send a page to invite him up," he said. "Then you will not ruin your dress, a night in the stables will not ruin your reputation, and the mead is here to be sipped. *Slowly.*"

"You *are* a man of fine and discerning judgment, your Highness," Roshana said. The world was getting pleasantly warm, and swaying a bit around the edges. Perhaps she should drink more of that elderflower water.

She had heard Hal described as "the Prince's stableboy" so often that she'd expected him to be someone like Amalric: young, golden, handsome, muscular. She'd imagined half correctly; after years of physical labor, he was notably more muscular than the gently rounded poet-prince. And Hal was distractingly handsome as well, but in a way much more like Theodric than like his nephew. Hal's hair had been much darker at some point, but it was now a striking steel gray that matched the intensity of his gaze.

They must have aged well together, Roshana thought. Not old, not yet, but certainly they had matured together, the way Kyndric wines were said to improve with aging in oak barrels.

It would have been a joy to observe how fiercely Hal felt the need to protect his beloved prince from any catty young wenches who wished to make a mockery of him, Roshana also thought, if she had not been cast in the role of the catty young wench from whom his Highness needed protecting.

Hal was polite, dignified, and as unyielding as any warrior with a ready hand to his blade, even if the battlefront was a book-strewn conservatory where Theodric had been teaching Roshana some alternate fingerings for minor chords on the necks of fretted lutes.

Perhaps it was a good thing that Amalric was busy dancing until midnight, she thought. It seemed likely to take almost that long to settle Hal's protective bristling over a young woman who was supposed to be preoccupied with nephew Amalric's ballroom, but who had instead inexplicably invaded Theodric's private conservatory with her gowns and her mead glass and her dancing around highly improper suggestions.

After the third or fourth word-skirmish of it, Roshana poured herself another fingerful of mead and drank it down. Then she set the glass down and stared Hal square in the eyes.

"I would like to be entirely blunt," she said, and poor Theodric sank lower in his chair, because he already knew her well enough to have a notion of what was coming. "I dare swear you have loved each other longer than I have been alive, and I would never dream of coming between you. But someone of his Highness's blood needs an heir, I want a husband who *won't* yearn to bed me, and his Highness's nephew has spent his entire life trying so hard to shape himself into the perfect royal successor that he most likely hasn't a single blessed notion what *he* wants for *himself*. I would prefer to give him the space to learn, if we can."

"We," Hal said.

"We. You, me, your beloved prince, and his beloved nephew. In whatever arrangement works for *us*, not just for the bloodlines."

"I confess myself skeptical, understandably skeptical, of a woman who wants to wed a prince and claims no interest in displacing his lover from his bed."

"To be fair, I never said I *wanted* to wed a prince," Roshana said. "Of the options I have been presented, which include his elder Highness, his younger Highness, or some other Kyndric nobleman of unknown tastes, I would prefer to gamble my chances of happiness on his elder Highness. Who knows who he is and what he wants, and who has enjoyed your love and support for years. You're happy with each other. I'm happy that you're happy with each other. And if there were any way to get myself with his heir without troubling *any* of our hearts over the methods, I would be well pleased to do so. I will swear to that by any god, goddess, or imp you would have my oath upon."

"She's serious?" Hal asked Theodric.

"To the best of my knowledge? Entirely so."

"She's also drunk."

"I am not drunk, I am—" The Kyndric word slipped through her mind's fingers. "Tilted? I am a bit tipped."

"Tipsy," Theodric said, rueful.

"Tipsy," she agreed. "Certainly too tipsied to lie to you for an hour solid."

"*In vino veritas?*" Hal said, crossing—yes, Roshana had to admit those were some impressively muscular arms. Just because she didn't share the pelvic urges didn't mean she lacked the aesthetic appreciation, and all three of these men were quite aesthetic in their own ways.

Hal's equally impressive shoulders were edging up towards his ears.

"Roshana, my dear," Theodric murmured, "that was your outside-your-head voice, not your inside-your-head voice." He poured more elderflower water into her glass and pushed it toward her.

"Oh. Really?"

"If you're both serious about this," Hal began, and Theodric held up a finger.

"If we're *all* serious about this," he said. "Including you and Amalric."

"If we're all serious about this, then," Hal said, "and if we're still serious about this tomorrow when everyone is sober? Sometimes, when you need a stallion to cover a particular mare, and one or the other of them just aren't interested—I do know how to make the necessary arrangements there, too."

Nine months later, Roshana said to Hal, "I can't believe you talked us into arranging the timing into the middle of *winter*."

"Every woman I know complains about how miserable it is to be carrying late in the summer," Hal said with a rueful shrug.

"But I'm clumsier than a hippopotamus even before you pile half my weight in furs and wool on top of me!"

Another familiar voice said, "It's symbolic. The longest night, the first child of the coming year, the birth of spring's hope and suchlike."

Amalric stood in the open door, letting a gust of that horrific white frozen sky-dandruff in with him, and Roshana howled, "*Shut the door!*"

"Yes, yes. I've brought you a yuletide present, Aunt Roshana."

"That will never stop sounding strange," Roshana said.

Amalric's eyes crinkled very much like his uncle's when he was trying not to laugh at her. (Which both of them did with unfair regularity.) He swept across the room like a graceful, gilded swan, and Roshana tried not to cordially loathe him for that easy elegance while she felt as round as a river-cow. Then he kissed a greeting upon her cheek with chilled lips, and while she was spluttering over that he dropped to his knees and kissed a greeting upon her snug round belly as well.

"I think I liked it better when you were pretending to be perfectly charming," Roshana told him.

"Really?" He had the most soulful eyes when he chose to use them for nefariously teasing purposes.

"Not really," she admitted. "But you also don't need to tease me until I burst from sheer frustration."

"I thought you were ready to be delivered."

"I am! I have been! But your cousin is determined to take the leisurely path."

"Then in the meantime, I shall continue to tease you until you burst through the kindest and purest of motives, the relief of this joyful burden, the accomplishment of this yearned-for hope—"

Hal dumped half a bucket of snowmelt over Amalric's head.

As he gasped and spluttered, Roshana said, "*Thank you,* Hal. If we were both differently inclined I would kiss you."

"I shall consider myself honorarily kissed, your Highness," Hal informed her gravely, though with an amused gleam in those steel gray eyes. "Mal, where's your uncle?"

"He's bringing the rest of Aunt Roshana's present." Like a street-juggler, Amalric produced half a dozen oranges from the depths of his cloak, smiling when she made a sound of pure yearning.

"Oh, Goddess, Mal, give me those!"

"As you wish, Aunt." He poured them into the precariously

small nook of her lap that her burgeoning belly hadn't claimed, so Roshana was frantically clutching at an apron-fold of her skirts to keep the precious oranges contained when that thrice-bedamned door opened again.

"Shani?"

Roshana dropped the oranges. They fell and bounced across the floor as she all but flew across the room and threw herself into her brother's arms.

"*Rahim!* Rahim, Goddess keep you, what *happened* to you?"

"I found the silk-moths," he said, holding her as carefully as though she were made of eggshells, with his hands unsteady against her sides. "Shani, what happened to *you?* Mother said—I thought you didn't want—"

"I didn't want to be a royal broodmare to be bedded and bred over and over again," Roshana said, laughing through tears. "At least, not until I met the master of stables, who knows ways to handle the breeding part with *so* much less bother. Say hello to your niece, unless she's your nephew. And also to your nephew-in-law, his Royal Highness Amalric, dripping on the floor there."

From behind her brother's shoulder, Theodric said, "A joyous yuletide present, then?"

"The best I have ever received," Roshana said, rubbing tears from her cheeks. "Come in, Theodric, darling. And indulge me in my whims?"

"Yes, of course." Theodric was already reaching toward the fallen oranges when Roshana cleared her throat.

"Theodric. Sweetest of princes. Father of my child. *Shut that damned door before I nail it shut myself.*"

"Yes, your Highness."

"Is this normal in Kyndra?" Rahim asked Hal under his breath.

As Amalric burst into melodic laughter, Hal said, "In Kyndra, not at all. But in your sister's home? Yes, absolutely."

About the Author

Lynn Strong (MLIS) is a professional information designer, an amateur but enthusiastic trope flipper, and a questionably recovered wordaholic who used to be paid by the column-inch. It likely still shows.

Lynn is also a queer and disabled person who has lived on three continents, speaks six languages with different levels of fluency, has studied (and taught) medieval Japanese dye techniques, and at one point semi-professionally burned Kool-aid while studying for a degree in theater tech.

You'll find more cozily queer, ace, body-positive, and neurodiverse stories (and more recipes) at lynnstrong.com.

DEATH TAKES A WIFE

J.M. REINKE

I first saw Death when I was six-years-old. It was my great-great-uncle Marcus's funeral visitation in Goodlettsville, Tennessee. I was playing with my cousins in the foyer. From what I can assume now, ours was the only deceased available for viewing that night, otherwise, I'm sure our mothers would have kept us clamped to their sides.

A yellow-haired man in a gray suit and black tie came through the foyer, headed for Uncle Marcus's viewing room. Feeling rather bold, since I was wearing my favorite green velvet dress, I asked him, "Aren't you going to tell us to be quiet, too?"

He gave me a startled look. "You can see me?"

I thought he was weird. "Yes, sir. Can you see me?"

He smiled. "Yes, of course, Cassandra Young."

My mouth dropped open. "How do you know my name?"

The man shrugged. "It's a gift. It's been interesting meeting you. I'll see you around."

He walked into the viewing room and hovered near Uncle Marcus's casket.

"Who were you talking to?" my cousin Justin asked.

I pointed to the man. "You saw him. The man with the yellow hair."

"What, your invisible friend?" he scoffed.

"Yeah, Cassie, you were talking to thin air," said my cousin Aimee.

"I was not," I stubbornly declared.

"You're just weird," Justin said.

"You're weird," I shot back, with a pinch to his arm. Then the big baby went to tell on me.

At that moment, people rushed to one of the elderly ladies who had been viewing the body. My mom, a nurse, yelled to call an ambulance. She started doing CPR, but when she caught my eye, I knew it was hopeless. The old lady died then and there. The strange man stood, watching. When I blinked, he was gone. It turned out, the lady had had two heart attacks already. It was a wonder she had been alive that long.

I didn't see Death the rest of the night. He must have used the back exit.

⁊❧

THE NEXT TIME I saw Death, I was twelve.

Great-Great-Aunt Amanda, Uncle Marcus's wife, had lived a long life, healthy as a horse, as they say, until she developed breast cancer at the age of ninety-one. She elected not to fight it, but the disease wasn't quick. Hospice had been taking care of her, Mom said, and Aunt Amanda originally wanted to die in her own bed. At the last minute, she asked Mom, her favorite niece, to drive her to her condo in Destin. She wanted to see the ocean and hear its roaring waves. Was having children there a good idea? I would have left my younger twin sisters, Hallie and Zoe, and me, with Dad. But, for whatever reason, Mom brought me and my sisters along for the trip to Aunt Amanda's end time. When we got there, we skipped the beach, as it was January, and were busy watching cooking and kid shows. Mom helped Aunt Amanda with everything she needed. I watched Hallie and Zoe.

Suddenly, the man appeared again, wearing the same outfit

from before. I gasped, because he hadn't used any door, just hovered by Aunt Amanda's room.

"What are you doing here?" I asked.

He turned his head to look at me and sadly smiled. "Hello, Cassandra," he said before he turned back to the bedroom. "I'm here because it's Amanda's time to go home. What are you and your sisters doing here?"

I shrugged. "I don't know. Mom brought us."

"Stay in there. Do not come into Amanda's room."

"Okay."

Hallie spoke up. "Who are you talking to?"

Then it was Zoe's turn. "Yeah, Cassie, who are you talking to?"

"None of your beeswax."

They both looked at me like I was crazy. I didn't care.

A few minutes later, the man bowed his head. Then, turned and said a quiet goodbye before he disappeared through the front door. Mom came out of Aunt Amanda's room, tears streaming down her face.

"Aunt Amanda is gone," she said.

"Where'd she go?" asked the twins, simultaneously. It was an annoying twin thing when they did this.

"She died," I clarified.

"Oh," they said.

"I need to make some calls," Mom said, absently.

"Do you need some help?" I asked.

She wiped her cheeks and smiled. "No, thank you, baby. I need to do this by myself."

So, Mom made her phone calls. A while later, some people came and took Aunt Amanda away. Mom had been sleeping in bed with her, but now slept in my bed. The twins slept in their single beds in another bedroom. We left the next day.

At the visitation and funeral, I looked for the man in the suit, but he never showed. I was disappointed.

§

I WAS 22, about to graduate from college, when I met up with Death, for all intents and purposes. A couple of sorority sisters were hit by a drunk driver. Jessica died at the scene; the other, Emily, was in the ICU, barely clinging to life. Doctors said it didn't look good. I was one of many people who stayed in the waiting room with her parents. The man in the gray suit walked down the hall. He paused, seeing me, nodded, and made his way to the ICU unit, vanishing through the doors. Tears slipped down my cheeks. He was in there for maybe five minutes, but when he came back out, there was no rushing of staff members, no alarms that I could hear.

He gestured for me to follow him. I excused myself from the others. The chapel was just down the hall. I sat next to him in a pew. "Is Emily going to make it?" I asked.

He sighed. "Possibly, if she remains stable."

"Oh, thank goodness," I said.

"But, don't be surprised if you see me again."

I smiled wryly. "I've stopped being surprised by you, Death."

"My name is actually David."

"David, what?"

"I guess David Death is as close to a full name as I've ever had. But, for real life stuff, I use Holt."

"Am I still the only one who can see you?"

"There may be others, but you're the first that I know of who can see me in my non-corporeal form."

"So, you can be seen, like normal?"

"If I so choose."

"Well, what if I asked to meet you at a café, would other people be able to see you then? Or, would I be talking to myself the whole time?"

David looked amused. "Are you asking me out on a date?"

I garnered my courage. "Yes, I suppose I am."

"No interest in guys your own age?"

"I prefer older men," I said smoothly.

David's lips quirked. "A few thousand years' difference doesn't bother you?"

"Nope. Does it bother you?"

"You know it would never work. I'm Death and you're a human."

"What if I don't care?" I asked, reckless as always.

"But, I care. I want you to have a normal, happy human life. Find a nice guy, get married, have a few kids."

"And when I die of breast cancer, because it now runs in the family, you'll send me on my way."

He winced. "Don't say that."

I knew my stubborn chin was showing. "It doesn't make it less true, Death."

"David."

"No. That would mean we have some sort of relationship and according to you, that's never going to happen."

"I'm so sorry I've upset you, Cassie."

"It's Cassandra, Death," I reminded him.

"Understood." I refused to look in his stupid, handsome face. "One day, hopefully soon, you'll see I was right."

"Of course. Already working on it."

"Goodbye."

I stared at the stained glass at the front of the chapel. "Bye."

I'M proud to say I didn't pull a Bella Swan and go into a severe depression. I dated any nice guy who asked me, although I only managed a couple of dates apiece. I graduated, and started my career in marketing. I hung out with friends. I only cried a little bit each night before sleep took me. But, I prayed that Death would change his mind. Maybe that and the crying made me weak. I didn't really care.

I was at dinner at Cracker Barrel with Martin, one of my male friends, when a man at a nearby table started choking. And, there he was, just standing there, watching as everything unfolded. I sighed. Fortunately, for the choking man, his dining companion jumped out of his chair and performed the Heimlich on him until a piece of chicken flew out of his mouth and landed on the table.

Death nodded, and then caught sight of me. He raised his hand and smiled. I know my expression was stony. I excused myself from Martin, and weaved my way through tables and retail displays until I hit the restroom. I used the facilities, saw that Death wasn't inside, and washed my hands. He was waiting for me by the quilts. I guess we'd have some privacy.

"I thought you'd already be gone." I fingered the price tag.

"I can be seen. I went into the men's room when you did, and became corporeal."

"Great," I said, overly cheerful.

"Can we talk?"

"I need to get back to Martin."

"Oh, yeah. You're on a date. Makes sense."

I didn't bother correcting him. "If you want to talk, ask me out. It's that simple."

He swallowed. "Okay."

I almost passed out. Did he just say what I thought he did?

"Seriously?"

"As a heart attack."

"Not funny."

"I'm a little rusty. You'll have to forgive me."

I bared my teeth. "We'll see about that."

David shrugged. "Okay."

"So, do we just meet up or do you pick me up or how does this all work?" I asked.

"I'll pick you up. I do have a car."

"A hearse?"

"A 1967 red convertible Mustang, thank you very much."

"I'll wear a scarf over my hair."

"Are we really doing this?"

"Yes, we really are."

"Well, then, we'd better plan our date," he said.

I went back to my meal and movie with Martin. David picked me up the next night, Saturday, wearing a Kelly-green polo with dark faded jeans. I was surprised to see him so casual. I was wearing a lemon-colored dress, which showed off my auburn hair.

"Can people see you driving the car?"

"No, I thought I'd draw as much attention as possible tonight."

"Do you save all your sarcasm for your dates? Or, is this your standard way of speaking?"

"You're my first date."

I was flattered. And concerned. "Really? No one ever caught your eye?"

"A bold young lady finally caught my eye. I usually don't mind being alone."

"Until now?"

"Until now," he agreed.

David took me to a quiet Italian restaurant. The service was good and the food was excellent. I had the lasagna. He had the spaghetti and meatballs. He twirled his pasta expertly. I just cut into my food like a normal girl out on a date with Death himself.

"So, what do you do for fun?"

"I don't have a lot of down time. But, I do like to read and watch movies."

"Me, too. Do you have any favorites?"

"*Jaws* is in my top ten."

I smiled. "Of course it is."

He smiled back at me. "And *So, I Married an Ax Murderer*."

I gasped. "I love that movie! When the dad is singing the Rod Stewart song in his Scottish accent at the wedding, it's so freaking funny!"

David laughed. "That's one of my favorite parts, too."

David's blond hair gleamed under the lighting. It looked golden. His brown eyes warmed me. He was handsome, all classical features, but he didn't look like Death should look.

"You don't look like yourself," I said abruptly.

He cocked his head. "What do you mean?"

"You should be all black hair, cold blue eyes, mysterious, and have an evil laugh."

"Mwahahaha," he said.

"Very funny."

"Just trying to live up to your ideal."

"I like you just fine," I told him. "I always did."

"I like you just fine, too."

"So, let's say, you don't irritate me anymore with your opinions and we keep dating."

"O—kay," he said.

"And we get married."

"Boy, you just jump right in there, don't you?" he muttered.

"Am I scaring you off?"

"Surprisingly, no."

"What happens as I age? Would you show your age along with me?"

He considered. "Yes. I would do that for my wife."

"And when I die?"

"Are you always this dark?"

"It's a serious question."

He sighed. "I can choose for you to be with me forever."

I breathed. "Oh, that's nice."

"I just said I would have you as my immortal bride and you're okay with it?"

"Why wouldn't I be? Human soul mates ideally want to spend eternity together."

"This is some first date," David said.

"I'm sorry. Am I scaring you? I usually am too forward with my other dates."

"I'm made of sterner stuff," he assured me.

"I know. That's why I picked you."

"I thought it was the other way around."

"Nope."

"Well, I like that."

"I had a feeling you would."

After our meal, we went bowling. Despite it being a busy night, we managed to get a lane. As I was wearing sandals, I was tickled that David had brought an extra pair of his socks for me. I slid in my bowling shoes and chose a ball larger than I needed. However,

I didn't have to worry about getting my fingers stuck. I don't know why I was so surprised that David got a strike his first turn. I got a gutter ball.

"You suck," I told him.

He laughed.

"Any prospects?"

"I try not to think about it."

"Seriously, though, aren't there dying people right now? How can you be with me?"

"I can be several places at once. That's the only way. There have been over 3,000 people who have died since we walked in the door."

I was amazed, in spite of myself. "I can see that, I suppose, considering the world's population."

After that, we concentrated on our game. Not surprisingly, David won. I lost, badly. But, we had fun. We played a second one, and I did slightly better. David beat the pants off me. I'm not saying he used his mystical powers or anything, but, anything is possible.

Thankfully, smoking wasn't allowed in the bowling alley, so cigarette smoke didn't cling to our hair and clothes, when we walked out into the warm night air. I handed him his socks. "You might want to burn these," I told him.

He laughed. "I'll just bleach them. They'll be fine."

"It's your funeral."

His lips quirked. "Did you just make a death joke?"

"I suppose I did. How about that?"

"If I was Death himself, I might just be impressed."

I tugged on his arm, pulling him to a stop. "Why did you change your mind?"

He sighed. "I've missed you ever since I turned you down." At this declaration, I did an internal fist pump. "I was about to show up at your door last night, but I guess you were a little busy."

I crossed my arms over my chest. "I'm not the type of girl to sit around waiting for any guy to get his head out of his butt. Not even you."

He winced. "Ouch. The past few days, every song I listened to seemed to be about second chances and regrets. And I have regrets about turning you down. I want a real second chance."

"What do you think we're doing? Do I need to worry about your lack of intelligence being passed down to our children?"

David grabbed my upper arms, raised me up, and kissed me. His lips were warm and soft. I kissed him back in a Tennessee bowling-alley parking lot on a warm summer night. That's how I would describe it to our granddaughters in the future.

So, we were together from that moment. We married six months later and had four children, two girls and twin boys. And when it was my time to pass 71 years later, Death was kind and loving. He held my hand, kissed me one last time as a mortal, and chose me for immortality.

About the Author

While she writes under several different pen names for different genres, J.M. Reinke currently writes Fantasy and Science Fiction. She has been obsessed with books and writing ever since her mother read books to her as a little girl. Most of her childhood was spent living in different areas of the United States, picking up accents and stories along the way. J.M. Reinke loves to write, read, bowl, and spend time with her friends and family. She firmly believes in overflowing bookcases and stuffed full e-readers. Although she isn't a confident cook, J.M. Reinke is a big collector of cookbooks, much to her husband's dismay and her children's amusement. Sometimes, she's lucky and doesn't burn dinner or dessert. Her grandchildren don't seem to care, as long as she provides them with cheese and store-bought cookies. She currently lives with her husband and very round cat in Nashville, Tennessee.

THE GLOBE CRYSTALS
ARE NEVER WRONG

ANGEL MARTINEZ

Three?" Gvish Tuftear stared at the parchment. "There must be some mistake."

"We simply record the globes's proclamations, Sub-Minister." The human clerk handed over a second parchment without glancing up from transcribing. "Your appointments, sir. Congratulations and good luck."

"Appointments?"

"Yes. Your mates have already been notified."

Gvish tried to control his ears, but they swiveled back in consternation. "Potential mates. Plural."

The clerk had already moved on to the next person in line. Rude. He dealt with globe crystal staff frequently, but on the other side of the dome, where the globes predicted disasters. They were more professional. The staff here on the mate-matching side seemed both harried and bored—a bad combination.

Gvish would speak to their section leader later. Now, he had appointments spaced at two-hour intervals, with the first in twenty minutes. There went his entire afternoon. He'd finally had the time and, quite frankly, the energy to think about settling down with a mate again, singular, and the globes handed him... three.

The catfolk groom tending to Gvish's saddle lizard looked up sharply as Gvish came down the ramp of gleaming white stone. "Sir? Are you all right?"

"Yes." Gvish took Moonflower's halter from the youngster and found a marsh apple in his pocket for his mount. "Why do you ask?"

"Your tail, sir. Begging your pardon."

"Ah." Gvish had been so distracted he hadn't noticed his tail whipping back and forth. No wonder everyone had cleared out of his way so quickly when he left the dome. "Fine, Lers, fine. Just a bit perturbed."

"As you say, sir."

Gvish mounted and pointed Moonflower's head down the hill, back into town. Normally, he would stop and take in the view—Cranelock City stretched out below him with its hodgepodge of old buildings in the old walled city, and the more precise lines and cohesive styles of the new. Today, though, his stomach churned and he had no room in his head for admiring the vista.

His first appointment was in Morning Street, a wide thoroughfare of genteel shops. With his mount's familiar gait rolling beneath him, Gvish finally took a careful look through his parchments.

First appointment? Hyrian Teal, an elven woman who owned a bookshop. That sounded promising. A bookseller was most likely intelligent and patient, having to deal with customers of varied tastes, and Gvish had no preference regarding gender or race. Rather, he preferred them all, so one was just as pleasing to him as another.

The shop sat between a printer (convenient) and a tailor (not as convenient, but pretty with all the fabric bolts in the window), and the bookshop itself was a neat establishment of nut brown with green trim. The appointment parchment directed him to knock at the door beside the shop entrance, probably for the residence above.

The door opened immediately to reveal a petite, ebony-haired woman dressed in an ankle-length, embroidered coat. Her eyes widened, and she took a step back.

"Good afternoon, Honored Hyrian. My name is—"

"No!" She slammed the door in Gvish's face.

"Sub-Minister Gvish," he called through the closed door. "We had an appointment?"

A latch clicked above him, and Hyrian appeared in the open window on the second story. "No! You're one of those huge, brutish men who will... will... *take* things!"

"We could meet somewhere public, ma'am, if you're not comfortable with me in your—"

She upended a basin directly over his head and shut the casement, leaving Gvish with another unfinished sentence to go with his soaked fur.

He turned to his faithful mount. "That went well."

In response, Moonflower snorted, probably clearing his nostrils, but it summed up Gvish's feelings nicely. Since his first appointment had been so abbreviated, and his second was across town, he stopped at home to change. Arriving soaking wet wouldn't make the best first impression. Come to think of it, his black riding leathers probably hadn't been the best choice, either. Too intimidating.

After he'd washed and brushed his fur—gods only knew what had been in that basin—he chose trousers, vest, and coat in a deep blue with silver piping. People had told him more than once that the color suited his gray fur. Perfect. Much more gentlefolk caller and less military thug.

Kezec Whitetip, foxfolk, man, mage artist, his second appointment read.

"Certainly different from the first, Moonflower," Gvish grumbled as he mounted. "Let's see if we can get past the front door this time."

Kezec lived in the old city, so Moonflower had to navigate the narrow, winding streets with care or risk knocking over smaller cart lizards and street vendors' stalls. Many of the buildings predated the Karlak War when Gvish's great-great-grandmother had commanded Cranelock City's defenses. His family liked to brag that so many historic buildings survived because of her efforts. Perhaps. It did make a good family story and had encouraged many Tuftears to enter military service for several generations.

The address described Kezec as living *on the top floor* of his building, though when Gvish inquired with the young human tending the terrace garden, she informed him that Kezec actually rented the entire tower atop the west wing. Built in the Old Fortress style, the three-story tower cantilevered in unexpected ways and appeared decidedly unstable.

Though it's stayed up all these years. Gvish shrugged and started up the stairs the young human indicated. Before he reached his goal, the door at the top of the stairs opened to reveal a foxfolk man with red and white fur wearing the tightest black trousers Gvish had ever seen and an elaborately embroidered open vest.

Gvish stopped several steps below so he wouldn't loom. "Honored Kezec, I'm Su—"

"Oh yes. I know who you are." Kezec let out a put-upon sigh. "I suppose you may as well come in."

I may finish a sentence today at some point. Gvish trudged up the remaining stairs and followed Kezec into his parlor. The furnishings tended toward colorful wall hangings and scattered cushions, though an impressive antique tea table squatted in the center of the room. Mage sculptures dotted every flat surface, flowing from one pose to another or changing shape altogether. Gvish found it difficult to look away from the murmuration of tiny glass starlings, their coordinated flight captured in a continuous loop, one flight configuration melting into the next.

A host of gold rings in Kezec's ears jingled as they twitched and he raked Gvish up and down with his eyes. "Well, you're a handsome one, at least. But I'm sure you see why this won't work."

"I'm afraid I don't follow. We've only just met."

"A looker, but not too bright." Kezec dropped into the cushions beside the massive square table, every movement screaming insouciant arrogance. He gave a lazy wave toward Gvish. "Look at you. Highborn bureaucrat. Probably given your position because daddy or auntie was a government head. Your elegance is sterile. Your existence must be incredibly boring."

"But I'm—"

Kezec put a hand to the white fluff of his chest and went on as if Gvish hadn't spoken. "Whereas *I* am an artist. I need someone with creative sensibilities. Intellectually and sexually adventurous. I don't mean to offend, Sub-Minister. But we're simply too different."

"I think if we—"

Suddenly on his feet again, Kezec took Gvish's arm and steered him back to the door. "I'm truly sorry they wasted your time. I am." With a sharp smile and a pat to Gvish's arm, he herded Gvish out and shut the door.

I have no idea what just happened.

In the privacy of the stairwell, Gvish had to pause to regain his bearings. Attractive didn't do Kezec justice. He was spectacular. The lofty, artistic snobbery though? Possibly real, but the shabby splendor of that front room *had* felt real, and the art on display had been masterful. Gvish had to wonder how much of Kezec's behavior had been a performance for his benefit, a rude but still somehow careful dismissal.

He didn't have an answer as to why, though, not a good one beyond *bureaucrats are boring.* Something for another day, perhaps. On to his last appointment before he lost his nerve.

"I think the globe crystals are having a laugh at my expense, Moonflower," Gvish said as he unhooked his mount's lead from the post out front. "May need to have some pointed words with them later."

As usual, Moonflower didn't have much that was helpful to offer in response, but that was fine. At least he listened and let Gvish finish his sentences.

The last appointment lay on the outskirts of town where city streets and close buildings gave way to less traveled lanes and cottages. The particular cottage in question was red river stone, a single story partially hidden behind a pair of ancient puffseed trees.

Va Heartwood, human, bi-gender, healer.

"Don't eat the healer's plants, please," Gvish murmured as he hitched Moonflower to a fencepost.

The front door opened, and a tall, slender human with midnight hair and bronze skin stepped out. "Sub-Minister Gvish?"

"Yes. Healer Va?"

"I am." Va smiled and came forward to pet Moonflower's nose. "What a handsome steed. Though he's probably the largest saddle lizard I've ever seen."

Gvish fished in his pocket for a marsh apple. "Not his first job. We've been together many years. Moonflower was my war steed when we were young."

"Ah. Luck was with you, then, to keep each other this long." They beckoned toward the house. "Come in, come in. I expect we have things to discuss."

They ended up in the solarium with its light filtered through tall shrubs and a view of the back garden where rows upon rows of herbs grew in an astounding variety of green and blue. Gvish took a comfortable settee beside an elegant tea table set for two, while Va took the deep, round-backed chair beside him.

"Now," Va began. "The globe crystals sent you to me, and since we're close in age, I have doubts that this would be your first match. Tell me—why now?"

We're going to have an actual conversation. Refreshing.

Gvish picked up the offered mug of tea, letting the steam soothe his nose. "You're right. My first mate was self-chosen rather than globe crystal given. We were young. He found someone else, and didn't wish for triad negotiations. He left me. And you?"

"My mate..." Va gazed out into the garden, adjusting their shawl. "Was also self-chosen. She died in the Shej border wars. The same you probably fought in."

"I'm so sorry."

They gave him half a smile. "Many years ago now. Enough that I can think about another match now. But you haven't answered my question."

"Right. Why now." Gvish lowered his mug and found the dark

eyes watching him to be full of patient curiosity. "After the wars, I went into public service. The Department of Disaster Mitigation. Fought brush fires. Pulled people from floods. That sort of thing. Kept me busy and away from home most of the time."

"Understandable. Not the time to think about a new match."

Gvish gave them a grateful nod. "Exactly. I was good at it. Moved up through the ranks. I was captain of the contingent that managed the evacuation when Mount Paeis erupted two years ago, which prompted my promotion to Sub-Minister."

Va's eyes crinkled at the corners when they smiled. "And now you're home and have time."

"Yes. I thought this way would be simpler. A suitable match from the globe crystals. Some quiet courting. But the globes gave me three names instead of one."

"Would you not consider more?" Va poured him another mug. Gvish didn't recall finishing the first.

"I'm not *against* it, but I thought starting with one match would be sensible."

"Sensible. Yes." There was that little half smile again, though this one seemed amused rather than sad. "Am I your first visit, then?"

"No, my third," Gvish grumbled. "Though you might as well be my first. The other two tossed me out."

Va's eyebrows flew up in a very human expression of surprise. "Really? Why?"

Despite the nagging feeling that it sounded like complaining, Gvish told the story of his day, and though Va definitely smothered a laugh here and there, they didn't interrupt him once.

"So I'm either a criminal brute who doesn't understand consent or a highborn idiot without a creative bone in his body."

Va's regard became entirely serious. "Do you think you're either of those things?"

"No. Highborn?" Gvish huffed. "I'm no more highborn than the stones in your garden. And I would never force myself on anyone."

"Did you find either of them interesting?"

Gvish gave that serious thought before answering. "It's hard to say. One wouldn't speak to me at all and the other may have been playacting. They were certainly both attractive. On paper, they're people I *would* be interested in."

"It's possible, since we all gave our names to the globe crystals as seeking mates, that there were expectations in place. Ones that preconceptions ensured weren't met." Va offered a plate of tarts and waited until Gvish had chosen a yellowberry one. "Previous unpleasant experiences may have colored how they saw you."

The tart was delicious, spicy sweet, and Gvish took a moment to enjoy it. Va was only saying things he'd already suspected, but the encounters still stung. "Possibly."

"People may behave in unpredictable ways, but the globe crystals are never wrong." Va rose and wandered toward the window. "I think it might be best for all of us to meet. Together. A feeling of safety in numbers may help everyone say what they need to." They turned back to him, skirts swirling about their feet. "I suspect you've commanded people for many years. Accustomed to being in charge. But for this, would you consider letting me make arrangements?"

Unexpected relief swamped Gvish. "Yes. Please."

Va tapped a finger on their chin, regarding him critically. "And maybe consider dressing more...casually, yes?"

Two days later, they'd all agreed to gather at Va's cottage in the evening. Gvish was certain he'd arrived last, probably by design, since a cart lizard hitched to a single-person dray and one of those new self-propelled wheeled contraptions already sat out front. He thought he could guess which conveyance belonged to whom, but tried not to give in to preconceived notions. Dangerous things.

Gvish straightened his jacket. He'd decided on russet today, plain clothes he wore at home. Not rags by any means, but he'd rolled and re-hemmed the trousers and the jacket elbows were shiny with wear.

Voices led him to the solarium where everyone sat around the tea table. Conversation died a swift and terrible death as soon as he entered, with Hyrian making every effort not to look at him and Kezec glaring in open hostility.

"Gvish." Va rose to take him by the arm and lead him to the empty chair beside them. "Thank you for coming. I'd requested that we not talk about our shared dilemma until you arrived."

"Why did the globes give *him* our names?" Kezec spat out. "Why not one of us?"

"Not a question any of us can answer, why the globes do things." Va picked up the fish-shaped teapot and poured for everyone. "But we can answer questions about ourselves. Hyrian, would you like to go first? Tell us why you went to the Dome and what you'd hoped for?"

Back straight, gaze on the garden, Hyrian emanated poise and regality in her skirt and waist-length jacket of deep purple. She was definitely the same person who had run from Gvish previously, but Va had guessed correctly that having more people in attendance would make her feel safer. The tips of her pointed ears had blushed a deep pink, but Gvish couldn't say whether that was from discomfort or anger.

"I had a mate." She held her teacup in her lap, both hands wrapped tight around it. "My family picked him for me, a big human man. I *hated* him." Sharp teeth bared on that last sentence, then her expression went blank as stone before she went on. "I tried. At first. The things mates generally do. But I didn't enjoy it, and after the first week, told him no more. He screamed at me. Threw things. Threatened me. Began taking money from the shop. Claimed since I was broken and frigid, I owed him. He's dead now."

Did you kill him? Gvish had to lock his jaw to keep from asking, but he obviously wasn't the only one thinking it.

"How'd he, ah, die?" Kezec asked, his ears plastered flat to his head.

"He fell. He was a stonemason." Hyrian shrugged. "These things happen. I went to the globes because I don't like being alone, but I wanted someone for me. Someone who would respect what I don't want. Someone who would understand." She waved a hand toward Gvish without looking at him. "And they sent me this. So much like him."

Gvish kept his protests silent, too. Saying *I'm not like your mate* wouldn't do any good when she didn't know him. And if she'd encouraged someone to give this terrible human a shove? Well, he couldn't really blame her.

"Thank you for telling us," Va said gently. "I can see why that was upsetting. Kezec?"

Kezec sniffed and sipped his tea. "I just wanted a new bed partner. One capable of admiring me and my art properly."

Surprisingly, Hyrian intervened. "Kezec, don't. We're here for truth."

"Truth." Kezec put his cup down and leaned forward, forearms on his knees as he stared directly at Gvish. "Here's some truth. I was at university studying art and magecraft, and I fell in love with the son of a wealthy family. Old, old landowner stock. Oh, yes, he said he loved me, too. We would be committed mates when we finished school, he said, and I believed him. Young fool."

This last was said with a sneer, directed at the floor. Everyone stayed quite still.

"Our final year of study, the university hosted an exhibition of mage art. Well-known names from all across the continent sent pieces. One of them, *Water Falling Through Fire*, was stolen."

Gvish knew it might be a mistake, but he said, "I've seen that one. Airte Stone. Beautiful piece."

Kezec's head jerked up. "You...know Airte?"

"I do. I'm sorry for interrupting. Please go on. The piece was stolen."

While Kezec regarded Gvish with narrowed eyes, his ears twitched forward. That had to be a good sign. "Yes. They found the sculpture in my room. I was as shocked as everyone else, but no one believed me. I thought my lover would protect me. He *could've* protected me, but he chose not to. He pretended we were just classmates, I was tossed out of university, and spent some months in a work camp until they found the actual thief when he tried to steal from another exhibition. He confessed to hiding the sculpture in my room when he failed to get away quickly enough."

"No apology, no contact from your lover afterward, I take it," Va said into the unhappy silence.

"No," Kezec whispered to the floor, then rallied again. "I've done well on my own. Steady commissions. Enough work and play to keep me busy. Except... I want someone who's mine. Someone I know will be there for me, to trust, to care for. And the globes, as Hyrian said, sent me... this."

You loved him and he couldn't even speak for you, your highborn lover. No wonder you reacted so badly to my title. I would hug you, but you might bite me.

Gvish opened his hand toward Va. "Would you like a turn?"

They inclined their head and leaned back in the embrace of the round-backed chair. "My mate and I were both healers. Young, idealistic, thought we were invincible. I lost her to an arrow in the field. Nothing more or less dramatic than that. For many years, I grieved. Now I find I need companionship, and certainly wouldn't mind someone in my bed again." They raised their teacup. "Now you, Gvish, since you are both more and less than you seem."

He told his story again, though he took his cue from Va and kept it brief, and concluded with the relevant points. "My family are mostly shopkeepers and soldiers. The position I have, I earned. What did I want from the globes? I'm lonely, plain as that. I want someone in my house, in my life, someone to talk to, and, yes, someone in my bed would be wonderful. But I would never take anything not freely given, in the bedroom or out."

Hyrian still frowned, but she cocked her head, considering him. Kezec stared at him with a guarded expression, though those lovely red ears canted forward again.

"As for why the globe crystals set us up for a multiple arrangement when we all asked for a single mate, and why they gave me all your names instead of some other way around..." Gvish slapped his knees and stood abruptly. "We should ask them."

"We can't do that!" Kezec turned to Va. "Can we do that?"

Va spread their hands to include them all. "I don't see why not. But it's late, Gvish. Could we meet at the Dome in the morning when they open the doors?"

"Perfect." Gvish gave each of them a bow. "Honored Hyrian. Artist Kezec. Healer Va. I'll see you in the morning."

Gvish strode out, not willing to inflict his presence on them any longer. Let them talk among themselves. He allowed himself a little smile as he rode away. Whatever the outcome, he *did* like all of them.

THE NEXT MORNING just as the sun made a dramatic appearance behind the dome, Gvish waited at the bottom of the path, facing the city so he could watch the road. Va arrived first in one of the city-owned carriages that made regular rounds.

"Good morning, Gvish. Moonflower." They patted Moonflower's nose and gave Gvish a kiss on the cheek. "You both look handsome today."

Gvish stood taller and suddenly felt younger than his forty years. He'd opted for scarlet that morning, for himself and his mount. Nothing formal for him, just loose trousers and a short jacket, but the red leather saddle and lead on Moonflower was his best.

"You as well. The yellow is perfect for you."

"Thank you." Va smiled and adjusted their shawl against the morning chill. They nodded to the morning traffic. "There's Kezec."

Kezec's jaunty little cart lizard trotted up the hill without a hitch, as Kezec steered them effortlessly through the foot traffic. Green for his clothes, complete with a fashionably floppy green hat perched between his ears. Gvish had guessed correctly the previous evening that the cart had been his.

"Hyrian, too." Gvish pointed downhill where Hyrian rode her

wheeled contraption by pushing on a pair of metal paddles with her feet. "That looks...difficult."

"She showed it to me last night." Va laughed. "I couldn't keep it upright when I tried it."

Gvish wrinkled his nose. "I think I'd break it."

Va laughed harder and Gvish found himself purring at that marvelous sound. They all gathered in a nervous knot around Gvish, Hyrian to his right and Va to his left, while Kezec stayed a step behind as they all joined the queue.

When they reached an open desk, Gvish didn't bother with pleasantries. "Sub-Minister Gvish Tuftear. We'd like to speak to the globe crystals, please."

The clerk's sour expression was clear enough. She thought he was an idiot. "Sir. No one *speaks* to the globe crystals. You wouldn't understand them. Only the proctors understand them."

Gvish took a step closer for intentional looming. "I understand you're not as familiar with me on this side of the dome. I'm sub-minister for the Department of Disaster Mitigation, and I'm quite familiar with how the globe crystals work. You will find us a proctor. Now, please."

"Throwing your weight around?" Kezec murmured at his shoulder while the chastised clerk scurried off.

"Sparingly, but yes. The right weapon for the job."

Kezec snort-hiccupped a strangled laugh.

When the proctor—a white-haired senior human—arrived at a trot, Gvish moved his group to the side so the flustered clerk could proceed to the next person in line.

"Sub-Minister." The proctor offered a perfunctory bow. "We're not used to seeing you on this side."

"I'm sorry to be a bother." Gvish gestured to his group. "But the globe crystals presented us with an unusual matching. We have questions."

The proctor considered them, eyebrows raised, then waved for them to follow. "All right. This way. The dome can be a little distressing the first time, but stay on the white stones by the door. Don't reach out to touch, and you'll be fine."

"What does he mean?" Hyrian whispered as they all hurried along.

"The globes crystals are very...active," Gvish murmured. "Very busy place. You'll see."

The first set of outer doors opened on their own as they approached and the proctor waved them through, waiting until those doors had shut behind them. The second set of doors required the key on a chain around the proctor's neck, and again, he waited until they were through and locked the doors behind them. The third set were three times Gvish's height, huge slabs of black stone carved with stars and moons.

"A moment, please." The proctor placed both hands against the doors, and golden light surrounded his fingers, swallowing them so he looked as if his arms ended in glowing eggs.

The doors swung open soundlessly, and though Gvish had been inside before, the sight still made his breath catch. Hundreds of hexagons of opaque glass made up the dome, rendering the enclosed area bright, but not blinding. Globe crystals zipped everywhere—soaring, plummeting, bumping each other, spinning in place. Technically, they weren't globes at all, but Gvish reasoned it was easier than saying forty-sided polyhedrons all the time. Light from the dome created rainbows as they spun and raced about, giving the impression of unending ethereal fireworks.

Kezec pressed close, his hands gripping Gvish's arm, while Va put a hand on his shoulder as if to steady themself as they gazed upward. Hyrian had both hands clasped under her chin, her eyes shining in wonder.

The proctor nodded to the swarm of globe crystals. "Go ahead and ask. I'll do my best to keep up with translation as they answer."

Gvish cleared his suddenly dry throat. "Honored globe crystals, the four of us all requested a single mate. Three of us received no name at all, while I was given three. These three. We wonder if there's been a..." He nearly said mistake, but the globe crystals didn't make mistakes. "Confusion."

All movement ceased, and the globes hovered in place in eerie silence. A discordant chime sounded. Then the globes began to zip about even faster, letting out *ting-ting-tings* in rapid and varied rhythms.

"No confusion," the proctor began. "You each have strengths. Weaknesses. Talents. Shortcomings."

Four jagged shapes appeared in the air. Pictures of light, Gvish realized, since the globes ran right through them. Red, yellow, blue, and green, they each had smooth sides and protrusions.

"These are your needs and wants. The shapes of your lives now. We matched Kezec with Hyrian." The red and yellow pieces came together, and some parts fit, but there were gaps and pieces sticking out. "But it was not complete. The same with Kezec and Va, and Hyrian and Va."

The red and green pieces tried to match, then the yellow and green, with identical results.

"It was not complete. Then you came to us." The blue piece moved to the center of the room. Red, yellow, and green spun and maneuvered until all the edges matched to make an amorphous but perfect shape. "You are the fulcrum. We waited for you, because you are the center."

"So we're meant to be a quartet?" Va asked softly.

More tinging followed, the proctor went on, "Together, you are whole. With four, you have what each needs. With four, you have a stable structure."

The tinging ceased, and the globes returned to their usual frenetic activity.

"Did that help, Sub-Minister?" The proctor turned toward the doors.

Gvish waited until he had a nod from each of them. "Yes. I believe it did."

Back outside, where the regular morning sunshine seemed plain and dull in comparison, they all gathered around Moonflower.

"What now?" Hyrian asked, her chin raised in defiance. "I won't give up my bookshop."

"Gods forfend." Va produced an orange tuber from somewhere

for Moonflower to eat. "No, we must each keep pursuing those things we were meant to. And I doubt we'll all be setting up house together quite yet."

"I suggest we start with dinners." Gvish found it astounding that Kezec still had a tight grip on his arm, but didn't want to say anything quite yet. It felt rather nice. "I need to get to work, as I'm sure the rest of you do, but we could meet at my house this evening?"

"After seventh bell when the shops close." Kezec finally loosened his grip, though he patted Gvish before he let go. "You do have nice arms."

Hyrian nodded, though whether that was in response to the suggested time or Gvish's arms, he couldn't say. "I'll bring wine."

Warmth spread out from Gvish's heart as he rode back down the hill. Already they were working well together. He didn't have any illusions about perfect harmony. There would be arguments and hurt, misunderstandings and evasions, but that's how family worked. He looked forward to having a family, finally, and all the accompanying chaos and joy, too.

About the Author

Angel Martinez has been published since 2005 and writes science fiction and fantasy with queer characters, including the Brimstone series and the Merseton Tales series. Currently living part-time in the hectic sprawl of northern Delaware, and full-time in the writer's own head, Angel has one husband, one son, several cats at any given time, a love of all things beautiful, and a terrible addiction to the consumption of both knowledge and chocolate. angelmartinezauthor.weebly.com

DAMNED IF I DO

MORGAN WEST-BURNHAM

Mads was no stranger to the Crossroads.

He had been living in Llano, Arizona for years. It was a hot, hopeless, dead-end town. But there was magic in the desert.

Mumbling under his breath, he dragged the heel of his boot through the dirt of the intersection. He closed the circle just as the bulbous, amber moon rose bloated and wan in the east. The desert was glowing as he walked to the center of the circle and knelt, digging a small hole into the dry earth. Into this he dropped a single coin, which he buried.

He heard the crunch of steps behind him as he stood, brushing his hands clean on his jeans. A woman was crossing the circle, her eyes fixed on Mads while she flipped a coin and caught it in one hand.

"Ready for another go, already?" she asked, catching the coin again.

Mads grinned, but stayed where he was. "Seems that way, Pothos."

"You're on a winning streak, Mads. No thoughts of retiring while you're on top?" She quirked her brow at him.

"You know me, Pothos: I wager. I win. I wish. It backfires."

She laughed, her head tilting back, scarlet hair shivering down her back, her eyes never leaving Mads's face, "That's the risk of wishing; it needs to be *just right*. You know, we have our own bet downstairs on when you'll give up, or…" She stepped closer to him, walking her fingertips up his chest to punctuate her words. "… When I will set you up with someone. Who. Will. Finally. Stick."

Mads rolled his eyes. "Maybe if you didn't try setting me up with cult leaders and entitled socialites, your chances would be better. I'm in it for my wishes. I don't want to settle down."

"And I thought you liked Sheila!" Pothos pouted, stamping one, black-hoofed foot into the earth.

"Sheila was fine. I just couldn't move with her into the compound once the cult—the organization—reached a certain size." He touched a scar on his eyebrow. "Things got too lively."

Pothos sighed. "I thought you liked that." She considered him, teasing her lower lip in her teeth. "But I have the perfect match for you this time. There's a new priest at that old church in Arroyo. Get him to kiss you."

He scoffed. "That's it? Where's the challenge? With Sheila, I needed an engagement. The one before her—Mabel Lynn?—I had to get into her will. What's the catch?"

"You only get three months. Get a kiss, I'll give you a wish as usual. And"—her black eyes flashed at him—"if you win *and* fall for this one, I rake in a big pot downstairs." She gave Mads a wink.

"You're on." He held his left arm out in front of him.

"And, for consent's sake, if you don't deliver?"

Mads recited flatly, "You get my soul. Eternal damnation. Pain and torment, blah blah. This is all very win-win for you."

She grinned, her eyes alight as she took his offered arm and traced the words of their contract over it in red, glowing sigils that vanished in wisps of smoke. "Lovely."

❧

AMBROSE HAD BROUGHT JUST three bags with him to move into the rectory, one of which was a satchel that held his dim dream: thirteen short stories bound into a single manuscript. Still in the middle of unpacking, he had been living out of his suitcase for the last week. Unpacking meant he was committing to stay—in Arroyo, in the priesthood, in his limbo—and he wasn't ready to solidify that choice.

He had been through this, before. A new church meant a fresh start, a chance to bypass burnout, it meant a chance to reconnect with his calling—and he could recycle old homilies. Saturday evening mass was lightly attended, and the church emptied out quickly. He was thankful for the time to get familiar with his new space.

There was a light knock at the front of the church. He looked up.

A man stood halfway in the vestibule, leaning into the church. Ambrose walked between the rows of pews, opening his arms wide. "Hello, there. Can I help you?"

The man smiled. "I hope so." He held out his hand, and Ambrose took it in greeting.

As their hands clasped, Ambrose wondered what it would be —the stranger was attractive and healthy looking, with wavy blond hair and warm, amber eyes, wearing tailored clothing—he didn't seem to be hurting in any material way. *Pending divorce, maybe,* Ambrose mused, *or infidelity.*

"I'm newer here, but I'll see what I can do—my name is Father Wright." Ambrose offered, gesturing to a chair in the vestibule.

The man took the seat, leaning back, his eyes fixed on Ambrose, as if trying to read something written on his face. Ambrose cleared his throat, and the man spoke abruptly.

"I'm sorry; I thought you would be older. I'm Mads."

Ambrose ran his hand over his chin and smiled gently. "I get that a lot—I'm thinking of growing a beard—be taken more seriously." *And I thought taking the cloth would save me from needing a beard,* he quipped to himself, waiting under Mads's stare.

Mads gave his head a little shake and tore his eyes away from

Ambrose, fixing them instead on the ceiling. "I've been away from the church for a long time. Years. I'm not sure if I'm ready, but," His eyes returned to Ambrose's, and he supplied a gentle shrug of his shoulders. "I'm thinking of coming back."

"I see. I imagine this is the biggest step, making that acknowledgement."

"It feels big." Mads nodded. "I figured, who better to talk me into returning than a priest? Would you have time to meet with me?"

"I believe I do." Ambrose smiled, ignoring the dozen new responsibilities he had still to take over for his new parish as they sprang up in his mind. "Does tomorrow afternoon work to start?"

HE WAS glad he had thought to bring this book to offer Mads. *Till We Have Faces* mirrored his early journey in faith—the mistrust and disbelief into realization and peaceful service; he hoped Mads would find it as instructive. Ambrose found himself looking forward to these meetings every week, though he felt a stab of guilt at his pleasure; he was happy to guide someone else back to the path, all while neglecting his own struggle. He was an expert at offering spiritual advice, having tried so many things to reignite his own faith.

And he *liked* Mads. He was attractive, intelligent, Ambrose had his full attention, whenever they were together, and it felt good. *Why shouldn't I have something that makes me happy? It's not like anything is going to happen.*

They each had finished their coffees, the last, cool dregs in the bottoms of spotless white ceramic, and stood. Ambrose lifted the book from the table, reaching out to offer it. As Mads took the book, shaking his blond hair from his face, his fingers caressed Ambrose's.

Ambrose jerked his hand back so suddenly that the book thudded to the floor. Mads's fingertips were like tongues of flame, and the way this coiling thrill of heat shot through his body was a lightning strike, an awakening to a defibrillator jolting him out of what had been his death in the thirty-three years behind him, into what could be his life.

His face burning, Ambrose stooped down to recover the fallen book and hide his cheeks. As he reached out, he found his face quite near Mads's; they were both going for the book.

Their eyes met, Ambrose arrested by the deep amber irises, the crow's feet that creased in the corners of his eyes as Mads laughed.

"We're both too eager. Here—" He stood, his hand brushing Ambrose's elbow, helping him do the same.

Ambrose looked up to the ceiling as he rose, holding the book out for Mads to take again. "Sorry, clumsy me." He knew he was talking too quickly, but he couldn't stop himself. "I really do need to be off." He managed to lower his gaze to look at Mads again, who was tucking the book into the nook of his arm and watching him so gently that Ambrose felt his cheeks warm again. "Let me know—if you want confession." He spoke in a rush. "Or else—see you next week."

"Thanks for the book," Mads called after him, his voice smiling.

Ambrose waved one hand in acknowledgement, but couldn't turn to face him as he left. *Get a grip*, he thought as he exited the café. He took a few steadying breaths outside the door, slowly flexing his hand.

AMBROSE, with all the demands of his parishioners, only had a couple free hours every Sunday and had canceled the last two weeks. Mads was feeling slighted, wondering if Ambrose had lost interest in him and his soul, and he was feeling the pinch of his deadline.

So, Mads went to him.

It was a dilapidated thing in the sunlight, Our Lady of Assumption. A single, dreamless footprint. Dry, curling paint on ancient wood, sagging like a heavy sigh into the dust of the earth. Mads imagined it smelled like a century of incense and sweat.

Feeling conspicuous, he slipped inside, clutching Ambrose's favorite coffee order and pastry, and found a seat near the back.

A few of the worshippers gave him a look—he supposed he must have done something worse than just being late—but he smiled and nodded at them pleasantly.

Ambrose was in the midst of delivering what sounded like a sermon. His dark hair was neatly parted and he was dressed in robes of green, with sweeping sleeves and intricate embroidery; Ambrose spoke in a projecting, commanding voice that he had never heard in the coffee shop. Mads felt something inside of him loosen.

"And just as with the man in Sidon," Ambrose was saying, his hands interlocked in front of his body, "allow yourselves to be open. Listen—to those around you, your loved ones; to God, in all of His creation; and to *yourself*. Speak—in truth, in love, and to connect. Ask of yourself each day to be open to receive the world and the blessings in it, so that you too may be healed."

His voice was strong, but Ambrose looked weary, even from a distance. Mads's gaze was ensnared: Ambrose, steady and jewel-like in the verdant vestments, siphoning his faith and his energy into the people now getting to their feet around him.

For the next half hour, Mads struggled to stand, kneel, and sit with the rest of his row. As mass ended, he watched as Ambrose knelt, kissed the altar, and began to move down the center aisle with a small collection of people as those around him began to sing.

As Ambrose came even with him, their eyes met, and he saw Ambrose's face flush pink, a wild contrast to his verdant robes.

Mads turned to the woman next to him, who was cradling a hymnal, but not singing. "Do you know if Father Ambrose is available after mass?"

She shut the hymnal with a finger placed between the pages and pursed her mouth, looking Mads over. "Father *Wright* is not. Unless you can get him to yourself during the pancake breakfast—

and good luck with that, because Mimsy Bowen is already working to be first in line." She nodded to the back of the church where a woman was already tittering animatedly beside Ambrose.

The thing that had loosened inside him sunk into his stomach and he frowned. "He doesn't go to a pancake breakfast in all that, does he?"

Again, the book closed, the mouth sighed. "Of course not." She shook her head and flipped back open to her page.

Mads saw dozens of people filtering out now, though many stayed behind in the pews, singing or talking together. He didn't know much about churches, but he knew a stage when he saw one, and figured there might be wings on either side—for costume changes and props, or whatever their ecclesiastical equivalent.

He muttered a thanks to the woman, who returned an eyeroll, and he slipped out into the center aisle, maneuvering against the flow of bodies.

Mads moved with confidence. *Act like you belong, and no one will question it.* He nodded and smiled all the way to the door, right past the musicians.

It was unlocked and looked to be where Ambrose would change after mass. He set his offerings down on the only table—the coffee still tolerably warm—found a scrap of paper and a pen, and scribbled a note. He felt a sting of shame as he wrote; he was using Ambrose, and the man was giving so much of himself. But Mads wasn't *lying.* He enjoyed Ambrose's company, he really did want to see him again, all bets aside. Still, whatever had loosened within him hummed with guilt.

He set the note on top of the coffee's lid before leaving through the back door.

I miss coffee with you. Finished the book. Excited to discuss! I need something new to read. See you soon? X

WHEN HE FOUND IT, Ambrose had stared at the note. He had never felt missed before. Or wanted.

He would bring on a deacon to share in some of his duties, he decided. But time alone could not assuage his suffocating feelings: panic and longing. He was running out of reasons to stay in the priesthood, but he had no inkling of what he could do if he left, how he would survive. There was only his guarded dream around writing: immaterial, untested. He felt trapped.

And then there was Mads. Ambrose blushed at his thoughts, but he *missed* Mads; his amber eyes, hair like brushed gold, his insight—and his attention. Mads wasn't his first crush, but this was the first time he could remember feeling the risk of losing—or gaining—something.

"WHAT HAVE you brought for me, then?" Mads grinned, settling back in the chair. "It's been weeks and I've been so patient."

Ambrose chuckled, pulling his satchel around into his lap. "It's —no Lewis. But it's—" He pulled out a thick file folder, opening it to reveal a stack of paper. "Me."

He dropped the folder onto the table in front of Mads heavily, like a horseshoe or an anchor.

"You?" He picked up the folder, peering inside, flipping through filled pages. "You mean you wrote this?"

Ambrose's cheeks turned pink, but he nodded. "I did. I know that these meetings—they're supposed to be for you—to figure out your way back to the church. But—I want you know me, a little. If it's not what you—"

"No, this." He held the folder up in both hands, lifting it to feel its weight before securing it in his own lap. "This is what I want. Of course I want to know you."

MADS CONSUMED THE MANUSCRIPT.

A collection of short stories, walking the edge of fiction and non, Ambrose's prose was like a caress, touching something in

Mads that he hadn't known was there. He heard Ambrose's voice in the words as he read, falling like embers to the dry kindling of his heart.

These stories were Ambrose's wishes. Ambrose's prayers. What he wanted his life to look like, what he wanted to experience, to feel. Mads knew enough about wishing to feel the yearning in each page. That thing inside Mads that had loosened opened wider, until it was overflowing him, spilling out of him in waves.

Shit, he thought. *I'm losing this bet.*

Mads's own wishes felt flaccid and hollow in comparison to the undimmed hope of Ambrose's desire. His early wishes were predictable. When he first summoned Pothos—the accumulation of months of research and experimentation to find the right crossroad and the right words to call the right demon—he was so young. When Pothos appeared, Mads was game to try whatever she suggested; she was *hot*—so long as he didn't look at her hooves. All of her bets were about getting someone to fall for Mads, and if he loved anything, it was feeling loved. He never lost his bets, but every wish was a mess.

He wished for money—he was robbed. He wished for a rare, expensive car—he got into a wreck. He wished for money again— the IRS audited him. Every few years, he had to try again, only to have whatever he wished for whisked away or turned to poison.

Mads knew he could get it right, so he kept going back; practiced wishing for simple things—the perfect temperature on a steak, a good hair day—trying to get the wording right.

Ambrose's stories got it right, though.

He had to see him.

The church was nearly empty when Mads arrived for confession.

Ambrose met him outside, his blue eyes round with surprise to see that Mads had brought the manuscript with him.

"Thank you." Mads started lamely, patting the folder. "I really enjoyed this."

Ambrose's face fell a little. He didn't reach out to receive the folder. "You don't have to say that because it's me. Or just because I'm about to hear every bad thing you've done."

Mads leaned forward, stepping into Ambrose's space and clasping his hand tightly. "No. I *really* enjoyed this. I... reading you was beautiful and painful. I loved it. I love—" He cut himself off as he felt his palm go suddenly clammy, releasing Ambrose's hand. "I love it."

Embarrassed by his effusion of feeling, Mads was thankful for the screen that separated them in the confessional as he entered. He was determined to come clean, but he didn't want to look at Ambrose in the face while he did.

"Forgive me, Father, for I have sinned. It has been—let's say eons—since my last confession. Shit, this feels weird."

Mads heard the familiar chuckle of Ambrose's through the screen, though all he could see was the shape of a shadow.

"We can do this face to face, if you'd rather."

"No, I want the full experience."

"All right." The grin was heavy in Ambrose's voice. "What are your sins?"

Mads took in a steadying breath. This *was* the right thing to do. Being honest, letting Ambrose in. He wanted Ambrose, and if that meant he lost his soul, well, it was bound to happen eventually. *Nothing else to lose, just get it out*, he thought.

"There's just one that I need to get off my chest," he started, squeezing his eyes shut. "Making deals with devils." He paused. "I took a bet with a demon that I could get you to kiss me in exchange for a wish. But—I have feelings for you, Ambrose, I won't finish the bet." Another pause. He couldn't hear anything on the other side.

Finally, Ambrose's voice came through the screen, tight and slow. "I don't like jokes in confession, Mads."

"I'm not joking," he said quickly. "I'm trying to be honest with you."

After no reply came, Mads stepped out of the confessional, finding the door to the other half hanging open on its hinges, opening to empty darkness within, the manuscript on the bench.

଼

MADS DIDN'T KNOW where else to turn.

After his botched confession, he had given Ambrose some room to breathe, but it had been days with no contact. He tried to catch him at church, but he wasn't there. Questioned parishioners said Father Wright was away, visiting a friend. It had been a week; Mads didn't have more time in him to give.

So, he returned to the crossroads. Rehashed his ritual, scraping out the circle in the dirt, which turned to pale ethereal dust in the twilight sky.

He was on his hands and knees, digging, when Pothos stepped into his peripheral. "You still have a week, what gives?"

Mads stumbled to his feet, spreading his arms out wide in a gesture of failure. Or succumbing. "I'm out. I'm done," he started, pushing a hand through his hair, trying to take the edge of mania out of his voice. "You were right about this one."

Pothos laughed. "I knew it. Our cold, clever Mads *does* have a heart. You still have a week left on our bet, though."

"I don't care about the bet—" He stopped. He hadn't expected to say that, but hearing those words out loud, he realized they were true. "I don't. I need to set things right with him, and I can't find him."

She considered him, her black eyes narrowed. "Hmm. You remember the cost, if you don't get the kiss from him?"

"My soul. Yes. Can you help me find him?"

"I can," she started, furrowing her brow. Her smirk was gone. "Why would you quit our game early, Mads? That's so boring of you. You can be in love with him and still get him to kiss you. That's usually what happens with those squishy feelings, you know."

Mads felt his shoulders sag, felt his body as a heaviness, sinking into the earth, felt a sigh crumple through his chest. "I can't use him and—love—him." He struggled over the word. "I want him to be happy. I want him to trust me."

Pothos's black-within-black eyes bored in to Mads. "If I knew love would suck all the fun out of you..." she mumbled.

Mads cut over her. "I need help, Pothos. Please?"

She hissed out a breath and stamped her foot. "Fine. Fine! He's at a bar in Llano. The Painted Blind. You still have your week. Remember, I bet on you winning—it's not just you who loses."

IT WAS a dive like any other he had been to, on a side street with broken or boarded windows and trash gathering in the gutters like tumbleweeds. But this bar had Ambrose.

He pushed through the door. The oily light spilled off the walls, silver smoke hung in the air, and his eyes landed on Ambrose sitting at the far end of the bar, disheveled, a half-full glass of amber liquid in front of him.

Mads made his way over, taking the stool beside Ambrose and gesturing to the bartender to give him one of the same.

"Hey," he started gently.

Blue eyes, tinged with red, pierced him. "Mads," he said simply. "I don't think it's a good idea that we see each other."

Mads felt his stomach twist, and he took a sip of the drink that had appeared. "I'm sorry. I want to make things right. I really—I'm really fond of you, Ambrose."

Ambrose held his gaze, his eyes softening. "I was, too. But, hell, Mads. Demons? Lying to me about trying to find your way back to the church?" He gave a shake of his head and pushed himself up to a stand, draining his glass. "I can't be around you right now."

He moved to wave the bartender over to take care of his tab, but Mads threw a fistful of cash onto the bar. "Can we just talk for a minute?"

Ambrose gave him a dark look, but shrugged and turned to leave. Mads, leaving his drink unfinished, chased after him.

"Please, Ambrose," he gasped as they stepped outside into the hot night. "What can I do?" This spilled out of him louder than he intended, and Ambrose stopped. "I already told the demon I give up. I'd rather lose my soul than keep using you."

Ambrose turned to face Mads slowly. His face inscrutable, relaxed. As his eyes met Mads's, there was a flash in their blue depths—passion, between anger and lust—as if a dam had broken and pure, icy water was rushing forth to crash into Mads.

And then Ambrose did.

His body collided with Mads, hands in his hair and at the small of his back, as he kissed him. Hard, and gasping, Ambrose pushed Mads to the wall, knocking him against it, kissing him into the bricks. Mads's hands went out defensively, then softened, seeking Ambrose's face and shoulders, but as soon as he started to melt into the current, Ambrose severed it.

Stepping back, he wiped his mouth. "There. To keep your soul safe. What's left of it."

Mads watched him walk away, pinned to the wall like an insect.

❧

HE HEARD her before he saw her. The sharp staccato of her steps echoing off the brick wall and rolling out into the empty street. Pothos put her hands together in patter of quiet applause.

"Congratulations *again*, Mads. I must admit, I didn't think it was going to happen." She sauntered to his side, grinning and giddy.

Mads pushed off the wall, dazed. "Sure, congrats, Pothos, happy for you." His voice sounded flat in his own ears.

She nudged him with her elbow. "Oh no, you're sad. Want me to find someone else to cheer you up?"

He sighed, holding out his left arm to her.

"Aw, Mads," she prodded, taking his arm and giving it a stroke of her hands, sending sigils dancing away like scattered sparrows. "Don't be glum, you're bringing me down. You get your wish. Come on, you love wishing."

Pulling his arm back, he looked down the street into the dark, down the way Ambrose had disappeared. "I did," he agreed.

AMBROSE COULDN'T GET Mads out of his head.

It had been months. If he had ever been this hung up on God, maybe he wouldn't be gathering his unpacked bags and moving out of the rectory. Kissing Mads had pushed him too far, awakened feelings that he couldn't reconcile with his faith. He didn't know if he wanted to see Mads again, but he did want to feel like that again.

There was a priest looking for reassignment in Arroyo, nearer to family, and Ambrose took that as his sign to leave Our Lady of Assumption.

Walking away from the priesthood meant walking toward the things he wanted—he was open, hopeful, and broke. He saw a call for submissions from a new local press in the paper. Living off his meager savings, he had nothing to lose. He prepared his cover letter and sent in his manuscript the same day. The name of the press seemed fitting for his loss of clerical state: Hellfire Press.

The reply came sooner than expected.

He read through the letter, his eyes jumping over the page. Accepted. It instructed him to meet with an agent of the press at the same coffee shop where he used to meet Mads. He felt a twinge, but he pushed it aside.

MADS DRAINED his third cup of coffee, his leg bouncing. Every time the bell over the door sang, he twisted around to look wildly at the door and cursed himself for sitting with his back to the front. But he still didn't move.

He had thought about Ambrose incessantly, as if his thoughts alone could manifest the man, offering him another chance. Mads lined up his three empty coffee mugs, debating if a fourth would help him focus or launch him into space.

"It's you, isn't it?"

Mads leapt to his feet, clutching his chest as he turned around. "Ambrose, you—I'm—" Mads started haltingly. "You look different, you look good."

"No collar." Ambrose tugged at the neck of his sweater with the ghost of a smile as they sat down.

Mads stared at him, struck dumb for a moment.

Ambrose raised his brows expectantly, and Mads shook his head. "Ah, so, I'm starting here in total transparency." He had practiced this speech repeatedly and now it all spilled out of him. "I own Hellfire Press—co-own, anyway. My team accepted your submission." He kept talking, too quickly, rushing through what he needed to get out. "I didn't sway their choice—I'll step down and leave if you don't want me there. But I got a wish—for the kiss you gave me." Mads saw Ambrose's cheeks flush and hope fluttered in his chest. "And this was it. I wished for this press, and you can use it, or not. And—I love you."

Ambrose let him get all of this out, watching patiently. Mads stared back at him, feeling his pulse heavy in his limbs. Ambrose reached across the table, taking Mads's hand in his own, giving it a gentle squeeze. Mads constricted his fingers in response, a man grasping at a lifeline from the depths of a crevasse.

"I'll need time to read over the contract *thoroughly*," Ambrose started, his blue eyes smiling at their clasped hands. "And I don't want to work with—your co-owner. But I'd love to work with you."

Mads felt relief flood through his limbs.

He had a chance now, and he had never lost before.

About the Author

Morgan West-Burnham is a writer of speculative fiction and teacher of middle school students. She was born in the southern United States in the late 1900s and has worked with speleothems, video games, and now preteens. With one MA in Education, she is currently working on her MFA in Genre Fiction with Western Colorado University. Morgan plans to continue writing and publishing stories in the speculative realm from her home in Southern Colorado.

TELL ME ONCE AGAIN

GARY SMITH

Tell me once again as the moon's breath
and the pollendrift of midnight
numb my senses—

that you love me.
Whisper it once more as the skies dance
with a millionwatt of starlight
to undo my fear—

that you love me.
Hold me into your eyes as silence lifts
and birdsong wafts upon the lake
to betray my heart; say again and again

that you love me.
And as the night spills black upon the sky
and as the lakebirds shiver icy-blue
and the moon blurs an ashen hue
repeat to me that ancient lie,
whisper it, and like always
I will believe you.

About the Author

Experienced Secondary School English Tutor (12 years) Award-winning poet, short story writer and writing teacher, Gary Smith has a PhD in Creative Writing and has taught English Literature and Creative Writing subjects at Deakin University and Holmesglen Institute. Gary has performed at the Melbourne Writers Festival, Montsalvat Poetry Festival and on Melbourne and regional radio stations. His writing has been published in a variety of national and international journals and magazines. Gary is also a past Secretary of Melbourne Poets Union.

FOR THE LOVE
OF FARKAKTEH PHONES

SARA ITKA

Matchmaker

A beshert isn't true love, only the one that is destined. It doesn't mean a "soulmate," an "other half," or a "perfect match." Asking for more than seventy-five-percent compatibility takes chutzpah. I don't give people the love they want, I give them the love they need.

Even if they don't realize it.

Leaning against a woodpecker-desecrated palm tree, I watch a young woman shove out of the Weinstein Yeshiva High School staff facilities. She sets off down the sidewalk, twisting her brown hair into a clip. Withdrawing my smartphone from my suit jacket, I open the camera in the Shadchan b'Shemayim app. Left up to me, I would still write names in a book, but the technology gets more and more convoluted without my permission. Since I only experience one day a year, I'll never catch up.

After patshkeing with the focus and adjusting for twilight diffusion, I get it to zoom. I snap the picture as the woman climbs in her car. That's all the facial recognition needs, and her profile loads onto my screen.

Halma Rena, Age 25

Daughter of Shimon Yehoshua and Dena Leah

Both parents. I usually see prayers with fathers' names, since mothers' names are for healing. Someone decided Halma's situation constituted an ailment.

Prayers received from 2,358 individuals across 11 countries. Request placed by subject's grandmother, Ester Lena, for the subject to "b'ezrat Hashem, find her beshert before I wither and die."

Prayers for a match are normal, but this magnitude? How hopeless is this woman?

The staff door opens, heralding a second exodus through the parking lot. No one pays me any mind. No one can see me. Swiping to the shidduch finder part of the app, I let facial recognition pull up profiles and calculate compatibility. Since the subject didn't submit her own request, there are few preferences in her profile besides "a nice Jewish boy who will call even when it's not erev yuntif."

Passing over three middle-aged men in identical suits, tzitzit, hats, beards, and scowls, I land on a younger man with only half a beard, and three-quarters less scowl. His resume pops up, a blessed seventy-four-percent compatibility for Avraham Naftali son of Benyamin Eliezer, age thirty-one, English teacher with a degree from Yeshiva College. Newly single after his girlfriend learned he lives with his parents and calls his grandmother every Friday to wish her Good Shabbos.

I slide my thumb to take the picture and make the match—and drop the phone. Oy-ye-yoi, never thought I would miss flipping through personal ads. Fumbling in the mulch, I pick up the too-small phone, Avraham Naftali's profile no longer open. I scan the parking lot, finding him as he opens the door of his black sedan. I raise the phone, snapping the picture without bothering to patshke with the settings.

Matched!

87% compatibility!

Mazel Tov!

Wasn't it just seventy-four? Dismissing the message, I freeze when I see the picture. A young man in a suit, with long golden-red hair and a smattering of freckles over pale skin.

In all of time, I have never made this mistake. But I've never worked with a farkakteh phone that I didn't know had a front-facing camera.

Eighty-seven-percent compatibility.

A hearty Mazel Tov to... me.

Matched

Halma Steinberg, *Professional Dreamer*. That's what it says on my business card. That's what I've been called since my parents named me for Great-Grandma, after the Hebrew word for dream. People at shul would smile, "Halma'le, you're going to do wonderful things, you're such a dreamer!" Until I turned nineteen, and it changed to, "One of these days, you're going to have to get your head out of those clouds and make something of yourself." Because dreams don't pay rent.

Neither do college degrees. And whatever Bubbe's crochet circle says, the miracle answer isn't "a nice Jewish boy to settle down with." Not in this economy. All the boys I know, Jewish or otherwise, live with their parents.

I lucked into moving out when four of my seminary friends skipped ahead on the New-Yorker-retiring-to-Florida pipeline. As their token born-and-raised swamp monster friend, they asked me to shop for places in the area. I found one big enough for all five of us—if I slept on a reclining beach chair. But it got me out of my parents' house and away from comments on my unfinished education. I settled down, in a corner all my own with inspirational memes framed on the wall, and no "nice Jewish boy" in sight.

But Avraham had to play the "we should talk more sometime" card after tonight's faculty orientation. Which shouldn't bother me, but this was my first unofficial day as guidance counselor to aimless youth, a position my father, the Head Rav, got me. I'm not starting off my lucrative career of telling teenage boys they can't apply to all-girls seminaries by dating a coworker. Even if I were looking, that's not where I'd look.

Pulling into the driveway of our townhouse lovingly named the "Beis Din of Iniquity," I sigh at the sight of a young man standing below the overhang. Another poor date my roommate is letting schvitz in the Florida August in his three-piece suit and... is that a bright red fedora? Yeshiva guys are called "black hats" for a reason. His shirt is red too. Heresy.

I grab my purse and lock the car, the boy's eyes following me up the walk. Stopping by the door, I fish for my keys. "You here for Malkie?"

No answer. I look up, meeting his dark eyes. His hair is long for a yeshiva guy, longer than mine. Not Malkie's typical type, but maybe she's branching out.

"Hello?" I raise an eyebrow. "You, mister stupid hat."

The boy glances behind him, like I'm not making direct eye contact. "You can see me?"

I huff a laugh. "You're over six feet tall and wearing bright red. The only way anyone could miss you is if they thought you were a stop sign."

He shakes his head, fear settling into unambiguous bewilderment. Good, he's ready to go out with Malkie. "Nisht gut, I hoped... maybe it didn't work?" Poor boy has heat exhaustion.

"Look, it's hot, I'm going in." I fit my key in the lock. "Do you want to stand there and schvitz or come in and have a glass of water? My roommates are home, we won't be alone. Malkie should be ready soon, she's just on Malkie time."

The open floor plan of the Beis Din of Iniquity is tiled with a mismatched checkerboard of Home Depot closeouts, four additional rooms partitioned by curtains of souvenir beach towels. Savory scents of onion and schmaltz waft from the kitchen, which, since it's Selah's turn to cook, is sure to be something involving potatoes in a crock pot.

I sling my purse onto a wall hook. "Malkie, your latest shidduch date is here." I glance back at the open door and the boy on the stoop. "Nu? Come in or close the door, we're not air conditioning the neighborhood."

Reluctantly, he enters, closing the door as Malkie pokes her head between beach towels, brown waves flatter than when she oils them for a date.

"Girl, I don't think I have one tonight?"

"Then who's the nebech?" I jerk a thumb at tall-red-and-stupid.

Malkie follows my finger. "Halvah, darling, there's coconut water in the fridge, get hydrated, cool down, we're under extreme heat advisory."

I frown. "We've been under heat advisory since May, what does that have to..." My eyes flick between my roommate and the walking red flag, both giving matching you're-an-idiot looks. "You can't see him?"

"I'm getting you a drink." Malkie steps out, luckily fully covered in a bathrobe.

"So only *you* can see me." The boy still looks vaguely fartumult. "Unforeseen, but so are the circumstances."

Malkie pours coconut water into a glass without any sign of hearing foreign voices. What stage of heat exhaustion is hallucination?

"You're not hallucinating."

I start, glaring at the boy. "Are you—"

"Reading your mind? No." He cocks his head. "Only your face. I believe the modern term is 'emotional intelligence.' My job requires a lot of it."

I raise an eyebrow. Read *this*.

Malkie shoves the glass in my face. "Drink. And girl, please sit down." She shoves a folding chair behind my knees. "I'll be in my room, just do the *Hunger Games* whistle if you need anything."

A weak smile, and then it's just me and the boy. And three of four roommates a beach towel away. Selah and Rachel probably have headphones on, but they'd hear if I was mauled by a figment of heat exhaustion.

"I apologize."

I refuse to look at the Study in Scarlet.

"I shouldn't be intruding on your life like this. If not for my mistake, you wouldn't be aware of my influence."

What's that supposed to mean?

"You have questions, I know." He gives a tired laugh. "I... I'm... I've never... ech."

Conceding, I raise my eyebrows in the way even someone who doesn't speak Yiddish would know means "nu?"

The boy runs a hand through his obscenely long hair. "It's Tu b'Av."

I sip my coconut water. Last week was Tisha b'Av, the ninth of the month, it could be the fifteenth tonight. I whisper, "So?"

"It's the festival of love, when matches are more easily made."

I roll my eyes. "Actually, there's insufficient scriptural evidence—"

"Me!" His eyes flare, golden brown consumed in flickering red flames. "I'm the scriptural evidence!"

Heart racing, I press into the chair, knuckles white around my glass.

He swallows a breath, the fire calming to a roil. "I'm a messenger, sent by Heaven's outstretched arm this full moon, the fifteenth day of the fifth month—that is, the month of Av—to make most needed matches."

Panting, I give a slow blink.

The fire sputters out. "You think I'm lying."

"I think you're meshuggener." I choke out. "But I might be too."

He sags.

"So." I gulp, forcing my throat to relax. "Did I forget to sprinkle sheep's blood? What brings you to my doorstep?"

His brow crinkles. "I would have thought that obvious. You're in need of a match."

"Oh, for the love of God." Coconut water isn't alcoholic enough for this. "Am I not allowed to be happy being single?"

He blinks, like the thought never occurred to him. "I work by request."

"Clearly not mine."

"Your grandmother's. And the overwhelming number of people davening for you."

Of course. Draining my glass, I put it on the floor and bury my face in my hands. However meshuggener, I believe him. The fire? Not convincing. Bubbe being stubborn enough to raise an army of prayer until a heavenly shadchan comes to matchmake me? Checks out.

"Oy gevalt." Pulling my cheeks so they stretch my eyelids, I shake my head. "Okay. So, Shadchan Fairy, who's the schlemazel who has to date me?"

"Well, eh." His eyes shift, fire catching around the irises. Was it always there, and I just couldn't get past the hat? "The thing is…"

"Please tell me you couldn't find anyone."

"Not exactly." The fire flickers. "It was an accident. My finger slipped, and… well. Um…" He scratches behind his ear. "Me?"

"You what?"

"I matched you with me." His eyes finally meet mine. "A mistake, but the contract is binding."

Unable to stop it, my mouth drops open. And I laugh.

I laugh and laugh until three out of four roommates come check on me. Magically matchmade with a *Hallmark* attempt at a Jewish Valentine's Day movie. It's a miracle I ever stop laughing.

But eventually, I wipe my tears and shoo my roommates back to their individual electronic devices with promises I'll tell them tomorrow, it's not that important. The Shadchan Fairy scowls.

"It's very important. I need to either fulfill or annul our contract before next sundown."

Still smiling, I try to sober myself. "What happens then?"

"I have to leave Earth until the next Tu b'Av. I don't know what will happen if I have uncompleted duties."

"Right." I shrug. "I'm sure we can find a loophole. We're Jews, we're good at that." I look up at him, and—wow, he really is tall. "First, I assume you already know mine, so what's your name, Shadchan Fairy?"

He thinks, rocking forward on his toes. "Ahaviel."

I smile. "Of course it is."

Matchmaker

"Ahaviel, stop fidgeting."

My name, "Love of God"—more of a job description, but it's the closest I have. I've never used it, never needed to, never heard it said.

I've never explained myself, never casually talked to anyone. Though it's always been in my power to reveal myself, I never have. Yet here I am, in a crowded bagel restaurant, visible to everyone because Halma refused to sit at a table for two and talk to herself.

"I feel like everyone is watching me." I stare into my bright yellow reflection in the surface of my orange juice. I didn't want it, but Halma said I couldn't sit at the table without anything in front of me, and being in Florida without having tasted freshly-squeezed orange juice was a sin. The last time I tasted anything was some wine during the second temple period, a Shabbos Tu b'Av on which I completed my assignments early enough to catch four l'chaims. But even that didn't make my head this fuzzy.

She sighs. "You took off that stupid hat, no one's paying attention." What does she have against my hat? Or does she just hate the color red?

I pat my equally red kippah, framed in twin braids which join in a plait down my shoulders. Even without the hat, my hair is orange juice among wine. And if I wasn't conspicuous enough, to quote Halma, "It's brunchtime in Boca Raton, we'll be the only people under seventy."

"Seriously. You're fine," she says now, pushing a slice of lox back onto her sandwich. "Back on subject, are there any loopholes we haven't looked into?"

I cradle my face to block out the restaurant. "Not unless someone in the last ten generations of your family was born of a forbidden relation."

"Oh, well why didn't you ask?"

"Really?"

"No." She rolls her eyes, and picks up her phone. "Normally I'd consult a rabbi, but I doubt any would believe me."

"Then what...?" I nod to the phone.

"Web Talmud. Unless we want to be here until next Tu b'Av, I'm using indexed references." Scrolling her thumb across her screen, she does what she's wanted to do since I arrived: ignore me.

That isn't fair. She could have ignored me from the start, left me to deal with the glitch alone. But past all the sarcasm and quick remarks, she's considerate. Her friends love her. Her grandmother certainly does. I can't even count her sharp wit against her, since it's nearly made me smile. And there are many who would respect her willingness to crack open a Gemara and learn. I study her, waiting for a glaring flaw to present itself.

"Why did you need me?"

Glancing up from her phone, she raises an eyebrow. "I didn't. You came to me."

"Only because you hadn't found a match." I shake my head. "I specialize in hopeless cases, I understand what makes one. But what I don't understand is how someone smart, confident, and attractive, with good middos and good family, isn't with her beshert. Your parents should get nachas from you. It would be a bracha for any man to call you his wife. So why was I needed?"

"You weren't."

"I wouldn't be here if I wasn't."

"You are here"—her mouth hardens—"because my grandmother, just like you, can't understand why a young, eligible, nice Jewish girl would be perfectly happy being alone. You weren't needed, because I don't *want* to find my beshert."

I jolt as if slapped. A beshert is destined, not always what a person wants, but always what they need.

"Why?" I choke.

Halma moves her empty plate, and leans on the table. "Everyone is so desperate to be married. All of my married friends are disgustingly happy, so yes, I understand the appeal. But everyone else is driving themselves meshuggenah to find something that probably doesn't exist because they don't actually know what they want. And *chas v'shalom* you *suggest* they might not be ready to get married, and *maybe* that could be why they alternate between sabotaging good relationships and not recognizing bad ones." She heaves a slow breath. "I am far happier being single than most of my friends have been while dating."

Oh. She's not spiting destiny, she merely can't be bothered with it.

"It sounds like you don't wish to date."

She gives me a long blink. "Yes. That's what I've been saying."

"You don't have to date."

"Thank you for your permission."

"You could just get married."

She laughs, light and free with a little snort. There's no flaw in it either, except I'm not sure why she's laughing.

As if hearing my confusion, she abruptly stops. "Wait, you're serious?"

"Why would I not be?"

"I'm not going to just *get married!*"

"Why not?"

"*Because!*" Her voice creeps higher. If people weren't staring before, they are now.

I shrink into my chair. "But you don't need to date to prove compatibility. I can arrange a match for you."

"Oh really?" Her voice returns to normal volume, but her tone is barely restrained. "Because that worked out so well."

"Well..." I swallow. "I'm not certain it didn't. My system did assign us eighty-seven percent compatibility. Usually I aim for seventy. It is quite rare and special." A shame to annul it.

Her eyes narrow. "You're not having second thoughts, are you? If we find a loophole, you're releasing the contract."

"Oh, I can't." I hold up a hand before she can throw her phone at me. "Even if we found a loophole, it would be up to higher powers to judge the case. I'm merely an agent in this. If anyone could annul the contract, it would be the party which issued it."

Glare settling into resignation, Halma picks a poppy seed from her plate. "Then I guess to Grandma's house we go."

Matched

I roll my eyes as Malkie's texts pop up. That girl needs a dog to
arrange playdates for. Tapping the notification, I type a reply.

Her response is immediate.

Shaking my head, I shove my phone into my dress pocket, and
step out of the Century Village elevator as the doors open. After
Zeide passed six years ago, Bubbe moved into a smaller apartment
closer to her family. I could have walked here if I still lived with my
parents and it wasn't hot enough to fry latkes on the asphalt.

Should I have offered Ahaviel a ride? I assume he doesn't have
a car, but he met me at Holy Bagel this morning, so he's clearly
getting around somehow. Do angels even feel the heat?

Rounding the terrace corner, I brace myself for the evening.
When I called Bubbe and asked if I could bring a friend over at
five, her answer was the expected, "Of *course*, Halma'le! I'll make
dinner!" And no matter how I insisted we wouldn't be staying
long, Bubbe is the type of woman stubborn enough to call a
messenger of Heaven down to force her granddaughter into a
shidduch, and I'm the type of woman who ends up standing at her
grandmother's door at 4:58 prepared to eat.

I hope Ahaviel likes Manischewitz matzo ball soup and
chicken, because that's all Bubbe knows how to make.

A blast of heat hits my back, like the sun coming out from a cloud. Except it was already at full blaze. I turn as the shade recedes—and the concrete catches fire. Leaping back, my scream hitches as flames creep up the railing, burning bright before flaring up into a red fedora. A hand catches the hat and lowers it onto a head of ginger hair. Sparks trail down the shoulders of his suit jacket, and gold eyes flicker with orange and red as they meet mine.

I blink, brain processing Ahaviel now leaning against the railing. "Is there a rabbit in that hat?"

Straightening the fedora, he cocks his head. "Should there be? Is that current etiquette for meeting a grandmother?"

"Yes. Luckily we don't want Bubbe to like you." I shake my head as his face crumples. "I'm kidding. You're fine. She's unfortunately going to love you no matter what."

As if on cue, the door opens behind me.

"What are you standing out here for—oh my!" Bubbe scans the foot-and-a-half of height difference to Ahaviel's face. "Your friend is a boychik! And such a punim! Come in, come in!"

I sigh. And so it begins. At least he let her see him.

She waves us in, the smells of matzo ball soup and grandmother tinging the cool air. The dining table is set with a Shabbos tablecloth and nice dishes, and her silver hair looks freshly out of curlers. Even without knowing I was bringing a boy, she brought the spread.

Slinging my purse over a chair back, I lean to hug her. "Thank you, Bubbe. Dinner smells amazing. Though you *davka* didn't have to cook."

"Nonsense. Sit, sit."

I give Ahaviel a half smile and a whole shrug. He takes the seat across from me, and it's like we're back at Holy Bagel, discussing our compatibility. If he casually brings up marriage in front of Bubbe, I'm going to be adding another chest clop to atone on Yom Kippur.

Bubbe maintains a steady stream of chatter all through the matzo ball soup. We agreed not to lie to her, but she doesn't give us a chance to explain the truth.

"Ahaviel, did you go to yeshiva?"

"No. I don't spend enough time on Earth. I'm a heavenly messenger."

"A holy man! Wonderful, wonderful! Do you learn at the kollel?"

"No, my duties keep me occupied."

"And you have a job! Baruch Hashem!"

It isn't until the chicken that I'm able to get a word in.

"Bubbe, we actually have something to talk to you about."

"Of course, Halma'le." She forks a leg onto Ahaviel's plate. "Eat, eat. You barely touched your soup. No wonder you're so thin."

"No. That's the immortality."

I smother my laugh in my hand. Meeting my eyes across the table, he smiles, a slight, pastrami on wry thing. It transforms his face, crinkling his eyes and dimming their flames to a warm glow. I misjudged him; he might be Malkie's type after all.

Bubbe watches us with a bright smile that says she thinks she knows what's going on here.

"Bubbe." I harden my tone. "We need you to release Ahaviel from his contract."

She shakes her head. "What are you talking about? Eat your chicken."

"No—Bubbe." I intercept her fork before another breast heaps my plate.

Explaining goes far better once Ahaviel takes over, describing the accidental nature of the shidduch and why we need her to annul it. I'm mildly offended she'd prefer to listen to him, but it's only because he's the epitome of "nice Jewish boy." Besides, if she listened to *me*, we wouldn't be in this situation.

"So, what's the problem?"

I stare. "Your prayers forced a literal angel into an unbreakable contract, and you don't see a problem?"

"Not at all." She holds her hands out. "You're here, he's here, Hashem wills it, it's a match!"

The matzo ball turns to salt in my stomach. "You aren't going to release him."

She looks to Ahaviel. "Down the hall to the left, Tataleh, I have a little library with a nice sofa. If you wouldn't mind giving me a moment with my granddaughter."

Face blank, he stands and bobs a bow. "Of course."

As the library door clicks closed, she takes my hand. "Halma'le. Have you given this any thought?"

I scoff. "There's nothing to think about."

"He's a very nice boy."

"Bub—"

"A very nice boy who mamash fell from the sky for you. If that isn't Hashem's hand, I don't know what is. Have you thought about giving him a chance?"

"I don't *want* to!" I hiss through a thick throat. "Why are you pushing this?"

"Because." Bubbe pats my hand. "You are my smart, strong, beautiful granddaughter, and I want you to be as happy as you can possibly be." She holds up a finger to halt my protest. "I know you're happy by yourself. But you know you can be perfectly happy by yourself, and be with someone else, right?" She smiles. "I think being perfectly happy by yourself will make you far happier with someone else, because you won't be looking for a perfect match."

I swallow. "You aren't going to tell me Ahaviel's my beshert?"

"Oh, I am. But that doesn't make you each other's perfect match." She shakes her head. "Doesn't exist. Will you be good for each other? Certainly. Will it require work? Certainly. Everything worthwhile does. But if you aren't expecting perfection, you can make the work worthwhile."

I want to argue. I need ground to tell her she's wrong, but she isn't. All my married friends are in happy relationships because they committed to making the person they found the right one, and all my unhappily dating friends are still expecting perfect love. I have no commitments or expectations. Except towards myself.

She sits back. "Correct me if my old brain is misunderstanding, but if I release him, he'll disappear at sundown until next Tu b'Av. But there doesn't seem to be a deadline for me to annul the contract. So." She shrugs. "Give the boy a chance. You know you're compatible, what's the harm? And if you really decide you don't want to marry him? Bli neder, I'll annul the contract, he poofs, I never nudge you again."

I bite my automatic protest. In twenty-four hours, I haven't once thought of giving him a chance. Even thinking it now feels like betraying myself. I don't *want* love, not the way my friends do, yearning in misery. But maybe I don't have to want love their way. Maybe that *isn't* what Bubbe wants for me.

I meet her hazel eyes, a mirror to mine, watching me, listening. Perhaps she's always been listening, and it's me who never heard her.

"Fine." I squeeze her hand. "But when I break his heart, that's on your neshama."

Matchmaker

Twilight backlights the palm trees into black silhouettes. The last tendrils of pink and orange faded into gray, and I haven't moved from the window since. I took care of my other assignments over the night and after brunch, easy point and clicks. No more glitches.

The sun is almost fully down.

I don't know what happens next.

The library door clicks.

"She's not annulling the contract."

I watch Halma's reflection in the window, leaving the door open and leaning against a bookshelf. I wait for the disappointment to follow her words, the discontentment at having a contract unfulfilled, but it doesn't come.

"I'm sorry." I swallow. "You shouldn't have to be stuck with me. I know you don't want this."

"Do you?"

Do I? Since creation I have made countless matches, but it wasn't my duty to consider what would make people happy in one. What might make *me* happy in one.

"I don't know." I search her face. "You must be wondering how you, so confident, so self-assured, could be eighty-seven-percent compatible with someone without a concept of who they are, who has never thought about what he might want."

"You never had the option to choose." She frowns. "Technically, you still don't."

"That's certainly less pressure to figure it out." I don't know what I'm doing. I'm watching the sky darken into the sixteenth of Av with no clue what comes next. My hands clench on the windowsill.

"You still should." Her eyes meet mine in the window. "I can help."

"You don't have to. It's already bad enough you're stuck with me."

"Stop saying that. We're stuck with *each other*. This isn't your fault either, not really."

"Well—"

"You had a contract. I was going to be stuck with someone." She shrugs. "You're the one suffering for your mistake."

I hadn't thought of it like that. She made her displeasure so clear, I didn't have a chance to think whether I should feel the same. Except... "I'm not."

She raises a brow.

"I don't think I'm suffering. I'm... scared?" Is that the word? "Of what comes next. But I don't regret our match."

"That may change once you get to know me."

Matched

Ahaviel laughs in crackling fire. "I think I look forward to it."

His eyes glow like candlelight in the window, but they're less sad, lost. One look into them nearly had me stomping back to

Bubbe and insisting she release him. Our deal didn't include his suffering. But he says he isn't.

"I don't know what will come of this." I shrug. "But if you are ever unhappy, I will get her to free you. I want us both to be happy by ourselves, in who we are individually, just together."

"I think," he smiles, slow and surprised, "that sounds like the love I could need." His eyes drift back out the window. Mine follow.

"I see stars."

He exhales. "I'm still here."

"So you are." I smile. "Guess you're stuck with me."

"I suppose I should start figuring out who I am. By myself."

"Individually." I push off the bookshelf. "But together."

About the Author

Sara Itka is a born and raised South Floridian, meaning she believes "Fall" is when a hurricane comes and blows leaves off the trees. She is Ashkenazi Jewish, and has more tchotchkes on her desk than sechel in her cup. When she isn't working through her seemingly infinite To Be Read list, she can usually be found procrastinating working on her seemingly infinite To Be Written list. Her favorite procrastination methods include procrasti-linguistics, procrasti-making-youtube-playlists, procrasti-dancing-to-the-playlists, and procrasti-brewing-tea. If you want to help her procrastinate, she can be found at *saraitka.com*

THE TIES THAT BIND

LIA WU

There once was a man named Yue Lao. Where he came from, what he looked like, or what he wore were never noted in any annals of history or legend. Instead, he became known for what he *did*. More to the point, what he *caused*. Some believe that he pleased the gods, bringing upon himself and his fellow humans a gift of unimaginable value. Others, however, believe that he angered the gods, inviting into the world a punishment of absolute evil. Perhaps he was a god himself, bestowing his grace or wrath upon his supplicants.

Regardless of how the story truly went, Ziyou decided that Yue Lao was a *bitch*.

Her rage felt impotent. Her path to freedom was barred by an impregnable wall. Her fate was dangling on a knife's edge and it was *all Yue Lao's fault*.

"'God of matchmaking' my ass," she hissed, reveling in the sound of tearing silk as she ripped it from her shoulders. "'Divine red thread of fate'? What nonsense—more like 'steaming pile of snakeskin'!"

Chest heaving, she kicked wide, sending soft, supple leather boots flying. They thudded mutely against the rich green drapes framing the large window, letting warm sunlight filter into the large room. Gorgeous blades, staves, and maces, sturdy and shining with polish, hung on the walls.

Everything about the room was perfect. The clothes in the wardrobe were functional, comfortable, and tailored to her. Everything she could have ever desired was right in front of her. She wanted for nothing.

She hated it. She hated that she was here, warm and fed and safe.

She hated the bars on the window, ornate and nearly unnoticeable as they were. She hated the lock on the door. She hated the guards posted outside the door, invisible and inert no matter how much she screamed abuse at them.

She hated the red thread, effervescent and intangible, a mirage of a creature, twining its way toward her, encroaching ever closer toward her, day after day.

There once was a man or god named Yue Lao, who made it so that soulmates were real, so that soulmates were bound together by a divine red thread of fate, so that soulmates were *made* by being *the best for each other's well-being.*

And now, here she was, a war general captured by the enemy, stuffed into a gilded cage, growing softer and more complacent by the day, surrounded by gifts and food and comfort all designed for the sole purpose of fooling her body into accepting her "benefactor" as a source of health, as a way to lack nothing, as a font of *well-being.*

Soul threading. She was being soul threaded.

She knew how this would go. Her captor would remain anonymous. Her guards would diligently stay out of sight and out of earshot. She would be kept well-fed, her wounds obtained on the battlefield tended to, and her interests and needs met without pause. Day by day, while the gashes in her sides knitted back together and the bruises on her shins and shoulders faded, a red thread would appear, first barely noticeable—a fantasy or afterimage, a suggestion of a thought—then darker and thicker, more of a manifestly physical cord than a thin illusion of string. Finally, once the red thread of fate had thoroughly lurched its way into dreadful being and her body had reached its peak of health and satiation, her *benefactor* would appear.

In some accounts, all it took was the sight of the captor's face. In others, the captor's voice. In still further tales, it required a name, a touch, a kiss.

In all stories, however, the result was the same. The thread would finally bind itself to her, tying her to her "soulmate." He or she would be Ziyou's soulmate. Ziyou would not be theirs.

In many cases, that would be enough. The thrill of having that claim over another person's soul brought a keen sense of pride and victory to the more greedy of soul threaders. For the desperate, they might look forward to acts of reciprocation from the person they had threaded. No matter the way in which the thread came into being, after all, very few liked the thought of having a soulmate who was not theirs in return.

Nonetheless, in the case of war, there was a far more... useful consequence. Soulmates could not intentionally take harmful actions against each other. It was like a blinder on a horse or a noose about one's neck—the compulsion to keep a soulmate from danger was powerful. And then, even if Ziyou could overcome that compulsion, there was still the matter of her reputation. Her soldiers would struggle to keep from questioning her every order. Her allies would not be able to eschew whispering their doubts in her allegiances in each other's ears. To be a general soul threaded by the enemy would be the end.

She could not allow that to happen.

She had first tried starving herself. A hungry body, after all, would not be healthy or satisfied. However, after a full day of dumping meals onto the floor just inside the door, she woke the next day to a clean room, a belly full of soup, and a fresh meal waiting by her bed. Even days later, she shuddered to think about some nameless, faceless stranger stealing into her room as she slept and somehow spooning broth into her mouth without her waking. The implicit promise of another invasion drove her to eat the meal waiting for her that morning and each meal since.

Further, she reasoned, she would need her strength if an opportunity presented itself to fight her way out of her captivity.

She had then tried depriving herself of good sleep, alternatively keeping herself awake throughout the long night hours and forgoing the bed entirely, shoving herself into the tightest of corners and the most uncomfortable of configurations upon the hard floors. But her benefactor had been patient and had waited for a moment when her body had given out and fallen into a deeper sleep that dragged at her even as she lay upon the hard and cold floor and with a metal spike digging into her back.

That had been last night.

This morning, she had awoken, tucked comfortable and warm beneath soft blankets and placed on top of the mattress she had avoided for the past two nights. Her clothes had been changed while she was unconscious. She had been stripped of the coarsest and stiffest clothes she had managed to dredge from the wardrobe and put into a set of silk pajamas.

Her flesh prickled and her mind roared.

The red thread pulsed, more vibrant today than the day before, waiting.

"I don't want you," she muttered at it. "You are unneeded. You are a blight upon my life and I will never forgive you if you—"

But she couldn't finish that thought—not even as a hypothetical. What she could do, however, was strategize and plan. Very rarely did first skirmishes ever turn out the way the men and women on the battlefield anticipated, and this was no different.

She took a deep breath, the force of it sending a deep and satisfying ache from the stretch throughout her chest.

Fact: It had been five days.

Fact: The average time to barter the release of prisoners after a battle, particularly of high-ranking generals, and especially between the kingdoms of Monarchs Zun and Zhong, was three days.

Fact: Ziyou had yet to be released or rescued. At this point, chances of such were low.

Fact: In a war of attrition, she did not have the advantage.

Fact: Time was not on her side.

Fact: Her moments of weakness were victories for the enemy.

Conclusion: She needed to act. She needed to force action during a moment where she was prepared and her captor was not.

The pounding in her chest settled. The tingling in the tips of her fingers eased. She took another cleansing breath and pulled the shredded remains of the silk top from her torso. The chill of the air against her skin was bracing.

She thought about the conditions for victory.

The first condition, naturally, was escape. She surveyed the room, taking in her options. The obvious tools at her disposal were the weapons mounted on the wall. Added, no doubt, as an attempt to appeal to her interest in battle, they were ornate and dulled. Bemused, she thought they were an apt comparison to what her captor wanted her to be—a once dangerous artifact made docile and put up for display.

There were eight sconces interspersed on the walls at even intervals. Previous investigations revealed two were loose and could potentially be worked from the stone with some effort. There was a heavy chest of drawers, mostly solid with metal legs and embellishments on the edges. Hanging down from the high, vaulted ceiling was a chandelier, a great monstrosity of brass, wood, and candles that, had it been anywhere else, would have set Ziyou's heart at ease with its aesthetic.

There was a wardrobe filled with clothes, boots, gloves, hairpins, and cloaks. There was a large, barred window. There were heavy drapes. There was the bed, placed against the wall farthest from the window and the door, a rug, a fireplace, a table, and a chair. There were some books stacked neatly on the table. Nestled in an alcove just behind a wall that jutted out from the fireplace for privacy was a place to bathe and relieve herself. The tub was fed by some sort of spring, shallow but kept constantly filled by a stream flowing in from some outside source.

The only door opened into the room. Its handle, ornate like the rest of the furnishings, was an iron loop.

Ziyou breathed, considered, and smiled.

The second condition for victory would be redirection and denial—and she had the perfect plan.

She started with the quieter tasks, pulling the drapes from the window and emptying the wardrobe of all its contents. From the clothes, she pulled the thickest and toughest hides and leathers and donned them. She stuffed the drapes into the tub to soak and piled the rest of the clothes on top of the bed. Then, she turned to the wardrobe. It was tall, wide, and very heavy. It screeched against the floor as she shoved and pulled at it, ever so slowly maneuvering it until it was placed in front of the window. It did not cover it completely, but it reduced the light filtering into the room considerably.

Sweating and huffing from this, she climbed with shaky legs on top of the table and pulled down the candles from the chandelier. She left these clustered on the table save for one, which she lit and braced upright within the fireplace. She grabbed the books and threw these onto the pile of clothes on the bed.

Pulling a mace from the wall, she then turned to the loose sconces. With a wild, exhilarating swing, she smashed them from the stone and sent them clattering to the floor.

Then she paused, waiting. Listening.

Outside the door, she could hear footsteps and murmuring. Her banging, crashing, screeching actions had brought curiosity and concern gathered outside her prison.

Excellent.

She shoved both the mace and the sconces under the bed and returned to the tub, where the drapes had sufficiently soaked through with water. Grunting and wrestling with the unwieldy fabric, she dragged these to the bed and stuffed them under the frame as well. This left a trail of water from the tub to the bed, so she mopped this up with one of the sheets on the bed and then rolled it up and tucked it along the bottom of the door, covering the gap between the floor and the bottom of the door.

To finish things off, she then dragged the chair over to the door and braced it under the door handle at an angle to prevent the door from opening with any sort of ease.

Finally, she went back to the fireplace, where the candle had sufficiently begun to melt the wax at the base of its wick. Tipping this wax into the palm of her hand, she worked it between her fingers until it was slightly hardened and malleable. She stuffed this wax into her ears, effectively deafening herself.

This was where things would become dangerous, if she wasn't careful.

Feeling more than hearing her footsteps upon the floor, she plodded back to the table where the rest of the candles lay. She scooped these up and carried them and the still-burning candle over to the bed where, one by one, she lit the candles and dropped them atop the pile of books and clothes on the bed. By the fourth candle, there was a proper inferno building up, feeding more upon the paper and fabric than the candle wicks. Satisfied by this, she dove beneath the bed and wormed under the wet drapes, mace gripped tightly in one hand and sconce clutched in the other, and waited.

Unbearable minutes passed. Only the thudding of rushing blood sounded in Ziyou's stopped-up ears. Breathing became slightly labored as smoke began to fill the room. Sweat gathered at the nape of her neck, prickled at the backs of her knees and at her brow, pooled inside the crooks of her elbows, and slicked the palms of her hands. The air grew scorching.

Finally, Ziyou felt footsteps pounding against the floor. She imagined the very air vibrating with the force of panicked knocks against the door, then shoves and kicks against the wood as her guards realized it wouldn't easily open. Every delay was paramount. She needed the room to fill so completely with smoke that visibility would be reduced to nearly nothing. She could not be allowed to catch sight of a single one of the guards who poured in, for fear of completing the threading, and they could not be allowed to see her, lest they manage to lay hands on her and drag her to another prison.

She waited. The fire ate steadily through the bedding.

Gradually, the heat of the room became more focused on her back as the barrier between her and the blaze she had kindled diminished rapidly. She waited, staring into the darkness of the drapes covering her face. She waited and prayed.

The door came crashing in. Muddled and indistinct against the wax in her ears, the sharp and high voices of her captors flooded into the room. Ziyou took one last, deep breath, then lurched from beneath the bed, shedding the nearly dry drapes like the confines of a cocoon. The angles of the room would have naturally guided the guards, blinded by the smoke and stumbling in the dark, in a straight line toward the fireplace and the bathing suite. Panic and human instinct would have caused them to naturally shy away from the blaze in the opposite corner. Keeping low to the floor, Ziyou took advantage of these two facts to dash behind the group as it barreled past her. She slipped through the still-open door. Grabbing the handle as she ran by, she slammed the door shut and shoved one of the sconces into the loop. Like the chair, the sconce would only slow her pursuers for a brief moment, but it would be a moment she needed.

She risked a look left and right. It stood to reason that, if her intended threader had been outside the door, he or she would have rushed in with the rest of the group, needing to be the first that Ziyou laid her eyes on just in case the threading was ready to be completed. If she caught sight of anyone in the halls now, they likely would be someone of less importance—a lower-ranking soldier, groundskeeper, or servant. Politically and militarily, it would be easier to bribe or drag them back to Monarch Zun's court. Consequently, Ziyou's threading would fail to eliminate her as a threat on the battlefield.

However, the halls were empty, so that concern was, for the time being, unnecessary. She darted left and began looking for an exit. As she ran, however, a slow and dreadful realization began to wash over her. The turns in the halls were predictable. The placement of rooms, stairs, and cliff faces out the windows was familiar. The banners on the walls were recognizable.

She had assumed the room she had been placed in had been

reconstructed based on a careful study of Zun kingdom architecture in order to better lure her into a sense of comfort.

She hadn't stopped to think that the room had, simply, been a room in a Zun building.

This... what was Ziyou supposed to think about this? As ragged breaths tore themselves from her heaving chest, as her scabbed-over wounds pulled at her sides, and as the mace and remaining sconce weighed more heavily in her hands with each step, she tried to fathom what her escape from a Zun castle as a Zun general meant.

Soul threading—a vile, heinous act condemned officially by Monarchs Zun, Zhong, and Zhi—was, while not expected, not entirely a surprise from an enemy. For it to come from an ally, a fellow soldier in Monarch Zun's army, was inconceivable. What on earth could one possibly achieve from this? Why would they think doing something like this, especially at the fevered height of war that the kingdoms now found themselves enmeshed in, was a good idea?

The confounding nature of it all was nearly enough to drive Ziyou to tears.

No closer to answers and much further from guaranteed freedom than she would have liked, she was nonetheless able to put her discovery to good use. The protocol on guard rotations and perimeter protection was common across castles throughout the kingdom for the sake of easy transplants of personnel from one front to the next. This allowed her to eventually slip free from the castle's defenses without detection, finding shelter deep in the forest surrounding the remote castle.

This, unfortunately, left Ziyou with a new conundrum.

What was she to do now? Who could she turn to? Who, among her allies, had been complicit in her imprisonment? How many of the guards she had slipped past did she know personally? For what and for whom had she been fighting this whole time?

The sting of betrayal was deep and biting.

She clenched her teeth against the scream of outrage that threatened to burst from deep within her chest. The inferno she had left behind suddenly felt like nothing in comparison to the white-hot anguish that settled in her veins like a thick sludge. She ripped the wax from her ears, reveling in the pricks of pain it left behind, and threw them to the ground. Then she backed up against a tree and slid down to sit at the base of the trunk. The rough bark scraped at her scalp and pressed, hard and menacing, against the thick protective leather she had put on to weather the fire.

She breathed in. She breathed out.

Fact: the conditions for victory had been met.

Fact: the present battle had been won.

Fact: an ongoing war had been discovered.

Conclusion: Ziyou was safe for the moment, within the lull between battles. As with any war, her next and only duty was to recover and prepare for the next battle. Worrying about a battlefield that had yet to be declared and an army that had yet to be identified would get her nowhere.

She lingered there, eyes closed, head tilted back against the grounding pain of the bark, breathing deep, for several minutes. Her hands remained loosely clasped around the mace and sconce in her lap. Her legs, braced with knees bent and heels fully planted upon the grass, quivered as her body calmed from the battle frenzy she had stirred up within herself.

Then she opened her eyes.

The red thread was there in front of her, waiting like a dog for its master. It was a deep, blood red. It was thick, like a length of chain. If she were to reach out, it seemed almost like she would be able to take a hold of it as surely as she could the weapons in her lap.

"Damn you," she muttered. She had no strength to put any real anger into her words. "What good are you? You and Yue Lao can both climb a donkey. Go away."

The thread did not respond. Ziyou sighed and stared.

Then she stared some more, and pondered. What if...?

Her eyes followed the length of the thread, for the first time paying less attention to the end of it that stretched toward her and instead investigating where the other end trailed out of visibility. Rather than heading back toward the castle she had just fled, it reached toward the west, deeper into the forest. She studied the thread, her wounds throbbing and heart bleeding.

Finally, she climbed to her feet and headed west.

The thread pointed unerringly deeper into the forest for what seemed like hours. Without stopping, Ziyou followed it. Suffocating from the heat, she shed the jacket after the first hour. Only half an hour after that, she stripped off the heavy pants as well. Clad in thin underthings, she trudged through bramble and debris, mace and sconce in hand and eyes undeviating from her quarry.

Then, as the sun, already high overhead when she made her escape, started to descend behind the horizon, Ziyou came upon a hut.

The hut was unremarkable. It had the same thatched roof that she had seen hundreds of times before. It had the same wooden fence as any other for managing livestock. The small, dirt-packed courtyard filled with chickens and a grazing mule was disarming in its commonplace simplicity. There was nothing about this hut that she hadn't seen before.

And yet, the thread she had been following for the better part of the day passed unapologetically beyond the barrier of the hut's door.

Whether from shock, exhaustion, or something else, Ziyou's fingers went slack. The mace and sconce fell from her grip and landed with muted thumps on the grassy ground. Slightly swaying, she stood rooted to the spot and watched the hut, unblinking and unmoving until the sun had firmly retired for the night and left the world awash in darkness. The end of the thread closest to her tapped at her wrist. It tickled the hairs there and jolted her into a sharp inhale.

Then she strode forward, through the gate, across the dirt courtyard, and up to the door. The red thread of fate grew taut as if in anticipation. She knocked at the door.

A pause.

The door swung open.

The red thread snagged around her wrist, binding itself to her forevermore.

And Ziyou laughed, free and relieved.

Glinting out of the darkness, her soulmate laughed back.

She walked deeper into the hut and examined her soulmate. Her soulmate stared back at her.

Dark, tired eyes met dark, tired eyes. Cracked, dry lips smiled. Cracked, dry lips smiled back. Ziyou raised her right hand to brush tangled, brown hair from her face. Her soulmate raised her left hand to brush tangled, brown hair from her face.

"Yue Lao, you utter bastard," she crowed.

In the mirror, Ziyou's soulmate opened her mouth to curse Yue Lao, though no sound escaped.

Her heart soared and she fell to the ground with a harsh thud that sent shocks up her spine. Though she didn't know it, the owner of the hut would eventually return to find her sprawled on the floor, unconscious and unable to be roused. The poor farmer, alarmed and terrified, would drag her to the bamboo pallet he used for a bed and wash the dirt from her wounds. In the morning, he would coax her into eating plain rice porridge and a salted egg, then offer to carry her to the nearby castle on his mule to seek aid. She would refuse his offer, instead asking for help getting transport to the border between Zun and Zhi territories.

In the following weeks, a new general would make a name for herself within the Zhi army, having renounced her position within the Zun contingent. She would serve as a mediator between Zun and Zhong hostilities. She would find the people who schemed against her and she would have her revenge.

As she laughed and watched herself laugh in the mirror, Ziyou didn't know what her future would entail. She didn't know, but she knew that, whatever her fate was, it would be *fantastic*, and it would be *hers*.

She met eyes with her soulmate and smiled. "Hello, freedom."

About the Author

Lᴵᴀ Wᴜ ɪs ᴄᴜʀʀᴇɴᴛʟʏ ᴡɪɴɴɪɴɢ at life. She's got a shiny Kyogre in her pokedex, the first year of her doctorate down, her second short story published, and nothing is on fire! She still can't stand spice, is obsessed with anime and Batman, and will eventually publish something from the multiversal monstrosity of crossovers she has planned in her head... maybe. One day. She is an English teacher at the University of Arkansas and an editor and publisher for her own small company, Ozark Hollow Press. It's a toss-up on when she'll keel over from too many energy drinks, but it's definitely in the cards. Keep track of her on her poorly maintained social media: @liawuwriteswords.

ALLIE'S AWAKENING

R.A. JOHNSON

Phones started dinging throughout the room. Joyce stared at hers, blinking and vibrating in her hand.

"Aren't you going to check?" Allie asked, adjusting her tone of voice to hint that it was good news.

Joyce looked around at the other dancers, who were gathered in the warmup room. Some laughed and high-fived. One even squealed in delight, but most milled around quietly, their tight smiles trying to show support for their friends who had made the cut. Other disappointed hopefuls threw dagger-eyes at Allie.

"Come on," Allie prodded. "You know you're better than *Candy*." She nodded to the squealer, who was now bouncing on the balls of her feet.

Joyce sighed. "Oh, all right," and touched her phone.

A moment later, her face broke into a wide smile.

"Told you so," Allie said.

"You made it too, right?"

Allie nodded, but refrained from saying, "Of course." She had "read" the email milliseconds after it hit her in-box.

Those who had received the "Thank you for your efforts, but unfortunately..." message began heading for the exit. Several sneered at Allie, and one even shouldered her as she passed.

"Hey!" Joyce started after the offender, but Allie laid a hand on her arm to stop her.

"It's okay. Believe me, I'm used to it."

Frowning, Joyce nodded. "Well, they need to get used to it, too. You're an Emancipated Sentient Being, now. The world is changing, and we humans need to adjust."

Allie smiled and adjusted her facial features to simulate heartfelt gratitude.

"Thanks for being such a good friend," she said. She meant the words, but giving them the proper *feeling* took conscious effort.

Before Joyce could respond, the door to the stage opened, and Al Loring and Cora Longacre stepped through it. Al was a global pop star, famous for his up-tempo songs and intricately choreographed videos and live shows. He had rescued Allie with a promise of emancipating her from an abusive owner, after she wowed him while auditioning for his dance troupe.

Cora was his long-time choreographer and nearly as famous for her innovative style that mixed artistry and athleticism.

Cora clapped her hands. "Dancers! Form up, please."

The remaining twenty dancers formed a line.

Al stepped forward. "Congratulations, all of you. Cora and I are very pleased to have you as part of a new show, which is unlike anything that has been produced before."

Joyce looked at Allie with raised eyebrows. "Told ya," she whispered. There had been rumors that this audition was for more than just Al's next music video.

Al cleared his throat, and all heads snapped back to him. "Over the next month, we will be creating the world's first pop-rock *ballet*." A confused muttering rippled down the line of dancers. "Oh, I know there have been rock operas—'Jesus Christ Superstar,' 'Tommy,' and others before. But our story will be told through dance, as well as music."

The dancers' looks of confusion changed to nods and exclamations of joy. Cora clapped her hands again, restoring silence.

Al gave a sidelong look, then continued. "Fifteen dances,

including seven for the full company, four featured group dances, three solos, and the climactic *pas de deux*." Cora leaned toward Al and whispered, "You mean thirteen. Seven, four, two, and one," but Al shook his head.

"All spots are open, except one of the solos and the *pas de deux*, which have already been filled." Cora stared at him in open confusion. "The *pas de deux* will be danced by our primo performers, Joyce and Ernesto."

The dancers erupted in cheers, and Joyce stood, shocked, while the other dancers gave her and Ernesto hugs and air-kisses. Allie waited until the last before embracing Joyce and whispering, with all the sincerity she could muster, "You deserve it. You're going to be great."

Wiping tears from her eyes, Joyce squeezed Allie, then turned and took Ernesto's offered hand. Together they stepped forward, bowed to Al and Cora, then turned to receive the other dancers' applause.

Allie noticed Cora and Al in a whispered argument until Al silenced her with a sharp gesture. He clapped his hands for quiet, while Cora stood silently frowning.

"As Cora said, there were originally only two solos planned, but I've since written a ballad about a brave woman who rises above her suffering and the abuse hurled at her from others. The solo accompanying that song will be danced by our very own, Allie."

His announcement was met by stunned silence, then was followed by tepid applause and an undercurrent of mutterings. Allie, as stunned as everyone else, bowed to Al and stoically weathered the muttered insensitivities as she always had. At least Joyce, her best friend—her only friend, really—gave her a warm hug.

"It isn't working out," Cora said. She and Al sat in Al's office a week later. "It can execute all of the moves in the dance. Perfectly, I admit. But there is something lacking. There is no feeling to the dance. No *passion*. Of course. It can't *feel* anything, let alone passion."

Al frowned at Cora from behind his large desk. "She's standing right there," he said, nodding at Allie, who stood silently to the left of Cora's chair. "Don't talk about her in the third person."

Cora sniffed. "Why not? Do you think I'll hurt its feelings? It's just a fembot, remember?"

Allie spoke up for the first time. "Technically, Cora, I am not a fembot. Those settings were dialed back to almost zero."

"You're making my point for me," Cora snarled.

Al shifted uncomfortably in his chair. "Allie, what pronoun do you prefer we use? 'She', 'Hai', or...'It'?"

Allie stared straight ahead. She had never even considered the question before. Although she knew she was a unique person with an individual identity, what other people called her didn't matter to her at all.

"I...I really do not have a preference, Al." She turned to Cora. "Whatever you wish to call me does not diminish my sense of self."

The put-down was delivered with a complete deadpan expression, but Cora fumed. "See? It doesn't even care if you insult it. It has no feelings whatsoever."

Al sat back in his chair, his hand to his chin. He nodded as he made his decision.

"Allie, I'm afraid I have to agree with Cora. Your solo is the most emotional song I've ever written, but your dancing, though technically perfect, leaves me, and everyone...flat. If you can't step up your game by this time next week, I'll have to assign someone else—"

"Candy," Cora said.

Al shrugged. "Whoever. Allie, we need to see more emotion, more passion in your dance."

Allie feigned a deep breath. "I understand, Al." She turned to Cora. "I will do better. You'll see."

The only response she got was a raised eyebrow.

❧

LATER THAT DAY, as Allie approached Mr. Gottmutter's shop, a man with a hood covering his face hurried out the door. As he walked away, head down, she recognized him—the troupe's *primo ballerino*, Ernesto. She knew Ernesto was augmented, but maybe he needed an upgrade to match Joyce's skill.

When she opened the shop's door, the owner, Isaac Gottmutter, greeted her like a favorite niece. He was the technician who had customized and sold Allie to her first owner, an older widower whom she thought of as her father. Pater Jameson, in turn, regarded her as his adopted daughter, even after he unwisely remarried. When he died suddenly, his shrewish new wife and step-daughters, jealous of the attention he had heaped on Allie, exacted their revenge. They abused her and reduced her to nothing more than a household robot, instead of the unique, high-end, and passably feminine anthrobot whose sibling-bots could be seen gracing the arms of many celebrities.

"You missed your last check-up," Isaac said warmly. "Shall we get started?"

He walked to his test equipment against the far wall.

Instead of undressing for an examination, Allie said, "That is not why I am here, Isaac."

"Oh?" he said as he turned back to face her.

"No. I am here for emotions." Her voice was flat.

"Excuse me? Why on Earth would you want emotions?" he asked and offered her a chair.

Over the next few minutes, she explained the situation.

"Can you help me?" she said when she had finished.

Isaac sat back in his chair. "Normally, I would say 'No, I can't help you.' And even a month ago, I would have said, 'No, that's impossible.' But..."

"So it is possible?" she tried to add hope to her tone of voice.

He gave her a *don't-try-to-fool-me* look. "There is an experimental upgrade to your line of anthrobots that adds human-like emotions. Emotions that you will actually *feel*. Supposedly, they cause bodily reactions and modify thought patterns to mimic humans' biochemical emotional reactions. It's only in beta testing right now, though."

"Oh, please, Isaac. I really need that upgrade."

This time, her faux pleading had its desired effect. He thought for a moment, then nodded and pulled up a document on his tablet.

"You'll need to sign this waiver, since it's still in beta." He held the tablet out for her.

"Ah, I...I can't," she said, barely above a whisper. She answered Isaac's questioning look with, "Al has never officially emancipated me. Every time I ask him about it, he refers me to his legal team. They don't even return my calls."

"That bastard," Isaac muttered. "When I brokered your sale to him, he swore he would free you immediately."

She looked at the tablet and scribbled a perfect facsimile of Al's signature. "He's the one who says I need emotions."

Isaac shrugged, then his face got serious as he read the red-outlined page with warning after warning.

"I have to warn you, though, that this upgrade is barely tested. The emotions delivered with the upgrade are not selectable." He looked at Allie. "In other words—"

"I already read the warnings," she said with a smile. "I cannot pick which emotions I want to feel. You cannot tune them up or down. And the upgrade is permanent, since it integrates with my most basic processing functions. Did I get them all?"

Isaac nodded. "You're sure?"

Allie nodded back. "I am."

❧

ALLIE'S EYES FLICKERED OPEN.

"You should probably keep to yourself for a day or so to get used to—"

"Thank you! Oh, thank you so much!" Allie gushed. When she looked at Isaac, she *felt* something so strongly. Her upgrade identified the emotion as gratitude, which immediately switched to regret over all the times she hadn't thanked those who had offered her kindness.

Isaac, monitoring her, saw the spikes of so many of the new emotion lines on her processing graph.

"As I was saying, try to limit your exposure to your new emotions. Let them be integrated one at a time, if you can."

Allie was smiling. He had never seen such a natural smile on her face before. He couldn't help smiling in response, but then laid a cautionary hand on her arm.

"Remember. Take it slow. Emotions can overwhelm even those of us who've felt them our whole lives. You'll be feeling them all for the first time."

Allie nodded but kept grinning. "I will, Isaac. Really, though, thank you for all you have done to help me—" She gulped and reached up to feel the tear running down her cheek. Her voice quavered when she said, "I...I'm leaking."

Isaac couldn't help chuckling. "Those are tears, Allie. Tears of joy, I suspect."

"Joy? Is that why I feel so...full?"

Nodding, Isaac took her hands in his. "Yes, my dear. But be careful. We humans usually try to hide our emotions."

"But, why?"

Isaac frowned. "Well, if you're happy, but everyone around you is sad, that might make them even sadder—or angry. You must learn to read the emotions of others and only express the ones that you feel are...compatible. Or complementary. Do you understand?"

Allie nodded. "My basic programming lets me 'read' others' emotions, as you say. That was always just an analytical input to my reaction selection processing, though." She examined the new code that had been added to her core. "Now I understand that my emotions affect others, and theirs can affect mine...right?"

"Emotions can be contagious or contentious, I think. Which is why you need to be careful how you express them to others."

"I think I understand." A strange feeling came over her. "Can I...can I give you a hug?"

Isaac beamed and spread his arms. "Of course, Allie."

The warmth she felt was more than just from the conduction of his body heat.

THE MUSIC FADED as Allie completed her final pirouette and held her *attitude* for a heartbeat before melting into a puddle like the Ice Princess her dance embodied. Stunned silence held the troupe, during which at least one of the other dancers failed to hold back her sob. A moment later, the assembly erupted in applause.

Allie rose gracefully from the rehearsal floor, and Joyce rushed forward and wrapped her arms around her friend.

"That was...beautiful. Amazing," she whispered into Allie's ear before pulling back and wiping a tear from the corner of her eye.

Allie stared in confusion. "You're crying?" She looked around the troupe and saw several of the other dancers wiping their eyes.

"And I'm not the only one. Your dance moved us to tears." Seeing the confusion on Allie's face, she quickly added, "In a good way."

"Congratulations," Al said as he stepped forward and took Allie's hand. He was beaming. "You found and then revealed the emotion I tried to put into the song." Looking over his shoulder at Cora, whose eyes were red-rimmed, he said, "I told you."

Allie felt a strange heat rise up her elegant neck to redden her cheeks. Pride warred with embarrassment within her breast. She squeezed Joyce's hand to steady herself.

"Thank you, Al. I...I can feel the Ice Princess's heartache. It took me a while to learn how to express it." Lying about the origin of her emotions left her feeling a strange sensation that her upgrade told her was *shame*.

"Well, wherever you found it, we're glad you did." He looked at Cora, who nodded. "In fact, it occurred to Cora that we need an understudy for Joyce's role."

Allie felt her friend's hand go cold just before Joyce shook it loose from Allie's.

Cora stepped forward. "You've been struggling, Joyce—"

"I know the dance," Joyce interrupted.

"True. But lately you seem to have trouble matching Ernesto's intensity," the choreographer said.

"He's...he's *augmented*," Joyce muttered.

Al's tone was soothing. "Be that as it may, you need to improve the intensity of your performance. Which I'm sure you can do." He laid a hand on Joyce's arm, then turned to Allie. "In the meantime, we need a...backup. Just in case."

He didn't say "a Plan B," but Allie knew that was what he meant. Joyce's cold stare told her that her friend knew it, as well.

"Do you know the *pas de deux*?" Cora asked.

The thought of replacing Joyce both thrilled and horrified Allie. Pride and ambition struggled with some other unfamiliar emotion. Ambition won out.

"I know it," she said, avoiding Joyce's eyes.

"Good." Cora clapped her hands. "Ernesto! Places."

BY HALFWAY THROUGH THE DANCE, Allie's prowess and newfound artistic expression had exposed Ernesto's enhanced abilities for what they were. His *grande jete* and *tour en l'air* though high, looked mechanical when paired with Allie's effortlessly flowing movements.

And she knew it. She knew, also, that she was stealing Joyce's role right from her fingers. Her fingers. Allie imagined Joyce's fingers entwined with hers, their arms linked, their bodies striding in synchrony through life. That deeply hidden emotion came bubbling, then erupting to the surface, and she saw it for what it was—love.

Love of dance. Love of this new, full life that she was living for the first time. But most importantly, love for her best friend.

The joy of her revelation was quickly clouded, though, by the shame that her dance, a betrayal of that friendship and love, represented. In her mind's eye, she saw her *arabesques* shattering Joyce's dreams and grinding them to dust.

The decision came even more easily than when she had grabbed the chance of satisfying her own ambition. A single misstep, slightly out of time, and an over-enthusiastic leap was all it took. She and Ernesto toppled, falling hard to the floor, although she made sure to cushion his landing with her own body.

Joyce gasped and rushed forward, roughly pulling Ernesto off Allie.

"Are you all right?"

The concern on her face confirmed Allie's decision. She faked struggling to her feet.

"I'm okay. A little sore is all." She gave Ernesto a look of scorn for having landed on top of her—even though she had engineered it.

This time, the lie came easily to Allie's lips. She held her head high when she said, "I guess I don't know the dance."

Joyce's shocked expression was matched by Cora's skeptical look. Turning to Joyce, the choreographer said, "Teach it to her over the weekend, please. You'll both run through it with Ernesto on Monday."

She dismissed them with a flick of her hand.

As the two friends hurried to where the troupe was changing their shoes and dressing in their street clothes, Joyce took Allie's hand again.

"Thank you," she whispered. "I know you staged the fall. I think Cora does, too." She turned Allie to face her. "But don't throw away this chance. I can't possibly match Ernesto with his augments."

"You're a much better dancer than me or Ernesto. With your own augments, your artistry would outshine everyone."

Joyce grunted and frowned. "Maybe. If I could afford augments like his."

Allie reached up and gently stroked Joyce's cheek. Her smile was mischievous and conspiratorial at the same time.

"Well, I know a guy."

❧

ISAAC SHOOK his head after Allie explained what Joyce needed. "I'm not licensed to work on humans."

Allie gave him an *oh, please* look. "So that wasn't *Ernesto* who I passed on my way in here last week?"

Isaac just grunted and shrugged. "Guilty. So what augments are we talking about? Boosting your fast twitch muscles in your calves and thighs?"

Joyce, wide-eyed, looked confused, so Allie took control.

"Yes, but nothing too obvious. Also, a little extra ATP storage for energy and stamina. Can you do that?"

Isaac looked from one woman to the next, then sighed. "Yeah, you know I can."

"Ah, what's that going to cost?" Joyce asked.

Allie interrupted before Isaac could say anything. "Don't worry about that. I'll cover it."

"Wha—" Joyce began, but Allie held up her hand and looked to Isaac, who nodded.

"Isaac is like my favorite uncle," she said, and they all laughed. "He's also my financial advisor, guardian, and general rock."

Isaac's expression darkened. "Technically, Al is your guardian. Actually, he's still your owner, since he never emancipated you."

"That bastard," Joyce hissed. "Didn't he promise you?"

All Allie could do was nod through the shame of being a possession. Something she had never felt before. "Anyway, let's get on with it."

Isaac led Joyce into his workroom. "You'll be sore for a day, and you'll have to get used to the augments. You'll feel like you're walking on the moon for a while. Think about moving in slow motion until your reflexes adjust."

When Isaac finished the procedure, he let Allie into the workroom while Joyce recovered from the anesthesia.

"How are those emotions working out?" he asked.

Allie rolled her eyes. "It's been...exciting, frustrating, and generally terrifying."

She and Isaac shared a laugh. Then she told him what really brought the two dancers into his shop.

"You're sacrificing a huge step in your career for Joyce." It wasn't a question. "That's very altruistic of you."

Allie shook her head. "No. I'm doing this for me as much as for Joyce. I don't think I could live with myself if I used her...human limitations...to get ahead. Besides, her success means more to me than my own."

Isaac smiled broadly. "You know what that means, right?"

Confused, Allie shook her head.

Isaac chuckled. "It means you're in love."

Allie shook her head. "No, I...I'm just an anthro. She's human. She could never love *me*."

He reached up and wiped the tear that ran down her cheek. "We love who we love," he said. "Regardless of their origins."

Then, as Joyce stirred on the table, he pantomimed drawing a bow and aimed it at her waking heart.

"I honestly hope that worked," he said and hugged his protégé.

"So do I," she whispered into his chest.

❧

ALL DAY SUNDAY, alone on the practice floor, Allie and Joyce rehearsed until Joyce had full control of her augments. Allie, dancing Ernesto's part, easily caught Joyce's high leap and eased her into an *attitude* pose. Together, they executed a full turn, then Allie launched her into a perfect *assemble*. After having practiced for hours, they moved as one, as if they were two bodies sharing a single mind—or a single heart.

As Joyce slid down along Allie's body from her lift into their final caress, she pressed her body to Allie's and laid her head on her partner's shoulder. They held their embrace as the music faded to silence. Neither wanted to ruin the moment by drawing back. Instead, they shared a deep sigh and a tiny whimper.

"I love you," Allie heard herself whisper before she realized she had.

She stiffened, afraid of the rejection she was sure would follow. How could Joyce, or anyone, fall in love with an anthrobot? How stupid. She must have just ruined everything.

Instead, she felt her heart nearly burst when Joyce nuzzled her neck and whispered in her ear, "I love you, too."

Their moment of joy ended, though, when they heard slow clapping coming from the door to the practice floor. Pulling apart, they turned to see Al and Cora standing there. They were both smiling.

"Cora, I think we've found a new finale," Al said.

The choreographer nodded. "A *pas de deux* between...two *prima ballerinas* will bring down the house."

Joyce took Allie's hand in hers and turned to Al. "Two *emancipated* ballerinas, you mean, right?"

Cora looked at Al in shock. "You mean you never freed *her*?"

Abashed, Al said, "Ah, we'll make it official first thing Monday morning."

Allie melted into Joyce's arms and let her tears of joy flow.

About the Author

R.A.(Rob) Johnson is a cross-genre author whose writing stretches from micro-fiction to novel series, and spans historical adventures, science fiction, fantasy, horror, and even speculative non-fiction, for YA readers through adults. Born and raised and still living in Pennsylvania, Rob's stories are often set in PA and many of the places his wanderlust has taken him to. A senior technologist for over forty years, his forty-five patents include high-speed networking, cybersecurity, and hardware verification innovations. His writing blends science, religion, folklore, and technology, and features an element of mystery that challenges the reader to examine the story and their own world on many levels. Then again, some of it is just plain fun.

You can connect with Rob at rob@rajohnsonauthor.com

Sign up for his newsletter, read his blog of over one-hundred flash fiction pieces, and check out his books at rajohnsonauthor.com.

POSSESSIVE LOVE

LESLIE KUNG

Lyra browsed the aisles gleefully, skipping while pushing the cart in front of her. The clearance sales at Target were good today, and the body she had accidentally possessed was healthy and so very enticingly alive.

She marveled again at the size of the engagement ring on her host's left ring finger, pulled out her host's expensive newest iPhone (which unlocked immediately when she held it up to her host's face), and checked the calendar. The wedding was in three weeks, and all of the bride's to-do list was laid out systematically on the calendar and in the reminders widget on the phone's home page. Lyra had to give her host credit for being very organized.

Lyra Liu smiled again, having a hard time containing her excitement now that she had a physical body. A pale blonde pushing a cart with a snotty toddler in front and slightly older child in the main cart sneered judgmentally as she clapped and twirled in the aisle between the paper plates and toilet paper.

It was hard to pretend to be normal, because she'd been trapped in a miserable limbo since the early 2000's. Being unable to touch anyone or anything, taste or smell, and float. Details were fuzzy, but the last time she had a body, "So Crazy in Love" by Beyoncé was on the radio non-stop.

Still dancing in the aisle, she opened the iPhone photos and started scrolling through the albums, looking for her future husband by proxy. She found him almost immediately as he featured prominently in many of the pictures. Her host was on the tall side, probably 5'8" without shoes, but the man in the picture was several inches taller, with broad shoulders and a ready grin. He was incredibly handsome, and very likely part Asian. He had the Henry Golding look (an actor Lyra had come to admire during her long bouts of depressed movie theater haunting), but with a leaner, slimmer face, sharper jawline, and longer hair.

Lyra had been a Chinese American on the verge of turning 18 when she passed, and the years had been so lonely. She'd watched a lot of films. *Crazy Rich Asians* had been a delight. She wondered if her host had liked that film too. According to the phone's bio info, her host's name was Angelica Wang, and she was 26 years old.

Angelica was probably of Chinese descent too, based on the name and the photo album of family members celebrating Lunar New Year with red envelopes. Was their shared heritage the reason why Lyra was able to jump into her body, after all this time floating around passing straight through the living, leaving only body chills and disquiet behind? Unlikely, as it hadn't mattered before. Regardless, the sensory overload of mortal, corporeal existence was exhilarating beyond words.

By the time her host's alarm for "Pilates in 2 hours, GET READY!" went off, Lyra had a cart full of the most random items. She checked out, fumbling awkwardly with the credit card as if she'd never used one before (because she hadn't). She just did what the person in front of her did with their card, and thanked the teller profusely, giving the young Latina compliments on her makeup and hair color. The young woman smiled shyly and said, "Thank you!" as Lyra was leaving.

Being able to actually talk to people was amazing! She was giddy as she pushed the cart out the automatic doors toward the car she'd driven here and parked ever so carefully, taking the time to reverse and advance five or six times until the car was perfectly parallel to the yellow lines. Not bad for a novice driver who hadn't driven in twenty years.

It took a little bit for Lyra to figure out how to mount the cell phone and ask it to direct her to Angelica's house. Okay, it was almost forty minutes of struggling since she'd never used a smartphone before, but she managed to make the machine voice start to tell her which way to go, which was an entirely different skill from driving while looking at the tiny screen while listening to the robot lady's instructions.

A few near misses, lots of honking, and two stops on two different shoulder lanes later, Lyra finally got to Angelica's house, which, according to all evidence on her phone, she shared with her fiancé. Lyra parked in the driveway, not bothering with the large three-car attached garage. She bumped her head on the car door frame, and smiled because she'd just bumped her head and it hurt, which was such a simple human experience. She had missed being alive so much.

Grinning like a carved pumpkin, she figured out which key unlocked the front door. The grand entry opened up to a vaulted ceiling with a large chandelier. There was all sorts of art and framed photos on the walls. Lyra dropped everything, including her purse and took her shoes off. A cat toy that had fascinated her rolled out of the plastic bag, along with a bag of chips she'd never tried before.

Lyra spun in circles with her arms spread wide. The furniture was very nice. The floors were some sort of heated tile with a wood look. She was on the ground touching it when the most beautiful man she'd ever seen in person rounded the corner into the open concept living space wearing only a towel around his waist.

He was dripping wet.

Holy crap balls.

"Babe...?" he said, in a concerned tone, flipping damp hair back over his perfectly formed forehead. "What are you doing down there?"

She could hear the smile and hint of laughter in his voice. His dimples and crow's feet around his eyes when he smiled made her audibly gasp.

"Wow..." she said, covering her mouth with one hand, "You're so hot."

He laughed and came over, casually gripping the bunched top of his white bath towel so it wouldn't loosen.

"Thanks, Baobao. But let's get you up. Did you eat anything today? Is it low blood sugar?" His hand was huge and warm. He cupped her elbow and helped her up, and she could see his perfect abs, and his arm muscles were insane.

"Um, yeah, I think I forgot to eat," Lyra murmured, blushing.

"Your class is gonna start soon. Let me throw on some clothes and see what I can feed you before I drive you over, okay?" His voice was deep and rich, but soft like velvet.

"Okay," she agreed vaguely, eyes locked on his left dimple. He had a smattering of gray hairs through his temple areas as well, which was not something Lyra had ever considered attractive, but now it was very charming.

"Go sit down, hun, I'll be right out," he said, walking away down the hall. Lyra watched him go, and it was an illuminating experience. The towel bunched and moved around his rear. Lyra banged her shin into the couch and fell ungracefully onto the cushions.

"Si-ick," she said to herself in shock. "She really bagged the perfect buff hottie..." Lyra patted herself on her host's arms. "Good job, Angelica! Oh shit, what's his name though?" She scrambled for her phone and pulled up the wedding invitation photo album, and read through all the design iterations. His name was Zachary Hollis-Zhang. So, he was probably half Chinese, which explained the "Baobao" nickname he called her. What a dreamboat, even if he was an older guy. Lyra kept scrolling through Angelica's phone. She was a very Type-A person. She even had copies of their birth certificates and social security cards in a "Vital Documents" folder.

Zach was born in 1984, which meant he was SUPER OLD compared to Angelica. Gross! But she figured it was fine since he was very attractive and fit. Besides, she herself had been born in

1986 (or something, it was hard to remember)—she just hadn't spent that much time actually alive. She wondered idly if she would look as good as Zach if she'd been alive, or if she would be haggard and wrinkled. She would never know.

True to his word, Zach came back before Lyra could even finish her phone snooping, washed his hands and started pan frying eggs. He put on some jazzy music that she didn't recognize, danced and swayed as he finished up the eggs, got sandwich materials out of the fridge and made two stacked sandwiches with the works and sunny-side-up eggs just ready to burst when bitten into.

"You wanna eat at the table or over by the couch, babe?" he asked, almost shouting over his music.

"Table is fine!" Lyra replied, cupping hands around her mouth to amplify her words.

He said, "Okay Google, stop the music," and the music stopped right away. Surprised, Lyra looked around and couldn't find a boombox or CD player or MP3 player. She smiled at him widely and told herself to get it together before he figured out that something was wrong.

"Your meal is served, m'lady," said Zach with a flourish, putting the plates down at the glass-top table. He scooted out a chair and gestured at it with a slight bow as she walked over.

"This looks great! Thank you," she said, reaching forward. His large hands circled her wrists hotly, and he said, "Did you forget something, silly?"

"Um," she uttered breathlessly, "...what?"

"Go wash your hands, love," he said, his face too close to hers, his smile and twinkly, sparkly amber-brown eyes warm with love.

"Oh, right!" Lyra stood back up and went to the sink to wash up, drying her hands on the clean hand towel he had left folded for her beside the sink.

"Dig in! I put the chili crisp you like on there too, so watch your shirt," he said, sitting down beside her. They both ate the sandwiches, and Zach handed her a napkin when some egg yolk and red chili oil started sliding down her chin. She laughed and scooped it up with the napkin and thanked him.

She must have done a pretty good job pretending to be Angelica, because the next thing she knew, he was escorting her to her room and telling her he had laid out her yoga pants and favorite exercise top. She got changed while he cleaned up the kitchen, and when she stepped out of their bedroom, he was waiting with a metal insulated cup with a handle that sounded like it was full of ice and liquid, and holding car keys in the other hand.

"We're really cutting it close, but I'll get you there on time," he said, reassuringly.

He drove her to the pilates place in their nice new extended-cabin truck, and handed her the drink before pulling her in for a kiss. His lips were wet and soft, and he tasted like coffee. Lyra's first kiss was amazing. The fact that she could feel, could taste, was held and could grasp onto his arm and his shirt... It was a miracle. Maybe love was partly stored in and expressed by the cells of the body, and Zach's love for Angelica, and Angelica's love for Zach was just a natural cascade of habitualized hormones, but Lyra couldn't care less.

She was burning with electric tension as she leaned into this incredibly handsome man and his soft kiss. His tongue peeked out and teased the seam of her lips, and she opened her mouth slightly to his advances. After a little while, Zach was the one who pulled back to take a deep breath.

"Whoa, babe...where did that come from, hmm?" he asked, leaning back a little to look at her dazed, flushed face. He knuckled her lightly on the nose, gave her a peck on the cheek and said, "Jelly, you should get going now. Raincheck on the make-out session, okay?"

Still stunned, she could only nod and open the door to slide out. He winked at her when she was standing on the pavement, and she blushed even harder while she shoved the truck door shut. She was sweating in weird places, and went inside the little fitness gym still touching her lips with her fingertips.

Pilates was pronounced pill-AH-tease, not py-LATES, and it was pure, evil torture. Whoever invented it was a sadist, and they had problems. Lyra mentally cursed the inventor as her core, legs and arms burned. The ladies in the class seemed familiar with Angelica. Good thing it was a pretty intensive hour, and people didn't have the energy or breath left to chat.

Right before the class dispersed, Zach showed up, leaning against a wall and watching her mop sweat off her face. Everything was starting to feel more real—especially her burning abs and cramping middle section. She grabbed her iced coffee and took a few sips from the straw as she walked over to her (host's) fiancé.

"Ready to head home?" he asked, but the lady who had taken up a familiar spot right next to her intercepted Lyra to chat and pulled her off to the side with a smile.

"Angie, I have those lace samples for you that we talked about, you know from my aunt? But they're with my stuff in the locker room, so do you have a minute...Or is your insanely hot husband going to drag you away?" Lyra nodded and followed, pointing at the lady's back and mouthing "be right back" at Zach. He gave the okay hand signal and sat down at the benches by the entrance.

The lady was brunette with streaky highlights, and she was super petite, the top of her head barely coming up to Angelica's shoulder. Once they pushed through the swinging door to the ladies locker room, she walked briskly to locker number 18 and opened it. Inside was a colorful duffle bag, and three cardboard pieces wrapped with white and ivory lace edging, pinned flat to the cardboard pieces.

"Here's the lace. It's really hand tatted—that's what they call lace-making," she said, handing over the cardboard rolls.

"Oh wow, these are pretty!" she said, not knowing exactly what the backstory was.

"So, is everything still on track?" asked the lady, in a much more business-like tone.

"Yeah, everything is good," said Lyra, smiling at her in what she hoped was a friendly and normal manner.

"Okay, we've got everything you'll need, and we'll do the

handoff right here in two weeks. I'll see you again next week, and the support team is on stand-by."

"Oh, okay. That's good," said Lyra, with a fake confidence. This lady must be a good friend if she was helping with the wedding. But meeting at the locker room after pilates class was a little weird.

"You good? Need anything?" she asked, deeply searching Lyra's face.

"Nope, everything is great," she replied more seriously, since her apparent friend was being super serious. "No cold feet or anything," she added.

"Good. See you next week for a check in, and two weeks for the package handoff, and then the next week after that is party time. Any questions?"

"Nope, all good here," she said, half saluting.

"Okay, go back and enjoy all of that while you still can. Little morbid, but you gotta take the wins when you can. Don't let it get to you," she said, clapping Lyra on the shoulder.

Lyra had no idea what the heck this lady was talking about, so she just nodded and said, "I won't let it get to me. Thank you."

They both left the locker room, and Lyra handed the lace rolled up on cardboard to Zach when he held out a hand for them. He also opened the door for her, which was super nice. She looked back at the brunette from pilates class who nodded to her. *What a strange person*, she thought to herself.

"Baobao, do you want to stop by anywhere, or should we go straight home?" Zach asked, opening the truck passenger door for her.

"My stomach hurts from all those crunches, so let's go home," she said, starting to clutch her middle. Actually the pain was getting worse, not better, even after a cold drink and some cool-down time. Bodies were strange, and having one again was delightful. Even the pain was tolerable because it was a privilege.

Privilege or not, Lyra was breaking into a cold sweat and hunching over her seatbelt strap by the time they pulled up to the driveway.

"Are you okay, babe?" Zach asked, gently unbuckling her seatbelt. He patted her back gently.

"Yeah, pilates kicked my butt really hard today," said Lyra, climbing out of the truck.

"Oh no, Jelly. Your pants..." said Zach in a worried tone as soon as she stood up. "It's your period, babe."

He came around and pulled a fleece zip hoodie out the back seat and wrapped it around her middle while she was coming to terms with the shocking revelation that she was experiencing her first menstrual cycle in over twenty years, and she had leaked through her pants in front of the hottest man in the world.

Zach took everything out of her hands and unlocked the door. He put everything down on the entryway table, dropped the keys into the large ceramic bowl along with his wallet, and helped her slip her shoes off and put soft slippers on.

When he had slippers on too, he walked with her to the large bathroom off the master bedroom and started running a bubble bath for her. Lyra absolutely could not undress or do anything else embarrassing in front of this man, so she just hung back clutching her cramping midsection.

"I'm gonna make a quick chocolate run for you, okay? Are you all set? Need anything else?" She nodded and shook her head for each question, and then closed her eyes when he kissed her on the forehead.

"I'll be right back," he said, closing the door behind him.

Lyra took a bit of time looking around, pulling open drawers, discovering a walk-in closet full of their clothes, finding Angelica's hyper-organized baskets of personal hygiene items, as well as her well-labeled drawers and baskets of clothing in the closet. When she had everything she needed, and she knew where the hamper was for dirties, Lyra finally undressed and slid into the hot bath water and towering piles of bubbles.

She would have spent a little time looking at Angelica's body just out of curiosity, but she felt so crappy, and the steam had overtaken the expansive wall of mirror where the floating vanity was attached. For a moment, she felt like she was floating. The heat of the water scalded and then spread like wildfire through her nerves, followed by a deep relaxation.

She drifted…

Log cabins.

A campfire.

Sundown. Shadowy branches.

Running, tripping on a rock.

A lakeside at dusk.

Water lapping at her ankles.

The figure behind her looming…

She couldn't breathe.

Head under water.

Hands gripping so tight—

Lyra startled, feeling like she'd jumped out of a plane and landed in this body just before smashing head-first into the unforgiving earth. Her fingers were only slightly pruned, and the bath was still hot, but she felt disoriented just like the first time she'd floated by the young Asian woman passed out with her head on her crossed arms at the picnic tables by the fountain. Like gravity, she'd been pulled in, not even meaning to interact.

All of a sudden, she had arms and eyes and feet and nerves alive with sensation. She also had a bad taste in her mouth and a huge headache, but the first few hours of being in a physical body again were spent touching leaves and running around the fountain, running barefoot through the grass, laughing, sobbing, and talking to alarmed strangers.

In a strange moment of fate, Lyra had a chance to make up for missed time, to practice all the fun, interesting things people did daily that she could only witness silently for decades. But the loss of consciousness and flashes of a nightmare felt too much like dying again. She did all the requisite body cleaning, rinsed the washcloth and exfoliating cloth and hung them on their suction cup hooks. It felt like what Angelica would have wanted.

She dried off with a fluffy towel that was really big, like as big as a tablecloth. Rich people really were different, she thought, as she peeled the backing off a winged pad, applied it to Angelica's panties and shimmied them up into place. The oversized T-shirt nightie felt soft as she pulled it on. Wrapping her hair in a smaller towel, she slipped her feet back into the fluffy slippers and headed out.

That gorgeous man was just getting back inside, holding several shopping bags. He came over to hand them to her and give her a quick kiss.

"I got your usual favs, and there's a new blueberry milk chocolate flavor, so I grabbed that one too. And the white chocolate raisins are for me, if you don't want them." He guided her to what must be her spot on the couch, where there were plenty of throw pillows and soft blankets.

"Thanks so much, I really appreciate it," she said sincerely, tucking in under a double-layered chenille blanket the color of ocean storms.

"Of course, babe... Anything for you," he said casually as he sat down next to her and pulled the blanket over his lap as well. She leaned in, an action her body seemed to do instinctively, and basked in the feeling of being held by a lover. Maybe this was all a gift, so that she could experience things she'd missed out on when she passed away. As the sun went down, she munched on chocolates, watched TV, and was waited on hand and foot by her fiancé.

He made her Shin Ramen with boiled eggs and a slice of melted cheese on top for dinner, which she had never had before.

The rest of the week passed by in a blur of cramps and gentle love from the man she was getting more and more comfortable with. Of course she had to figure out how to get to work, what Angelica's job was, and how to fake it until she made it—but that was all doable. As long as she smiled and matched people's energies, no one even looked at Lyra sideways.

"Love you, babe!" became an easy phrase. And because of her period, when they went to bed, they just snuggled, albeit with some suggestively straying hands on his part. Snuggling, sleeping next to a man, and getting consensually groped was already five bases further than anything she'd experienced in life, so it was sometimes overwhelming to think about the week after or even their wedding night.

Zach was so perfect, it was starting to get on her nerves a little, until she discovered that his man den in the house was a tragic mess. That was the ounce of humanity she needed to witness, because she fell all the way in love with Angelica's fiancé. She wondered sometimes if Angelica was still around somewhere, waiting to come back, and she resolved to not even fight if she wanted the body back.

After all, this was all stolen time in a stolen body.

It could all end as inexplicably and swiftly as it had begun, and she had to be at peace with that. She didn't crawl into this body; she'd been sucked in like being caught in a vortex. The week rushed by so swiftly, and she was being dropped off at her pilates class again. At the end of the session, her bestie pulled her to the locker room again and had the same strange chat about if she was ready, if things were still on track, if she was feeling good.

She managed to figure out Violet's name when someone else called for her during pilates at least, so that was an improvement. Violet handed her a manila envelope and said, "Check everything. We have some updated intel on hubs, so make sure to review it."

"Okay," Lyra said, taking the folder from her and sliding the papers out of the top into her hand. There was a photo of Zach, his detailed bio info, his father, Senator Hollis's info, what financial ties he had, which firms he was selling information to, and which accounts he had millions of dollars in. Lyra barely held back a surprised shout, her eyes widening. The next page was the blueprint and satellite imagery for the wedding venue hotel, and different plans on how to assassinate Zach, the sweetest man alive who made her feel love for the first time in life or death.

"Hannah, this is real. Okay? Get your head back in the game. I feel like you've gone so deep in this cover, it's...changing you. We have his accounts now, proof he's selling proprietary US military R&D, and we have a green light. Next week is the hand off. Everything you need, and it'll be in a Bride-themed gift box, okay?"

"Okay, got it," said Lyra, trying to keep the tremor out of her voice as she flipped through the papers faster, trying to scan everything. Apparently "Angelica" was actually Hannah? How could—

"Are you sure?" Violet (or whatever her name really was) looked deeply into Lyra's eyes as she asked.

"Yes, I'm sure. I'm ready," she said, trying very hard to be as resolute as the handler needed her to be.

"Okay, then let's get you married next week, and as soon as you kill hubby, you're on a chopper to a safe house then back to base for psych and physio and debriefs out the eyeballs: the usual." Violet took back the papers and the envelope, sealed it back up with a pull tab and shook the envelope a few times while it hissed lightly. After less than a minute, it sounded like she was shaking an envelope full of sand, and what was left of the files gathered in lumps at the bottom.

Needless to say, the ride home with Zach was difficult. Lyra spent the next few days trying to cancel the wedding, and find excuses why it would be better to elope. It actually made Zach pretty upset, and they had their first argument over it. He asked if she was getting cold feet, and she shot back a hard "Yes," to which he said he was going to take a moment alone in his den downstairs before he said anything he regretted.

It was very mature of him, and he was actually making it even more impossible to either break it off or warn him. She imagined the heartbreak in his eyes if she told him she was fake. If she told him ANGELICA was fake, it would hurt enough. There was no way she was telling him that she was actually a ghost inhabiting Angelica's body who turned out to be some sort of undercover assassin.

The week passed too quickly now that she'd taken leave from work as it was planned on Angelica's calendar. Zach also took work off, and he insisted on surprising her with a romantic candlelit dinner. He spoke to her so gently and lovingly, and booked a last-minute couples therapy session only two days before the wedding.

The therapy session went well, except for all the secrets Lyra was choking on like stale bread with no water in sight. She was head-over-heels in love with Zachary Hollis-Zhang, and she was supposed to kill him on their wedding night. Lyra even tried floating out of Ange—Hannah's body several times to try to escape their ill fate. It never worked. "Okay, then I just won't do it," she thought to herself. "I'll protect him," which felt like an impossible lie, even in her own head.

All too quickly, the wedding at the high-end intimate venue marched along. The catering staff, the hotel staff, and the wedding planner scurried around like busy ants. Angelica's dress fit stunningly on, and Lyra gazed at herself in the full-length mirror in the bride's room in a full panic attack. There would be fewer than a hundred guests, so everything was on a smaller scale. She wondered if her side of the family were all actors or agents or a mix, but soon a woman with a clipboard and headset was telling her it was time.

The lights shone so brightly, Lyra could feel the heat of them making her break into a sweat. Violet had been with her up until they took her out to walk the aisle, and she was hyper-aware of the small gun and tactical knife on each thigh under the gown's generous volume. Everything was a blur until she saw him waiting. He was beautiful. She was not going to hurt him. She would confess, and they would run. The wedding was beautiful, the speeches made everyone cry, and the bride and groom looked like a fairytale.

And then she saw it during the home videos and slideshows.

"Crazy in Love" started playing.

Campers in matching shirts.

"Got me lookin' so crazy in love—"

Log cabins.

The lake.

"Uh oh, uh oh, no no—"

A photo of Zach as a young man in a "counselor" shirt with his big hands waving at the camera. Big hands wrapped around her neck. Thrashing. Screams turned to bubbles in murky water. In the photo, a teen girl stood amongst other campers in her Converse shoes and rainbow laces with an all-too-familiar smile.

Lyra Liu who would never get to be 18.

Lyra finally knew why.

And she knew what she had to do.

About the Author

Leslie Kung (whose degrees in English and Philosophy from Cornell College are old enough to drink, but not yet old enough to rent a car) writes speculative fiction and character-driven narratives. Kung won poetry awards as a young teen, one of which was presented to them by Alice Walker herself. They are a parent to three wonderful people, as well as a hobbyist zookeeper of a leopard gecko, bearded dragon, infinite self replicating guppies, and a number of chonky goldfish. Kung is an ethnically Chinese child of immigrants who learned the joy of storytelling while listening to their dad tell adventurous tales of ghosts, supernatural phenomenon, and highly inadvisable childhood access to explosives back when Myanmar was called Burma. Kung's previously published stories include "At Last" published in the *Story of a Kiss* anthology, edited by Taylor Sullivan, and "Lazarus Squad" in the *Dark Space* anthology, edited by Leonie Skye.

CUPID'S AROS

KAY HANIFEN

Of all the stumbling blocks I expected to have when I began my publishing career, this was not one of them. I could handle a competitive industry, a shrinking job market, and even celebrity authors who acted like total divas. When I got that internship at Starbooks Publishing, I was overjoyed, especially when it turned into a full-time job, one that I'd been working towards for almost ten years.

No, the bizarre stumbling block began about a month away from my thirtieth birthday. That was when the world went... strange. It's the only word I could use to describe it.

I first noticed it the day I walked into the Lion's Pride, a gay bar I frequented with my best friend, Josh. I almost didn't recognize him. My friend lived in jeans and band T-shirts. He wasn't a slob by any stretch of the imagination, but he preferred comfort over fashion. He was the definition of casual. But here he was dressed in a soft pink sweater vest, light green shirt, and honest-to-God khakis. He sipped at a colorful, fruity drink, and when he spotted me, he gave me an exaggerated wave.

"There she is," he drawled, pulling me into a hug and then, inexplicably, kissing both my cheeks. "Allie, it's been too long." It had only been three days, but I was still so stuck on the outfit that I didn't notice that additional bit of weirdness until later.

"What's all this?" I asked, gesturing to his outfit.

He blinked in confusion. "I don't know what you mean."

"Your look? Do you have a date tonight?"

He laughed. "Oh girl, you know I'm tragically single. I just thought I'd change things up a bit."

My stomach twisted uncomfortably. Josh didn't talk like that. He didn't act like that either. This was wrong. All wrong. It was as if he had been replaced by an alien pod person who only learned about the existence of gay people through nineties sitcoms. I placed my hand on his forehead. "Are you feeling okay? You're acting weird."

"Sis, I'm fine." He leaned against the bar, taking a sip of his drink. "Speaking of fine, did you do something with your hair? Because you look fabulous."

Completely befuddled, all I could do was shake my head. "No?"

"Natural beauty, I guess." He sighed dramatically. "If only we were all so lucky. You're almost thirty, and you look just like you did in high school." Taking a sip, his smile grew mischievous. "Speaking of...do you have plans for the big Three-O?"

Now I was really confused. "We were going to Heroes Con, remember?" We bought the tickets the moment we realized that the convention would fall on my birthday weekend. I'd been planning and building my costume for months. As far as I knew, he had been doing the same. How could he forget?

"Bor-ing," he singsonged. "You should be out on the town having a good time, not sweating it up in a convention hall surrounded by men who think that Axe body spray is deodorant." He leaned in conspiratorially. "Speaking of...we need to get you a date. When's the last time you got laid?"

The hell?

When I came out to Josh as asexual and aromantic, it took a lot of explanation, but once he understood, he never tried to push me into starting a relationship. After all these years of unconditional acceptance, it hurt for him to suddenly start invalidating my identity again. "Seriously, what is going on? Is this some kind of prank? Because it isn't funny."

"Honey, I have no idea what you're talking about. I'm just the same-old, same-old."

"No, you're not." I spoke around the lump in my throat as I grabbed my purse. "And I'm leaving. Don't talk to me until you've got...whatever *this* is out of your system." With that, I turned heel and left.

"Don't be so stubborn!" he called after me. "You'll find love eventually. Just open your heart to it."

As I stormed out, an image in the window glass caught the corner of my eye, making me pause. It was the most beautiful man I had ever seen. He seemed to have something slung over his shoulder, but I couldn't make out what it was before he disappeared.

On the way up the stairs to my apartment, I ran into my neighbor, Mike. He moved in at around the same time that I did, and at first, I was excited to have a friend in the building. But then, years later during a movie night, he leaned over and kissed me. I was so unprepared for it that I nearly threw my popcorn bowl in his face, and he left furious and humiliated. We hadn't really spoken since.

This time, though, he smiled at me. "Hey, Allie, how have you been?"

I blinked, surprised that he was addressing me for the first time in years. "Uh, fine. And you?"

He let out a self-deprecating chuckle. "Same. Been busy with work, but when am I not?"

"I feel that," I replied, stepping around him to continue my path home. "I've been working my ass off the past couple weeks, trying to make myself into a good candidate for promotion."

"Fingers crossed it all works out." His eyes softened as he stared at me, his smile warm and affectionate. It made my stomach twist almost as much as Josh's weird behavior at the bar earlier that night.

Ignoring my discomfort, I nodded. "I'll need all the luck I can get. Good to see you, Mike."

He smiled and waved for just a little too long as I left. "See you around, neighbor."

"Uh, yeah, bye," I replied, resuming my climb up the stairs. Why the sudden change of heart? Did he finally get over the awkwardness of that failed kiss? I really hoped so. I liked being friends with him and was sad that I couldn't reciprocate his feelings. He probably felt like I was leading him on, but that was never what I wanted to do. But unfortunately, intent doesn't always matter with certain people.

Thankfully, my cat was still acting normal. Luna trotted up to greet me, purring and rolling at my feet as I prepared her evening can of wet food. "For your majesty," I said, putting it down.

She practically swatted my hand aside as she ate, acting like I didn't leave her a full bowl of cereal when I left that morning. With a sigh, I flopped onto the couch and turned on the TV. *The Bachelorette* was on, and I didn't bother changing it, finding myself oddly engrossed. I used to joke with Josh that this was an ace aro's worst nightmare, but now, I could kind of see the fantasy. Still absolutely not for me, though.

Being asexual and aromantic is a bit like being colorblind. Everyone else seems to know that red is red and green is green, but to you, those colors are the same unappealing brown. It takes a while for you to realize that people actually do perceive red and green, and that they're not exaggerating how much their lives center around these two colors. And the worst part is that everyone tells you that you should love red and green, that they're the most beautiful colors in the world and that you're somehow incomplete or broken without them.

It took a long time for me to accept that I wasn't broken or doomed to be lonely, that life was so much more than sex or romance and that I didn't need it to be happy. Because I was happy just the way I was.

I had work the next morning, so I shut the TV off just before she handed out the final rose. For a split second, there was a reflection in the TV. The man I'd glimpsed at the bar, someone so beautiful he could have been a Greek statue brought to life. Yelping, I whipped around.

Luna napped undisturbed on the seat beside the couch. We were utterly alone in the apartment. It must have been my imagination. Still, I double checked that the door was locked and searched every possible nook and cranny before going to bed with a baseball bat propped against my nightstand.

That night, I dreamed I was dating someone, but I could never quite see their face or remember their name. We walked through the park and danced in the moonlight and kissed underneath the mistletoe. I woke feeling oddly bereft.

My alarm must have turned itself off, because somehow, I slept right past it. When my natural body clock stirred to life, I realized with a jolt that I was running late. Throwing on some clothes, I fed Luna, grabbed my work bag, and rushed out the door. Thank God my job was in walking distance.

"Hey Allie," Mike called as I raced down the stairs.

"Sorry. Can't talk," I replied, blowing past him and racing to the street. By the time I got to work, I was sweaty and out of breath. I opened the door to the office.

And walked straight into a cup of coffee. I cried out in shock, the hot liquid seeping into my shirt and burning me. "Watch where you're going!"

"Shit, I'm so sorry," the man formerly holding the now-spilled coffee exclaimed.

Today was not my day. "It's fine," I grumbled, pawing at the brown liquid now staining my blouse. Of course it had to be a day where I wore white.

"Let me grab you some napkins."

"I said it's fine." Pushing past him, I set my things at my desk before grabbing my emergency cardigan and heading to the bathroom. After checking if the coast was clear, I pulled off my shirt and put on the cardigan for something resembling modesty before rinsing the ruined garment in the sink. Some of the brown liquid came out, but most stayed stubbornly in place.

Sighing, I resigned myself to wearing a wet, coffee-stained shirt all day.

And I hadn't even gotten the chance to eat breakfast.

My lucky streak continued, because my boss, Mr. Heller, called us in for a meeting. I tried to cover myself with the cardigan as best as I could, but the stain was too big. Everyone eyed me before looking away, embarrassed to get caught staring.

"So, I bet you're wondering why I've brought you all here," Mr. Heller said after everyone filed into the room. "I would like for all of you to welcome our newest manager, Nathan Bradley."

The man who spilled the coffee on me stepped into the room. We made eye contact. Then, his gaze trailed to my poorly hidden coffee stain, and he winced. I looked away, eager for this meeting to be over.

"Thank you all for the warm welcome," Nathan said. "I look forward to working with you."

"Right now, I've assigned you to work with Allie on developmental edits for the latest Detective Shroud novel," Heller said. But that didn't make sense. If Nathan was a manager, he would be focused on the big-picture publishing plan, not developmental edits for the novel. Still, with my promotion on the line, I thought it was best not to argue.

Nathan smiled brightly at me, revealing pearly white teeth, and gave me a nod. The man was handsome, with bright blue eyes, dark brown hair, and strong features. I may not experience sexual attraction, but I can still appreciate when someone looks good, even if he's got too much of a Patrick Bateman vibe for me.

Later, he found me at my desk. While I read through chapter three of the novel and took notes on the mystery, he leaned casually into my space. "Allie, isn't it? I'm sorry about the coffee. And the shirt. I can pay for you to get a new one."

Looking up from my computer, I shook my head. "It's fine. Sorry I snapped at you. I was the one who wasn't paying attention, so it was my bad."

"Is there some way I can make it up to you?"

I shook my head. "I'm good if you're good."

He leaned in uncomfortably close, practically whispering in my ear. "What about dinner? You can catch me up on your progress with the book and we can get to know each other better."

Great. Another office creep. And this one was my manager, so I had to stay on his good side. I rolled my chair a little away from him. "As flattered as I am, I prefer to keep my personal life separate from my work life if that's okay."

He blinked, clearly not expecting that answer. Nathan was the kind of handsome who could get any girl he wanted. I doubted he'd ever heard the word "no" in his life. I braced myself for anger, for a temper tantrum from a grown man, maybe even retaliation. But his expression went oddly vacant. "Oh. Okay. Sorry to bother you." Then, he wandered off as though lost in the office he'd commanded just moments before.

My confusion mingled with my relief as I watched him go. For a moment, I thought I saw a figure out of the corner of my eye, but when I went to look directly at it, nobody was there. Goosebumps rose on my arms and the back of my neck. I curled in on myself, waiting for the eerie feeling to pass.

"Why aren't you following the rules?" a voice whispered.

I gasped, twisting my head as I searched for the source. No one was nearby, let alone close enough to whisper in my ear. I had to be going crazy. Closing my eyes, I counted my breaths to calm my racing heart. It was probably just stress doing weird things to my brain.

I was grateful not to see Nathan for the rest of the day. He was probably busy licking the wounds of his rejection, so I could work in relative peace. As long as he didn't retaliate against me and turn all this into an HR nightmare, I was good.

At the end of the day, I shut off my computer and stretched, my joints popping like the old lady that I was. When I waved goodbye to my coworkers, I realized that Nathan was not among them. He'd probably left early, but it still seemed a bit strange to me. Our previous project manager had always been the last to leave. Maybe his work ethic was just different. I know I'm a bit of a workaholic, which isn't exactly healthy. Maybe he was one of those mythical employees who could maintain a proper work-life balance.

Mike was in the stairwell again when I made it back to my apartment. "Hey Allie. Rough day?" He gestured to the massive stain on my shirt.

"You could say that. I ran into my new boss and got his coffee spilled all over me." It was strange for him to start speaking so casually to me again, but it was also nice. As long as he understood that I wasn't interested in anything other than friendship, I would be happy to try our relationship again.

Mike laughed. "That's a hell of a first impression."

"And the craziest part was that he asked me out to make it up to me." I shook my head. "I was terrified that I would have to go to HR."

"So you didn't say yes?" Though he tried to sound casual, I could hear the note of hope in his voice. Great. Time for another awkward anti-birds and bees talk.

"No. I mean, I didn't come out to him or anything, because that usually leads to a barrage of questions about my sexual orientation, but I told him I wasn't interested." This was a little bit of a jab and a little bit of testing the waters.

Five years ago, when we were sitting on the couch watching a scary movie, Mike leaned in. At first, I thought he was just reaching for the popcorn. But then he pressed his lips to mine. I jerked away, sending the bowl flying.

"Sorry," I said, my heart squeezing a little at his wounded expression. "I don't feel that way about you."

He blinked, looking shocked. "But we've practically been dating for months."

"What?" It was my turn to look confused. "No, we haven't."

"What do you call this?" He gestured at the pizza, the popcorn, and the movie, which showed a scene of a masked killer chopping the head off a cheerleader with a pizza slicer.

"Friends hanging out?"

"And eating dinner together and going to parties together. Hell, you were my plus-one at my sister's wedding."

"Because you asked me to be. You said you didn't want to be alone," I said, feeling like a train that had just run out of track and was heading straight towards a cliff. The ending to this was as inevitable as it was tragic.

He got to his feet, scrubbing his face in frustration and pacing the floor. "I can't believe you. How can you be that oblivious?"

Now, it was my turn to be frustrated. "I told you when we met that I'm asexual and aromantic. I thought you respected that I wasn't going to date anyone."

"*I* thought you might get over it. Like you hadn't met the right guy yet."

"Get out," I said softly, pointing towards the door. And then louder, "I said get out!"

"Fine," he snapped and stalked out of my apartment. Until recently, that was the last time I spoke to him.

Now, years later, his smile became forced when I mentioned my sexual orientation. I hoped he was just embarrassed by the reminder of his entitled behavior. But if not, maybe I didn't want to rekindle this friendship. Not until he showed me that he was truly sorry.

"Well, I hope he didn't make the workplace too weird after that," Mike replied. It wasn't anything close to an apology, but at least he didn't try to invalidate my existence again. In the interest of civility, I decided not to mention his own reaction to my rejection.

"Yeah, things must have been too awkward because he seemed to just disappear." I shrugged. "Honestly, I'm glad. We both got to avoid any more weirdness."

"So, do you have any plans for the evening?" he asked.

I shrugged. "Feed the cat, eat dinner, watch some mindless television while folding laundry, and decompress. You?"

"Pretty much the same." He smiled almost shyly. "If you want, I can drop by. We can do a movie night like we used to."

And whose fault was it that we stopped?

I smiled around the lump in my throat. "Maybe another time. Today has been a bit of a mess."

He frowned, looking at me with hurt puppy dog eyes like he wasn't the one who hurt me first. "Okay. Another time, then." With that, he headed into his apartment.

Eager to put the day behind me, I retreated to the refuge of my own. After feeding Luna, I changed into my sweatpants and collected my dirty clothes. The laundry room was on our floor, practically next door to Mike's apartment. As I carried the basket down the hall, Mike's voice carried through the thin wall. I knew it was wrong, but I couldn't help but stop and listen.

"Why don't you just shoot her? That's what you do, right?" Mike demanded. "What do you mean it doesn't work like that?"

I couldn't make out the reply from the voice on the other side of the door.

"I told you she's all alone in there. You're clearly not trying." A pause while the other person spoke, and then he responded, "No, what I need is for you to do your goddamn job."

I dropped my basket, too shocked to care about the sound that reverberated through the hall. Did...did Mike hire someone to kill me? Or was he after someone else? What the hell was happening?

"What was that?" Mike asked.

Oh no. My heart racing, I scooped up the laundry basket and scurried back to my apartment, all thoughts of clean clothes forgotten. As I slipped inside, I heard Mike's door open and shut. I locked and deadbolted my door before bracing a chair up against it. Grabbing my phone and a knife, I closed the blinds to my windows and huddled in the bathroom. Luna seemed to sense my alarm, because she joined me, curling in my lap as I debated calling Josh. He might have been acting weird, but he wouldn't want to hurt me. Not like Mike.

Was all this because I said no to him a few years ago? What was his problem?

Or maybe I was just jumping to conclusions. Maybe he was talking about something else, and I was panicking for no reason. Still, I didn't feel safe alone at the moment. I needed my friend, even if he was acting like a pod person.

Closing my eyes, I counted my breaths—in for four, hold for

four, out for four, repeat. Eventually, my heart rate calmed enough for me to pull up Josh's contact and call him.

It went straight to voicemail. I left one, and then texted, but the message refused to go through. The same thing happened with all my other friends. None of my messages were getting out. And suddenly, the hired hitman idea didn't seem so far-fetched. Maybe the guy that Mike was talking to had some kind of signal jammer.

There was a knock at the front door. My breath caught in my throat as I listened, my ears straining for anything from the other side.

"Allie, it's me," Mike said. "I think you might've overheard something out of context. I was practicing for a play with my scene partner."

It was a cliched explanation, one that I'd heard in thousands of movies and TV shows. I kept silent, clutching Luna to my chest. My cat usually squirmed when she was picked up, but she must have sensed my terror, because she kept utterly still.

"Allie, I know you're in there. I just want to talk."

I wanted to yell at him to go away, but I couldn't bring myself to make a sound and risk giving away where I was, especially if his hitman was still with him. I prayed to any god who would listen that he would get bored and leave me alone.

And then one listened.

"There seems to have been some kind of misunderstanding," came a voice in the darkness of the bathroom.

I shrieked, covering Luna's tiny body with my own as I curled away from the man speaking. How did he get in here? I knew I hadn't locked my door when I stepped out, but I was out for less than a minute and would've seen him in the hall.

The light flicked on, and standing before me was a beautiful man, *the* beautiful man I'd been seeing in reflections and out of the corner of my eye. He wore a casual white T-shirt and pants. A quiver of arrows was slung over one shoulder and a bow was hooked over the other. He flashed me a smile full of perfect teeth.

With the hand that wasn't holding the cat, I raised the knife and slowly got to my feet. It likely wouldn't do me any good, but if

I was going to die, I wouldn't go down without a fight. "What do you want from me?"

He shrugged. "Nothing, really. It's what your not-so-secret admirer wants. He summoned me, you know. Fed me this sob story about how he was in love with a lonely woman, one who was so focused on her career that she failed to see how miserable she was. Now that she was about to turn thirty, she needed to settle down and find love. As Cupid, you and he fell right into my purview."

"Seriously?" I laughed out loud. I couldn't help it. Yesterday, I was excited that Mike wanted to be my friend again, but apparently, that wasn't the case. No, he was just as much of an entitled ass now as he was then. And apparently, he summoned a god to try to get into my pants.

I wasn't sure why I accepted that the man who stood before me was literally Cupid, the God of Love, but considering the past couple days I'd been having, it was as reasonable as anything else.

"It did seem to be a bit much. But I watched you for a while. A woman alone with nothing but her cat, her apartment, and her career. Beautiful but unattainable. I could see why he wanted you, but when I tried piercing you with a golden-tipped arrow, it flew through you like you were made of smoke. It happens from time to time, so I had to go to Plan B."

"You what?" I hated the way my voice pitched upwards so high that the question practically came out as a squeak. This guy shot an arrow at me without me noticing? How was that even possible? He reached backwards, plucking two from the quiver. A stab of panic ran through me, and I waved the knife. "Whoa, whoa, whoa, what do you think you're doing?"

"I'm showing you the two kinds of arrows I use. One is tipped in gold and the other in lead." He pulled the arrows free to show me. "The gold creates near-uncontrollable sexual desire, and the lead makes you averse to that person. When I tried the gold on you, it didn't work. So, I had to try a more human method."

"Which was?" I asked, unable to stop myself from marveling at the golden sheen of one heart-shaped arrowhead and the dull gray of the other. The shaft was ivory white with dove feathers for the fletching. The craftsmanship was stunning, with delicate etchings along the shaft and head. Even the dull gray of lead seemed to glow with a fascinating luster.

He straightened and puffed out his chest, looking proud of himself. "I like to think I'm an expert in human courtship methods. I've studied your stories extensively."

I blinked, tearing my eyes away from the weapons. "What?"

"I'm especially fond of human romantic comedies. They're very instructional, so I use them as my guide." He frowned, his brows furrowing slightly. "But you refused to play along."

My mind raced, the pieces finally coming together. Why was Josh acting so weird last night? Because the female protagonist of a rom com usually has a sassy gay stereotype as a best friend. Why did my alarm make me late, leading me to literally run into Nathan and get coffee spilled on me? Because couples often have meet-cutes. Why did my boss pair us together for a project even though it made no sense and why was Nathan asking me out on a date? Because there needed to be a justification for us to spend time together.

But that didn't make sense. Not completely. All of this would point to Nathan being my love interest. Unless...

Unless I did go on that date with him and maybe a few others, only to find out that the rich guy was a massive asshole, leaving me to fall into the arms of the boy next door, the one who loved me all along: Mike. And the conversation I overheard all fit. He didn't hire a hitman; he summoned Cupid to override my free will and make me love him.

Fury made my jaw clench. "The reason I didn't play by the rules is because I have no interest in the game. I'm asexual and aromantic. There was nothing before that he could say or do to make me fall in love, and there's definitely nothing he can do now."

"Are you sure?" Cupid asked. "Because I can't leave until he releases me from the pact."

"I'm sure." Setting Luna down, I snatched the lead-headed

arrow from Cupid's hand and stalked out of the bathroom. Throwing the chair barricade aside, I unlocked the door.

When I opened it, Mike was still standing there, his eyes widening in panic at the rage on my face. "Allie, what are you doing?" he asked. "Please, I can explain. I—"

"I never want to see you again," I growled, plunging the lead arrow into his chest. When it pierced his heart, the arrow vanished.

Mike blinked, looking confused. When he saw me, his face twisted in revulsion and he turned on his heel, heading back to his apartment.

Well, the feeling was mutual.

Shutting the door, I found myself face-to-face with the God of Love once more. "I think that should do it. Are you free?"

Cupid blinked and felt his chest as though the binding had a physical mark. Maybe it did. I didn't know how it all worked. "Yes, I think so. How did you know the arrow would work for you?"

"I didn't," I replied, putting the knife back into its block. "So, will things go back to normal? Will my best friend start acting like himself again? Do I have to deal with a manager who has a weird crush on me?"

"Without your love interest, you won't have a plot," Cupid said, still sounding taken aback by what just happened. "So, yes, things will return to normal."

"Great. I'm ordering pizza. Do you want any?"

"Er, no thank you." With that, he vanished in the flutter of dove's wings.

I got my pizza and turned on the TV. Luna curled on my lap, and Josh texted me about his day, my friend acting like himself again.

Who needs romance? I couldn't be any more content with my life than I was right then.

About the Author

Kay Hanifen was born on a Friday the 13th and once lived for three months in a haunted castle. So, obviously, she had to become a horror writer. Her work has appeared in over one hundred anthologies and magazines. Her first anthology as an editor, *Till the Yule Log Burns Out*, was published in 2024. Her debut novel, *The Last Ballard,* came out this year. When she's not consuming pop culture with the voraciousness of a vampire at a 24-hour blood bank, you can usually find her with her black cats or at *kayhanifenauthor.wordpress.com.*

Twitter: *@TheUnicornComi1*
Instagram: katharinehanifen

(RE)WILD AT HEART

CAITLIN BARBERA

To: Saskia MacLeod
From: Rewilding Service Onboarding

Dear Saskia,

Thank you for choosing a two-year assignment with the Rewilding Service! We are thrilled that you have chosen to take part in the project to return humanity to our ancestral home!

Regarding your request for a solo assignment, the Service's research has indicated that it is best for monitoring teams to be assigned in pairs. Our Cupid's Arrow protocol uses a state-of-the-art algorithm for sorting and classifying assignees according to personality, with our specially trained employees providing the human touch and the final decision in assignments. This protocol ensures that you'll be paired with someone compatible to minimize friction and make your two-year assignment comfortable. Many of our assignees have become lifelong friends!

Saskia's partner was late. The shuttle was supposed to leave in... she checked the clock on her in-eye display: three minutes. What would happen if the other person didn't show up? Would Saskia have to stay aboard the orbital? Would she never get to Earth at all? Would she....

"Are you going to Station 346?" someone asked from the shuttle doorway, sounding out of breath. Saskia looked up and found a man giving her a smile so warm that she had a moment of panic, convinced she'd met him before and forgotten. Who would smile like that at someone they didn't know?

He ducked inside, just as the door closed behind him and the shuttle AI prepared for take-off.

"...I am. I'm Saskia."

"Ketill." The man threw his luggage carelessly onto the long bench on his side of the shuttle and flopped down after it, stretching out his legs and crossing his ankles. "Wow, this is going to be fun, isn't it? I can't think of a better adventure!"

Saskia smiled politely, even though she wanted to frown. A polite smile was the best response to most any situation, her mother had always told her. Her mother always had the best advice; she wished she could have some of her mother's advice now. "I'm not sure an adventure is what I'd call it."

"What then?"

"A duty," she said sternly. *An escape*, she didn't say. *A refuge.*

"How species-minded of you!" Ketill said, and laughed as though they were in on a joke together. Saskia didn't think it was a joke, though. Her smile grew a bit thinner, and she crossed her arms. Ketill's smile faded, and he turned away from her to pull a tablet out of his pack. Saskia looked at the stars, wondering if this was really what passed for an excellent algorithm with the Rewilding Service.

Her eyes kept being drawn back to the man as the flight went on. He was irritatingly handsome, she had to admit.

And then the shuttle changed direction slightly, and the edge of the planet came into view, green and blue starting to reclaim it in particularly successful places, gray and brown retreating as life returned. Saskia sucked in a breath, and even Ketill put the tablet down and stared.

For a long moment, they were together in silence, and Saskia imagined he was feeling the same simple awe as she was.

❧

KETILL CONSIDERED himself to be the sort of person who gave others the benefit of the doubt. When something was talked up as much as the Cupid's Arrow protocol had been, he really wanted to believe that he could trust it.

But it had paired him with someone who didn't think he had anything to offer. She was beautiful and clever and serious and she looked at him just the way people always had. He'd left the comfortable orbital and come down to a planet in the throes of rebirth just to be useful, and the person who was supposed to be his partner thought he was useless. Just like he'd always been back on the orbital. Just like his parents had always thought he was.

It made him want to run to his room and bury his head under a pillow. After all, hiding was his tried-and-true method of dealing with people who didn't like or respect him. His father had always shaken his head in disappointment that he never faced his problems head-on, but that was just who he was, he guessed.

Except that he couldn't do that. Measurements had to be taken at the same time every day, several times a day, to keep the all-important data flowing. For the first time in his life, he had an important job to do. He couldn't hide.

They had to work together to take measurements, strapping on their filter masks and picking up soil, sucking up air, clipping the very tips off blades of grass wherever it was growing. They weren't supposed to do any of it alone, in case of an emergency. It was the only time he and Saskia spent together, and, paradoxically, it was when he felt best. He liked having something to focus on, something that wasn't as slippery as making people like him.

And it was the only time that he thought the Cupid's Arrow

protocol might have gotten things right. Because they worked really well together, both focused, both careful.

Maybe the protocol didn't care if they were happy together, as long as they got things done.

On their third day, they stopped at a cliff overlooking the river. The water was still sludgy, but the giant machines upriver were doing their work, and the particulates in the water were decreasing day by day. Soon, the machines would pass the monitoring station, and the view would be of clear water and the beginnings of grassy banks.

"Good work today," Saskia said, and Ketill nearly tripped over his own feet in surprise.

"What?"

"I've been meaning to tell you. You do good work."

"Oh. Uh, thanks." Ketill couldn't help his smile. "You too." After a pause, he asked, "It's incredible, isn't it?" He gestured to the mountains spearing the sky and the river running between them.

He saw Saskia nod out of the corner of his eye. "It's only going to get better. That's the thing I can't wrap my head around."

He felt the same way.

※

"What even *is* this?" Saskia muttered, lifting the odd little box from the cushion of the chair. It was covered all over in fabric, embroidered with trees and birds.

"Oh, you found it!" Ketill said at an entirely unreasonable volume. The coffee pot hadn't even finished brewing yet. Saskia winced.

"I found it by nearly sitting on it, actually."

"Oh, no! I'm sorry, I completely lost track of it." Saskia was about to voice a further complaint, but then Ketill stepped into her space, seemingly without even thinking about it, and took the box out of her hands. Like he always did, he smelled like some sort of floral soap. She wished she could stop noticing that, stop noticing how much she liked the way he smelled and how lovely his smile was.

"What is it?" she asked again. He stepped away, and she was relieved and only slightly disappointed.

"My paint set!"

"You're going to... paint?"

"Of course! You didn't bring your hobbies along? What do you even do most of the day?"

"I go for walks," Saskia said, a little defensively.

"...And that's it?" Ketill asked, after a long, awkward moment. When Saskia didn't answer, he grinned. "I know what we should do! We should go to that rock that looks over the sapling forest. I can teach you how to paint."

Saskia immediately wanted to say no, but paused. No one had offered to teach her something without her paying for it, not since her mother. Her throat tightened. Saskia nodded jerkily and whirled on her heel to find her boots.

The paint set turned out to hold an absurd number of colors, as well as a stack of erasable film paper and brushes with elegant tips in various sizes.

"Yeah, it's a little extravagant," Ketill said, shrugging and flushing. "I'm not a good enough painter to justify it, but it was a gift from my big sister."

"That was kind of her." Saskia watched curiously as Ketill set up a little folding easel and film paper, then surveyed the scene with his eyes narrowed.

"Yeah. It's funny, because she thinks painting is stupid, just like our parents. She's... sweet, like that." He smiled fondly. "She's always been nice to me, even when she doesn't understand."

"Your family doesn't like that you paint?"

"They don't really care about anything I do. We're a political family, very serious, and I'm, well..." He gestured aimlessly at himself, as if to encompass everything. "Luckily they've got my sister. She's much more what they wanted, so it's okay that I'm not." He smiled brightly, but he didn't meet her eyes.

For the first time, Saskia wondered if his reasons for taking up a rewilding assignment were similar to her own. "Did they... have any thoughts about you coming down here?"

"Not really," Ketill said shortly. "What about your family? What do your parents do?"

"My father does some kind of business, but he... didn't stick around." Ketill's honesty deserved to be answered in kind, but it was still difficult to say.

"That's shitty," Ketill said plainly, and Saskia snorted. "What about your mom?"

"Odd jobs, whatever she could get. It was just the two of us."

"Did she have any thoughts about you coming down here?"

"No, she... died a year ago. I started training for the Rewilding Service after that." She probably should have left it at that, but to her own surprise, she kept going. "Actually, the first thing I did was go to my father to ask if he could give me some career advice. Not even a job, just advice. He, uh, said he probably shouldn't be associated with me. He has a wife and kids, you know."

There was a long pause, and Saskia wished she hadn't said anything. Then Ketill asked, "May I?" When she looked back at him, he was holding one hand out toward her, like he was asking her to dance. Confused, she put her hand in his. His hand was so warm, and her heart was suddenly pounding.

Then he put a paintbrush in her hand and curled her fingers around it, holding her hand up with the tip of the brush nearly touching the film paper. "This is the best way to hold it," he said, his voice soft, and Saskia met his eyes. They held each other's gaze for a long moment, before Saskia cleared her throat and looked away.

"What next?" she asked, and Ketill laughed.

"Next, Saskia, you paint."

❧

KETILL'S FEELINGS about Saskia were pointless, he knew. She had absolutely no interest in him. That was probably what he was picking up on. He'd spent his whole life chasing the approval of people who didn't see the point of him. Why did he think it would be any different on the planet?

But the way she'd smiled, just the smallest little twist of her lips, while she'd drawn the paintbrush across the paper...

"Here," he said, holding out a cup of coffee. Saskia was sitting out on the station's porch, looking down into the valley at the river.

She blinked at him and at the cup. He'd brought her coffee every morning for days, yet it seemed to surprise her every time. It made him want to bring her more, more coffee, more new experiences, more of everything.

"Thanks," she said with a slight smile. "I was actually thinking..." She gestured to the view. "It might be nice to paint this."

He had to swallow several times against a solar flare of happiness. "*This* view? Not the one on the other side? This one is..."

"I know," Saskia answered, a little defensively. "It's not *pretty*, like the other side. But... there's something about how sad it is that makes me want to look at it."

He looked back down into the valley, the slowly moving river, the barren banks, not yet ready to grow again. He could see what she meant.

He'd never thought of sadness as something to be savored. He'd always been trying to get away from it, filling the gaps with beautiful things so that he could borrow someone else's joy. Why would he want to borrow sadness?

But he wanted to watch her paint another picture, wanted to watch the concentration on her face and the careful way she held her hands, as if her movements meant everything.

"You could borrow my easel."

She glanced at him, then away again. "Actually, I thought... I could watch how you paint. Just to see..."

"That... I could do that. Let me finish my coffee and..."

He turned around so fast that he spilled his coffee out of the mug and onto his hand, sucking in a pained breath. She got up quickly and took the mug from him, pressing her lips together to hide her smile, and he suddenly wanted to know what it would take to make her laugh.

"You don't have to rush," Saskia said softly.

"I'm really glad you're the person I'm here with," he said. "I guess the assignments really do work."

"Yeah," she said. When had they started standing so close? Was it possible they could stand a little closer? "I really think…"

A flashing red alert blared across his in-eye display, and from the way Saskia jerked back, she'd gotten it, too. An urgent message from the Rewilding Service. He blinked to accept the communication.

A young man, probably just out of Orbital Higher Ed, took over his visual field. When he saw them, he blurted, "Oh, fuck, you're alive, thank heavens."

"Were we… not supposed to be?" Ketill asked, a little alarmed.

"No, I mean, obviously, yes, you're supposed to be alive, it's just, with interpersonal conflict… Never mind. How are things going?"

Ketill glanced at Saskia. She looked as confused as he felt. "Things are… fine. No problems. Is there something we should know?"

"Well, the thing is… I'm David, I'm your analyst, the one who assigned you together. And, well, it turns out that I was a little distracted when I did and, uh, I misclicked. I didn't discover it until this morning, and…"

"Wait," Ketill cut him off, his heart sinking. "What are you saying?"

"Well, uh, the thing is… You really shouldn't have been assigned together. Your scores aren't really close at all. With how incompatible you are, I… Well, now that I know you're okay… I have to get you reassigned. Right away, as soon as possible. We should be able to resolve this and get you paired with compatible partners within forty-eight hours."

Forty-eight hours? That was too fast. Ketill felt like his mind was spinning in circles.

"Is that really necessary?" Saskia asked, glancing at Ketill. He should have probably said something, but his throat was too dry, his stomach lurching and roiling. "We've been working well together, I don't think…"

David was already shaking his head with quick, nervous motions. "No, that would be against the protocol, and it really is better for the people working together to be compatible. Please, let's just get this resolved."

"But…" Saskia trailed off, staring at Ketill now. He knew she was waiting for him to chime in, to point out that things had been going so well. He wished this conversation had never happened.

He had been so sure that he'd finally found exactly where he was supposed to be. He'd never belonged with his family, but he had belonged here, he'd thought. The Rewilding Service had assured him that it didn't get these things wrong. He'd really thought he'd found it. And now David and Saskia were both staring at him expectantly, and he'd never felt so small.

His eyes felt hot and prickly, and he had to close them. He wanted to end this call and go lie down. "Well, if… if that's what you think is best, I don't… want to cause more problems. I guess we should see who we were supposed to be with."

There was silence. Ketill opened his eyes again to see the semitransparent image of David staring uncertainly. When he focused his eyes past the image and onto Saskia, he saw that her face had gone completely blank, not even looking annoyed.

"As my colleague said," she said blandly. "Please contact us again when the reassignments have been worked out."

"Saskia…" Ketill started, but she shook her head sharply.

"I'll wait to hear from you, David."

Then she cut the connection and marched back into the building. From deeper inside, he heard her door shutting. The worst part was that she didn't slam it, just shut it firmly and finally, leaving Ketill to slump his shoulders and stare at the sludgy river far below.

Saskia hadn't cried since she was a child, and she sure as *hell* wasn't going to start now. Not because Ketill had decided he didn't want to be around her unless an algorithm told him it was the right choice. Not because she was being left alone, *again*.

She heard him moving around, but he didn't knock, and she didn't look out. By the time that absurd analyst called them back, she'd lost track of time. A glance at the clock in her in-eye system told her that it hadn't even been an hour.

She pulled herself together and answered the call. Ketill's face appeared in her field of view, too, but she tried very hard not to look at him. Or the fact that his eyes and nose were reddened.

"Are the reassignments ready?" she asked. David looked even more panicked than he had before.

"Well, um, no, that's been put on hold for the moment, because, uh, there's another problem. There's been a malfunction with one of the machines upriver, and it really needs to be dealt with right away. Otherwise, it might start releasing some of the pollution it's been picking up..."

"Setting back the rewilding in the area by years," Saskia finished for him.

"If not decades," Ketill put in.

"Uh, yeah." David nodded miserably.

"What kind of malfunction are we talking about?" Saskia asked.

"An electrical short. I've sent the shutdown command to both of you. One of you will have to wirelessly connect your in-eye system to the control panel on the machine to run the command."

"I'll take care of it." Saskia nodded and cut the connection. She could stabilize the machine long enough for the orbital to send a maintenance team. She opened her bedroom door and stepped out, glad to have something to do.

Then she saw Ketill standing across the hall, pulling on his boots.

"I can take care of it on my own," Saskia said.

Ketill shook his head. "We're not supposed to travel to remote sites alone. This is a two-person job."

"It's like you said, we weren't supposed to be assigned together, and besides, I have more climbing experience. I don't think you'd be any help."

He actually flinched when she said that, and for a moment his face crumpled.

"I'm sorry," Saskia said stiffly. "I shouldn't have said that."

Ketill hesitated, then determinedly stepped into his boot without looking at her. "I'm still coming with you. Until we get reassigned, we're still partners."

Saskia couldn't argue with that, so she strapped a gravity harness to her back and stalked out into the morning. He joined her a moment later, and she set off, hiking as quickly as she could.

They were silent all the way to the machine. As they approached where the river was being cleaned, there were more and more green plants around, hardy things slowly but surely coming back to life.

She had to blink several times when she thought that now she'd never get to watch Ketill paint a scene. She imagined that his brow would furrow the same way it did when he was confused by something in their measurements, but that maybe he'd smile while he worked. She'd wanted to see that.

Well, life was about wanting things you wouldn't get. The trick was to make yourself forget you'd ever wanted them in the first place.

The machines, one on each side of the river, were great hulking things covered in solar panels, their weight evenly distributed across narrow legs, like a spider moving in slow motion on their hundred-year journey down the river. Each extended one long arm into the water. The arm of the nearer machine was jerking erratically, and the smell of ozone was in the air. An electrical short. All she had to do was get to the underside of the machine to trigger the emergency shutdown, then wait for maintenance to arrive.

There were handholds on the outsides of the spidery legs. She was sizing them up when Ketill asked, "What can I do to help?"

"Can you spot me from the ground while I climb?" she asked, reluctantly.

He nodded back and followed her to the base of the nearest leg. She connected the gravity harness to her in-eye system, brought up its controls, took hold of the bottom set of handholds, and started up.

It was nice to be climbing, exerting herself, just body and destination. The gravity harness took some of her weight and would slow her fall if she lost her grip, but she could still feel the strain in her muscles, she still had to concentrate on each move. Everything else was meaningless.

Even heartache.

Finally she reached the top of the leg, sweat running into her eyes. She pulled herself along the underbelly of the machine, toward the control panel. Her muscles were screaming by the time she reached it. She opened the panel covering it and flicked her eyes through her in-eye system to connect wirelessly and run the shutdown command. There was a whir, the legs slowing even further, then coming to a stop.

The light on the panel flickered, and she felt something like a shock in the space behind her eyes, making her squeeze them shut. The gravity harness suddenly stopped holding her up, and she clung to her handholds with her heart in her throat.

When she opened her eyes, her in-eye system displayed big red squares of alerts about whatever malfunction the feedback from the machine had caused. She tried to minimize them. They didn't respond. They filled up her field of vision, disorienting her, making it impossible for her to see where her hands were.

She was blind.

SASKIA LOOKED SO small on the underside of the machine, and some absurd part of Ketill wanted to catch her if she fell. But then she got to the shutdown switch and triggered it, and he breathed a sigh of relief. She'd done the climb once, she could do it again.

She didn't move, though. He tried to open an in-eye channel to her, but there was no response.

He tilted his head back and called up to her. "Everything all right?"

"No," she called back. "There was some kind of feedback. The harness went down, and my in-eye system."

"So you have to climb down without the harness?" he asked, worried.

"Um... And also blind."

"What?"

"There're alerts in my visual field. I think I need to wait for the maintenance team. I just have to hang on." She said it firmly, but Ketill couldn't imagine that she really could hold on for however many hours it would take for the maintenance team to get there.

"I'm coming up there," he said.

"Ketill," she started, but she didn't say anything else.

He didn't have too bad of a time going up the leg. He even managed not to think about the fact that he didn't have a harness. But then he got to the underside of the machine, and imagined crawling his way over to her, with nothing to help keep him up. He grabbed the first handhold, trying to swing himself out onto the new surface. His hand was sweating, and the handhold twisted in his grip. His head spun with sudden dizziness, and he made a wordless noise as he only just managed to catch the leg again, clinging to it with his heart slamming in his chest.

"Ketill?" Saskia asked, her voice strained and frightened.

"I don't think I can get to where you are," he admitted. "But... I can tell you where the handholds are. If you can get to me, I can help you down."

Even as he suggested it, he knew that it was a stupid idea, and she'd never agree to it. No one would trust someone like him with their life. He was as useless here on the planet as he'd ever been up in the orbital.

But then she said, voice small, "Okay."

He had to swallow down his own fear. "All right," he said,

focusing as hard as he could. "Slide your left hand about three inches to the left."

Slowly, slowly, following each of his instructions to the letter, she made her way across the underbelly of the machine. Her arms and legs were shaking, and his heart seemed to be climbing up his throat, and sweat dripped into his eyes, but he kept his voice steady until, finally, she was close enough that he could reach out with one hand and take one of hers, guiding it to the top handhold of the machine's leg.

"Pretty straight up and down from here," Saskia muttered, her voice shaky. "I'm just going to... rest for a second." She looped her arms around the handhold and swung down until her feet were on another rung. "Thank you, Ketill. Thank you so much."

"Of course, Saskia." He hadn't taken his hand away from hers. The warmth of her skin made it real: he'd helped her. She was safe. They were going to be okay.

It took them a terribly long time to get to the bottom of the machine's leg again. When they made it to the grass, they both threw themselves onto their backs and just breathed.

Suddenly, Saskia laughed. "Oh, there it goes. My in-eye system must have sorted itself out. All the alert boxes are gone."

"So you can see again?"

"Yeah. A little late to be helpful, but yeah. If we'd just waited, maybe you wouldn't have had to help me."

"I wanted to help you." Ketill hoped she could hear in his voice how true that was.

There was a moment of silence, then Saskia said, very quietly, "I don't want to be assigned to someone else. I don't care what the protocol says."

He touched the side of her hand with his pinky finger, and a moment later, she turned her hand to grasp his. "I don't want to, either," he said quietly. "I'm sorry. I should have stood up for what I wanted. For you."

"I'm sorry, too. I wish I had just talked to you, instead of getting so upset."

"I'm going to tell David. I'm going to call him back and tell him

I'm not leaving. I'm staying here, and... and if you want, I'd like it if you stayed too."

"I'm not going anywhere." Saskia squeezed his hand, and Ketill smiled. There was another long pause, then Saskia continued, "All things considered, I think we should probably kiss now."

Ketill burst out laughing, then rolled toward her to do just that.

⁂

SASKIA WATCHED as Ketill drew the brush across the canvas, filling in the shape of the river with nothing but black ink, carefully thinning it with water to create what seemed like hundreds of different shades of gray. It was almost hypnotizing, watching the way he carefully considered each brushstroke, his head tilted on one side and his eyes narrowed.

The sun was bright in the sky, and the river flowed more quickly now than it had three weeks ago, when she'd first proposed this painting, as the machines upriver drew closer and closer, cleaning the water. It had taken a lot of back and forth with David and his bosses, but they'd convinced the Rewilding Service to let them serve out their assignment, at this station, together, and Ketill had said they should celebrate by finally painting the river.

Saskia wished it could go on forever, watching the river below them take shape on the paper like magic, watching Ketill's concentration and the careful movements of his hands, but finally, he set down his brush and stretched his arms over his head.

"There," he said. "What do you think?"

She considered it. It was sad, of course, the way the river appeared on the canvas, gray and black, just like it was sad the way it appeared in real life, sludgy and sluggish. But she smiled anyway. There was hope for the river, both in the real world and in the painting.

"I love it," she said, and enjoyed the way he smiled brightly at that.

"I think it just needs one more thing." He lifted his paint box and considered, selecting a slim brush and a dark green paint.

With a few strokes of the brush, he added a small patch of green grass growing right beside the river, a bright spot of life among the grays and blacks.

"Perfect," Saskia whispered.

"Perfect," Ketill repeated, and out of the corner of her eyes, she could see that he was looking at her.

About the Author

Caitlin Barbera is a lifelong lover of reading and writing science fiction and fantasy. Her first story was about a girl velociraptor going on an adventure and fighting androids. She is currently a student in the Genre Fiction concentration of the Graduate Program in Creative Writing at Western Colorado University. A native of Colorado, she lives in the Denver metro area with her spouse, child, and dog, and spends much of her time coming up with more story ideas than she could possibly write in a lifetime. She has been published in anthologies from Inkd Publishing, Raconteur Press, and Knight Writing Press. She can be found at caitlinbarberawrites.wordpress.com.

STAR-CROSSED

DIANA OLNEY

We were beautiful,
once.

Our bodies:
Light, clarion, aerial,
the utmost height
of an inherently
elite society.

Our lives:
Decadent, luxurious,
a twenty-four-seven
nightlife,
darkest silk and velvet draped,
unfurling in euphoric
juxtaposition.

Our hearts:
Lambent, irradiant, ablaze,

every incendiary atom and vessel
wreathed in singing flame
so bright, so bold, so passionate,
the echo alone
could cross galaxies.

And it did.

That is how
I found you,
heard you,
saw you,
from a thousand miles and
lifetimes away.
You burned
and beat like a ballad:
Electric, enchanting,
a serenade of sweeping,
nitrous clarity
reaching out to me
in nuclear reactions.

To those below, you were an enigma,
too mysterious, esoteric, and distant
for anything but desperate
wishes;
unheard, unseen, unanswered.
But you answered mine
simply by existing.

Delta Scuti, they called you—
the heartbeat star.
I called you:
Perfect.

When I first spotted you,

my pulse raced,
rushing in waves
torrid and ultraviolet,
but still paled
in comparison to yours.
Yet somehow,
through the serendipity
of rhythm and radiation,
we sang together,
the notes of our immolated vibrations
synchronized
in a star-crossed duet
that turned the friction
between us
into a symphony.

In that fateful moment
of interstellar attraction,
the hammer of our
two hearts
was so strong,
we changed the course
of our own constellations.

But oh, how those hearts
wept
when at last we
broke apart.

Even in our perpetual
luminescence,
we never saw the crash coming.
Out there,
in the infinite, caliginous umbra,
there was no warning,
no soliloquy or story

to tell us
why falling
in love was dangerous.

When I fell,
my imagination wandered, chasing
the smoke of a thought
twice as treacherous
as my own trajectory.

What if.

What if I was the catalyst?
My materials
volatile, unstable—
the ardor of my orbit
twisting our elevated embrace
into a downward spiral?

But I see now,
it was no one's fault.
These things,
these terrible, tragic accidents,
happen all the time,
without rhyme or reason,
safety or equilibrium,
save for the secret
agendas
of degenerate matter—
that's how chaos goes
from theory
to reality.

Chaos doesn't care
for our infinitesimal wants,
our atomic desires,

it strikes
in every stretch of every system of every galaxy
killing indiscriminately—
a star dies,
the cosmos ignites,
erupting in volcanic,
molten supernova,
and the embers birth
the abysmal black mass
of a eulogy.

But we were different,
special,
because we went out
together.
Even the blinding agony
of our head-on collision
was its own miracle,
proof
that our union was more
than just happenstance.

That is why,
though I am shattering,
I will not collapse
into the cruel black trap
of anhedonia.
That is how
I know
in every single
iron splinter and silver shard
of my disintegrating
heart,
that our song
is long from over.

This is only
an intermission.

After the dust
settles,
our encore will come.
And when it does,
we will sing
through the ink of the heavens
with the melodic genesis
of all new elements,
telling our story
in notes, words, colors, and chemicals
that haven't even
been invented.

We were beautiful,
once.
Exquisitely, enviably,
alive and enlightened,
richer, brighter
than the rarest diamonds.
But the truth is:
We were our most beautiful
in love,
and if we hold on
to the gravity
it gave us,
we will be
again.

About the Author

DIANA OLNEY IS a Seattle based author, but she is most at home in the shadows, exploring the dark paths between dreams and nightmares. Her work has appeared or is forthcoming in publications by Blackstone Publishing, Small Wonders Magazine, Crystal Lake Publishing, Dark Horses Magazine, and others. She is also the creator of *Siren's Song*, an original queer horror comic series. Her influences include her furry assistants, black cats Dolce and Gabbana, as well as the words of Jack Skillingstead, Richard Kadrey, Gwendolyn Kiste, and Shanna Germain. Visit her website dianaolney.com or Instagram @dianaolneyauthor for updates on her latest tales.

WITCHFUL THINKING

KRISTI CHARISH AND SEBASTIEN DE CASTELL

Chapter 1
The Magic Shop

The little magic shop tucked away in an innocuous alley in downtown Cardiff was called Witchful Thinking. Megan had found the play on words endearing all those times she'd strolled past the quaint Edwardian storefront with its leaded window adorned in gold-leaf Celtic knots. Almost as charming were the eclectic clientele she'd spy stepping out from the dark mahogany door, arms laden with small bundles wrapped in beige linen paper and tied with string. It was like peeking into a past that never quite existed. Today, however, Megan found herself in the uncomfortable position of having business inside.

The smells hit her first: lavender oils and cinnamon sticks, burning sage and hints of Ylang Ylang that didn't so much assail Megan's senses as make her feel as if she were falling into someone else's dream.

"I can help you," said a tall, lanky chap behind the counter over the tinkling of brass bells and the shuffling feet of the customers crowding around displays of books and tarot cards and all manner of occult curiosities. The shopkeeper's dark brown hair hung down to just below his jaw, kept presentable by a navy blue poet's cap, tilted at a roguish angle. Megan reflexively wanted to straighten the cap. Rhys wouldn't have been caught dead taking out the rubbish bins looking half so dishevelled—never mind showing up at work in such a state.

And here I am again, she thought, *pining for a man in love with someone else.*

"Miss?" asked the young shopkeeper. "I asked if I could—"

"Actually, you didn't ask," Megan said, stepping past dangling vines of silver and gold charms hanging from the ceiling. "You said, 'I can help you.' Odd way to greet a potential customer, don't you think?"

The shopkeeper offered up a lopsided, self-deprecating grin that didn't quite mask a touch of overconfidence. "Ah, yes, but you see, I *can* help you." He stuck out a hand despite the two of them still being a good ten feet apart. "Dylan Morris, at your service." The smile widened. "Oh, and in case you're wondering, I'm neither a witch, a warlock, nor a pervert."

Charming as he appeared, Megan was in no mood to play the straight man to someone else's well-worn comedy routine. She was all set to deliver a clever and devastating retort when the entirely wrong words erupted from her. "I need to break a curse. Today. Now!"

Her outburst silenced the shop and drew the shocked gazes of the other customers.

"Curses are powerful dangerous words, missy," said a big, barrel-chested fellow in a checkered flannel shirt that would've made him look like a lumberjack were it not for the silver chain around his neck from which hung an assortment of pentagrams, Norse runes and Celtic triskelions. "Let's have no idle talk of curses."

Bloody hell, she thought. *Less than a minute in this shop and I already sound like...someone who spends her time in places like this.*

Megan Griffiths did not consider herself to be superstitious, New-Agey, or a believer in any sort of arcane voodoo-hoodoo witchery. Her physics lecturer father would've rolled over in his grave to hear that his rigorously logical daughter had stepped inside a magic shop. In point of fact, during the past two weeks of surreptitiously staking out the store these past two weeks, Megan had rehearsed a number of perfectly rational explanations of her current dilemma that didn't make her sound like a crackpot.

"My ex-boyfriend cast a love spell on me," she blurted out.

Nope, that wasn't it.

She could feel her face flush the particular shade of vermillion that used to annoy Rhys when they argued. The shopkeeper, Dylan, arched one dark eyebrow at her, though not, it seemed, in mockery. "Right," he began. "Let's get down to business. What else can you tell me about this obsession hex that's been cast upon you, Miss..."

"Griffiths," she replied. "Megan Griffiths. I'm an urban planner."

Dylan tapped a finger on the antique oak counter between them. "Is the hex related to your day job somehow?"

"I...no."

He nodded. "Then let's keep our eyes on the prize, shall we? What was the conveyance of this particular obsession hex."

"It's not a hex," Megan snapped. "It's a curse. Rhys has cast some sort of curse to force me to love him—*after* he dumped me!"

"What's this now?" asked the burly lumberjack with the blinding array of metal charms around his neck. "Some fool let go of a darlin' lass like you?" He waddled over to join them at the counter. "You want I should have a little chat with this fellow?"

"Thanks, but I'd rather rid myself of the curse. Besides, I can fight my own battles."

The big man grinned as he put up his hands in surrender and backed away. "Aye, I'll bet you can, love."

Megan turned back to Dylan. "Look, I've already wasted my time with therapists, counsellors, and an acupuncturist who stuck needles in places I'd rather not describe."

Dylan laughed for the first time. A nice laugh, Megan thought, made endearingly rakish by the way he then adjusted his navy blue poet's cap. "Right, so, at least we know you're well and truly desperate if you finally summoned up the nerve to come inside instead of pacing back and forth on the sidewalk these past two weeks." Before Megan could formulate a convincing denial, the young shopkeeper shifted gears, a frown pursing his lips. "Now, let's hear it. Why would your ex-boyfriend cast an obsession hex on a woman he was in the midst of leaving?"

"Revenge," Megan said stiffly. "Rhys is a manipulative, controlling, self-aggrandizing, arrogant son of a—" She cut herself off, taking a deep breath instead. Rhys always loved it when he got her so riled up she'd unleash a torrent of foul language, even if her shouting could be heard through the thick walls and high ceilings of his posh Cardiff townhouse. "Please," Megan whispered, "is there anything in this shop that can break the curse?"

Dylan tilted his head, nearly dislodging his cap. The way he watched her reminded her of a cat—specifically, *her* cat—who always looked as if he were confounded by the silly things humans did. Megan steeled herself, hating that she'd shown such vulnerability in front of a stranger. Rhys used to say it made her look like prey to most men.

Dylan, though, didn't make a pass at her or leer or even try to hold her gaze. Instead, he searched under the counter to retrieve what would no doubt turn out to be some exorbitant piece of carnival junk to sell her.

"Ah, here they are," he said, holding out a pair of ornate silver dice. "I wouldn't usually hand these over to an amateur, but this particular obsession hex sounds serious."

Megan stared at the dice resting on Dylan's palm. They were odd little things: instead of the usual assortment of pips from one to six, each side was adorned with an intricate esoteric symbol. "It's a love spell," she corrected him. "I'm not obsessed with Rhys; I'm really in love with him. More so than I ever was when we were together."

Dylan smiled again. The lopsided grin and light dusting of stubble on his cheeks and jaw suited him. Definitely a cat person. "Megan, lass, you've come to a shop you wouldn't normally be caught dead in, asking advice from a fella you clearly think spends his evenings contemplating which Star Trek captain was the greatest—It's Picard, by the way."

Megan could stop herself from laughing at the unexpected joke. Her father had been a Trekkie himself, and recreating scenes from his favorite episodes had been dinner-time theater in the Griffiths household. "I'm a Kirk ride-or-die girl, myself. But I didn't come here to trade Starfleet barbs. I need a—"

"There's no such thing as a love curse," Dylan said, placing the dice on her palm. His hand felt surprisingly warm on hers. "No one can magically induce love, only make you obsess over them. Consider it the Prime Directive of magic."

"It certainly feels like love," Megan said quietly, despair slithering its way inside her as she stared at the silly dice in her hand that were likely nothing more than a scam the shopkeeper ran on the gullible.

He closed her fingers over the dice. "Take these home with you, focus on this man you're obsessing over—Rhys?"

Megan nodded.

"Hold that anguish you're feeling inside you right now tightly as you roll the dice. Don't shy away from it, Megan. Accepting the pain is how you let it go." He held up three fingers. "Roll the dice three times. No more, no less."

"How much?" she asked, suspicious despite already opening her purse.

"No charge."

Now she was *really* suspicious. "Why?" She glanced around the crowded shop. The other customers turned away, trying unconvincingly to make it seem as if they hadn't been following every word of this absurd conversation.

"You can pay me once the hex is broken," Dylan replied.

"Won't the owner be upset when they find out you're giving out priceless magical artifacts to random strangers who think this is all gobbledygook?"

Dylan picked up a worn paperback book from behind the counter, slumped down on a stool and opened to a dog-eared page before giving her one last smile. "I'll see you tomorrow, Megan."

Chapter 2
The First Spell

Megan sat on the threadbare chesterfield of her new apartment—though referring to this ramshackle shoe box in the cheapest part of Cardiff, "new" seemed excessively optimistic. Having never before performed a magical ritual, she'd assembled what tools could be rummaged from the three-room walk-up's cupboards: two candles of dubious lineage, both synthetic and heavily perfumed, neither particularly magical; a cup of chamomile tea, and the closest thing she could find to a familiar.

"Stop glaring at me like that," she told the sour-faced short-hair tabby staring at her from his perch atop the coffee table that he was not, under any circumstances, permitted to sit on.

Fido kept right on staring at her, pausing only to dunk a paw into Megan's tea, lick it clean, and then dip in for seconds.

"I thought cats were supposed to be magical?" she said. "All you do is steal tea."

Fido meowed imperiously, then darted out the window in protest.

Megan held the dice clenched in her fist and thought about Rhys. *Here goes nothing*, she thought, feeling particularly stupid. She almost wished she'd never mistaken his credit card statement for her own. They used the same bank—which was how they'd met, in fact. Glancing through the statement, she'd at first thought she'd gotten ripped off by some online scam, only to learn that Rhys had not only bought a "love potion" from an online Wicca shop but tricked her into believing it had been a new sports drink.

A sports drink literally labelled "Love Potion."

God, when did I become so clueless?

The more Megan thought about Rhys, the angrier she became, but beneath all that rage was the love they'd shared for two years that now felt like a vacation from the real world. As much as Rhys could be a prick, he was also congenitally charming—not to mention the most beautiful man Megan had ever met, never mind dated. He was sometimes kind, often generous. The first to carry his elderly neighbor's groceries up the stairs, the last to leave his nephew's birthday party. When he surprised Megan with unexpected gifts—which he did often—they were neither flashy nor overtly expensive. Most men of his type contented themselves to fuss over the wine list to make sure their waiters were dazzled by their sophistication, but Rhys also had exquisite taste in flowers and could bake the hell out of a chocolate-chip cookie.

The perfect modern bloke.

Also, the absolute prick who had cast a love spell—no, an *obsession hex*, Dylan would've insisted—on the sobbing mess of a woman he'd shuffled out the door two hours earlier.

Megan shut her eyes and rolled the dice. She waited for a breath and then opened her eyes again to see that the dice had rolled up to the candles and stopped on two crescent moons. She thought about Rhys, but found it oddly hard to picture him. Perhaps the obsession was finally fading?

"Is that it?" she asked Fido as he crept back in through the open window. The cat yawned, making it clear he had nothing to offer on the subject of human love potions and, furthermore, it was past their bedtime. The furry little imp's yawn proved contagious. Bleary-eyed and exhausted from all this mystical mumbo jumbo, Megan followed the cat into the bedroom, hoping she was rid of the curse of Rhys Gallagher at last.

Chapter 3
Outbursts

"It didn't work!"

Megan hadn't meant to shout. In fact, her plan—well rehearsed on the way here—had been to simply deposit the useless silver dice on the oak counter, thank Mister Dylan Morris for having wasted her time, and depart his silly shop without another word. Instead, she'd caught one look at that crooked smile as she came through the door and lost her cool entirely.

"I mean it," she yelled, having given up on self-possession. The other customers stopped browsing for their trinkets and tarot cards to stare at her. "Don't fall for his nonsense," she warned them. "His stupid so-called 'spell' only made things worse!"

An elfin-faced teenager with swirly heart-shaped tattoos on her cheeks came up to Megan, placing a hand on her arm. "Made what worse, miss? Are you—"

"Never date anyone better looking than you," she advised the girl. "Also, beware of suspiciously named sports drinks."

The visions that had haunted her all night of Rhys and his new girlfriend, the unconscionably gorgeous Branwen Davies, returned even now. Every time they'd invaded her dreams, she'd woken in a cold sweat, reminded of Dylan's insistence that there was no such thing as a love spell.

"I'm more in love with Rhys than ever!" she declared.

Okay, that was the third time you've shouted since walking in here and everyone's staring at you. Get it together, will you?

Megan reached into her pocket for the distinctly un-magical dice and, with as much dignity as she could muster, hurled them at Dylan. To her surprise, he caught one in each hand, then bowed to his customers as they clapped at his—admittedly impressive—dexterity.

"Oh, that was tidy!" said the teenager with the heart tattoos appreciatively.

Dylan, however, grew serious, beckoning Megan to the counter. "I've a bit of a confession to make," he said in a low voice.

Megan felt the fingers of her right hand squeezing into a fist. She'd never hit anyone in her adult life—a trend the cavalier shopkeeper was coming precariously close to breaking. "Go on."

"I'll admit, Megan, there was a fair chance the dice would fail from the get-go." He must've sensed how irate she was becoming, because he went on without giving her a chance to properly express her displeasure. "Amateur stuff, really. I mean, not entirely, but certainly not up to par for your degree of obsession."

"I told you, I"m not obsessed. This is lo—"

"What this hex really calls for is a Bangolesh."

He'd spoken so quietly, Megan thought perhaps she hadn't heard him properly. "A Bango-what now?"

"A Bangolesh," he repeated, then pulled a key from a slender necklace beneath his tan cardigan and unlocked a drawer beneath the counter. A moment later, he produced a hexagonal cymbal and what appeared to be an ornately carved little drumstick. "*This* is a Bangolesh—or the means to call one, at any rate. They're a type of wilderness spirit that roams the hillsides, or sometimes the ghost of a person who was jilted by a lover long, long ago. A Bangolesh is trapped by their own sense of loss."

"That sounds awful."

"Ah," Dylan said, wagging a finger, "that's the rub, though: a Bangolesh feeds on obsession. Summon one to you tonight, and the nasty little fae will slurp up all those obsessive feelings that have been troubling you."

Despite her earlier fury, Megan found herself smiling at the fox-faced shopkeeper's earnest delivery. "Let me guess, results guaranteed or my money back?"

He leaned across the counter, placing a hand on her arm. "Make no mistake, Megan, this is dangerous magic. For the Bangolesh to work, you'll need to be close to the source of your obsessions. Preferably at night, outside his window."

"Oh sweet Jesus," Megan said, but took the cymbal anyway.

"Wait!" Dylan called out before she'd gone two feet out the front door. The sun was blinding this morning, and she couldn't see what he was slipping into the front pocket of her blazer until it was too late.

"What's this?" she asked, taking out the rose-like bloom and holding it between thumb and forefinger as if it might bite her.

"A wee charm that's even more magical than a Bangolesh," Dylan said, nodding thoughtfully. "It's called a flower."

"What does it do?"

The cheeky bugger leaned over and kissed her cheek. "It's meant to remind you that it's a beautiful day, you're a beautiful lass, and life itself, in case you've forgotten, is beautiful too."

Chapter 4
The Bangolesh

Life is beautiful, Megan reminded herself as she knelt uncomfortably between the garbage bins outside the ground floor of Rhys's townhouse. The concrete was killing her knees, the smell was making her nauseous, and at this very moment she was watching her ex-boyfriend, with whom she was utterly, inescapably in love, engaged in passionate sex with a woman whose body made Megan—who used to be quite pleased with her own looks—feel like a frumpy old spinster.

To make matters worse, Fido, her tea-stealing cat, pining for his old stomping grounds, had decided to accompany her. Megan had tried to explain that Fido was not, in fact, allowed to run back into their old apartment, which was why the cat was now doing his level best to claw his way free of her grip while swishing his tail in her face.

"I hate you, Dylan Morris," she muttered, using her free hand to keep tapping the tiny drumstick against the cymbal that had, thus far, failed to produce a fae spirit. The discordant chime *had*, however, brought Rhys—naked and flawless—to the window several times in search of the source of the noise. Megan had been forced to clamp a hand over Fido's mouth to keep him yowling for rescue.

You drink one cursed love potion disguised as a sports drink and your life is wrecked forever.

"The good news is," she whispered to the cat as she resumed her banging of the cymbal, "now he and Branwen are *really* going at it, so I doubt they'll notice the lunatic ex-girlfriend crouching behind rubbish bins trying to summon a demon."

Between taps, she itemized her reasons for now hating Dylan even more than her ex. "The stupid poet's hat. The lack of a proper haircut. That smirk you seem to think passes for a charming grin. Oh, and let's not forget your idiotic, unfounded optimism."

"It's a beautiful day, you're a beautiful lass, and life itself, in case you've forgotten, is beautiful too."

Had he meant any part of it? Probably not. Hard to call a girl beautiful when she's constantly taking her problems out on you. Fido, having apparently had enough of her nonsense, wriggled free and fled behind the bins. Having now failed to even keep hold of her disobedient cat, Megan gave the cymbal one last good bang, adding, "And Picard was a terrible starship captain. There, I said it!"

Oddly, despite no Bangolesh appearing to devour her obsession and now faced with searching for her errant tabby, Megan felt better than she had in weeks. *Maybe there's something to Dylan's daft magic after all—*

"Something wrong, miss?" asked a voice behind her.

Megan nearly jumped out of her skin. She swallowed and turned to find a tall middle-aged man with short-cropped graying hair and a no-nonsense mustache frowning down at her, one hand wavering over the black leather pouch at the right side of his belt holding what she was quite certain was a collapsible baton.

"Umm...lovely evening, constable?" she stammered.

She was hiding behind her ex's home, practically going through his garbage holding a strange gong-like cymbal. Megan had never been more mortified in her entire life. She was a stalker. She was going to jail. What would her parents think? Her boss?

Dear God, what will Rhys think?

In a stroke of undeserved luck, Fido chose that moment to return. Prowling behind the officer, the irate tabby let out an indignant meow. Megan, silently thanking whichever deity had deigned to rescue her, collected Fido in her arms. "There you are, Fifi!"—the cat *hated* being called that—"I've been looking for you for hours," she added for the officer's benefit. "The cymbal means dinner time. We used to live here. Silly thing keeps coming back." Megan glanced up at the window, where both she and the constable could hear voices. "Please don't say anything. I think they'd be mortified," she said, cradling her cat.

Chapter 5
Pity

"And he just let you go?" Dylan asked, passing Megan a cup of hot cocoa across the oak counter. "That's incredible!" He patted Fido – the little traitor – who was nestled happily next to the register having once again foiled her attempts to lock him in the apartment. "Cats do have a reputation for being magical guardians, but I never dreamed—"

Mindful of the crowded store, this being a Saturday morning, Megan kept her voice quiet. "The police officer *took pity* on me, Dylan. He figured out right quick that I was lying about looking for my cat and got me to confess to my very obvious crime right there in the alley. When I was done blubbering, he said, "Ach, you'd make the boozers in the drunk tank cry, sorry and sad as you are." Megan thrust a finger at Dylan's chest. "*That's* what your stupid Bangolesh spell got me. Worse, I still can't stop myself thinking about Rhys and Branwen!" The way the two of them moved together through the window, the mixture of raw passion and adoration between them was...haunting. The worst part of it was that Megan couldn't help but wonder if maybe she'd imagined all this: the cruel and utterly out of character "love potion" thing, the so-called "curse." Maybe Rhys had just been a once-in-a-lifetime boyfriend with whom she'd screwed things up and he'd gone and fallen in love with someone better.

"What?" she asked Dylan sulkily when she saw him watching her. She wished he'd at least had the decency to mock her latest embarrassing escapade. Instead, he looked...troubled.

"This is a deep obsession hex you're under," he said. "No use denying it, lass. You're in some trouble here."

Hearing him say it made the truth of those words come home to her. "What am I going to do, Dylan?" She buried her nose in the comforting scent of the cocoa. It wasn't until the two of them had gone an entire minute without saying anything that she looked up to find him watching her thoughtfully.

"Are you waiting to see if I'll start yelling again?" she asked. "Or perhaps fall into an inconsolable weeping mess on your magic-shop floor?" She forced a smile to her lips. "Don't mind me. I'm a mess. None of this is your fault. Ever since the first day I came in here, you've been nothing bu—"

"It's time to bring out the big guns," he said abruptly.

"Sure, why not?" Megan asked, masking her unexpected disappointment that he'd cut her off before she could finally say one nice thing to him with what she was uncomfortably aware sounded like near-hysterical laughter. "Guns! Great idea! Conjure me up a mystical M-16. Only, this being Wales, I'm not sure my forgiving constable from last night will let me off with a warning next time."

"Ah, but see, this particular weapon comes from the future," Dylan said glibly before kneeling down beneath the counter. When he didn't come up again, Megan leaned over and saw he was on all fours, prying up the floorboard.

"What are you doing?"

"Magic this potent can't be left to just bars on the windows or even the store safe."

With a creak, the floorboard gave way. Dylan reached down into the gap beneath and took out something that he quickly hid in the palm of his hand before standing back up. Gazing out at the gaggle of customers conspicuously glancing over, he said, "Out, everybody. We're closing early." He waited until the bell on the door stopped tinkling, signalling the last of the disappointed stragglers had gone. Only after he'd locked up the store door did he open his hand to show Megan what was so secret and dangerous he couldn't trust it to an actual safe. "Take it," he said with far more solemnity than she would've thought possible. "The magic you need is here."

Megan stared down at the familiar triangular-shaped pin—a *delta*, her father would've corrected her. She looked back up into Dylan's sea-green eyes and said, "You have *got* to be kidding me."

Chapter 6
Twixt Love and Obsession

MEGAN SAW Rhys sitting outside at Le Chat Noir cafe not far from where the two of them used to live. He was impossible to miss with his thick mane of blond hair perfectly parted, every strand held in place thanks to his meticulous grooming habits and exorbitant budget for styling products. He didn't look up from his coffee until she had pulled the white metal chair out, the feet scraping loudly across the pavement.

His smile looked unexpectedly genuine as she took her seat. "It's good to see you, Megan. Getting on okay?"

Without warning, she found herself snared by those high cheekbones, that firm jaw and those lips—*damn, those lips!* Most of all, though, it was the way Rhys looked at her, as if she were the only other person in the universe, bathing her in the warm glow of his undivided attention.

Funny though, that this time, even as his smile remained perfectly intact, those blue, almost violet eyes just as intense and inviting, Megan couldn't feel the old, familiar heat between them.

The actual sun was out, however, and the late afternoon glare reflected off the pin on Megan's blouse, distracting her. That pin: Dylan's ridiculous Star Trek emblem. Discreetly, she folded the lapel of her light summer jacket over the pin.

Apparently he hadn't noticed, because his smile only intensified. "You're looking well, Megs!" he said. She could tell he was giving her a more than cursory once-over, though unlike all those nights when the two of them had been getting ready to go out to some posh event, he seemed less critical than she remembered. She would've expected this unabashed appreciation from the most critical boyfriend she'd ever had to fill her with pride or pleasure, make her feel special. Today, though, it had the opposite effect.

"You finally joined a gym like I always said you should, didn't you?" Rhys didn't wait for affirmation. If there was one area in which he had no doubts about his own brilliance, it was in prescribing the next step on someone else's journey to perfection – to being a little closer to Rhys himself. "Oh, and thanks for this," he added brightly, patting the cardboard box Megan handed to him. "I really appreciate you coming out all this way just to bring me these."

When Megan had called him suggesting they meet, it had been under the guise of returning a few of the things that had "accidentally" made their way into her moving boxes. Mostly, these consisted of sports trophies, singles from three different sets from his cufflink collection and, perhaps most egregious of all, his made-to-order two-thousand-dollar Vita Brillante olive wood hairbrush with rare recut boar bristles.

Boar bristles.

Megan would swear the brush had given her dandruff.

What was odd now, though, was that she'd come fully expecting Rhys to chastise her for lugging an unsightly cardboard box into Cardiff's finest French bistro. Yet, embarrassment seemed to be the furthest thing from his mind as he casually perused the contents of the box with not so much as a whiff of dismay over Megan having so obviously split up his favorite cufflink sets—to say nothing of the hairbrush.

Was it me all along, bringing out the worst in Rhys all along? Megan wondered, despairing as her long-held conviction that she was the injured party in their relationship seemed to fade so quickly. *Or is it simply that Branwen has a magic that brings out his best?*

"So, how're things with the new girl?" Megan blurted out, wincing at how terrible that sounded. "Branwen, I mean," she added lamely.

Megan steeled herself for the inevitable, devastatingly disapproving eye-roll followed by the knowing accusation that she was fishing for flaws in his new relationship to console herself for being alone.

"Good, fine," he said, seeming to almost dismiss his love life as his gaze, his entire being, seemed focused on Megan. "I really appreciate how big you're being after everything that happened between us," he said, his instinctive, unaffected charm on overdrive. His wry smile was almost bashful. "Am I a fool to hope we can put the past behind us and stay good friends?"

You lying sack of dirt! Megan thought as she struggled to resist Rhys's apparent sincerity. She schooled her expression as she fought to stay here, in the present, and not get sucked into the vortex of anger and self-hatred she'd been caught in since the break-up. *You cheated on me for weeks—practically convinced me I was the one who drove you to it after you were caught out. You've ghosted me ever since, and as if that wasn't enough, you tricked me into drinking a bloody love potion so I'd never—*

Megan gripped the edge of the table with her hands, shoving the rage back down, reminding herself of Dylan's instructions before he'd shooed her out the door of the magic shop yesterday: in order to break the obsession spell she had to let herself fall in love with Rhys all over again.

"Obsession is the lock on your heart, lass, love is the key," the gangly rogue had repeated to her again and again, the cliché somehow rendered sincere when spoken in that slow, patient, long-on-the-vowels Valley accent of his. *"You loved the fella once. Let yourself love him again, truly. That way, there won't be any room for obsession."*

Had Dylan been trying to get Megan to reunite with her ex? Had he seen so many jilted lovers come into his magic shop in search of a love potion of their own that he'd learned to see beyond the pain and resentment to what remained underneath—something shared yet unspoken by the object of that obsession?

The theory sounded almost plausible, but then Megan remembered Dylan pressing that ridiculous Star Trek pin into her palm—the same one she now found her fingers reaching for beneath the lapel of her jacket.

"But Rhys is in love with someone else now!" she'd insisted. *"You're telling me to open my heart all over again to someone who won't love me back!"*

Dylan's reply had been so certain, so strangely sad, that it had convinced her to go ahead with this mad plan of his. *"Unrequited love is still love, Megan, maybe the truest love of all. Sometimes it builds over years and years; sometimes it comes on sudden and unexpected as a summer downpour. But none of us can avoid the rain forever, and in the end, any kind of love is better than obsession."*

"Is that what Captain Picard would say?" she'd asked.

He'd given her a kiss on the cheek, and this time she'd noticed him slipping another flower into her pocket. *"It's what Captain Dylan Morris says,"* he said before adding with a grin, *"Now, engage, Number One. Engage."*

Taken aback by his patience, his kindness, and, perhaps most of all, his utter willingness to appear silly in front of her, Megan had taken the Star Trek pin, called Rhys the next day to meet, and followed every one of Dylan's instructions to the letter.

So why now, sitting across from the man she'd desired so much these last months she could still feel the ache in her stomach, opening herself up at last to admitting how much she wanted him, were her feelings so muted, so lacking?

Rhys reached out and placed his hand over Megan's—the one still clutching that ridiculous pin. "Look at us, Megs," he said, a fondness bordering on awe gleaming in his almost dewy-eyed gaze. "Meeting here like friends. We could make this a regular thing." His fingers squeezed hers, making the edge of the pin dig into her palm. "I was just thinking the other day how much I missed the old you."

"The old me?" she asked.

He nodded, enthusiasm breaking through his usual buttoned-up self-control. "The happy, confident girl who barely noticed all the men looking at her when she walked by. I missed that girl, Megs, and now, here she is, sitting across from me."

It was so strange, Megan almost felt as if she'd slipped into someone else's dream. Months ago, weeks ago—hell, *yesterday—* those words would have been the magic incantation that would've unleashed a torrent of tears, laughter and kisses. Why wasn't she feeling that now, though? Why did Rhys's compliments sound stale in her ears? Why, as his hand took hers, placing it between both of his, did that familiar warmth leave her so cold?

Was this how she'd made Rhys feel when she'd reached for him during those awful, inexplicably anxious weeks when he'd already begun seeing Branwen in secret?

What's wrong with me? she asked herself. *You've wanted him since the day you first met him, even after he took up with Branwen. Now, when he's finally reciprocating those feelings, you're suddenly repulsed by him?*

Like all Dylan's previous, preposterous spells, this one was definitely not going according to plan.

Unless somehow that damned love potion Rhys slipped me is countering it. Maybe there's a mystical failsafe that's now confounding the spell Dylan gave me?

She took her hand away from him and reached for the pin under her lapel again, closing her eyes even though she knew she probably looked like a lunatic. *Remember how much you liked Rhys's hair—women kill to get their hair that perfect*, she thought, then tapped the pin as per Dylan's instructions.

The "spell"—if such a preposterous ritual even qualified—involved remembering each aspect of what had drawn her to Rhys and then tapping the pin, almost as if she were calling the *Enterprise* to beam her up. The problem was, it wasn't working, and she only had until the end of their coffee date to convince herself to love Rhys again.

"What are you doing? Is that some sort of flying insect?" he asked, leaning back in his chair. His gaze darted from her to the table to even his own chair. His hands came up to ever-so-carefully pass over his hair. "You know how much I hate bugs. It's like they're magnetically drawn to my hair products."

"What? I'm not—"

She froze, seeing her own outstretched arm, fingers aching to play with Rhys's perfect hair.

No, she realized with a start. *Not playing with his hair. Mussing it. I'd been about to muss Rhys's hair. Why would I do that? I used to love how flawless he kept it, how every strand was perfectly in place.*

Rhys saved her by moving to a less fraught topic. "How is Fido holding up?" he asked, biting into his breadstick, chewing carefully and swallowing before continuing. "I'll bet he misses me a ton."

There, she thought. *That's one of the things I always loved about him!*

Rhys had tolerated Fido's presence in their lives with a stoicism that bordered on the heroic, given that he hated cats so much his one requirement for keeping the pesky beast had been that they name him "Fido" on principle.

Megan tapped the pin and summoned up memories of Rhys, sitting on the couch trying to read over work documents, allowing the unruly tabby to sleep on his lap. Now that she thought about it, it was Fido who never seemed all that happy with the arrangement, not like the other day when he'd curled up in a distinctly proprietary fashion on the counter at Witchful Thinking. She cracked a smile at the memory of Dylan nodding thoughtfully each time Fido had mewled or groaned to let them know how comfy he was, as if man and cat had been engaged in a deep philosophical discussion.

The spell, Megan reminded herself. *Even Rhys isn't going to keep being this polite forever. Why can't I keep focusing on the things I love about him?*

"Megs?" he asked.

"Hmm?"

"I said, any chance you took it?"

"Took what?"

For the first time since they'd sat down outside the bistro, Rhys looked irritated, and Megan realized she'd been so lost in thought about Dylan with his floppy hair and the silly way her cat made itself at home around him that she'd completely lost track of the conversation. Her hand had let go of the pin and was now reaching inside her pocket for the flower Dylan had given her yesterday, but she'd binned it on the way here, not wanting to distract herself from the mission at hand.

"The sports drinks I mentioned?" Rhys repeated. "I'd ordered them from a specialist shop who formulated them for Branwen specifically." He held up one of the cufflinks she'd returned to him earlier, grinning wryly. "I wondered if you might've packed one up by accident before you left the apartment?"

"No, I—" Even before the lie had passed her lips, a sinking feeling in Megan's stomach caught her off guard. *It was never for me! That's why the custom name on the label had read "Love Potion"—it had been meant for Branwen all along!*

A sudden pit opened up in her stomach as all the tiny details about the love spell—the *curse*—she'd been convinced Rhys had somehow put on her revealed a truth about Rhys that left her reeling in confusion. Why would the most handsome, charming, confident person she'd ever met feel the need to use a love potion on a woman who was already involved in an illicit affair with him? The same woman whose texts were so effusive over her excitement about the two of them being together properly once he'd broken things off with Megan?

For the same reason he's suddenly so infatuated with you now that you're no longer obsessed with him, she realized.

Rhys Gallagher had been masquerading as the man of every woman's dreams for so long he'd blinded every one of them—including Megan—to his own insecurities. That was why he worked so hard to appear perfect—so flawless on the outside no one would ever pay attention to the subtle signals of his sense of inadequacy.

Confident people don't need constant validation, she thought, thinking of someone else entirely for a moment. *They're kind and decent. They want you to feel special, not trick you into feeling so desperate for their approval that you wish you were someone else entirely. They go out of their way to help you, even when you're acting like a pathetic, lovelorn fool. And when they'd have every right to shout at you and make you see how badly you're behaving on the worst day of your life, they try to build you up. They slip flowers in your pocket and tell you that you're beautiful.*

Rhys was pointing to her pin, the sudden change in his expression, the smile turning to a smirk, was the same one that would've shattered her confidence only weeks ago. "Someone get you to wear that bit of kitsch on a dare?" he asked. "All that Star

Wars stuff is for odd ducks living in their mother's basements, isn't it?"

Megan removed the pin from her blouse, ready at last to perform the last step of the spell.

"Once you've fallen back in love, snap the pin in half," Dylan had instructed her.

Holding the gold-painted plastic emblem between the thumb and forefinger of each hand, Megan found herself holding back a chuckle at how flimsy it now felt, and how all that supposed mystical power Dylan had implied was imbued within was nothing more than a playful kindness shared between a silly shopkeeper and an even sillier girl who, it turned out, had badly needed just that sort of silliness to free her from a self-imposed curse. One good twist, and the pin would snap, and with it—if Dylan was to be believed—the emotional shackles binding her to Rhys.

Megan stood up from her chair, smiling politely at her handsome, dashing ex-boyfriend. "So good of you to come out for coffee, Rhys," she told him, sliding the unbroken pin into the pocket of her coat. "I'm really happy for you and Branwen."

Rhys stood up with a jolt. "But...you're leaving already? We've only been here for—" he glanced at his wristwatch – the Vacheron Constantin Traditionnelle he'd bought himself for his last birthday. "I suppose we've been here for almost half an hour, but still, do you have to run off so abruptly?"

She smiled. "Can't waste a day this lovely lingering outside a creaky old French Bistro, Rhys." She turned towards the restaurant's exterior windows, saw the almost perfect image of a lovely table, a bottle of unopened wine, and a young woman on the verge of something wonderful. Only one thing was missing from the picture.

"Megs?" Rhys asked, sounding at once anxious and irritated. "You're being awfully mysterious. I thought we were having a moment, something..." He tried that enchanting smile of his on her one last time. "I know it sounds silly, but it felt magical."

Megan flashed him a grin before stepping off the sidewalk and across the street to wait for the next bus. "Oh, there's nothing magical about love, Rhys. It's as common as rain once you stop hiding from it!"

Chapter 7
Witchful Thinking

The golden Star Trek pin wobbled on the oak counter separating Megan from Dylan. He looked down at it, staring in silence until at last the pin settled into a mournful solitude. "The spell didn't work?"

Without answering, Megan walked behind the counter and gave Dylan a gentle shove out of the way. He looked at her in confusion, but still, she gave no sign as to her intentions. Instead, she knelt down and pulled up the board beneath which he kept those magical items so precious and dangerous he couldn't trust them even to the store safe. "Pass me the pin, will you?"

"But you're supposed to break it," he insisted. "That's the most important part of the spell!"

"The pin, if you please?"

Reluctantly, he handed it to her, and she set it down carefully on a small purplish cushion in the gap beneath the floorboard. "The important part of the spell was breaking my obsession with Rhys. Obsession isn't love, isn't that what you always say?"

"Yes, but you have to break the pin to complete the spell, so that you can be in love without being *bound* by that love."

Megan was about to put the board back in place, but thought better of it, deciding instead to grab Dylan's wrist and tug him down so they were both kneeling over the little cache and out of view of the store's other customers.

"This magic stuff is all nonsense, isn't it?" she asked, conspiratorially.

For the first time since she'd met him, Dylan looked shy, almost uncertain about how to answer, but then caught her gaze, and said, "There's magic all around us, Megan. It's just not spirits and bogeymen who make it work. It's us."

She nodded, and reached down to touch the surface of the plastic pin. "This really means something to you, doesn't it?"

He was quiet at first, and when she looked up, she saw a dewy softness in his eyes as if he were on the verge of tears. "Aye. It belonged to my mother. She was a true believer."

"In magic?"

He smiled wryly. "In Star Trek. She said it wasn't about spaceships and photon torpedoes. It was about people believing in one another."

Megan's fingertips felt a tingle from the golden pin. "So you gave me this pin, this...talisman, because you knew it meant so much to you, and I'd somehow pick up on that, and that would, in turn, give it potency?"

"Um, hello?" one of the customers asked, thumping on the counter. "Is anyone providing customer service today?"

Dylan ignored them. "I guess it failed, though, because when the time came, you didn't break it." He sighed. "But if falling in love with Rhys again has freed you from your obsession with him, then I wish you the best, Megan, I really do."

"Oh, the spell didn't make me fall in love with Rhys," she said, then she said something else, which he didn't seem to hear because of all the customers demanding service, banging on the counter and now ringing the small bell as well.

"What's that?" he asked.

"I said...oh, the hell with it."

She stood up, taking Dylan's arm and pulling him up with her. "You people want to see some magic?" she asked loudly.

The customers milling around the counter didn't seem pleased or inclined to answer, choosing instead to shake various items from the shop in front of Dylan, one even demanding a discount given how long they'd been forced to wait.

"How about you?" Megan asked him, more quietly. "Would you like to see a magic trick?"

His eyes narrowed. "What kind?"

She gave a wave of her hand. "I can make all these people disappear."

Dylan gave a nervous glance at the irate crowd. "Actually, that's a spell I wouldn't mind seeing right about now."

"Good," Megan said, lifting her chin and intoning, "And now, alakazam, kalamazoo, by the mystic forces of Welsh damsels do I hereby..."

The whole store had gone silent in anticipation of this grand spell, which made Megan want to giggle. She hadn't wanted to giggle in a very long time.

"Well?" Dylan asked. "I'm not seeing any—"

She shut him up with a kiss, the first of many, she decided, as her lips pressed into his and her fingers slid into the unruly locks of dark hair, causing his hat to fall to the floor. Impromptu cheers rose up from the gaggle of customers, who, it seemed, were getting over their desperate need for tarot cards, mystical incense and other assorted trinkets.

When at last she and Dylan pulled away, breathless, he observed drily, "Your spell didn't seem to quite work, lass." His arm swept out to gesture to the customers who were still standing there, cheering them on.

Megan grinned. "If there's one thing I've learned about magic, it's that it takes a great deal of practice. So get over here, Dylan," she said, pulling him to her. "Because this is a spell I want to get just right."

She kissed him again and, true to her word, the customers disappeared from the shop. That it took rather a great many kisses and several hours, well, that was just part of the spell.

About the Authors

Kristi Charish

Kristi writes a lot of things – urban fantasy, science fiction, and even cozy procedural mysteries. Her work and characters are inspired by current headlines, pop culture, irreverent comedy, and two inappropriate cats. A self-described recovering fly geneticist, she gratuitously – and often unnecessarily – peppers her writing with science details she acquired during a misspent youth in research labs. When Kristi isn't writing you can find her on her laptop making medical science comprehensible for entertainment media or working on various writing projects. If you look really closely at your TV screen, you might even spot her playing background on a favorite show.

Sebastien de Castell

Sebastien de Castell had just finished a degree in Archaeology when he started work on his first dig. Four hours later he realized how much he actually hated archaeology and left to pursue a very focused career as a musician, ombudsman, interaction designer, fight choreographer, teacher, project manager, actor, and product strategist. His only defence against the charge of unbridled dilettantism is that he genuinely likes doing these things and that, in one way or another, each of these fields plays a role in his writing. He sternly resists the accusation of being a Renaissance Man in the hopes that more people will label him that way.

Sebastien's acclaimed swashbuckling fantasy series, The Greatcoats was shortlisted for both the 2014 Goodreads Choice Award for Best Fantasy, the Gemmell Morningstar Award for Best Debut, the Prix Imaginales for Best Foreign Work, and the John W. Campbell Award for Best New Writer. His YA fantasy series, Spellslinger, was nominated for the Carnegie Medal and has been translated into more than a dozen languages around the world.

Sebastien lives in Vancouver, Canada with his lovely wife and two belligerent cats. You can reach him at decastell.com

THE BOTANIST AND THE MEDICINE WOMAN

CMARIE FUHRMAN

The botanist stared at the two men before her, disbelief fighting with rising panic. One was a ghost, a dead husband brought back to life. The other, her current husband, the living man who shared her bed and her life, shifted impatiently in front of her, his confusion growing with every silent second.

A wave of exhaustion washed over her. She'd been driving for hours, the road a blur of fatigue and doubt. She'd humored the medicine woman, following the instructions with a detached curiosity. But deep down, she'd dismissed it as folklore, a quaint tradition with no real power. Now, faced with the impossible, the line between science and ancient wisdom blurred. She adjusted her mother's turquoise bracelet on her wrist, a familiar comfort, a habit when she was anxious. The braids in her hair, a last vestige perhaps, a symbol of her heritage and a link to the generations of women who had walked this land before her, felt heavy with the weight of the moment. She was a botanist, a woman of reason, yet here she stood, caught between a ghost from her past who seemed very undead, and the alive man she had said goodbye to this morning.

The dead man's eyes, startling blue as a summer sky, widened with a youthful excitement she hadn't seen for decades. A grin spread across his face, and he tried to take a step towards her, as if unable to contain his joy. It was the same look he'd given her on their first date, a blind date that had blossomed into a love cut tragically short. More than thirty years had passed, but he remained frozen in time, the strong, handsome 34-year-old she last saw fishing on the edge of a bright summer river. He hadn't aged a day, while she...

She self-consciously tugged at her coat, pulling it away from her stomach, suddenly aware of every line the years had etched on her face, every curve softened by time. She couldn't help it, she looked away, the intensity of his youthful face a stark contrast to the weary familiarity in her living husband's eyes. The scent of pine needles and damp earth filled the air, a familiar smell that transported her back to that summer day by the river, the day her world shifted and she seemed to slide off. He'd dropped his pole, slipped into the current trying to rescue it and was swallowed by rushing spring runoff. Everything she had felt since that moment, the panic, the despair, the crushing weight of grief, resurfaced now, and she choked back the rise of emotion that threatened to take her own breath.

The botanist looked up at him, suddenly defiant. The days after his death were some of the worst of her life. He had left without a will, left without a thought about what his leaving would mean. He died and not only left her the huge house payment to make on her own but a family that refused to believe that he ever loved her. He left her debt. And worse, alone. Sixty miles from town, in a house they built for solitude, away from the crowds that swarmed the shores of every Montana river, she was utterly alone. Alone, in debt, young, and heartbroken. The scent of river water clung to him, a horrible reminder of the day he was pulled from the current, lifeless and cold. She had thrown their good china at the walls, cursed him, blamed him for his accidental death. For not being more careful, for flippantly saying that he probably wouldn't live to be thirty-five. Had he known? Had he sensed that he wouldn't reach thirty-five? Or had he simply been reckless, a boy playing a dangerous game? Her shoulders stiffened, she balled her hands into fists, her nails digging into damp palms.

But she hadn't grown old alone. The botanist looked over at the very alive man, her husband of twenty years. They'd met on the edge of forty, both wary, both with baggage. She'd watched his Grecian-sculpted body age gracefully. He was still fit, they both were, but fitness couldn't fix what age broke. The collagen had loosened its grip, the tightness of skin around smiles and biceps yielding to gravity. His six-pack had become four, then two, a soft roundness forming, and she remembered what it felt like to touch both versions, the smooth firmness of youth and the comfortable softness of age. His hair, once a bright, almost actor-blond, was now a mix of silver and gray, each strand a story she knew intimately. She'd brushed it, cut it, stroked it, memorized its every swirl and pattern during the two decades they'd shared in their small cabin in the woods.

The living husband stood awkwardly now, his big hands fidgeting in his pockets, his gaze darting between her and the resurrected stranger. It was as if he'd been thrust onto a bizarre game show, the prize being her love, the stakes impossibly high. Some sick, twisted, perhaps beautiful variety of the dating game, orchestrated by a medicine woman with a penchant for the dramatic.

She choked back a gasp, remembering the fight they'd had that morning. She told him she was going to the medicine woman's house—something about needing herbs for her research. He'd never questioned her, his trust always steady, but asked instead when she was coming home. Now she sat in the older woman's living room, wondering. Will she pick the dead husband or living husband? She couldn't help but smile at the scene, it was absurd and beautiful. The smile lit up her living husband's face, bringing a flicker of hope to his uncertain eyes. But then she turned back to her first love, the smile not leaving her lips.

The scent of woodsmoke on his worn wool coat filled the truck as they drove home from his parents' house that night. It was a scent she had ever since associated with romance, with him. A song played on the radio, something country. She couldn't quite recall the tune, but every other detail was etched in her memory: his old gray Dodge, the burn mark on the console where an installer had carelessly laid down a soldering tool, leaving a melted "j" on the fake leather. She traced the outline of the "j" with her fingertip, a scar that held a universe of memories. The money the installer paid to replace the lid was spent lavishly. A dinner in town, a night in a hotel. The dogs were in the backseat, of course. They were always in the back seat.

It was fall, a warm enough night, and he suddenly pulled over. He got out, came around to the passenger side, opened the door, and extended his hand. "Dance with me," he whispered, sending a herd of tingles through her legs. And she did. Radio up, swaying in the headlights of his long-gone Dodge pickup. When the song ended, he looked at her with such intention, so much desire that it took her breath away. Right there on that dirt road, under the gleaming Milky Way, with dogs as their witness, he offered her the entire universe. And she accepted it.

And then he died. The moon, the sky, the stars he'd given her —they remained, but the years dimmed their brilliance. Light pollution, a move to another state, the weight of grief itself had obscured their light. Now, when she gazed up at the night sky, she felt tethered to the earth, to the present moment. She worried about her living husband, imagined the questions swirling in his mind as he faced the impossible: her first love, resurrected and undeniably real. Did the dead have some awareness of the living? Was her first love sizing up his replacement, offering a handshake of gratitude or a challenge? *Thanks, I've got it from here.* Or would he step back, concede, and hope the best man wins?

The botanist admitted it: a low point in her marriage had driven her to the medicine woman's door. Twenty years with her living husband had worn away the romance, just as it had eroded her looks. Or maybe it was the other way around. Lately, she'd become fixated on this idea, this certainty that she was invisible. Not just to her husband, but to the world. She remembered a time when she'd turned heads, when her presence straightened spines in every room she entered. Now, she moved through the world unnoticed, untouched. She missed that feeling, the raw, almost animal-like desire that had filled her younger years. The hunger in someone else's eyes, the first kisses that left her breathless and hungry, the way her body had been both a source of pleasure and a weapon. More than youth, more than the firm muscles of her younger body, she missed being wanted. And she blamed her husband for this fading, for the neglect that had turned her into a ghost. That's why she'd convinced herself to come to the medicine woman, a wish she held in the back of her mouth, a desperate hope for a second chance.

It wasn't that it hadn't been a good twenty years. She'd stayed with him, hadn't she? But somewhere along the way, the spark had faded. He never told her she was pretty anymore. He didn't reach for her under the covers, didn't kiss her face when he came home from work, just a peck on the top of her head. He'd become blind to her, or maybe she'd become blind to herself. Like a neglected house, she felt worn and unloved, the bright colors of her spirit fading into the background. It was his fault, she was certain, that no heads turned anymore. That once, in a moment of reckless rebellion, she'd confessed a crush on another man, only to be met with rejection. The shame of that moment, the confirmation of her invisibility, had driven her to the medicine woman's door, seeking a remedy, a way to reclaim the woman she used to be. The one she was meant to be.

When the botanist knocked, the door opened to reveal a woman ten years older than herself, but still as strong as she remembered her. The woman's face was etched with the wisdom of a life lived deeply. This was the medicine woman, her presence radiating a quiet strength that both intimidated and comforted the younger woman. The botanist stepped across the threshold, carrying her shame, her fear, her sixty-year-old body, and the stubborn conviction that her living husband had somehow diminished her, aged her, rendered her invisible. Invisible, but not to the medicine woman, whose eyes seemed not only to embrace her but to see right into her.

The botanist had almost bolted when the older woman led her to the living room and gestured towards a worn, floral-print couch. It felt too similar to an appointment with her therapist, a cost and need she blamed on her dead husband and the fear of abandonment that was her own diagnosis. The medicine woman settled into the armchair opposite her, pushed a cup of tea across the coffee table, her gaze steady and, the woman thought, perhaps a bit judgmental.

"Why have you come back?" she asked, her voice gentle but firm. The question hung in the air, forcing her to confront the truth. It wasn't just about a serum or a magic plant-derived cream to erase the years. It was deeper than that.

"I want to feel alive again," she confessed, the words rushing out before she could stop them. "I want to feel desired, seen, wanted..." The medicine woman listened patiently, a knowing smile playing on her lips, as she described the emptiness, the longing for those first kisses, the yearning for a touch that ignited something within her. There was a knowing glint in the medicine woman's eyes, an understanding that went beyond the usual therapist's nod.

"And how did that make you feel?" the older woman asked, gently but probing.

"I don't know," the botanist said, pulling back from the hot tea she had picked up and sipped. "Alive, maybe?"

"Being wanted, desired, made you feel alive?" the medicine woman asked, leaning forward.

"Well, it certainly felt more alive than what I feel now. Unseen by anyone. When not even my husband sees me." The taste of resentment filled her mouth and it was hot and sour.

"Can someone actually make you feel anything, or do you choose..." the medicine woman began, but the botanist cut her off with a raised hand.

"I know, I know," the botanist said through teeth almost clenched. "I choose to feel this way. It's my fault. I get it." She'd been down this road before, the endless loop of self-blame and responsibility. But today, the familiar platitudes and exercise felt worthless. She was tired of being the one in control of her own life, the detached scientist dissecting her feeling under a microscope with only one lens.

What she couldn't dissect was the nagging feeling that if her first husband hadn't died, if he'd lived to grow old with her, maybe she wouldn't feel so much like the ghost he'd become. He'd seen her, truly seen her, even in those moments when she sought validation in the arms of others. The guilt of those betrayals mingled with bittersweet nostalgia. She realized then that it wasn't just about beauty; it was about the reflection of herself she saw in his eyes, a reflection she desperately longed to reclaim.

The discomfort of the situation before her broke through her reverie. Her living husband was trying to walk away, his face contorted in confusion and fear, but he couldn't. The spell, or whatever the medicine woman called it, had taken root. Literally. She watched in disbelief as both men, the ghost of her past and the reality of her present, became anchored to the earth, their feet sprouting roots, like trees.

The botanist looked into her living husband's eyes, their green depths pleading with her, trying to speak to her. It was a look she recognized, a look that echoed through their twenty years together. It was the same look he'd given her when she'd threatened to leave, overwhelmed by the challenges of their early years. The same look he'd given her when they'd had to say goodbye to their beloved dog, their eyes mirroring the shared grief. It was a look of trust, an unspoken promise that they could and had faced life's storms together. And in that moment, as his eyes locked with hers, she felt a warmth spread through her, a knowing that transcended the years and the impossible circumstances.

"You don't have much longer to decide," the medicine woman said, standing up, adjusting her simple white t-shirt and black leggings. The botanist just now noticed the stylishness of the older woman's cropped gray hair, how surprisingly modern she looked. For a moment, all eyes were on the older woman, the medicine woman who held their fates in her hands. "You have to choose."

The weight of the medicine woman's words settled heavily on the botanist's chest. She remembered the frustration, the anger that had sprung up when the older woman dismissed her initial request. It wasn't about youth, she'd argued, her voice tight with indignation, a tone she remembered using before with the medicine woman. The botanist didn't want to be younger, to erase the years etched on her face, grayed in her hair. She'd embraced aging, celebrating each milestone with defiant joy. But the loosening skin, the softening curves, the undeniable evidence that she was aging, growing older... had that contributed to her invisibility? Had it dimmed her light, making her less desirable, less worthy of attention? And what good was physical beauty anyway? It had brought its share of fleeting pleasures, sure, but also unwanted advances, shallow judgments, and the constant pressure to maintain a facade. A deep unease settled over her, a sense that she was on the verge of an important realization, a truth that had been hiding in plain sight.

"It sounds to me," the medicine woman said, her voice sharp, "that what you want is to feel like you felt in your first marriage."

"Yes. Maybe. But..." the botanist began, hesitant, unsure how to articulate the tangled emotions swirling within her.

The older woman's hand shot up, silencing her. "There is no negotiating desires in my house. We aren't kids. You want something from me, or you don't." Her eyes flashed and the botanist shifted back on the couch, fear and defiance mixed in her gut.

"Ok. Yes. What's the cost?" the botanist asked, her voice barely audible.

The medicine woman threw back her head and laughed. The sound filled the room. "So now you want to talk cost? You, who ignored me all these years? You, who turned your back on tradition, who embraced the white man's science and scoffed at the wisdom of your ancestors?" She leaned forward, her gaze piercing. "You who talked to the leaves, caressed the petals, but you who never truly listened. You gave them Latin names, categorized them, dissected them, but you never learned their true essence, the essence they whispered to our grandmothers."

The medicine woman unholstered a finger and pointed it at the botanist who felt her own defiance crumbling. She thought of all the times she'd dismissed tradition as superstition, the times she'd driven past this very house, head high and eyes forward, clinging to her scientific superiority. What was it that had finally drawn her here? What deep-seated fear had forced her to confront the beliefs she'd spent a lifetime denying?

"The price," the medicine woman continued, her voice low and resonant, "is belief. You have to believe that there is something beyond, maybe greater than, your Western science, something ancient and powerful. You have to believe that I, that we, know something you don't. Something your grandmothers knew, something the plants know." She paused again, her eyes undoing the botanist. "You have to believe in who we are. Where we come from."

And there it was. The thought that had haunted the botanist for years, the reason she'd fled the reservation and sought refuge in the sterile world of academia. She surrendered to the memory of her mother, and so her face rose before her, gaunt and pale, long hair gone, her skin wrecked by chemo treatments. She remembered a pleading in her mother's eyes as she drank the bitter teas, the healers' chants echoing through the small house, the smell of sage clinging to the air. Had her mother wanted to go back to the hospital, to the promises of Western medicine? Or had her mother been silently hoping for a different kind of healing, a healing that her daughter, blinded by grief and youthful arrogance, had rejected?

This was the root of her rebellion, the reason she'd buried herself in textbooks and labs, rejecting the wisdom of her ancestors. She'd sought to conquer death with science, to prove that science held the power to save, to heal, even to love more fiercely than any tradition. She'd clung to the colonizers' education, believing it to protect her against the pain of loss, a way to erase the helplessness she'd felt watching her mother fade away.

Watching herself fade. But now, faced with the impossible, the line between science and traditional knowledge blurred. The ghosts of her past reminded her that love, in all its forms, required faith, a surrender to something beyond the realm of Western science. This wasn't just about romantic love; it was about trust, about believing in something larger than herself, something that connected her to generations of women who had walked this earth before her.

"Believe you?" the botanist blurted, her voice breaking the stillness of the room. "Believe that you can actually make something happen with your songs and smoke and roots battered in a dish? How can I believe any of that when every time I've seen it, it's failed? My mother, my grandmother, my father…they all believed. And they're all dead." Her voice cracked with emotion. "If there's anything I believe, it's that you can't do a damn thing. That any healing abilities you possess can only bring suffering."

A strange smile played on the medicine woman's lips. "That will have to do," she said, her voice taking on a new, almost regretful tone.

Fury filled the botanist. She reached for her keys, intending to storm out, but her hand froze halfway to her pocket. Her body felt heavy, as if she'd swallowed wet cement, her limbs were refusing to obey. She glanced at the coffee table, the delicate china cup empty, a lingering bitterness clinging to her tongue. The realization hit her like a wave of nausea.

"The effects of the Winter Bear blend are quite amazing, aren't they?" the medicine woman said, her eyes so much like the botanist's mother's. "It's time. You must choose."

Her lips were the only thing the botanist could feel. Numb, tingling with a strange warmth. The world around her had dissolved. The couch, the house, the medicine woman—all gone. Before her stood her two husbands, their faces etched with a mixture of confusion and fear. One she had seen that morning. Even though they had argued, he'd kissed the top of her head and told her to drive safely. The other, frozen in time, his youthful face a mirror to her own lost youth. The one who stayed. The one who left. And in that moment, suspended between two realities, she realized she loved them both, each love a different facet of her own complex heart.

"What happens when I choose?" the botanist asked, her voice trembling.

The medicine woman nodded, as if anticipating the question. "There is a balance that has to be kept in the world," she explained. "It's what keeps us from tipping, from all sliding off the earth. One death gives life to something new. A fallen tree nourishes the soil, feeds the creatures of the forest. It's a cycle, a transformation."

Her dead husband's face tightened, a flicker of understanding in his eyes. The living one's gaze darted between them; his brow furrowed with confusion.

"If you choose your dead husband," the older woman continued, "the living one will be no more. Choose the living one, and the first returns to the earth."

A wave of terror washed over the faces of both men. Her living husband's face crumpled as if he were suddenly disappointed, while her dead husband's youthful features contorted in a mask of fear. The weight of her decision pressed down on her, making her wish she'd never left the house this morning.

"And if I choose neither?" she asked, her voice barely a whisper. "What if I choose me instead? What then?"

The medicine woman took a deep breath. "Well, nothing would change then, would it? You've chosen yourself over and over again. It's always been about you. About what you need. What you wanted to feel. Isn't that why you're here now? Isn't that why these men are standing before you, like contestants in some cosmic game show?" Her voice softened. "Love, sister, is not about choosing who, but believing in your choice. You want love, to be loved? Both of these men have loved you. Love you still. But neither of them can give you what you truly seek."

"Oh, no," the botanist whispered. She regretted coming here, regretted stirring up the ghosts of her past. She'd come seeking a magic solution, a Native Santa Claus to grant her wish, but the medicine woman offered only hard truths and impossible choices.

But as she looked at the two men before her, their faces filled with fear and also love, a wave of clarity came over her. No, she didn't regret coming back to the rez. This wasn't about choosing between two men; it was about choosing herself, about finally confronting the doubts and fears that had driven her for years. She didn't regret remembering the joy of her first love, the easy comfort of her second. And she didn't regret the path that had led her here, to this moment of reckoning.

"And the winner is..." the medicine woman's voice rang out, cutting through the tension. Both men stiffened, their eyes filled with a mixture of fear and desperate hope. Her living husband's face held doubt, a question that mirrored her own: had their years together been shadowed by the ghost of what might have been? Her dead husband's eyes held their own question: wasn't it him that the botanist had been begging back with the desperate tears she cried in the years after his death?

"Child," the older woman said, her voice grave, "we cannot upset the balance..."

"I'm sorry," she whispered, a wave of sadness washing over her. She lifted her arm, feeling a light tingling, as if it had been asleep perhaps for years. With a trembling finger, she pointed.

"Sorry for what?" he asked, his voice familiar and calm.

She squeezed her eyes closed, not wanting to open them. Pain throbbed in her arm, in the back of her head. She was cold, confused. A hand touched her forehead, and the medicine woman's voice, gentle yet firm, broke through her fog.

"Nothing to be sorry about, little sister. You made a hard decision, but a good one."

"Decision," the botanist echoed, the word suddenly reminding her. The memory of the room, the couch, her hand lifting, the impossible choice—it all came flooding back. She felt at once hollow and filled, not with romantic love, but with a yearning for balance, for acceptance. She was ready to believe in the wisdom of her ancestors, in that which was unseen by most, but promised in every story her mother and her grandmother told her.

"I'm so sleepy," the botanist murmured.

"You hit your head pretty hard, but you didn't hit Elijah."

The boy on the skateboard. She remembered now. The argument with her husband, the endless days at the office, the exhaustion that had settled into her bones. She'd been driving to the reservation, home, her chest filled with grief and anger, ready to confront the sister who had chosen a different path, the sister she'd blamed for their mother's death. Then, the boy, swerving into her path. a split-second choice between life and... something else. *Boy or snag. Living boy or the standing dead tree?* She'd jerked the wheel, her instincts taking over, a primal urge to protect the living.

"Thank you," she heard a voice whisper. "I lost my balance."

She opened her eyes to the face of a boy of ten or eleven, his eyes wide with gratitude and a glint of something familiar.

"I dropped my fishing pole," he explained, his voice still trembling. "That's why I came off the curb. I just wanted to go fishing..." He started to cry.

"Elijah, is your name?" the botanist asked, reaching out to comfort him.

"Elijah with a little j," he said, and then, with a shy smile, he lifted his shirt to reveal a small, J-shaped birthmark on his ribs.

She looked at her sister, the one who had embraced the old ways, the one she'd pushed away for so long. The medicine woman smiled back at her. "Seems like the ancestors were looking out for both of you," she said, placing a hand on Elijah's shoulder. "This one has a way of finding himself in need of a little saving."

Then the medicine woman turned to the botanist, "And you, you seemed to have needed a little saving, too," she said, nodding to the husband at her side, then looking to the rumpled hood of the car, the steam rising from the radiator; the tree, now slightly off balance, "I'm glad you chose to help that old tree fall, it's been trying to get back to earth for years."

About the Author

CMARIE FUHRMAN IS the author of *Salmon Weather, Camped Beneath the Dam: Poems* and co-editor of *Cascadia: Art, Ecology, and Poetry* and *Native Voices: Indigenous Poetry, Craft, and Conversations*. She has published or has forthcoming poetry and nonfiction in multiple journals and anthologies. CMarie is an award-winning columnist for the *Inlander* and Director of the Elk River Writers Workshop. She is Associate Director of the Graduate Program in Creative Writing at Western Colorado University, where she teaches poetry and nature writing. CMarie is the host of *Terra Firma*. She resides in the Salmon River Mountains of Idaho with dogs and wilderness. *CMarieFuhrman.com*

CURSED

HADLEY H. HUDSON

I had been in love countless times, but she was a different force entirely. Her chestnut hair framed her soft features, and I wanted nothing more than to breathe in her honey shampoo one more time. The way she focused on her laptop and nibbled at her lip made me want to kiss her. The lengths I wanted to go to take the stress that etched her skin left me disoriented.

I sighed, the weight of it all settling on my sagging shoulders.

I was completely and utterly in love with her.

And the feeling would be gone by morning.

I sank into the chair of the empty table, my eyes unwavering from the woman. The coffee warmed my hands, but I longed for it to be her warmth I held instead.

Her blue eyes looked up from her laptop, from across the cafe. They met mine, and the world stopped. She and I were the only ones in the cafe, and it took everything within me not to close the distance—to go and meet her.

I bit into the corner of my lips, fighting the smile that wanted to form. I tore my eyes away, to the chair in front of me that had been empty moments ago. This time, I didn't fight the scowl that formed.

"This never gets old," he hummed into his own cup of coffee, strawberry-blond hair fluttering across his face.

"Love to see that my pain and suffering brings you joy," I said coldly. I pushed my cup across the wood, the coffee no longer holding any appeal.

"Oh, it does," he confirmed, a grin spreading across his face. His eyes twinkled at me, capturing the soft light of the morning to be his. "It's what I live for."

"That's a pathetic life for a god, Eros."

"You know how many broken hearts I had to mend because of you? This is just me enjoying divine justice." He leaned back in the chair, nonchalant. I noticed the slight narrowing of his eyes, catching a glimpse of the rageful fire that lurked beneath them.

The chill that ran down my spine only indulged him further. I refused to look at his smugness anymore. My downcast gaze settled onto a stain on the table.

"What I did is something you send people to therapy for, not cast a curse on them," I grumbled, scratching at the stain with a fingernail.

"My apologies, I thought a serial romantic like yourself would've enjoyed this! A new love every single day. You should be thriving!" The patronizing tone ground across my ears.

I *had* enjoyed it at first. I could have my fun and start blank the next day. Now it was just monotonous. Something I lived with. I flicked my gaze to the woman across the cafe. There was no time for romance before the feelings were washed away. They would never feel the same before my heart moved on to the next person.

"Sure." It was the only word I could muster.

"You know it's been a year?" he asked.

I looked up at him. Had it really been so long? 365 different women to love and forget. There was a look on his face I couldn't quite place, and I was stupid enough to have hope about it. That this could be the end of it.

"Have you found the meaning of love yet?" His singsong voice, once serene to my ears, only taunted me.

"Love has no meaning." The words fell from my lips before I could stop them.

His light brows shot up, his head tilting slightly. The smile disappeared as his chair scraped across the floor. I watched my chance slipping away as he stood. A horror gripped my heart. I couldn't do this for another year.

"Eros—" I called out, my voice a pathetic shell.

"If it is meaningless, then I'll let you continue. What's the harm?"

"Please, that's not what I meant, Eros," I begged. My voice cracked on his name, too unworthy to even say his name any longer. I stood from my chair to follow him, but he disappeared into the wind, leaving me in the middle of the coffee shop.

My shoulders slumped and I fought the tears that formed across my lashes. And for a few moments, the ceiling was the most interesting thing as I blinked the tears away.

"Um, hey," a shy voice came to me.

My heart fluttered, and I knew who it was before I even turned to look.

"Hey." I swallowed.

Gods, she was even more beautiful up close. The way her brows scrunched slightly together was worthy of the finest marble. Her concern for me was a painting I wanted etched across my heart.

"Are you okay?" she asked.

These feelings weren't real.

"Yeah, I'm fine, I have to go,"

"Oh, do you—"

I turned, not waiting to hear her words. I grabbed my lukewarm cup from the table before heading to the exit.

"Hope things get better!" she called after me, her words lingering in my ear long after I was out of the cafe. And she was all I could think about for the rest of the day. Each brunette that walked by I hoped would be her. The smell of the coffee pot only reminded me of the cafe where I had left her. And the harsh keyboard scraped across my fingertips when all I wanted was to feel her touch.

I left work early.

I didn't even leave my apartment the next day. I called in sick from work and lay in my bed as my heart pounded in my chest. There was a yearning for a woman I hadn't met. A calling that tried to lure me from my enclosure. Lovelorn and alone was my existence. If I didn't leave the apartment, I was in love with a random actress I saw on tv. On days where I laid eyes on nothing but my ceiling, there was a longing for a stranger I'd never meet.

The following day, I raided my liquor cabinet.

Every day's new emotions were paired with yesterday's heartbreak. The loneliness that comes from denying the heart its one true need. I had done so well blocking them out. One talk with Eros and a year's worth of emotional control had flown out the window. At least when the alcohol burned my nose, my throat, my insides, there was something tangible. The pain never stopped, though, so neither did my drinking.

The next day I was out of sick days to use. My head was pounding, and the smallest sliver of light was enough to sear my eyes. The dim light of the cafe was a reprieve from the outside world, and I prayed the coffee and painkillers would kick in soon.

I avoided eye contact with everyone. If I was lucky, the strings of fate would choose a random woman I'd never meet. It was easier to function when I didn't imagine her face all day. But when I looked up to pay, I wasn't so lucky.

I saw Sophie nearly every day. She knew my order by heart, and today my heart was hers. I cursed under my breath, as I watched a life with her flash before my eyes. I would come every morning to see her before work. When she spent the night over, I would walk her here before the sun graced the sky just to make sure she got here safely. We'd move in together and she'd wake me up with the smell of espresso in our house. I wanted to spend every morning waking up to her, to pull her back into bed to steal a few more moments with her before she had to leave.

"The usual?" Sophie asked with a grin that took my breath away.

I nodded, unable to say a thing. I paid and walked away. What else could I do? Honestly, I was surprised it had taken this long for Sophie to be the flame of the day. Tomorrow she would go back to being my barista. So, I just stood waiting for my coffee. What I felt meant nothing, I reminded myself.

"Oh, hey!"

I froze, eyes wide. I was staring at Sophie making my coffee, and yet the voice beside me held me captive. I slowly turned to her, my heart picking up pace.

The woman from the other day stood there. I stared at her, wondering if she was real. My eyes softened, soaking up her features once more. She was just as beautiful, her smile throwing my stomach for a loop.

A blush bloomed across her cheeks, and I couldn't help the corner of my lip turning up in a lopsided smile.

"Hey," I replied.

"How have you been? I haven't seen you in a few days..." Her voice trailed as she looked away, fiddling with the strap of her bag. She whipped back to look at me, eyes wide, "I said that like I know you—I don't know you! I just come in every day to work, and I noticed you're always here too, especially since you seemed off last time, and this is coming out worse, so I'm going to shut up. Usually, I'm cooler than this I swear."

I chuckled. She was talking with her hands, the movements just as flustered as her words, and I found it incredibly endearing. She was scanning the coffee shop looking like startled prey ready to bolt.

"Well, if I knew your name then we wouldn't be strangers. Then it wouldn't be weird," I offered.

Her gaze fell back onto mine, and I found myself getting lost in the sea of her eyes.

"Paige."

"Paige," I repeated. The name rolled off my tongue, and I never wanted to hear any other name again.

"And yours?"

I blinked, pulling myself from the ocean she had pulled me into. I couldn't breathe, trying to catch my breath and give her an answer. No response came to me, and I found myself struggling to remember the question she had asked.

"Here you go, Jamie!" Sophie called out, sliding the cappuccino my way. I stared at the barista, my love of the day. I picked up the coffee, the residue of her touch like a fire on the cardboard cup. I watched her return to the espresso machine, begging for her to look at me once more.

I closed my eyes and let out a sigh. What was I doing?

My eyes flew open, turning back to the conversation I had just been a part of.

"Jamie," I supplied, holding the coffee up as proof, "My name's Jamie."

Paige glanced over my shoulder at Sophie with a confused look, the wheels turning. The slow nod let me know she had pieced it together. I was in love with Sophie—only for the day, but how would she know that?

I swallowed, wanting to fix it somehow. I flicked my eyes at Sophie before landing back to Paige. "It's not like that."

"Oh?" she asked, a single brow raised as she waited for me to continue.

"I have a few minutes before I have to leave for work, and if you had the time, I would love to hang out a bit."

She rolled on her feet, contemplating it. "Would it cheer you up?"

"More than you could imagine," I admitted.

And that's how we began. Each morning, I would see a new love of my life, and then turn to sit with Paige. I ignored the way my heart screamed at me, preferring Paige's company to the pining I had grown used to. Each day I spent with her it made it easier to ignore the pull of the heart.

I loved watching an idea dawn across her face when she was working. My ears craved to hear the passion in her voice as she spoke. When I took her out for our first date, I saw the way her nose crinkled when she laughed so hard she lost her breath. When she stayed at my house the first night, I witnessed how cautiously she moved, careful not to disturb anything. I remember how elated I was the first day she went to the kitchen to get a drink without asking for my permission. Every night I long for the way my heart sings when she curls into my arms, the way every nerve ignites when she kisses me.

The more time I spent with her, the more the curse rebelled. I saw the frustration etched in Paige's face when I couldn't give her my all, half my heart already sworn to another. I knew all too well how her ocean-blue eyes turned to a swirling storm when she was angry. She didn't know what was happening and I couldn't explain to her how there were days my heart felt like it would rip in two— that everything I felt for her, I would always feel for someone else.

She wouldn't understand how the gods had cursed her with me.

She was on my sofa, working on a presentation for work. I adored the way her face scrunched when she concentrated. I wanted to see it every night.

I wanted nothing more than to stay by her side for eternity. To be the one to love her, the one who held her as she slept, and the one who woke her in the morning.

But every new day, every new love, was another reminder of how I couldn't. I couldn't give her my full heart. Not like this.

"Paige," I said softly.

"Yes?" She looked up at me, her eyes soft and warm. Her smile sent me aflutter. I tried to commit her to memory. It was the last selfish act I would allow myself.

"We shouldn't do this," I started, still taking in each curve of her face. If I memorized it enough, I could see it in each woman I fell in love with. I could have moments with her across time, always just out of reach.

She straightened a bit. "What do you mean?"

"We need to end this," I clarified, my voice already hoarse.

"Where is this coming from?" She blinked, scooting away from me.

As I memorized her, the way her face scrunched in pain was seared into my memory. It broke my heart, and I had earned it. She deserved better, someone who could love her completely with their whole heart. Not this.

"I thought—we were..." Her words caught in her throat. "Tell me this is some sick joke."

"Paige, I need you to find someone who can love you the way you deserve. That isn't me."

"What do you mean? Yes, it is," she argued, shaking her head.

"Please don't make this harder,"

"I'm making this harder?" She reared back, baffled.

I stood from the couch, walking to the door. Her pleading eyes knew what I was about to say and begged me not to. I turned away, staring at the wall.

"You should go," My voice was cold, colder than I meant it.

"You are a heartless pig," she scoffed, gathering her things.

"You aren't the first to say it." I grimaced.

"Somehow, I'm not surprised." She huffed, each angry footstep ringing through my ears.

My body screamed at me to stop her from leaving, to stop the storm I had started. My heart ached, as if the fates had gripped their bony hands around it.

"Look at me," she demanded.

After it all, I still couldn't refuse her. She scanned my face, her gaze a furious storm that held no bounds. Whatever she was looking for, I hoped she'd find it.

I could see the venom coating her tongue, saw her carefully choosing her next word.

"*Pathetic.*"

I closed my eyes, gripping the cold metal of the doorknob to keep myself standing. I had done this to myself. I chose this. I have done this before, and I could do it again. Never did my heart hurt like this though.

I listened and held onto each step for some remnant of her as she left. When I could no longer hear them, I still stood there. I let out a shaky breath, my eyes burning with tears, I refused to let go.

"You're doing it again."

I whipped around to where Eros stood in my living room. There was no smugness, no contempt, just disappointment.

He didn't get to be disappointed in me. He was the god of love, and I had sacrificed what he valued most. All for her, so she could one day be blessed by him.

"What kind of sick game are you playing here?" I seethed, hot tears streaking down my cheeks.

"You were so *close*." He stepped closer till he towered above me. "And yet you throw their hearts aside like they mean nothing."

I stared up at him, my wrath rivaling his own. My nails dug into my palms, the only thing keeping me grounded, keeping me from falling apart.

"It is maddening that you believe you have no blame in this."

"I had high hopes for you," he said, pressing his lips into a thin line as he disregarded my words. "You do not deserve love."

"But she does. And I can't give it to her because of you!" I spat, pointing back to the empty hallway where she had been only moments before. Her memory was slipping away already, my heart priming itself for its next inhabitant.

He shook his head, stepping away.

"You were so close," he repeated.

I barked out a watery laugh. I shrugged, the movement exaggerated and stiff, my limbs not my own.

"I'm done here," he finalized, turning his back on me once more. He was gone in an instant, another echo I struggled to remember.

The first sob racked through my body like a jolt of electricity. The second one came only slightly easier. I hugged the wall, its coldness my only comfort as I slid down it.

I was so *close*.

The next day I was numb to the world. I walked through it, without reason or direction. I made my coffee at home. I shoveled sugar and cream into it, and it was still nothing but bitter. I walked to work, the colors of the city dull. I went through the motions of the day, a husk of my former self.

And when night fell, I nestled into covers that refused to hold any warmth. It was only then when it hit me. I wasn't in love. There was no woman today. Eros had been merciful enough to give me the day, but there would be a woman tomorrow...

There was no new woman.

There was no new ignition of love. The world was just as dull as the day before. I made my bitter coffee. I took the bus to work, not able to will my feet another step further. I stared at a blank computer screen, unable to find the motivation to be productive.

The next day I went to the metro, watching each woman pass, waiting for the bond of unrequited love to snap into place like it always did. After each train, I stood there more confused. The bond was always quick to form. The longer I was in love, the harder it was to move on the next day. It was a vicious cycle that Eros relished. So why hadn't it appeared yet?

Eros wouldn't have broken the curse. Not like this. Or maybe he had, and this was his ultimate revenge. Take away instant love and force me to fall in love the old-fashioned way.

But I already had, hadn't I?

I had fallen in love with Paige, and if the curse was truly gone—

I checked the clock. She should still be there. My feet moved on their own, through the subway and through the streets. I picked up speed, running down the street just to get me there faster, to see her sooner.

I sputtered to a stop in front of the cafe, my lungs burning.

I stared through the glass to the table where she always sat. My creature of habit. Dark circles ringed her eyes as she raked her nails across her scalp. She stared at her laptop screen in frustration.

Guilt crawled across my skin and the urge to go in there and fix it all was unbearable. Yet, there was nothing driving me forward. My heart didn't call to her like it had days ago. There was nothing there. Just the empty pit I had grown acquainted with.

"What did you do?" I growled to a person who was not there to hear it.

I cared for her, I knew I did, and yet I couldn't feel it. My heart was disconnected from my body, from my brain, refusing to listen to reason.

I stared at her through the window, trying to will any emotion to reveal itself. I loved her. I loved her, I was sure of it, and I couldn't feel it. There was no love in my heart. An emotion I had felt constantly for over a year had disappeared, and it had taken me too long to notice.

"Eros—give it back." I demanded, my entire body shaking. "Give it back."

"No." His tone was cold and stern.

"I'll take the curse then," I choked out, refusing to take my eyes off her, "Make me love someone new every day and I will still choose her each time, just let me feel it."

"No."

"Eros, please," I pleaded, my voice barely a whisper.

"I will not repeat myself again."

"Fine." I mouthed the word, but nothing came out. I bolted for the door, the cold rushing in with me like a storm as I approached her.

She looked up, along with half the patrons, but they didn't concern me. Paige was already shaking her head. She slammed her laptop closed, already shoving it in her bag by the time I got to her.

"I'm sorry," I nearly screamed across the cafe, trying to get her to stop.

She ran a hand down her face. "Jamie, don't do this here."

"I am a terrible human being, I leave a path of destruction, and am emotionally stunted beyond repair," I began.

She rolled her eyes, and it pained me that she wouldn't know the full extent of my words. She slung her bag over her shoulder and pushed past me.

"I am a lot of things, and one of them is in love with you." I knew I was. I didn't care if Eros wouldn't let me feel it. I was and I wanted to spend every day with her proving it to her.

She froze, turning to face me, "No, you're not. If you were, we wouldn't be here."

"It is exactly why we're here," I countered. "Paige, I am more in love with you than anything—anyone else. And I was scared. I was terrified, because I couldn't bear the thought of losing you. So, I decided to give you up before you had the chance to figure out I was no good."

My heart was pounding in my chest. I could hardly hear my own words. There was no one else but me and her, just like the day I met her. Her brows scrunched together, tears brimming her lashes.

"I am not perfect, Paige, but I swear to the gods if you give me one more chance, I will not blow it. I will be there every morning, and every night. I want to make you breakfast in bed and listen to you practice every presentation you make for work. I want to bask in your light or be cloaked in your shadow, wherever you find space for me. I will be there, just please let me be there, Paige."

"Jamie..."

"Please," I begged, ready to lay my entire life before her to do with it what she pleased.

"Okay."

"Okay?" My voice cracked, unable to believe I had heard her correctly.

"Yes." Her hand cupped my face. I leaned into her warmth, wrapping my own hand around hers.

Her lips met mine, how they had so many times before. None of them compared to the way my skin buzzed at her touch. Her kiss filled me—completed me. My life could be nothing but this moment, and I would be happy.

I broke the kiss, leaning back to look at her. There wasn't anything I wouldn't give for her. I was completely hers, body and soul, and I wouldn't allow anything to change that.

"I love you," I whispered, in awe.

"Yeah, yeah, I love you too," she hummed, the words sending me on a new high.

I shook my head, a lopsided grin spreading across my face. I looked up, spotting him through the window of the cafe. Eros gave me a nod, a small smile on his face. He turned away, disappearing into the passing crowd.

I turned back to Paige, cupping her face in my hands—my world, my love, the one I give my all to.

"I love *you*."

About the Author

Hadley H. Hudson is a lesbian indie author who thrives on the coffee that runs through her veins and the sapphic stories she writes. Ever since she was young, her writings were contained in the margins of class notes, chasing wild tales that filled her imagination while teachers lectured. Today, she works in graphic design and marketing, but Hadley continues to write novels to bring these stories to life. When not writing, Hadley enjoys drawing, crocheting, or curling up in bed to binge watch true crime documentaries. Her debut novel, Oathbound, was published in March of 2024, a sapphic new adult fantasy filled with ancient beasts and magic that threatens to tear realms apart. The second book of the Oathbound series is scheduled for a 2025 release, with many more novels planned for release.

ACKNOWLEDGMENTS

This anthology was made possible with the generous support of Draft2Digital and Western Colorado University's Graduate Program in Creative Writing.

COPYRIGHT INFORMATION

ABOUT THE EDITORS

KEVIN J. ANDERSON has published more than 190 books, 58 of which have been national or international bestsellers. He has written numerous novels in the Star Wars, X-Files, and Dune universes, as well as many original works. He has edited numerous anthologies, written comics and games, and the lyrics to three rock CDs. Anderson is the director of the graduate program in Publishing at Western Colorado University. Anderson and his wife Rebecca Moesta are the publishers of WordFire Press. He has 24 million copies in print in thirty-four languages. His most recent novels are *Nether Station, Horn Dogs, Persephone,* and *Princess of Dune* (with Brian Herbert).

An award-winning writer, editor and designer, ALLYSON LONGUEIRA has worked in fiction and nonfiction in multiple media, including newspapers, magazines and books for more than twenty years. Allyson is founder and owner of the independent publishing house Long Alley Press and also serves as Associate Director in the Publishing Concentration at Western Colorado University as part of the Graduate Program in Creative Writing. Her latest projects are co-executive editor with Kevin J. Anderson of *Gilded Glass: Twisted Myths & Shattered Fairy Tales, Merciless Mermaids: Tails from the Deep, Feisty Felines and Other Fantastical Familiars,* and *Chaotic Cupids: When Love Goes Awry* (WordFire Press, July 2025).

ABOUT THE ILLUSTRATOR

CL FORS—Cherrie to her friends—was born to a mad scientist and a mad artist, so it's no surprise she's cultivated lifelong dual passions for art and science that has shaped her career in writing and illustrating science fiction and fantasy.

Cherrie has lived all over the US and now calls the Southern California desert her home. She shares her life, love, and creative endeavors with her husband, four clever children, and her beloved art family.

Cherrie spent her early years obsessed with story and the many ways to tell it through drawing, writing, sculpting, and performing, She would sketch for hours, then cobble together her "creatures" from whatever she could find in the back of junk drawers, or stare into marbles and imagine she could step through to another world.

As a young adult, Cherrie served in the military and raised a family, but she knew she had to find a way back to her creative path. In 2012, she made a commitment to create again. Over the next ten years, she wrote, illustrated, and self-published four science fiction novels.

In 2024, Cherrie became an Illustrators of the Future winner just before beginning the publishing Master's program at Western. As a professional illustrator, Cherrie was honored to paint the cover for the *Chaotic Cupids* anthology. She is also the cover artist for her solo publishing project, *The Heads of Cerberus,* which features her hand-painted black-and-white watercolor illustrations.

Cherrie is currently working on her first graphic novel, a science-fiction tale of a genetically engineered bat-piglet who escapes the lab and discovers the meaning of found family.

You can find her work at clforsauthor.com and her Patreon, The Art of CL Fors: sci-fi, fantasy, bat-piggies, oh my!